PRAISE FOR MARY BURTON

I'LL NEVER LET YOU GO
"A sure bet for page-turning suspense coupled with titillating love scenes is author Mary Burton."

—*Library Journal*

BE AFRAID
"*Be Afraid* is vintage Mary Burton . . . a complex, riveting story . . . surprises and white-knuckle suspense with a capital *S*. Her characters are wicked smart. . . . Readers will be on tenterhooks. . . . Burton's story lines are finely tuned . . . a nail-biter . . . gritty, fast-paced suspense that will send chills down your spine."

—*USA Today*'s Happy Ever After

"Bestselling author Mary Burton is a master of her craft. She keeps her readers tingling with suspense while we try to figure out what will happen next."

—*Single Titles*

"Mary Burton [is] the modern-day Queen of Romantic Suspense."

—Bookreporter.com

COVER YOUR EYES
"If there's a category of 'page-turner,' Burton would always end up on the top of that list. This time is no different . . . a chilling puzzle . . . fantastic work with never a dull moment for the reader."

—*Suspense Magazine*

"With sharp detail, a nicely developed romance, and stellar plotting that distributes clues with chilling precision, Burton's latest 'lock your door and keep the lights on' thriller beautifully kicks off her new series of four Nashville-set mysteries dealing with the Morgan family."

—*Library Journal*

"In her latest, Burton pens a well-crafted mystery and an intricate plot set in Nashville with rough, gritty detective Deke and gutsy, vulnerable lawyer Rachel at the center. Her strong, dynamic storytelling and crisp dialogue are the highlights. Good pacing, distinctive secondary characters and chilling suspense make this story one heck of an exciting ride."

—*RT Book Reviews*

"Burton's trademark is providing the serial killer's viewpoint without giving anything away, and by feeding the reader tiny details one at a time, she keeps the tension building."

—*Publishers Weekly*

YOU'RE NOT SAFE
"Burton once again demonstrates her romantic suspense chops with this taut novel. Burton plays cat and mouse with the reader through a tight plot, credible suspects, and romantic spice keeping it real."

—*Publishers Weekly*

NO ESCAPE
"Burton always writes great, edgy suspense, and this book is no different. Pages will fly by as the danger around Jolene and Brody increases!"

—*The Parkersburg News and Sentinel*

THE
SHARK

Morgans of Nashville

Cover Your Eyes
Be Afraid
I'll Never Let You Go
Vulnerable

Texas Rangers

The Seventh Victim
No Escape
You're Not Safe

Alexandria Series

Senseless
Merciless
Before She Dies

Richmond Series

I'm Watching You
Dead Ringer
Dying Scream

MARY BURTON

THE SHARK

THE FORGOTTEN FILES BOOK I

Montlake
Romance

Published by Montlake Romance, Seattle

www.apub.com

Amazon, the Amazon logo, and Montlake Romance are trademarks of Amazon.com, Inc., or its affiliates.

ISBN-13: 9781503934474
ISBN-10: 1503934470

Cover design by Marc J. Cohen

Printed in the United States of America

CHAPTER ONE

Monday, September 12, 5:45 p.m.

When Riley Tatum vanished twelve years ago, no one sounded an alarm. No one called the cops, gathered a search party, or posted flyers. She simply disappeared from the streets into an abyss. Swallowed whole. She should have died. Been long forgotten. But for reasons she didn't understand, the darkness spat her out.

Now a Virginia State Police trooper, she and her five-year-old Labrador retriever, Cooper, enjoyed a solid reputation as a tracking team. They trained routinely in both rural and urban settings, reinforcing his skills and her ability to read his body language alerts when targets were close.

All that training was now in play as the sunlight faded above the canopy of trees, bathing the woods in deepening shadows. Even this late in the day, the temperature inched past ninety degrees while 100 percent humidity thickened the air into soup. A lightweight shirt wicked away moisture, battle dress uniforms protected her legs from the brush, hiking boots guarded against twisted ankles and snakebites, and a floppy hat covered her honey-tanned face and dark hair coiled in a knot.

A tug at the end of the tracking line directed her focus to Cooper. He dropped his nose to the ground, closed his mouth, and wagged his tail—all signs their quarry's scent was strong. They were close. She knelt on the narrow trail and inspected barely bent foliage angling toward the top of the ridge.

Their quarry was Jax Carter, a pimp and drug dealer. According to his prior arrest record, Carter worked the I-95 corridor between Richmond and Washington, DC. He and his girlfriend, Darla Johnson, prostituted two or three girls at any given time out of a motor home, often found parked at truck stops or large events. Carter and Johnson found their girls on social media, seducing each with words of love and promises of family. The couple kept the girls under close watch, and if any considered leaving, their tactics shifted from charming words to threats and brutal violence.

Riley first noticed Carter's motor home a month ago at a truck stop halfway between Richmond and DC. She was on a break and parked in the shadows when she spotted a young, scantily clad girl get out of a big rig cab. The girl hurried across the lot and vanished inside the motor home. Minutes later another girl, bone thin, followed a similar path. Riley had been ready to summon backup when a call came over the radio, pulling her to the scene of a five-vehicle accident. Hours later when she returned to the site, the motor home was gone.

Earlier today, a trooper had been called to help a badly beaten girl near Carter's motor home, which was parked near a truck stop diner. The eatery's surveillance camera caught Carter beating the girl, whose bony body absorbed several hard blows. It appeared as if the kid had been knocked unconscious, but as Carter moved closer, fist cocked, she pulled a blade from her pocket and stabbed him in the leg. He recoiled in pain, staggered a step, and regrouped to strike again when approaching sirens scared him off. He fled in a red Camaro, making his way west into the foothills of the Blue Ridge Mountains, where he abandoned his car in a deserted driveway overgrown with weeds.

Local news stations picked up a bystander's cell phone footage of the girl's beating and ran it several times. The video quickly went viral. Cops in four counties were alerted, and when Carter's Camaro was found, Riley and Cooper's tracking skills landed them on point position. By the time she arrived, a collection of sheriff's deputies clustered near the car, which was nosed under heavy brush. Media rolled up. It was a circus.

She hoped the knife wound would slow Carter enough so she and Cooper could catch up to him before nightfall.

The plan was for Riley and Cooper to guide three deputies up the trail. A private firm called Shield Security, headquartered near Quantico, had offered to assist, but she declined, fearing a civilian crew that she did not know could hinder the search.

Using one of Carter's shirts found in the car, Riley allowed Cooper to sniff and lock in on the scent. Barking, he led her and the three deputies into the woods.

Two hours into the search, one deputy twisted his ankle on a log. Three more hours in, the second succumbed to the heat and the third dropped back to assist a return to base. Riley should have quit the search, but when she pictured the girl's bloodied face she thought about another young girl, Hanna, a runaway she'd taken into her home and would soon adopt. Over the last five years, she'd seen Hanna blossom, though she could easily have ended up like the beaten girl in the video.

So Riley asked to continue. She wouldn't engage until additional deputies could be dispatched. When she received the green light, she checked her sidearm, a SIG Sauer with a ten-round magazine, and shifted Cooper's tracking line to her nondominant hand in case she needed to draw her weapon. She promised to check in every fifteen minutes.

A half hour later, she spotted the outlines of fresh boot prints. The trajectory of the impressions confirmed a westward bearing. The right foot impression was deep but the left shallow, a sign Carter was favoring the leg. His stride appeared shorter, suggesting his pace was slower.

Good.

As Riley's gaze now swept over the lush green foliage, she spotted red droplets of blood clinging to leaves ahead. Like all the markers on the trail, the color and patterns of blood told a story. Dark-red blood implied a punctured vein. Light red meant blood diluted with gastric fluids from an abdominal wound. Pink and foamy signaled a possible chest wound.

This blood was dark red. Unoxygenated. No doubt from the stab wound, which had sliced a vein. Ahead, the path forked and traces of red dotted leaves on both sides.

Close to Cooper's ear she whispered in Czech, the language he'd been trained to follow while working. *"Aport."* Fetch.

Cooper sniffed the ground around the first blood droplets and then around the second set. At the second location, his sniffing increased and his tail wagged. "Good boy," she whispered.

As they continued, crimson splashes were smeared on more leaves. The distance between drops shortened to less than four feet. The track was now in its sixth hour and had begun to open his wound. He was suffering, likely angry, and primed to make a mistake if pressed.

Even better.

She lifted a leaf and touched the blood. Still viscous. Fresh. She raised her boot to step when she heard the snap of a twig. She drew her weapon. Cooper's head rose and he glared toward the right. The dog watched the woods, but his body language didn't alert her that Carter was close.

Slowly she crouched, gently pulling the tense dog to her. Her heart revved from steady to overdrive, forcing her to slow her breath and listen to the wind whispering in the trees. Tense seconds passed. But there was no more movement. Only silence.

She could fall back, but that was a gamble. Carter's odds of escape greatly increased if he found his way out of the woods and got hold of a car. Cooper could track people, not vehicles.

Again, the grainy black-and-white surveillance footage of Carter's fist pounding the skinny girl jabbed her gut. If Carter escaped, he would find that girl and drop her into a hole so deep no one would ever find her.

Standing, she looked up the trail into the dense brush. At five foot nine, she was tall for a woman, and though she was in peak shape, wrangling an injured, possibly armed suspect off the mountain in the fading light would be reckless. She'd stay close but would not engage, knowing at worst an overnight without food and water would drain Carter's energy reserves, making him a softer target when backup arrived at first light.

Again, Cooper's gaze cut right. This time she caught a faint flicker of movement. Someone else was there. Freezing, she searched the dense thicket. Had additional police arrived, or worse, one of Carter's kin?

Her right hand tightened slightly around the gun's grip as she waited. Watched. There was stillness. Silence. As hard as she searched, she saw no threat. Finally, Cooper looked away. Mouth closed, he sniffed faster as his tail wagged.

Up the trail, the snap of twigs was followed by a painful grunt. Carter. He was up ahead. Close. Grabbing her cell, she texted an update to the base station and seconds later a reply fired back.

Two deputies are one hour out.

Cooper remained alert and silent, a sign her hours of continuous training had paid off.

She typed, Roger.

Wanting a visual on Carter, she tucked her phone back in her pocket before she and Cooper inched forward through the branches.

Monitoring her foot placement and her breathing, she made almost no sound. When she crested the next rise, she spotted Carter staggering toward a tree, one hand on a gun and the other on his bleeding thigh. He pressed his back to the thin trunk, slowly lowered to the ground, and pulled a water bottle from his pocket. He drained the container, then tipped his head back and closed his eyes. He thought he was alone. Safe.

Now it was a waiting game.

A sudden flash of movement flickered in her peripheral vision. Her head snapped right. This time, instead of fluttering leaves, she saw a very tall man. He wore fatigues, an olive-green T-shirt, black hiking boots, a jungle hat, and green camouflage paint on his face and hands. He wore a small backpack and a knife strapped to his thigh. Slung over his shoulder was a Colt M4 Carbine rifle.

What the hell? Adrenaline flooded her body as the stranger's dark gaze pinned her. He was alert and calm all at once. He wasn't an amateur.

With a stiff, precise flick of his hand, he pointed up toward Carter. He *knew*. *Who is this guy?*

And then it clicked. Shield Security's offer to send personnel. Despite a refusal, they hadn't listened. This guy had been at least an hour behind her, and yet he had easily caught up without her or Cooper detecting his presence until a few minutes ago. As they were for most of the former-military personnel at Shield, field operations and tracking were second nature to him.

His frown suggested he considered her a liability. If not for the need for silence, she'd have laughed. *Really, pal, you think I'm the problem?* She shook her head. *This is my show, and I'm not backing off.*

Without comment, he was on the move again, his long legs easily moving up the trail. Tightening her grip on her SIG, she moved parallel to him, heart hammering in her chest. He circled to the north, and without a word spoken she moved south. Their trajectories would converge near the top by Carter.

They'd never trained together, a recipe for getting one of them killed. Neither intimately knew the other's thoughts or patterns, nor did either want to be positioned directly across from the other if they had to fire on Carter in the middle.

She reached the top of the rise where the woods opened to a small clearing where timber had been harvested. Certainly big enough to give Carter time to see who approached.

Carter sat on the far edge of the clearing, his bloodied hand cupping an outstretched leg. Lying on the ground next to his right hand was the weapon. His breathing was labored, a sign he was running on empty.

She glanced to her right and discovered the stranger gone. She listened. Wind in the trees. No movement. A ghost. Whatever sounds he'd made before were intended to get her attention. Where the hell was he?

Dusk was closing in; soon it would be dark.

As she watched Carter's chin sink deeper into his chest, she recognized an opportunity to act. She tied the dog's tracking line to a tree and rose. She advanced several steps as she leveled her gun at Carter's chest.

In a blink, Carter's eyelids popped open. His gaze telegraphed wild, desperate fear, pain, and anger. Sweat dripped from his nose as his dirty, bloodstained hand reached for his gun.

"Don't touch it!" she shouted.

Carter's fingers were inches from the gun when a shot cut through the air and struck the ground by the weapon. Carter recoiled but reached out again. Another shot hit the ground by his leg. The well-placed bullets gave her the seconds she needed to reach the gun and secure it.

Carter stared up, his eyes burning into her. "Bitch!"

Out of the thick woods the stranger moved into position behind Riley, silent, alert. She grabbed the cuffs from her belt and tossed them at Carter. "Handcuff your right hand."

When he glared at her, the stranger moved forward a step, his weapon trained on Carter, his finger on the trigger.

"I won't ask again!" Riley said.

Carter cuffed his hand.

"Now wrap your arms around the tree and cuff the other hand."

"What the hell!"

"Do it!"

Carter grunted and, straddling the tree, reached around and cuffed his left hand.

The stranger moved to the spot where his bullets had struck, and unsheathing the knife from his leg holster, he dug both slugs out of the ground and pocketed them. She'd bet serious money the shell casings in the woods would never be found either.

"Who the fuck are you?" Carter demanded.

Riley stared at the stranger, trying hard to get a read on his features hidden under the paint, hat, and the growing shadows.

He leaned forward a fraction as he searched Carter for a second weapon and whispered something to the man she couldn't hear. Carter's face paled.

Riley kept her SIG trained on Carter. "Is he clear?"

"Yes. Do you have this?" The stranger's deep voice sounded calm.

His words electrified her senses and planted the unsteady feeling she knew this guy. "I'm good."

He motioned Riley out of earshot of Carter. "Keep this between us."

"You sure? Good publicity for Shield."

"I was never here."

"What about Carter?"

"He won't talk." Certainty underscored the words. "Right, Carter?"

Carter eyed the stranger as if fearful to take his gaze off him. "Right."

She wondered what he'd said to Carter.

With a nod the stranger turned and melted into the woods.

"You dumb bitch," Carter said. His face was pale, either from pain or the stranger's whispered warning.

Drawing in a steady breath to dilute the adrenaline, she moved toward Cooper and untied his tracking line. "I'm dumb? Who's the one cuffed to the tree?"

Carter tugged at the cuffs. He spoke in a low, gruff tone. "I'm going to kill you!"

Ignoring Carter, she inspected his leg. It was oozing blood, but his makeshift tourniquet had stopped most of the bleeding. "Where are the other girls you're running?"

Carter shifted, wincing as his leg rubbed the tree. "I don't have any damn girls."

"One's in the hospital now. Where are the others?"

He rolled his head from side to side. "I don't know what you're talking about."

She rose, staring at his leg and knotting her brow as if pondering. "That tourniquet ought to do you until the deputies arrive."

"When are they gonna be here?" He glanced toward the thick woods, which were growing darker by the moment.

"Don't know," she lied. "Could be all night. And I hear it's going to rain." An owl hooted. "Other than the black bears, the animals should leave you alone as long as you don't fall asleep."

The metal cuffs chewed into the bark as he again struggled to get free. "You can't leave me here!"

"Where are the girls?"

"Fuck you."

She turned back toward Cooper. "Have a good evening, Mr. Carter. Don't let the mosquitos bite."

CHAPTER TWO

Tuesday, September 13, 1:00 a.m.

Cigar smoke. The clink of poker chips. Soft music. Men arguing.

The pungent scent was the first to reach below the medicated haze and tug Vicky toward consciousness. Nose wrinkling, she coughed as smoke puffed across her face.

"Wake up."

Fatigue weighed heavily, coaxing her back toward the darkness where it was safe, warm, and quiet. It had been weeks since she had slept well. Jax kept her awake working night after night, having her make nice to whoever had money. To sleep on a soft cushion with no one touching her was a luxury. To surrender to the light felt cruel.

"Wake up!"

Sleep's iron hold loosened as she clung to it. She did not want to wake up. Awake meant a return to the streets and the dimming hope Jax loved her. But to resist tempted Jax's temper, and nobody wanted him mad. Jax's other girl, Jo-Jo, was always pushing him, and her back talk had earned her a couple of beatings.

More smoke blew against her face, seeping and slithering up her nostrils, prying her free from the safety and security of the darkness.

She coughed again, stumbling unwillingly toward consciousness as her eyes opened. Grimacing, she raised her hand like a shield as a half-hearted offer came automatically. "You want to party? I like to party."

"Wake up. Please." Another voice. Another man.

A deeply rooted survival instinct chased away the fatigue. Where was she?

She pushed herself up into a sitting position. Pain split and cracked through her skull as if one of Jax's fists had struck her. Drawing in a breath, she lowered her hand and focused on her surroundings.

The room was bathed in ivories and creams. Gilded trims. Lights glistening in crystal. Every detail in the room screamed expensive. Uptown. Not like the truck stop motels, her normal territory. The truckers she knew. Quick. Easy. But this . . . this was not good. God, where had Jax sent her?

She pressed trembling fingers to her forehead, rooting for her last clear memory. She had been with Jax and Jo-Jo. She and Jo-Jo were surprised when he took them to the diner and bought burgers, extra fries, and large sodas. The girls were so hungry they didn't think beyond the food. Toward the end of the meal, a guy joined them in the booth. A friend of Jax's.

Memories reached out, grabbing hold of the present. And then, in a blink, she remembered. The friend's name was Kevin. He was tall, well dressed, with gold cuff links and buffed nails. Dark-brown hair was cut short and slicked back, emphasizing blue eyes. She remembered thinking he didn't look like a Kevin.

Jax, looking a little nervous, ordered him coffee as if he were the grand host. As Kevin sipped the dark, bitter brew, he asked her and Jo-Jo questions. What's your name? Where're you from? The guy needed conversation. Not all the johns liked to talk, but this one did. Jax quickly grew tired of the questions and cut off her last answer.

"Which one do you want?"

Kevin sat back in the booth, studying her face as he tapped a nervous finger against the table. "She has the right look. How much?"

"Two grand."

No one had ever paid that kind of money for her before and she expected Kevin to laugh. But he wasn't put off by the price and handed Jax a handful of crisp one-hundred-dollar bills. "There's a little more. I'll need her a few extra hours."

Vicky shifted, nervous. Men paid that kind of money when they wanted something different, and she worried what that meant.

Jax grinned, his gold tooth winking in the light. "Sure. But I want her back in twenty-four hours."

"Right." Kevin's gaze dropped to his cup of coffee. He offered her another soda, but Jax said she'd had enough. Jax hustled them all out of the booth and the diner. Kevin opened the front door of a sleek black car and waited for her to settle inside. She nestled into the car's front seat. When he slid behind the wheel she reached for his crotch, but he brushed her hand away.

"I thought you wanted to party," she said.

"No."

That unexpected twist revved her fears.

Kevin gripped the steering wheel, but smiled. "Don't worry. I'm going to get you fixed up. Hair. Nails. A new dress."

"Okay, sure." She didn't argue, fearing he'd tell Jax if she did.

"You'll like the dress."

"Sure."

Later, after her nails and hair were styled, he watched her slip on the yellow dress at his hotel room. The material was soft and silky. As he handed her a glass of champagne, his smile was mild. She started to relax. And then it all went black.

Struggling now to sit, she realized she still wore the yellow dress, as well as gold teardrop earrings and silver high-heeled shoes. She wasn't bleeding, hurting, or sore. *What the hell?*

"Is she awake?" the old man asked.

"Yes, she's awake." The second voice was familiar. Kevin.

"Where am I?" she asked. Her words rumbled in her head, crashing into the sides of her skull. "What did you do to me?"

Kevin shoved his hands in his pockets. "Nothing. You've been sleeping."

"Good, she's focusing," the old man said. "It's important she's *aware.*"

Aware of what?

She craned her neck to see a large round mahogany table surrounded by four tufted chairs. Playing cards lay in three neat piles, suggesting two players and a dealer. In the center of the table lay a pile of light-blue and a few brown poker chips, and on top of the chips, a torn sheet of notebook paper. A marker.

"Water," she said. "My throat is dry."

Kevin's smooth fingers pushed a water bottle into her hand, and she drank without thinking. Cool liquid slid down her throat and eased the thirst. The familiar dread of facing a new john returned.

When she finished drinking, Kevin took the bottle. She looked up into Kevin's dark, now-worried eyes. Stubble darkened his chin. His loosened red tie dangled against a white rumpled shirt with sleeves rolled up to his elbows. How long had she been out?

This didn't make sense. "What happened to me?"

A smile tipped the edges of Kevin's lips. "Like I said, you've been sleeping."

They might not have hurt her yet, but that didn't mean shit. *Get the hell out of here.*

The warning voice echoed in her head. She moistened her lips. "Jax is gonna be mad if I don't call him. I'm supposed to call him every hour."

As if she'd not spoken, the old man said, "It's time. I won and winner chooses life or death."

"He'll hurt me if I don't call," Vicky said. "He's got a bad temper. I'll do whatever you want, but just let me check in with Jax."

"You and I could play another hand," Kevin said. "Double or nothing?"

"No." Impatience sharpened the word. "This was the last hand. You lost. Now I choose . . . death."

Death. The word jacked up her heart rate. Vicky pushed herself up on wobbly legs. "I need to get out of here. I'm going to be sick." Not true, but if they thought she'd barf on their floor, they might let her rush out of here. She took a step and her legs shook. Running was impossible. Walking a stretch.

The old man had a face pale as milk, but his eyes were black as coal. "Kevin, pay up now or I shoot you. You know how the game is played. We all agreed to the terms before the first card was dealt."

"I know. I know," he stammered.

The old man raised a gun and laid it on the table. A white shirt billowed over a thinning chest. "Do this or I'll kill everyone you love first. Your wife, Jennifer. Your brother, Nate, who just got out of jail. Then you die."

Hearing the names of his family robbed Kevin of words. And then, "Why does she have to die? I'll talk to her. She'll be quiet."

The old man rubbed his thumb against his clenched fist. "I thought you were ready for the game. I thought you wanted the high stakes."

He picked up a single chip and turned it over. "I do. I did. I thought . . ."

"That you'd win. Everyone thinks they'll win." He leaned back in his chair, gently turning a poker chip over. A thick cigar dangled from his other hand, the smoke trailing from the glowing tip. Trimmed nails and a gold signet ring caught the light.

Vicky's attention was so focused on the old man at the table, she didn't see Kevin approach. When she noticed his fine leather shoes standing beside her, she pivoted to run. Too quickly. Dizziness. She fell to her knees.

Kevin's trembling hands moved quickly, wrapping a thin strap of leather around her neck. He twisted. Tightened.

She coughed and grabbed the leather. "Kevin. Don't."

"I'm sorry, Vicky," he whispered close to her ear. "But I agreed. Winner chooses."

"Please." Her windpipe closed.

"Forgive me."

Her hands groped at the cord, and when she couldn't wedge her fingers under it, she reached for his wrists. She scratched and pulled but didn't have the strength to loosen the binding.

She gagged. Coughed. Thrashed.

Kevin hesitated, the cord slackened, and she drew in a desperate breath as she caught his reflection in the mirror. "Please," she said with the last wisp of air from her lungs.

His eyes were a swirl of regret and sorrow. "I have to do this." He leaned closer, nestling his lips close to her ears. "Don't fight, and the end will come faster."

The old man rose and moved toward them. More smoke coiled like a serpent as he raised the cigar to his mouth. His eyes danced with fascination and triumph. She thought this might be how he got off. Watching women suffer did it for some. But he wasn't hard and he made no move to touch himself. What kind of game was this?

The question must have reflected in her gaze as she looked at him. He smiled. "You were his stake in the poker game. His Lady Luck." His voice sounded as if it were rubbed raw with sandpaper. "We don't play for money. Too boring. We play for life and death."

Kevin tightened his grip quickly this time, cutting off her oxygen. Her vision blurred. She blinked, realizing she was going to die.

"I'm sorry," Kevin whispered. "It was a sure bet."

"They're all sure," the old man said. His hand trembled slightly as he stared at the glowing tip of the cigar. "Everyone thinks Lady Luck will give them the winning hand. Amateurs. Lady Luck screws us all in the end. Best we can do is squeeze the luck out of her as long as we can."

"I'm sorry." Kevin's fingers twisted the rope tighter.

She couldn't pull in any air. All her mother's warnings replayed alongside her father's predictions that she'd die young.

"Don't be sorry," the old man said. "You're doing her a favor. They're never the same after they've been on the streets."

With a determined grunt, Kevin yanked the strap deeper into her skin, crushing her windpipe. She arched back, her hands clawing at his arms. Veins in her neck bulged as her heart pounded in her chest, and her lungs hungry for oxygen burned.

She would have begged, pleaded, or traded her body or her soul to live. But Kevin's reflection in the mirror told her words would have no effect.

The old man reached for her hand and took it in a weak grip. Frustration burned in his eyes. As her vision blurred, she realized he wanted to be the one doing the killing, but he couldn't. Age or illness had robbed him of the ability.

The old man kissed her softly on the back of her hand. And more to himself, he said, "You look like my Lady Luck."

She was dying because she looked like someone else?

Vicky's world dimmed and her eyes closed. As her body slackened toward the ground, Kevin wept. One of his tears dripped on her cheek. And the abyss swallowed her.

***

Clay Bowman stood outside the small brick rancher, taking note of Riley Tatum's police cruiser parked in her driveway. The house was dark, but there was enough light from the sliver of moon to tell him something about the woman who had spent the better part of the day tracking in the woods. The lawn was cut and shrubs trimmed, but the three flowerpots clustered on the side of the house were an empty testament to a failed gardening attempt. He never imagined her tending flowers or a vegetable garden. Domesticity wasn't her style.

A second car in the driveway had him wondering if that car was hers or if she lived with someone. When he conjured up her image, he always pictured her single, but a woman like her didn't stay alone long. When he had spoken to her in the woods, she'd looked at him as if she recognized him, but the situation hadn't allowed room for the past. Not that it mattered. He'd had a chance to love her once and had tossed it away.

Yesterday's mission was to track her in the woods. Keep her safe. And he had done it, glad he was there for the takedown, which had sent a thrill of much-needed adrenaline through his body. Retirement, as it turned out, didn't suit him. Lazy days on the front porch, fixing up the old house, savoring sunsets—all sounded good when he was part of the FBI's Hostage Rescue Team hoofing it through the woods, carrying a one-hundred-pound pack, and chasing fugitives. When he'd turned in his badge, he thought he was done with the cops-and-robbers shit.

But three weeks of downtime was his limit. When Shield Security had offered him the job, he took it on the spot.

He was back in the game. So what the hell was he doing standing outside Riley's house like a crazed stalker?

As he turned to leave, a light clicked on in the house and he drew back toward the shadows. He checked his watch: 3:00 a.m. A silhouette of a woman passed in front of a window, and he recognized her long, lean frame.

She moved into the kitchen, dressed in a running top and jogging shorts. She switched on the coffeepot and threaded her fingers through her long dark hair, arching back slightly as she knotted it all into a ponytail. Minutes later she was sipping coffee, leaning against the counter and staring into the night. He took another step back.

Bowman had first met Riley five years ago. It had been six months after his wife died and he was training a group of police officers in search-and-rescue techniques at Quantico. Riley was one of his best students, and he noticed her the first day of class. He also caught her stealing glances at him. Several times she asked questions about the training, and it took effort for him to keep his gaze off the rise and swell of her breasts under the regulation T-shirt.

But they kept their distance until her last night at the school. She showed up at his motel room. Kissed him. And they fell into bed, pulling off clothes and going at it as if possessed. He drove into her, savoring the feel of her. She was so passionate.

He still remembered when he woke up, Riley nestled by his side, feeling happy for the first time since Karen's diagnosis. However, on the heels of this happiness was guilt. He felt disloyal to a dead wife who had loved him unconditionally.

When Riley awoke later, he was standing fully dressed by the window of his drab motel room. She came up behind him, pressing her full breasts against his back. His body responded immediately to her and he wanted to lean back, savor her touch, and go back to bed. But guilt shuddered through him as he glanced at his ring finger, which still bore the faint tan lines of the wedding band he'd worn for a decade.

Instead of loving Riley, he found himself resenting her vibrant health. She was full of life, and Karen was dead. And in the hours they'd been together, he'd forgotten about Karen and cared only about Riley and himself. How could he so easily abandon precious memories of a woman he'd cherished?

Unable to face Riley, he told her to leave. He had work, he said. He could sense the tension and confusion rippling through her body. She lingered another beat as if hoping she'd heard him wrong.

"Are you sure?" she whispered.

"Yeah."

She drew away, detecting the cut underscoring the words. Without any discussion, she reached for her clothes. He heard the jerk of jeans sliding up over her long legs and her rooting for the shirt and boots.

"I don't know why, but I thought this was more than a casual hookup." Under the formal tone simmered sadness. "I thought we had something," she said in a controlled, clear voice.

He dared a glance at her and saw raw pain glistening in her eyes. "I can't do this."

She didn't beg, plead, or make a case for them. A shrug of her shoulders and she tugged on her boots. "Right."

That was the last time he'd seen her until yesterday on the mountain.

Bowman wasn't sure why he'd tracked Riley to her home. She sure didn't need his help after the stunt he'd pulled at Quantico five years ago. She owned a home and had one hell of a job and a life. She had her shit together better than him.

And yet, here he stood in the shadows craving what he'd recklessly tossed away.

CHAPTER THREE

Tuesday, September 13, 2:00 p.m.

A body had been found in a field. Riley had received the radio call fifteen minutes ago. The dispatcher didn't have much more information, noting the caller sounded distraught.

Her lights flashing, she nosed her state police SUV onto the shoulder behind an old red Chevy pickup truck. She was the first officer at the scene.

She glanced in the rearview mirror at an alert Cooper. "Ready?" He thumped his tail and barked. Yesterday's chase had left her with slightly sunburned skin and briar scrapes, but she was good for duty today.

Out of the car, she glanced back toward the off-ramp leading from I-95. With no traffic approaching, she went to the passenger-side back door and hooked Cooper's tracking line. "Come on, boy, let's go to work."

Pulling her shoulders back, she settled her cap on her head and searched the truck for signs of the man who called in the report. To leave fingerprints and physical proof of contact, she touched the tailgate and rooftop with her hand, then peered in the driver's-side window.

Seeing no signs of him, she and Cooper moved toward the scrub of trees bordering the roadside.

Beyond the trees was a field filled with tall grass. A flicker of plaid and denim flashed to her right and she turned, hand on her weapon. An older man with a thick shock of white hair moved toward her, his shoulders stooped and his eyes wide with worry. A short, scruffy beard covered his angled jaw.

"About time," he said. "I called a half hour ago."

"I'm Trooper Tatum. Can you tell me what you found?" Cooper sat next to her, staring with a keen gaze at the man.

"Like I told the lady on the phone," he said, stealing looks at the dog, "I found a body. Jesus, scared the life out of me."

She fished a small notebook and pencil from her back pocket. "What's your name, sir?"

"Russell Hudson. I manage and own all the land on this stretch of road. I live off Route 602 about two miles from here."

She recorded his name and address. "What were you doing out here today?"

"I'm leasing the field to a promoter. A music festival is coming to the area in two weeks. I was fixing to cut the field with my tractor, but wanted to walk the land first."

"And that's when you found a body?"

"Yeah. I saw a flicker of white by the trees over there and went to check it out. The dead girl is leaning against the tree trunk." He pointed to a tall oak. "I can show you."

She pressed the radio button mounted on her vest and relayed her position. Dispatch confirmed the sheriff's deputy was en route. "Let's have a look, Mr. Hudson."

They moved through the thick grass until they came to a tree centered in a small clearing. At the base of the tree was the body of a young woman. Her head was slumped forward, sending long dark hair cascading over her face and breasts. Her neatly manicured hands rested in her lap, making her look almost polite, demure.

"Shit, the sight of her still makes me sick. I'll never forget this. I saw dead bodies when I was in the navy, but it was never a girl like this."

"Have you touched her or moved her in any way?"

He held up bent hands. "Hell, no. I'm not going near that."

"Stay here."

"Suits me fine."

Riley tugged on latex gloves, moving through the brush with Cooper. A sick, sweet scent wafted around her, a harbinger of the pungent scent of decomposition.

She knelt and touched the girl's wrist. Cold, stiff, and no pulse. By her looks she was young, not more than twenty. Faded jeans skimmed over slim hips and a peasant blouse clung to full breasts. There were no signs of trauma to the body, but as much as Riley wanted to tip back the cascade of hair and search for a cause of death, she'd leave that for the forensic team.

Rising, she clicked her radio on. "This is Trooper Tatum. I have visual on a young female victim. You can check with county, but I'm sure they'll need the state lab to do the forensic collection." She patrolled in a small rural county policed by a handful of deputies. They had the capability of collecting some forensic data, but a case like this would require more support.

She and Cooper walked back toward Mr. Hudson. "Do you have any idea who this girl might be?"

"Never saw her."

"Have you seen anyone else in this area since you arrived?"

"Nope, just me."

"When's the last time you were on the land?"

Hudson scratched his gray beard on his chin. "Two or three days ago, and I didn't see her."

"You're sure?"

"Damn straight. I wouldn't miss *that*." He rubbed his eyes as if trying to erase the girl's image. "This is the last problem I expected."

"Have you noticed any unfamiliar cars in the area?"

"No. Business as usual."

Long stretches of desolate country road didn't mean traffic went unnoticed. Someone usually saw something.

He pulled a handkerchief and wiped his brow with fingers bent of age and arthritis. "Do you mind if I get out of here? Seeing her gives me the creeps."

"Mr. Hudson, I'd like you to wait in your truck for a little bit longer. The local deputies might have questions for you."

"I've got work." He shook his head. "I'm counting on the money from the lease of the land. This contract will settle a lot of bills."

"Yes, sir, I understand. But you need to wait."

"How long do you think it'll be before I can cut this grass?"

"I don't know, sir, but you need to wait."

He shook his head again. "Jesus H. Christ. What a mess."

"Yes, sir."

As he slid into his truck, a sheriff's deputy arrived, nudging behind her SUV.

The responding deputy rose out of his car and settled his hat on his head. Riley recognized Deputy Harris DuPont's tall, lanky frame. They'd crossed paths over the years, and each time he made it clear he didn't like outsiders in his jurisdiction.

DuPont paused at the red truck to talk to Mr. Hudson. He laughed, touched the brim of his hat before settling his gaze on Riley.

As DuPont approached her, she adjusted her sunglasses, determined to make nice. "Harris, been a while. Molly and the baby doing well?"

He cleared his throat, his gaze skimming over her. A shake of his head betrayed disapproval. "They're both fine."

"Good to hear."

"Saw you and your dog on the news. You're the popular one." An edge lurked under his tone.

Absently, she tapped her finger on her gun belt. "Won't be long before we're yesterday's news."

He hitched his big hands on his belt. "Naw. Not you." His smile didn't mask the sarcasm. "I bet they promote you to agent within the year."

She'd considered applying for the promotion to agent, but moving up meant leaving Cooper to a new handler, and that she'd never do. As long as Cooper could work, she'd be with him. "Maybe, one day."

"Ah, come on. You have to admit your career is gonna get a boost."

"I was doing my job."

Blue eyes narrowed. "I heard you had help on that mountain."

"Really?"

"Two other deputies said they were there for the arrest. Said they pulled Carter off the mountain."

She smiled, refusing to let him annoy her. "They arrived later, but I don't recall seeing anyone around when I was cuffing Carter to a tree."

He took a step closer. "You don't get all the credit. Team effort."

"Right."

He tugged the brim of his hat lower over his eyes. "What can you tell me about the victim?"

"Victim is a young female. Brown hair. Wearing a white top and jeans. Brown boots."

Nodding, he dug crime scene tape from his trunk and crossed the field to within five feet of the body. "Looks like one of those hookers from the truck stops. The ones you're always trying to save."

Annoyed, she studied the mop of hair draped over the victim's face. In the few years Riley had been working the I-95 corridor, she'd learned none of the prostitutes were in the profession by choice. Pimps promising a better life coerced many of the young girls into the sex trade. But guys like DuPont didn't see sex slaves or human trafficking victims. They saw hookers or strippers looking to make quick cash.

All local law enforcement along the I-95, which cut a two-hundred-mile swath through the center of the state, knew she cared about cases like this one.

"Russell Hudson is anxious to get back to work. With the concert coming, he can't waste hours in the middle of the day," DuPont said.

"I asked him to stay for now."

"Doesn't make sense. Russell didn't kill that girl." His gaze scanned the field. "He's making a fortune leasing the land. We haven't had a murder in this county in a couple of years."

"Officer Tatum?" her radio squawked.

She pressed the microphone button at her chest. "Tatum."

"Forensics has been dispatched. About a half hour away."

"Roger."

DuPont's gaze narrowed as he glanced up at the clear, cloudless sky. "Nothing to do but sit and wait."

The idea of standing here and waiting made her skin crawl. She wasn't good with stillness, much less listening to DuPont's latest theory on politics. "I'm going to take my dog for a look around the field. He might find something."

"Suit yourself."

She tugged Cooper's line. "Ready to do some work?"

The dog barked and wagged his tail.

Cooper sniffed the air and tugged on the line. They moved back toward the tall grass, and Cooper took her straight to the body. He wasn't a cadaver dog, but the scent was strong and hard to ignore. She let him sniff the ground and the area before he turned from the body and guided her into a thicket of woods. She followed, not sure where they were going. They were thirty feet into the woods when she spotted the black backpack sitting on the ground. Cooper sat in front of it, barked, and wagged his tail. She rubbed him on the head and praised him for the find.

Kneeling, she opted not to touch the bag. She'd bet money it belonged to the victim. She waved to DuPont to mark the place, and when he finally made his way with an orange flag, she and Cooper kept searching.

By the time two more deputy patrol cars arrived, she and Cooper had searched a large grid area of the grassland and found nothing else. News of the Woodstock-like concert planned here in early October was exciting for many of the local businesses. Hotels within sixty miles were sold out, and restaurants and food vendors were gearing up. What would happen now was anyone's guess.

When she heard the engine of the forensic van arrive, she returned to the crime scene. She glanced across the field and saw Harris shake the technicians' hands. She looked toward the scene and spotted a familiar uniformed officer, the forensic investigator Martin Thompson, working the crime scene.

Martin moved toward the body with two large cases, one in each hand. The technicians trailed, each carrying a piece of equipment. Within minutes, a tent was set up along with a folding table stocked with equipment.

By the time she returned to the body, Martin was setting up a camera designed to take a 360-degree panoramic image of the scene. She stepped outside the crime scene tape and watched as the camera's eye swept the field around the dead girl.

"Trooper Tatum," Martin said finally. "What can you tell me about the scene?" He wore a short-sleeved blue shirt embossed with a state police logo, khakis, and boots. Dark hair and a thick mustache were both trimmed close, making his angled face look sharper and leaner.

"Body of a young woman was found by a local farmer walking the field. Beyond confirming she doesn't have a pulse, I let her be. Cooper found a backpack close by. I think it belongs to her."

Satisfied he had a good shot of the overall crime scene, he hefted a 35 mm digital camera and took a couple of practice shots. He moved toward the tape, focusing on specific elements of the scene. Click. Click. He captured shot after shot, working his way around the tape. The images might not be interesting to a civilian, but they could capture a critical clue missed by the naked eye.

Martin approached the body and with gloved hands brushed back her hair. "There are ligature marks on her neck," he said. "Medical examiner will make the call, but my money's on strangulation."

Sadness tugged at Riley.

"She's in full rigor mortis," he said. The stiffening of the limbs developed within two to six hours after death and eventually dissipated within twenty-four to forty-eight hours.

"So she died within the last day?" Riley asked.

"That's the best guess until the medical examiner takes a liver temperature. That will pinpoint time of death better."

"Okay."

"Harris looks annoyed," Martin said. "Looks like he ate a sour apple."

"You know how he loves having state police around." Her belt creaked as she shifted her stance. She needed a distraction from the lifeless body. "How's the running going? I heard you're training for a marathon." Outsiders rarely understood how cops could make small talk at a murder scene, but sometimes clinging to everyday life helped them deal with the horrors.

He opened a paper bag and pulled it over the victim's left hand. The bag would save any DNA trapped under her fingernails. "The running is doing its best to kill me."

Riley smiled. "Hang tough. You'll come to love it."

"If you say so." His tone was always indifferent, his expression stoic, and his sentences factual to the point of dry. "I understand you've filed adoption papers."

"That's right. Soon I'll be the proud mother of a seventeen-year-old. Hanna is thrilled. I'm hoping social services doesn't find any reason to reject my petition."

"I don't see why they would."

"My job has crazy hours."

"Raising a teenage daughter is an undertaking, but you've done well so far, right?"

"So far so good. You have teenage girls, right?"

"Three." Martin photographed the victim's body, arms, hands, and face. The girl's eyes were half-open, her jaw slack, but despite death, Riley recognized her. The invisible weight on her shoulders doubled. "I've seen her before working at a truck stop."

"Doing what?"

"Hooking."

He shook his head. "Girls like this don't fare well."

It had been four weeks since she'd seen this girl vanish into the motor home. She'd been ready to knock on the door and demand to see her. Then the call came from dispatch and she'd been pulled away. What would have happened if she'd been at the scene just another ten minutes? Would she have had time to check IDs and find out where the girl really belonged? "No, they do not."

Martin leaned in and checked the victim's front and back pockets. He retrieved a crumpled dollar bill, a stick of gum, and two condoms. "We might find ID in the backpack."

As he drew closer and studied the ligature marks on the neck, he said, "There's a tattoo on the back of her neck. There's an extra pair of gloves on my worktable over there. Put them on and you can have a look."

She moved to the table, noting the neatly organized bags, cameras, and sketch pads. Martin insisted on organization. She plucked a fresh pair of latex gloves from the box and pulled them onto her hands.

As she moved toward Martin, he lifted the curtain of hair off the neck. Above the ligature mark were the initials *JC*. The letters were crudely written, the dark ink thick and uneven. She knew them for what they were. *JC*. "Jax Carter's brand."

"The man you arrested?" Martin asked.

"I knew he controlled several girls. He put one in the hospital with broken bones, but he wouldn't tell me where the other girls were. I'll bet money the motor home I saw this girl vanish into belonged to him."

"Heard he spent the night cuffed to a tree," Martin said.

"The deputies were only an hour behind me."

Martin's dark eyes danced with amusement. "I heard they weren't in a real rush."

"Safety first. Didn't want anyone twisting an ankle."

The humor faded from his gaze as he shifted his attention back to the body. "Well, then he couldn't have killed this girl."

Riley agreed. "But he has a girlfriend named Darla Johnson. I pulled up her arrest record. She looks strong enough to have done it."

"How many girls does he have?"

"It's a guess, but I'd say two or three at a time. I stopped by the hospital to talk to the kid Jax beat up, but she's still out of it. Broken ribs and heroin withdrawal. It'll be a few days before she can talk."

Martin scowled. "That kid has a long road ahead of her."

"Police got a look at her cell phone," Riley said. "There're quite a few texts between Jax and the girl."

"Not a big surprise."

"No, it's not," Riley said. "I'd have waited, but the media arrived outside the hospital."

"I know you. You'll see her soon and get some answers."

"I will." Riley studied the victim's sightless gaze. A ring of purple bruises wrapped around her neck like a morbid piece of jewelry. Reaching for her phone, she snapped a picture of the girl's face.

"Who's investigating the murder?" Martin asked.

"I don't know if it's been assigned yet, but I bet the investigation gets tossed to state police. This case reaches beyond the county's jurisdiction, and no one is going to want an unsolved homicide before a big concert brings in lots of people and money."

Martin raised the camera as he snapped more pictures of the victim. High cheekbones tapered into parted full lips. Her peasant top rode up, exposing a narrow waist and the underside of full breasts. The jeans were a standard variety, not designer, but they looked new and clean. She wore no shoes, but her toenails were freshly painted a bright red, like her fingernails.

As Riley knelt next to the girl's face, a bone-deep sadness settled. "So damn young," she said, more to herself. A few more minutes and maybe she could have saved her.

Martin clicked through the last few camera images, studying them. "At her age I was more worried about passing my final chemistry exam or making sure I had a date on Saturday night."

Riley had worried over her share of tests, but dates had been a low priority after her mother died and her stepfather's ogling turned hungry.

In the days after the funeral, she'd hear him pacing in front of her door as if mustering his courage. When he finally burst into the room and moved toward her, she curled her fingers into a fist and punched him. He swore, cupping his bloodied nose as he retreated. Terrified, she slammed her door and pushed her dresser in front of it. And when he tried the knob and couldn't get in, he pounded on her door, demanding she let him inside. *You're like your mother. Selfish, cold. Never good enough.*

When her stepfather left for work the next day, she shoved clothes and whatever cash she could find into a backpack and left. Her plan was to get a job in one of the New Orleans diners or restaurants and find a new place to live. She was convinced any life was better than hers. However, like most kids who took to the streets, she underestimated the monsters lurking by the abyss.

Riley had sugarcoated her teen years when she'd met with Hanna's social worker. She had never lied but a lot went unsaid.

Squad car lights flashed on the trees, drawing her gaze over her shoulder. Sheriff Bobby Barrett's black SUV parked behind Deputy DuPont's vehicle, carving a spot out of the mud and gravel.

Sheriff Barrett stood close to six feet. Twenty-five years separated him from his training days, and though time had swapped muscle for bulk, he retained his determined jock gait that telegraphed to the world to stand clear.

"The party has started," Martin said.

"What, I don't count?" Riley asked.

"You're a baby in the eyes of the area sheriffs' offices. Ol' Bobby is the king of it all. Tell me you've had your shots. I hear he bites."

Rising, Riley dusted the dirt from her hands. "I bite back."

Martin shook his head. "Now that, I'd like to see."

Sheriff Barrett paused to talk to DuPont, and the two exchanged a hearty handshake along with a couple of easy smiles. However, Sheriff Barrett's smile vanished when he glanced past DuPont and saw her.

Refusing to look away, she pulled a brand-new small spiral notebook from her back pocket. She filled dozens of notebooks like this one each year.

She watched as DuPont raised the tape for Sheriff Barrett and smiled, easy and relaxed. The sheriff's long strides cut through the weeds, which she imagined magically parted for the guy who had been the sheriff for two decades.

"To what do we owe the honor of the state police?" the sheriff asked.

"Received a call from Russell Hudson. He found a body," Riley said.

"Where's Russ?" the sheriff asked.

"In his car. He's not happy about staying."

"Ah hell, there's no need to hold him." He turned and ordered DuPont to send Russ home. "We can find him anytime we need. And I know he sure didn't kill this girl."

Riley watched as DuPont hustled over to Russ's truck and gave him the good news. The man nodded, tossed her a glare, and drove off.

"So do we know the victim's identity?" Sheriff Barrett asked.

"No ID," Riley said. "But I crossed paths with her about four weeks ago. I didn't get a name, but she was hanging out with Jax Carter. My dog also found a backpack about fifty yards north."

"She's not from this area, or if she is, she's new," Barrett said.

She showed the sheriff the girl's tattoo and gave him the update on Jax.

"So she's a hooker," Sheriff Barrett concluded.

"She's a kid."

Hearing the anger humming under her tone, he planted thick fingers on his gun belt. "Don't you got bigger fish to fry?"

Contempt scraped the underside of her skin. If this victim's daddy were rich or gave a damn, this place would be covered with cops. "Not right now."

"My money says she's a hooker working the I-95 truck stops. With a concert that's supposed to bring in several thousand people, it makes sense that the traffickers like Carter would be moving girls into the area." The case was hours old and Barrett already sounded tired.

"We might learn more when we run her prints through AFIS," Riley said. The Automated Fingerprint Information System maintained fingerprints from a variety of sources, including arrests, employment, and background checks.

"Makes sense," he said.

"Wouldn't hurt for me to hit the hangouts where the runaways gather as I'm patrolling today." Someone always knew something, and it was simply a matter of finding the right person. The faster she moved, the better her chances of unearthing a lead before it went cold.

He shrugged as if his mind had already shifted to more important cases. "I won't say no. You'll keep me posted."

"Of course."

Martin straightened. "Let's have a look at the backpack."

Martin planted a number next to the backpack. Next he documented the item first in a sketch, then with more pictures. "Sheriff, you can open the backpack now."

The sheriff shook his head. "Let Tatum do the honors. She was first at the scene."

Riley unzipped the bag and examined the contents: a water bottle on top of worn jeans, a sweatshirt smelling of sweat and dirt, athletic shoes slightly worn on the bottom, a yellow dress, heels, and a toothbrush wrapped in a plastic bag.

Sheriff Barrett tugged off his glasses and leaned closer. The lines around his eyes and mouth deepened as he frowned. "ID?"

"Not in the bag," she said.

In a side pocket she found several crumpled one-dollar bills and a pamphlet for a youth emergency shelter she recognized.

Sheriff Barrett rested a hand on his holstered gun. "Trooper, what's the backpack tell you about her?"

"The bag suggests she's been moving around," Riley said. "She's thin, likely underfed by Jax, so she's been with him at least a month. But the pedicure looks fresh and professional. Most pimps like Jax don't make that kind of investment. Girls like her are lucky to get a shower and fed."

Martin straightened and lowered his camera, bending backward to stretch his back.

"I see the pamphlet is for Duke Spence's shelter," Sheriff Barrett said. "Spence is always handing out flyers at the truck stops, malls, and city streets." He looked at the victim. "There was something about that girl I couldn't put my finger on until now. She looks a little like you, Trooper."

Riley, grateful for the protection of her sunglasses, delayed her comment until her annoyance passed. "Not even close."

The sheriff shrugged. "Not saying that to rattle your cage, Tatum. I mean it."

Not convinced his intentions were sincere, she didn't look at the body. "Dark hair and tanned skin. That's about all we share."

Sheriff Barrett stared at the dead girl's face a long moment. "Hell, Tatum, she could be your sister."

His words burrowed under her skin and he knew it. Cops were always searching for weakness within their ranks, and she'd absorbed her share of hazing when she first rode patrol. With cops, the teasing never really stopped.

Grinning with satisfaction, he checked a worn black Timex watch. "When will the body be transported to the medical examiner's office?" he asked.

"About an hour," Martin said. "Team is on the way."

Eight years of working patrol had introduced her to death multiple times. Car accidents, shootings, domestic fights. Still, heaviness settled in Riley's chest as she struggled to remember the girl alive. No one deserved this.

Kids from the streets were invisible to most. Faceless. Nameless. Most of the politicians didn't care if a homeless kid, here or there, vanished. This girl's death would soon fall off the radar.

"Riley," Martin said. "Open the side pouch of the backpack while I photograph it."

Riley squatted and unzipped the pocket. She held the flap open while the camera snapped.

"Go ahead and remove the contents of the bag," Martin said.

She reached in and pulled out five playing cards, which she fanned. Thick paper stock. The face of each card was smooth, but carefully detailed. Tension rippled up her arm, and when she turned the cards over and stared at the ornate scroll pattern on the backing, her breath caught. The word *Loser* was written in bold black lettering on the back of each card. "A three of spades, a two of diamonds, a five of clubs, a four of hearts, and a king of diamonds."

The cards struck an unwelcome chord she thought long buried from a case dating back twelve years. As her heart kicked into gear, Riley was careful to keep her expression neutral as she bagged each one and handed them to Sheriff Barrett.

"If she was playing poker," Sheriff Barrett said, "she would've been a loser. She was holding about the worst possible hand."

"The deck of cards to a serious player is critical," Riley said.

"You a card player?" Sheriff Barrett sounded amused.

"Stepfather was a big gambler. According to him there were good cards and bad cards."

Sheriff Barrett shrugged. "They're all good. Depends on the combination you need."

The heat of the day faded; the sound of traffic on the main road vanished.

When she'd run away, street life was far tougher than she'd imagined. She quickly ran out of money and within days was so hungry. When a church volunteer had offered her bottled water, she'd taken it gladly. That was the last thing she remembered. She lost seven days.

At the end of those missing days when she'd crawled free of a void, she could barely focus, her system loaded with some narcotic cocktail. But one of her first memories was of finding five playing cards in her back pocket. Same deck as these, different spread. But there were no words scrawled on her cards.

CHAPTER FOUR

Tuesday, September 13, 3:00 p.m.

Riley stood in the field staring at the cards, burrowing into those lost days in her past, trying to remember any detail.

"Riley?"

She glanced up at the sheriff. "Yeah."

The lines around his eyes deepened. "You see something?"

She tore her gaze from the cards. "I thought I did, but no."

"You sure?" Sheriff Barrett had been a cop too long not to sense tension or smell an evasion.

"I thought they reminded me of an old case I came across a couple of years ago." Lies worked best when you kept the details scant and threaded in the truth when possible. "But I was wrong." She handed the cards back to him.

The sheriff held the plastic bag up to the light and glared at the cards as if searching for what she might have seen. "Where do you think they came from?"

Keeping her voice steady when she spoke, she said, "These are professional-grade cards. They don't come cheap."

"And the word *Loser?*"

"I don't know." The crisp lines of the white-and-black baroque were more likely linked to a high-stakes private game. She studied the delicate pattern.

"You sure?" Sheriff Barrett asked.

She looked toward the victim again, studying the color of her hair, the long, lean limbs, and the tapered hands. "Nothing catches my eye yet."

"Trooper, you're studying that face mighty hard," the sheriff said.

Riley straightened but made no comment.

"We don't get many murders in this county, but always stings more when they're young. I never get used to it."

"Once I have the scene processed," Martin said, "I'll let you know if we find anything else."

"Sounds good," Sheriff Barrett said.

Riley was puzzled by the body's position. "The killer took the time to pose her sitting up as if she were resting. She's also fully dressed. He could have abused the body, but he didn't. And her face was turned downward, so her eyes didn't look up at him."

"That's one way of looking at it, I guess," the sheriff said. "Or they could have been doing drugs or having sex and it went sideways."

She shook her head. "I don't think so. He strangles her, which is a very personal way of killing someone, but then he feels bad enough not to dump her body like a bag of trash."

"Maybe. Maybe not." Sheriff Barrett glanced back toward the interstate ramp. "The killer could have disposed of her body and been back on his way north or south in a matter of minutes."

"He could be three states away by now."

"Martin, any tire tracks?" the sheriff asked.

"Not in the field, but there are fresh ones on the side of the road just beyond Hudson's truck. I've dropped flags to preserve them. There are plenty of footprints, though. Someone walked around the body several times. Could have been Hudson, since the impressions were made by work boots, which I am assuming he's wearing."

"He is," Riley confirmed.

"I'll need impressions of Hudson's boots."

"I'll swing by his place and get them," Sheriff Barrett countered.

"Judging by the size of the footprints, I'd say a man's ten or eleven," Martin said.

"We should be able to clear Hudson as soon as I get his impressions," Sheriff Barrett said.

"A DNA swab wouldn't hurt," Martin added.

"Sure." The sheriff rolled his head from side to side. "Trooper, any other thoughts?"

"The victim is thin, so she wouldn't have been hard to carry," Riley said. Had he slung her over his shoulder or carried her in his arms? Both images, one suggesting disinterest and the other care, bothered her. She shook both off. As a cop, it was better to focus on facts rather than feelings. Easy enough during the daylight, but at night those denied emotions robbed her of sleep. "Can you tell if she died here?"

Martin examined the victim's back and side. The victim's right side was stippled with dark blue as if bruised. "When she died and her heart stopped, she was on her side. Likely stayed that way for a while—gave the blood time to settle. If she'd died here, like this, the blood would have settled in her hands and the bottom half of her legs. My guess is she died somewhere else."

"Gambling's not legal in this state," Sheriff Barrett observed as he studied the cards.

"Doesn't mean it can't happen. Private games go on all the time," Riley said. "The big players don't fuss with public venues."

"High stakes. In a fancy backroom game. Sounds far-fetched," he said, more to himself.

Riley blinked, remembering her stepfather had been a high roller who couldn't stay away from the tables. "These guys play with the best cards, and they hire the prettiest girls to serve them drinks and keep their mouth shut about what they see."

The sheriff's head cocked slightly as he studied her. "You pick all that up while on patrol?"

"I pay attention."

"All right," he said after a pause. "Keep me updated. I'll contact criminal investigations with the state and turn the case over to them."

"Sounds good."

Sheriff Barrett crossed the field, shook DuPont's hand, climbed in his car, and left.

"Are you okay, Riley?" Martin asked. "You look a little pale."

She cleared her throat and squared her shoulders. "Still worn out a little from yesterday. I'll be fine."

"Sure? Hell, you look like someone walked on your grave."

His concern pricked at her pride. "You're being dramatic."

"Yeah, that's me. Mr. Drama." A deadpan tone made the statement laughable.

"I can see that." Riley grinned, hoping to break the tension coiling inside her.

But the levity was fleeting. If not for the cards, she would have theorized that a john or one of Jax's friends had killed the girl. It was the most plausible conclusion. If not for the cards.

"Seriously, you okay?" Martin studied her like he would one of his crime scenes. "You ain't gonna faint on me, are you?"

She mustered another smile. "Hell, no."

"Thank God."

The crunch of gravel under tires had her turning to spot a television news van rolling up on the other side of the highway across from the spot Sheriff Barrett had vacated.

"Out of the frying pan and into the fire," Riley said.

"Good news travels fast."

"He's not here for this case. He's here for me. I saw him at the park yesterday, and he was at the hospital this morning."

"He wants to talk to the woman of the hour."

"Unfortunately. And thanks to the sheriff's perfect timing, I'm not going to be able to sneak away."

"Maybe DuPont will talk to him and run interference."

"DuPont isn't going to do me a favor."

"You handled the media well enough yesterday after the Carter arrest," Martin said.

"I didn't say a whole lot."

"Exactly. The less said the better."

"Even then, think twice."

The cards still playing on her mind, she moved back toward the road where DuPont and the other deputies stood, arms crossed, faces grim. In no mood to deal, she moved past them with a quick nod, knowing it would not serve her well to quip with a deputy while the media was close. Keeping her gaze trained ahead, she adjusted her sunglasses. "Have a good one."

No response followed as she approached her car and opened the backseat door to allow Cooper to jump inside. She switched on the engine and the air-conditioning.

The reporter, Eddie Potter, was a guy in his late forties who favored blue button-down shirts and khakis that hung loosely on his trim frame. He crossed toward her.

"Trooper!" he shouted, waving his hand. Behind him, an older, sturdy man unloaded the camera, and though he didn't stroll, he didn't race like the reporter. "I didn't get a chance to talk to you again this morning when they arrested Carter."

She settled Cooper in the backseat and closed the car door. "Yes, sir. What can I do for you?"

"Eddie Potter. I'm with local news."

"Yes, sir. I remember you from yesterday."

"Hell of a trek into the woods you made yesterday and a ballsy arrest." He glanced toward the backseat of her SUV. "That the famous Cooper?"

She moved to the right, blocking his view of the dog. "That's Cooper."

"I did a little digging. Human trafficking is your thing."

"My thing?"

"Bad choice of words. Your *cause*. Is that why you were determined to get Carter? We've all seen the video of him hitting that girl. Brutal."

"I can't comment."

Potter clicked the end of his pen several times. "You're interesting. I could do a whole profile on you."

She didn't want anyone digging into her life, especially with Hanna's adoption pending.

Deputy DuPont moved forward, his look more curious than threatening as he asked, "Can I help you?"

"Mr. Potter is curious about your crime scene," Riley said. "Do you have anything to add?"

DuPont shifted his weight and hitched his hands on his belt. "No comment."

Riley opened the car door, sliding into her seat and taking time to click her belt in place. "Have a nice day, Mr. Potter."

Putting the car in drive, she gave DuPont a wave and drove south back toward Richmond. Prints would be run and there would be an autopsy, but that likely wouldn't happen until tomorrow.

The rolling landscape was dotted with tall oaks and thick grass, and the North Anna River swept past. Fields quickly gave way to exit signs promising fast food, gas, and lodging. She took the Ashland exit and drove past strip malls toward the city's historic center. She lived in an old house near the train tracks that cut through the heart of the small town. But instead of turning toward her home, she went left to the town's center.

Cooper looked out the window, wagging his tail at the sight of the familiar streets.

"Sorry, Cooper, we aren't going home yet. Need to stop by Duke's."

She drove to a three-story converted warehouse nestled off the road near an open field. A red neon sign above the front door read "Duke's." On the aged brick were the faded letters hinting to the building's first years as a grain warehouse.

The parking lot was in need of paving—a project Duke kept swearing he'd tackle as soon as he won the lottery. Even though Duke joked about winning the lottery, he never played it. There was enough risk these days running a restaurant in a soft economy.

Out of her SUV, Riley hooked the tracking line to Cooper's collar and took him for a quick walk in the woods by the lot before putting him back in and cranking the AC. "Be right back."

She locked the door with the keyless entry and moved across the lot, her boots crunching gravel with each impatient step. Pushing through the door, she was greeted by the spicy scents of barbecue, fried potatoes, and at least five different kinds of pies.

Duke Spence opened Duke's twenty years ago when he moved to Ashland after years of working the blackjack tables in Las Vegas. He said he once received a vision from God when he woke up in a back alley battered and bruised. God told him to get his act together and open a place where people could get good, affordable food. He said he never played another hand of poker and moved back east the next day.

When Riley was seventeen, living in Duke's shelter and in need of a job, Duke gave one to her. When he offered her a spare room on the restaurant's second floor if she enrolled in high school, she refused. In those days, she didn't trust anyone. But in the coming weeks, he never pressed or gave her a reason to be afraid. So she asked if the deal was still on the table. They shook on it.

During the first nights living above the restaurant, she pushed the dresser in front of her door. It took another two weeks before she really fell into a deep sleep. He never said more than two words to her until her report card arrived. To say she blew it out of the park in terms of grades would have been a lie. Duke studied the paper closely and told her to get her grades up. He didn't threaten or cajole, but spoke to her like an adult. And she listened. Her grades improved, and she ended up living in that upstairs room for four years while working her way through community college and then the police academy.

Inside Duke's restaurant, Riley grinned at the kid behind the front register, Hanna Rogers, her soon-to-be daughter. Five years ago, Riley was working patrol when she stopped a white van with a busted taillight on the interstate. A couple of muscle-bound guys were in the front seat, and in the back, three young girls. One was Hanna.

Riley knew immediately the kid was underage, and when neither of the drivers could prove their relation to her, she called in for backup. All the girls were under eighteen. A background check told Riley that Hanna would not be going home. The kid's father was in prison, and the mother was a heroin addict living with a convicted child molester. She wasn't sure why, but she made the offer to foster the then-twelve-year-old girl. Hanna accepted, saying, "Until something better comes along." Riley hadn't argued, knowing the kid was all bluff and terrified.

Two weeks ago, Riley had filed adoption papers, which would officially make Hanna her daughter. The move didn't make sense to some, seeing as Hanna was close to eighteen, but it was important for both to have a real family. Neither wanted to mess the adoption up.

"Riley," Hanna said. "You look official."

Riley grinned. "Need to look the part."

"Oh, you totally do, Trooper Tatum. Caught any bad guys today?" Hanna reached for a set of silverware and rolled a paper napkin around them. If Riley had a nickel for all the silverware she had rolled when she lived above Duke's, she'd have the money to send Hanna to college free and clear.

"No bad guys yet. Give me until dinnertime."

Hanna glanced at the large round clock on the wall. "Coop in the car?"

"Yeah, doing what he does best. Sleeping."

"You're a little early for dinner."

"Didn't come to eat. Questions for Duke."

"About a case?"

"As a matter of fact, yes."

"That sounds exciting."

"No, it's very routine."

"Too bad. I think he could use a little excitement. He's in the back adding numbers and grumbling."

"How much is he grumbling?"

"Said Satan invented numbers to torture humans."

She arched a brow. "That bad?" His bark was worse than his bite.

Hanna shook her head. "It's the worst I've seen him in a while."

"Must be quarterly taxes. He hates those. What time do you get off today?"

"Six."

"How are the applications going?"

"Slow." She grimaced. "They want me to write all these essays about my life, but each time I do, it sounds all wrong."

"Why wrong?"

A shrug of her shoulders telegraphed worry, not apathy. "Not the most impressive background. Not exactly college material. And then when I add up the cost. You won't be getting a check from the state once the adoption papers are finalized."

"You write about your life and don't worry about if it fits the mold. Anyone can fit into a mold. And when you get accepted into a college, we'll figure out the money."

"It's overwhelming."

To say it was happily ever after once Hanna moved in would be inaccurate. The first months were rough, and if not for Cooper's endless affection, she wasn't sure the kid would have stuck around. Riley had introduced Hanna to Duke and asked him if she could have a summer job. Riley wanted the kid busy while she was at work. He agreed and his wife, Maria, also offered Hanna a bed in their house when Riley worked nights. Theirs wasn't a perfect, model family, but it worked; they were doing okay.

Riley winked and rapped her knuckles on the counter. "Remember, one step at a time."

"You make it sound easy."

"It is. Really." She did her best to make it look easy, but the truth was, she didn't know exactly where the money for Hanna's college would come from. She said she'd find a way, and she already figured she'd pick up part-time work after the girl started courses.

Riley left Hanna and wound her way through the thirty-plus tables, waving to a couple of the waitresses. Most were from the streets, and they lived at the shelter Duke ran down the street in a six-bedroom house he'd bought and renovated fifteen years ago. The shelter could house up to a dozen girls, and while they lived in his place, Duke gave them a job as they pieced their lives together. Some kids returned to the streets, but quite a few had gone on to finish high school and college.

Pushing through a set of swinging saloon doors and ignoring the "Employees Only" sign, she moved along the dim hallway to the door at the end of the hall on the left. She stopped at the threshold and saw the gray-haired man stooped over a set of books. He wore a black T-shirt that accentuated muscled arms covered in tattoos. She heard the tattoos extended across his back and over his chest.

Duke Spence was frowning as he cradled a cell phone close. He muttered a curse, hung up, and tossed the phone on his desk.

"Your face is going to stick if you keep scowling," she said as she leaned against the door frame and folded her arms.

Duke glanced up, tugging off half glasses, and tossed her one of his easy trademark grins. He was in his early sixties but kept himself in great shape by working out daily. His jeans were well worn but clean, and his biker boots finished off the look of a guy who had done more than could be confessed to in an afternoon.

He tipped back in his chair. "Well, ain't you official looking, Trooper Tatum. You giving those boys a run for their money?"

"Like you always said, fake it until you make it."

"You've nothing to fake, kid. You're smart as a whip and one day will be an investigator solving crimes faster than any of them. Don't let 'em rattle you."

"I'm never rattled." She pulled her cell from her back pocket and brought up the victim's photo. "I have a question for you about a case."

"Shoot."

"Do you know this girl? I saw her at one of the truck stops a couple of weeks ago."

Duke's chair squeaked as he rose and straightened to his full six-foot-one-inch frame. He slid his glasses back on. "That kind of question from a cop can't be good."

"It's not." She handed him the phone.

He took the phone in weathered hands and blew up the image. "She's dead?"

"Yeah."

"Pretty."

"And young."

Shaking his head, he handed the phone back to her. "I haven't seen her around the shelter."

"You sure?"

"Face is not familiar. And if she was on the streets, it doesn't look like she was on her own for very long."

"That's what I was thinking. She has a tattoo on the back of her neck. *JC.* Likely she's one of Jax Carter's girls."

"I've heard about Carter's arrest and saw the video of him beating that girl on the web. Sorry to hear she was mixed up with him."

"What have you heard?"

"He and his girlfriend, Darla Johnson, are new to the area. They've been around here a couple of times trying to talk to the kids, but I chased 'em off. Told him I'd bust his knees if he came back."

She didn't doubt it. "I pulled his record and hers. They've been running girls for years across the country but stay on the move."

He snapped his fingers. "Darla Johnson is from this area, I think. She can be a real charmer. You looking for her, too?"

"Not officially, but if I come across her, I'll have questions."

"I hope he rots in jail."

"It would be nice."

"How's the kid he worked over?"

"She's still unconscious. I have a few days off starting tomorrow. I'll swing by and see her as soon as she can have visitors."

"There's always a bed for her at the youth shelter if she wants it."

"Thanks."

Duke stared at the picture on her phone. "This one reminds me a little of you."

That was the second time today she'd been linked with the victim. "The victim had one of your pamphlets in her backpack."

"We deal with so many kids. I can't keep track of them all anymore." Frown lines deepened around his eyes. "How long has she been dead?"

"Rough estimate is a day."

He rubbed his hand over the back of his neck. "So Carter is off the hook?"

"So far. Would help if I knew the victim's name."

"If you can get me a hard copy of that photo, I'll ask around."

"Great. Thanks." She tucked the phone back in her pocket. Duke and his wife regularly visited the truck stops, bus stations, and street corners to hand out flyers to kids who looked as if they might need a place to stay.

"I wish I had more information for you."

"It was worth a shot."

He yanked off his glasses as if he'd seen too much. "How did she die?"

"The cops haven't released any details to the media yet so keep this under your hat."

"You know me, I'm a vault."

"She was strangled."

He winced. "Was she sexually assaulted?"

"Her clothes were intact but that doesn't mean much. I'd like to observe the autopsy and find out the answer to that question, but that will depend on who gets the case."

"If the powers that be are smart, they'll keep you in the loop. You always were a sharp kid."

"I thought you said I had rocks in my head."

A smile tweaked the edges of his lips. "Let's say you can be stubborn when you get an idea in your head." His expression hardened. "You could have ended up like that kid, but you wanted to get ahead and never gave up."

"Who's to say how long I could have kept it going if not for you and the shelter?"

Duke knocked on his wooden desk, an old gambling trick to get Lady Luck's attention. "You're a tough nut."

She considered asking him about the cards, but hesitated. Duke had made and lost his first, second, and third fortunes as a professional gambler in his younger days. He often said he'd still be at the tables if not for divine intervention. And then he'd met Maria, who hated the idea of the tables.

But it wasn't smart to share a key detail like the cards with anyone at this stage. "Hopefully, I'll have updates soon."

She waved her hand and left, taking a moment to check in with Hanna. "Straight home from here and homework, right?"

Hanna saluted. "Yes, ma'am."

Hanna, who had little structure in her life, had taken to Riley's house rules like a duck to water. For the first time in her life, someone cared about her, and she liked it. Once, early on, she tested Riley's resolve and did not come home. Riley had tracked the kid to a boy's house. Dressed in full uniform with Cooper at her side, she immediately had spotted Hanna in the crowd of drunken teens. What saved Hanna's ass was that she hadn't been drunk or high and she looked overwhelmed by the scene. The kid had been in over her head and didn't know how to get out and save face. Riley had given her a choice right there in front of the room full of people. Follow the rules or pack up her shit and get out of Riley's house. A sullen Hanna had followed Riley out of the party.

And now, the two of them had forged a kind of family that worked, and she would not let anything from the past ruin it. Hanna would be leaving for college next summer. The kid needed to build her own life, but Riley already knew she'd miss Hanna being around the house.

As Riley slid behind the wheel of her SUV and glanced at a sleeping Cooper in the rearview mirror, her phone buzzed. The display read Agent Dakota Sharp's name. He was four or five years older than her, and they'd gone through the police academy together. "Trooper Tatum."

"Where are you?" The deep southern drawl leaked over the line. He was tall, a mountain of a man who smiled little and was terrible at small talk. But he was one of the best investigators in the mid-Atlantic.

"I'm in Ashland."

"I spoke to Barrett," Sharp said. "Virginia State Police is now officially assisting the sheriff's office with the investigation."

"Good." To the media, the sheriff's office would take center stage, but behind the scenes, state police would actually handle the bulk of the investigation.

"I've spoken to Martin. He says you think Jax Carter is connected to the killing."

"His initials are tattooed on her body."

"He has an alibi for last night," Sharp said.

"Carter has a girlfriend, Darla Johnson. I'm not sure where she was last night, but you should talk to her."

A pause. "Okay. I'll run her name and see what pops. I'm on my way to the hospital to talk to Carter. Care to join me?"

"You bet I would."

"Thought you might like to see this case through. That big arrest in the woods earned you the right."

"I'd like that."

"The medical examiner has our Jane Doe on deck for tomorrow morning at ten. You can observe if you have time."

"I have time off. That works well."

"Good. I'm headed to the hospital. See you soon."

"Will do." She rang off and checked her watch. There was still time to drop Cooper off at home.

She swung by her house, a small one-level brick rancher, which she'd painted white last year. She did a good job of keeping the yard cut and edged. However, the flower garden Hanna had wanted to plant before the social services visit had died within weeks because both forgot to water it.

She'd bought the house six years ago, scraping together the financing by working extra patrol shifts and eating peanut butter and jelly sandwiches. The place barely took up fifteen hundred square feet, and it still needed work on the bathrooms and kitchen. Before Hanna, there'd been some money for extra projects. Now the best she could afford was a rewire of a secondhand lamp. The rest would have to wait until, well, until the kid was out of college.

After a quick walk with the dog, she opened the front door and let Cooper pass. Inside, a bedroom on the right and one on the left flanked a large family room furnished with pieces she'd found at flea markets and hand-me-downs from Duke. Not high design but clean and functional.

Cooper padded across the hardwood floor into the kitchen, and she opened his crate. He drank water from his bowl, then settled on his blankets with his chew toys.

The kitchen was retro with a black-and-white-checkered floor, white appliances, and a Formica countertop. The cabinets were original to the house, though she'd updated them with a coat of white paint and new hinges and pulls. The kitchen was in need of a redo, but like everything else that was serviceable, it would have to wait.

"I'll be back soon, Cooper."

The dog closed his eyes.

She texted Hanna, asking her to walk him when she arrived home, and headed south to Richmond and the state university hospital located in the city center. She parked and found her way to the lockdown floor where the prisoners were housed. Nurses checked her badge and credentials, and she was escorted through a set of locked doors to wait outside a room.

She heard the blare of a television broadcasting a game show coming from inside. Heavy footsteps echoed in the hallway, and she turned to see Agent Sharp approaching. Hair cropped short, he wore a simple black suit, white shirt, red tie, and his badge clipped to a belt that circled a fit waist. He carried a black vinyl notepad holder in his right hand, and with each long stride, his jacket billowed enough to offer glimpses of his sidearm.

"Trooper. Thanks for meeting me."

"Thanks for the invite."

Not bothering to knock on the hospital door, he entered the room. She followed.

Carter lay in a large bed, his right hand cuffed to the metal railing. He wore a hospital gown, and in front of him was a lunch tray consisting of what looked like meatloaf, mashed potatoes, bread, and cake.

He was about to shove a spoonful of potatoes in his mouth when he saw them. "If it isn't Trooper Tatum. Who's your friend?"

"This is Agent Sharp with the Virginia State Police, Mr. Carter."

Sharp's gaze wandered from the food to the television. "It looks like they're treating you well."

Carter dropped the spoon back on his plate. "Not my idea of fun, but it beats hugging a tree all night."

So he was sticking with his story about his night on the mountain.

"I hear you have a court date in a couple of days," Sharp said.

Carter grinned, a gold tooth winking in the fluorescent light. "So they tell me." He leaned back, staring at Riley. "Did you miss me, Trooper Tatum?"

Sharp nodded toward her, giving her the go-ahead to ask the questions.

"I ran across one of your girls," she said. "Pretty. Dark hair."

He arched a brow. "Girls? I don't know what you mean."

"One of the girls you and Darla pimp along I-95. She worked out of that camper you drive around."

His smile was wide, the proverbial Cheshire cat. "Don't know about that."

"This isn't the girl you put in the hospital. But another one."

He shifted, pushing his tray away. His smug smile faded. "What's she saying about me?"

"What do you think she's saying about you?" Riley asked.

"How the fuck would I know?" His agitation suggested he really was worried about what the girl would say. He believed at least one of his girls was still alive.

"Turns out, she's not said much," Sharp said, watching him closely. "She's dead."

Carter sat forward quickly, and a grimace proved the movement irritated his leg. "Who's dead?"

"The young girl I saw get into your motor home about a month ago," Riley said.

"We're running her prints," Sharp said. "Shouldn't be more than a few hours before we have her name. You can save us some time and give us a name."

Carter folded his arms over his chest, revealing a large snake tattoo that coiled around his forearm. "I don't know who you're talking about."

"You don't know?" Sharp asked.

"Lots of girls on the streets like what they see when they see Jax Carter. Got all kinds of dates coming and going."

Riley showed him the picture on her phone. "Look familiar?"

Barely glancing at the photo, he shook his head. "Nope."

"If you don't remember, the girl you beat up will," Riley said. "Is this girl the reason you beat Jo-Jo so badly? Was Jo-Jo asking too many questions about her?"

Carter was silent, but frowned at the mention of Jo-Jo's name.

"Jo-Jo's healing nicely by the way," Riley said, playing along as if she had more information than she really did.

"She's next on our list of people to talk to," Sharp added. "She'll tell us the girl's name."

Carter tapped a finger on the small bed table. "There's always girls hanging around at the truck stop near Fredericksburg. They was always asking for money or a cigarette, but I don't know no names."

She'd bet money he not only knew the girl well but also kept very close tabs on her whereabouts. Many of the working girls on the streets received a text every thirty minutes from their pimp, who expected an immediate response. Tardiness led to consequences. When cops had found Carter's car at the rest stop, there were several phones on the floor. Those records might help.

"You don't remember?" Riley asked. "I could swear I saw her getting into your motor home a month ago."

A half smile pulled at the edge of his lips. "Nope."

"All right. Maybe Jo-Jo will remember when you saw this girl last."

He shifted, again tugging at the wound in his leg. He cursed and settled back, muttering, "Jo-Jo don't remember shit because she don't know nothing. I can promise you that."

"You sound pretty sure of yourself," Sharp said.

"I'm sure."

Images of the girl lying dead in the field and the video of Jo-Jo's beating stoked anger, but she kept it in check. "Jo-Jo's not under your control right now, Jax. She's getting rest and good meals and healing. Drugs are leaving her system. No telling what a girl will say given a little encouragement from someone who actually cares about her."

"You're bluffing, bitch."

"Am I?" She moved forward a step, leaning against his leg. He hissed in a breath. "You think she won't talk? She's already started."

He shifted in the bed, turning a shade paler when he pulled his leg away from her. "Fuck you."

"I like it when you cuss," Riley said. "Confirms I've gotten under your skin."

Carter opened his mouth to speak but stopped.

"Rest up, Jax," Sharp said. "I don't think you'll get as much sleep in prison."

Carter shook his head. "I ain't going to prison."

"You keep telling yourself that," Riley said.

CHAPTER FIVE

Wednesday, September 14, 9:45 a.m.

After Hanna left for school, Riley spent an hour visiting the youth shelter, talking to street girls who might know Darla. Several of the girls had been off the streets for months and had severed all their connections. And the two newest girls, who'd moved in midsummer, had never crossed paths with Darla.

Riley handed out business cards to all the girls and told them to call day or night if they needed anything. The girls had been leery of her, many disappointed by family and friends before, so she wasn't holding out a lot of hope as she left the shelter and crossed the parking lot to her car. While driving to the state medical examiner's office in Richmond, a call to the hospital told her Jo-Jo was barely awake and still in no shape to answer questions.

Now, dressed in black slacks, white blouse, dark jacket, and low-heeled boots, Riley arrived at the medical examiner's office just before ten. She parked on a side street and then hurried to the Marshall Street entrance, pushing through the front doors and stopping at the front desk to show her badge.

The receptionist, an African American woman in her fifties, glanced up. "Who you here for?"

"A Jane Doe brought in yesterday. Brown hair, young. Teenager. Caucasian."

"Right. I heard about that one." She reached for a stack of papers and clipped them together. "She was brought in from up north. Who's the lead?"

"Agent Dakota Sharp."

"He's a hard-ass." Grinning, the woman shook her head. "A skinny little girl like you, well, he'll eat you right up if you aren't careful."

Riley smiled. "I'm all gristle. Don't worry about me."

"Well, good for you, baby doll." She handed Riley a visitor's pass.

"Thanks."

Riley stepped into the elevator and rode it to the lower level. The doors opened to a tiled hallway, fluorescent lights, and the smell of strong chemicals. Squaring her shoulders, she kept her pace steady and clipped. She had this under control. She did. Granted, she'd never witnessed a body being cracked open and taken apart by a doctor, but like any challenge, she'd figure it out. She hoped her stomach played along.

She pushed through the double metal doors and found herself facing a long stainless-steel counter outfitted with a sink and a hose attachment in the center. Angled next to the counter was a gurney carrying a body covered by a white sheet. Above the table were several adjustable lamps and a microphone ready for the doctor to dictate notes.

The room's air was heavy with an unnatural smell that coiled inside Riley's stomach. She pulled back her shoulders to ward off a gag reflex.

"Trooper Tatum, correct?"

So focused on the draped body, she didn't notice the woman enter from a side door. Automatically, she extended her hand. "Dr. Kincaid?"

"Yes. Agent Sharp said you'd be here."

Dr. Kincaid was tall and lean and in her midthirties. Under a white lab coat she wore simple khaki pants and a navy-blue blouse. Long dark hair feathered into lighter ends and curled around her angled face. A honey-olive skin tone accentuated her perceptive green eyes. Other than a trace of gloss on her lips and shadowing around her eyes, she wore little makeup. A gold chain looped through a gold ring, encircling her neck. The ring was wide, like a man's, and Riley bet it was a wedding band.

Dr. Kincaid regarded her closely. "We haven't worked together before."

"That would be correct. I'm a trooper, so I don't usually follow a case this far."

"Well, welcome."

The doors opened to Sharp, who looked tense and annoyed. Notebook in hand, he strode toward them. "Tatum."

"Agent," Dr. Kincaid said. "I'm running a little behind. Let me change into scrubs and we can get started."

"Sure."

The doctor vanished through a side door as a lab assistant pushed through another door. "Agent Sharp I know, but you, I don't. I'm Ken Matthews."

"Nice to meet you, Ken," Riley said, taking his hand.

He eyed her closely. "You have a slight pasty look. You a virgin?"

"Excuse me?" Riley asked.

Sharp lifted a brow, grinned, but had the good sense not to comment.

Matthews chuckled. "First time to the show?"

"Yep." Don't deny or apologize for the obvious. Acknowledge it and move on.

"I bet you do fine."

"There're gowns in the locker over there," Ken said. "It's a good idea if you put one on. You can also stow your purse and grab a barf bag if you need one."

Sharp moved toward the lockers and shrugged off his jacket. Without a word, he reached for a gown and slid his arms into it.

"Right. Sure." Riley turned from the table, glad to have it out of her line of sight. As she crossed to the locker and removed her jacket and slipped on a gown, a saw buzzed behind her. She flinched and glanced at the paper barf bags.

"Breathe," Sharp said. "Ken's trying to rattle you."

"Right." Her stomach turned at the thought of the saw cutting into flesh, but she left the bag behind.

She and Sharp were in gowns by the time Dr. Kincaid emerged, dressed in scrubs, her dark hair pinned under a surgical cap. At the instrument table, she unwrapped a pair of latex gloves and snapped them on over her slender fingers with practiced ease.

Turning, she moved toward the table with a steady, determined gait. "If you have questions, ask. We're gathering evidence."

"Sure." Questions were sometimes tricky. The benefit of an answer didn't always outweigh telegraphing the questioner's ignorance.

Dr. Kincaid removed the sheet and held up a pale hand. "She has a fresh manicure and pedicure."

The victim's hands were long, slim, and graceful. They were suited for playing a piano. Instead, Riley pictured those fingers picking through trash like many runaways did.

Sharp pulled on latex gloves, knitting his fingers together and working the slack from his gloves. He glared at Riley, studying her closely. "You good with this?"

"Never better."

Riley, drawn by curiosity, moved closer, inspecting the victim's now-cleaned face. Without makeup, the victim looked years younger. Eighteen, tops. Pierced ears, twice on the left. A small mole on her right cheek. A thin, inch-long white scar crossed the upper-left side of her forehead.

"Just a kid," Sharp said.

"No missing persons report on her yet?" Riley asked.

"None," he said.

"I stopped at the youth shelter this morning," Riley said. "No one knew her, but I'll keep trying."

"I've requested Jax Carter's phone records. Assuming she worked for him, we should find a connection."

Dr. Kincaid said her name into the microphone and stated the date and time along with the list of the four people in attendance for the autopsy. She leaned toward the body, studying the slim rings of bruises around the girl's neck. "Exterior exam suggests strangulation. Ken, do you have X-rays for me?"

"Sure do, doc." He turned and pushed two X-ray slides up onto a light box and switched it on.

The doctor turned, and as she examined the image, traced a horse-shoe-shaped bone in the center of the victim's neck. "Broken hyoid bone." Returning to the table, she said, "There're two rings of bruises on her neck."

Riley studied the bands of purple marks. "He wrapped a rope around her neck, squeezed, and then stopped?"

"Stopped, screwed up his courage, and started again," Sharp said. "Not all killers do clean work. Strangulation takes time and steady pressure. It's a very personal way of killing."

Dr. Kincaid pulled the sheet back farther and revealed the girl's too-thin nude body. In the twenty-four hours since the body was found, the chemicals triggering rigor mortis had eased. She now lay flat.

Lifting the right arm, Dr. Kincaid inspected it. "I don't see needle marks, but there's some bruising by the upper-right forearm." Moving to the other side, she noted a heart-shaped tattoo on the girl's right thigh and the crudely written letters *JC* on the back of her neck.

With slow precision the doctor moved up the left side of the body, indicating the presence of more bruises on the left hip and left arm, along with a fresh needle mark in the central vein at the elbow.

"There are no signs of scarring from old puncture wounds. However, there is faint scarring on her wrist. Crisscross pattern. None of the marks were enough to kill. It could have been a suicide attempt or she might have been cutting herself."

"The physical pain distracts from the mental turmoil," Riley said.

"So I've heard," Dr. Kincaid said.

"You'll run a toxicological screen?" Riley asked, inspecting the mark. "She could have been drugged."

Sharp shifted a curious gaze to Riley.

"Yes," Dr. Kincaid said. "Results could take a week or two."

Sharp frowned but didn't comment as Dr. Kincaid continued her exterior examination, noting three more tattoos on the body: a heart below her belly button, a rose and vine at the base of her spine, and a star at her ankle.

When Dr. Kincaid moved to the top of the body, she reached toward an instrument table for a scalpel. The polished metal glistened in the light as the doctor, with little fanfare or warning, pressed the tip of the blade to the spot between the breasts and sliced downward over the belly and to the pubic bone.

Riley's mouth watered as the doctor pulled back the flesh from the bone and inspected the tissue and internal organs. Nausea curled in the pit of her stomach, but she held her ground. Cops could be ruthless when they saw weakness, and the last damn thing she needed was to have it get around she'd lost her breakfast at her first autopsy in front of Dakota Sharp.

"You okay, Trooper?" Sharp asked.

"I'm fine." From somewhere, she summoned a smile. "But you look a little green."

He laughed. "Not me. Cast-iron stomach."

She would not be sick. She would not. Biting the inside of her cheek, she allowed her mind to wander as it did when she was a kid, hiding in the shed behind her mother's house, waiting for her stepfather to either sober up or pass out. She pictured a gentle breeze blowing and the sun on her face. If she could outwait William, she could handle the smells and sounds of an autopsy, which, by her way of thinking, wasn't hurting a soul. As her heart slowed, she focused on evidence collection and facts. *Learn what you can about the girl. It's the only way you're going to catch her killer.*

"Heart, lungs, liver all look normal and healthy. She wasn't pregnant."

Ken reached for another set of X-rays. "Your victim did have a couple of broken ribs at one point in her life. They've healed. She also suffered fractures in her left arm. It's a spiral fracture, suggesting someone may have twisted her arm."

"The injuries could explain why she ran," Riley said. "But doesn't explain who got ahold of her after she arrived in the city. What about sexual assault?"

Sharp's expression did not change, but he rolled his head from side to side, a habit she'd noticed him do at fatal car accidents.

"That's next on the list." Dr. Kincaid instructed Ken to stitch up the chest with dark thread.

The testing for rape was next. She knew basically what to expect, but the exam was the last indignity this girl would endure in her short and troubled life.

Sharp's features were granite, but his fingers flexed once or twice.

"There's presence of semen. I'll need to test DNA to see if it's from a single source or multiple sources. And there are no signs of vaginal tearing or trauma."

Riley knew a DNA profile fed into the national database could land her names of the men who had been with the girl before her death. But paying for sex with a young girl didn't mean they were killers. And solving the death of a runaway girl would not land on the top of anyone's priority list, so it could be months or years before a report surfaced.

When Dr. Kincaid completed the exam, Riley moved to the locker to strip off her gown. Her camisole and blouse were damp with sweat. A dull headache thudded at the base of her skull.

Dr. Kincaid tugged off her gloves and gown. "I've seen seasoned men drop like a sack of potatoes in here."

Her deadpan tone had Riley raising her gaze, wondering if the doctor was making fun of her in her sweat-stained shirt. "I hold my own."

Sharp stripped off his gown and gloves and tossed them in a waste bin. He pushed through the suite doors without a word.

Riley stared after him, wondering what she'd done wrong.

"You did fine," the doctor offered. "These cases always bother Sharp."

"They bother most cops."

"He lost a sister a long time ago. She was only about eighteen when she died. It strikes close to home."

"I didn't know that." Sharp was always short on the personal details.

"You didn't hear it from me."

"Understood."

Out in the hallway she found Sharp waiting by the elevator, an unlit cigarette dangling from his mouth and a lighter clutched in his hand. When the doors dinged open, neither spoke as they rode it up to the first floor and crossed the lobby.

Outside, Sharp cupped his hand around the end of his cigarette and lit up. He took a deep breath. "Fingerprints should help ID her, and we can put her picture on the evening news if you haven't totally pissed off Eddie. I hear you've been dodging him."

"Ah, Eddie loves me."

"Like a splinter."

She laughed. "He'll get over it for a headline. If you need me to call him, I will."

He drew in a deep lungful of air and held it for a beat before he let it out. "I'll call you if it comes to that. I'm hoping information pops on the phone records or the fingerprints."

"Thanks. I'd like to be kept in the loop on this case." She pulled her shoulders back a fraction. "I saw that girl getting into Jax's motor home a month ago. I got called away before I could ask any questions."

"It's not your fault."

"Five more minutes might have made the difference for her."

"Maybe, maybe not."

She fished her phone out of her back pocket and checked the time. Three hours since the autopsy began. Hanna wouldn't be home for two more hours, giving her time to hurry home, change, and walk Cooper. "Thanks, Sharp."

Nodding, he inhaled again and turned and walked up the street.

Moving to her car, she drew fresh air into her lungs and slid behind the wheel. She sat for a moment, allowing the day's heat to warm the chill from her body before she followed signs to I-95 north. Twenty minutes later she pulled into her driveway behind the 2000 VW Beetle she'd bought for Hanna. The car wasn't much to look at, but it was dependable.

When she pushed through the front door, Cooper barked. In the kitchen, she opened his crate and rubbed his ears. "How you doing, Coop? Enjoy the afternoon off?"

He barked while wagging his tail.

"Hanna? Are you home early?"

For a moment there was only silence, and then, "It's Wednesday. Half day of school, remember?"

She scratched Cooper between the ears. "Remind me why it's a half day?"

"Teacher workday."

"Right. Slipped my mind." Juggling motherhood and work never got easy. "Not parent-teacher conferences, right?"

"You didn't miss anything."

"Good."

The girl rounded the corner, her long hair tied up in a thick pony-tail that brushed her shoulders. "You're getting old."

Riley unhooked her sidearm and set it on top of the refrigerator. "Careful, brat. I'm still spry enough to take you."

Hanna laughed. "No way."

Riley shrugged off her jacket. "I'm taking Cooper for a run. Care to join us?"

Hanna scrunched her face. "Your workouts are too intense."

"For an old lady, you mean?"

"Right."

Riley changed into jogging shorts, a sports top, and running shoes, and ten minutes later she and Cooper were running toward the local park, which was a mile from her house. Her muscles were still stiff and cumbersome from Monday's outing. Cooper moved easily, showing no signs of stress after the hike. She kicked up her pace and ten minutes into the run her legs loosened up.

As she approached the back entrance of the park a dark car drove up behind her, slowing its pace to a near crawl. She slowed and glanced at the vehicle while noting the tinted windows. Instinctively, her hand went to her waist and to the sidearm that wasn't there. "What the hell are you looking at, pal?"

Cooper, detecting the tension in her tone, looked up, his ears perked.

As she spoke, the car picked up speed and turned at the next corner, vanishing. Most wouldn't have given the car a second thought, and maybe she wouldn't have either, but the hair on the back of her neck stood up. Stopping, she drew in a steady breath, watching the corner in case the car returned. Cooper looked up at her, as if waiting for an order.

When the car didn't double back, she shook off her apprehension and tugged on Cooper's line. "It's good, boy. Let's train." They ran along the small dirt path and into the woods until they found the trail. Memories of the young girl robbed of her life and lying on the medical examiner's table crowded out the car. She owed that kid. "I'll figure it out."

By the time she and Cooper burst out of the woods forty-five minutes later, she was covered in dirt and sweat. Cooper was barely panting.

As she pushed through the back door of the kitchen, she smelled chili. "Did Duke send home food, Hanna?"

"He just dropped it off before you got home. He said he made too much."

"Lucky for us." She unleashed the dog and filled his water bowl only partway. She watched as he lapped but pulled the bowl before he had his fill. After hard training, too much water could bloat a big dog's stomach and twist the gut, which was potentially fatal. The dog settled on his bed in the corner. "You have triathlon practice tonight, right?"

"Correct. It's a bike day."

As soon as Hanna came to live with her, Riley had insisted she pick a sport. The first attempt was soccer, but Hanna wasn't great at sharing the ball. Next came tennis, a sport Riley had played as a kid. Hanna didn't like the other girls on the team. Too snooty. And then, they happened on a youth triathlon team, which required no ball sharing and didn't attract stuck-up girls. A blessing. Hanna had taken to the sport and would be leaving in a few days for a big race in Georgia.

"Let me take a quick shower and then we can eat." She wanted to rinse away the sweat as well as the lingering smell of the coroner's office.

Cooper followed her and jumped up on her bed as she toed off her shoes and stepped into the small bathroom. Pulling off her clothes, she tossed them in the hamper and turned on the shower. When the room was steamed up, she stepped under the hot spray. As the water washed away the grime, memories of the girl lying on the medical examiner's table elbowed forward. She wanted desperately to believe finding the girl's body had been random. But it wasn't.

She grabbed the soap and lathered her hands, then washed her face, body, and hair. By the time she stepped out of the spray, the scents had spiraled down the drain, but the memories lingered. She twisted her hair back in a tight knot and slipped on sweats and a T-shirt.

Picking up her phone, she scrolled through the images until she reached the picture of the cards. "Damn it."

She moved to her closet and, rising up on tiptoes, pulled down an old box and set it on her bed. She'd been busy with Hanna last night, and honestly she'd just been too afraid to look inside. Her fingers hovered a moment over the top before she opened it and dug below the layers of old college papers to the cloth napkin. She carefully removed her small package and unwrapped the coarse fabric. Staring up at her were five playing cards. They weren't common, everyday cards, but expensive. Thick. Coated in plastic. A black-and-white baroque pattern on the back. Like the cards found in Jane Doe's backpack. The only difference between the two hands was that hers was a royal flush and there was no message scrawled on the back. Winning hands didn't get better than a royal flush.

She traced each card's face and studied the pattern on the back, which was almost identical to the cards now in an evidence bag in the state police forensic lab.

She looks like you.

"Dinner's ready!" Hanna shouted.

Riley started. "Be right there!" She carefully rewrapped the cards and tucked them in the back of the box, which she shoved in the closet. Her cards were from New Orleans, over a thousand miles away. There was nothing written on them. They couldn't be connected.

She found Hanna placing a bowl of chili and slice of bread at a place set for her. Hanna liked eating at the table, like a family, she often said. Their dinners were never silent affairs as Riley's had been in her stepfather's house. They laughed and talked about school, college, and any worries Hanna wanted to voice.

Riley sat at the table and draped the folded paper towel over her lap. "How was school?"

"Routine," Hanna said, sitting. Like Riley, she took time to place her napkin in her lap.

"What about those applications?"

"Applications." She dragged out the word as if it had twenty syllables. "I've downloaded the college applications."

"Good. Have you started on the essays?"

"I don't know what to say about myself." She dropped her gaze to her chili and swirled it around and around.

"You've had a pretty interesting life."

"It's been amazingly pathetic."

"I don't see it that way at all." Riley set her fork on her plate and pressed the napkin to her lips. "You're a survivor, Hanna. You're here and looking ahead, not over your shoulder. And that's worth a lot."

"But I've not had a regular life. I've not done all that real-kid stuff like soccer games, or cheering practice, or tennis."

"Where did you spend your twelfth birthday?"

"In the shelter. I was trying to do my homework while a couple of kids pulled knives in a fight over a shirt."

"Write about that. Believe me, the admissions staff will never, ever see another essay like it. You're unique. Don't try to shove yourself into a mold."

"But I want to be in a mold."

"No, you don't. Look at me. I don't exactly look like the mother of a teenager."

Hanna shrugged. "You're definitely way cooler."

"See?"

"But what if the essay sucks?"

Riley laid her hand on Hanna's. "Once it's done, I'll read it. It'll be great."

The girl stirred her spoon in her chili. "You sure?"

"It's going to be fine. Don't worry."

Tears glistened in Hanna's eyes, and she wiped one off her cheek with the back of her hand. "If you tell anyone I cried, I'll scream."

As much as Riley wanted to crack a joke to lighten the mood, she opted to baby the kid a little. "Your secret is safe with me."

"Thanks."

They ate in silence and when the bowls were cleaned, Hanna said, "You're quiet."

"Thinking about a case." She didn't want to burden Hanna with what she'd seen, but she also wanted her to never forget the dangers out there.

"Can you talk about it?"

"It's a young girl who was strangled."

Hanna's face paled. "That's awful."

"It is. So please be careful when you're running around town."

"I know. I *know*," she said, rolling her eyes. "Situational awareness."

"I mean it."

Hanna straightened. "I *know*."

"Good." Riley rose. "Homework?"

"Just a little."

"Get it done while I do a little computer work."

"Fine."

Riley cleaned the dishes and sat on the couch with her laptop. Cooper settled at her feet, chewing his favorite red rubber ring.

She typed in the particulars of this murder case into Google. *Strangulation. Young female. Playing cards.*

Not surprisingly, nothing came up.

It would be easy to chalk up Jane Doe's murder to an angry pimp or a crazed john. Girls like that died all the time without much notice. But this kid's death wasn't typical.

Her index finger lightly tapped the side of the keyboard. She wanted to believe this case was random. But she learned a long time ago the universe didn't care about her wants and needs.

She typed *New Orleans* and the year she'd left the Big Easy for good.

For a long moment her finger hovered over the "Enter" button. What would Sharp say if he knew about her set of cards? Would he see a connection or tell her she was worried over nothing? Shit. Either way, he'd pull her off the case. And what if social services got wind of this? She couldn't let either outcome happen. She pressed "Enter" and sat back as the adrenaline rushed through her body.

An icon on the screen swirled. But there were no matches in the search results.

She looks like you.

Riley shook off Sheriff Barrett's words and shut off the computer.

***

Kevin sat in the dark, swirling the amber scotch in a crystal glass. The ice clinked again and again, slowly melting and diluting the twenty-year-old liquor.

His losing streak had stalked him for a year and had taken a toll on his reputation. His ribs still ached from the beating he'd received ten days ago from the Vegas thugs who were looking for a couple hundred thousand dollars paid in full.

Then he heard about the life-and-death game, which hadn't been played in years. He thought he'd found his way back into the big leagues. The Shark spotted any challenger ten-to-one odds if they brought a very specific kind of girl to the game. Kevin had twenty grand left to his name, but he had the potential of turning that into two hundred grand. That would have been enough to pay off his debts with a healthy bonus to the girl.

The girl, his stake in the game, had been easy to find. Vicky cost him two grand and he promised her pimp he would return her within twenty-four hours. He was certain when they left the diner he'd win, and in the end he'd help her get free of the life.

The game began well enough. He won several of the opening hands. The wins emboldened him, and when the final hand was dealt, he was already thinking beyond the game to his new fortune. In his mind, he was on the verge of saving himself and the girl.

When the last card had turned, and he was looking at four queens, he was certain the Shark couldn't pull out a straight flush. What were the odds? But then the Shark's last card turned. A king.

The Shark had won.

He had lost.

Rising now, Kevin stared into his glass of scotch, then gulped the contents. He savored the familiar burn as it trickled down his throat.

The image of Vicky's face flashed in his mind. Her blue eyes were desperate and pleading as she gasped for the air he was slowly cutting off.

He thought once he placed her in the field as instructed with the cards tucked in her pocket that he could move on with his life. He'd lost considerable fortunes at poker plenty of times but had recovered. He had enough money to vanish. He should cut his losses.

He rose, grimacing as his bruised ribs pinched. So why was he still in town? Why couldn't he forget that girl? And why did losing to the old man continue to dig at his pride?

CHAPTER SIX

Wednesday, September 14, 6:00 p.m.

Clay Bowman's computer dinged, signaling a message from his boss, Joshua Shield. He reached for the fresh cup of coffee and sipped as he read the e-mail's subject line: `Riley Tatum`. His interest sharpened as he scanned the details of a murder scene she'd responded to yesterday.

"Have you had a chance to read the e-mail?"

Bowman looked up to see Shield standing in his doorway. The man had been an FBI agent for twenty-five years, joining at age twenty-seven after five years in the marines. Over the years, the challenge of the investigative work crumbled under the bureau's politics, so ten years ago, when he was on the verge of a huge promotion, he walked away and founded Shield Security. The company quickly earned a solid reputation and proved to all he'd not lost his mind but had made a solid choice. He'd grown the company to twenty-five employees in the last few years.

Shield, like Bowman's father, Zeb, had graduated from the Virginia Military Institute and had always had an interest in the younger Bowman's career. When Bowman left the bureau last month, Shield had been ready with this job offer.

Bowman rose. "You sent it less than a minute ago."

"And your point is?"

Bowman smiled. "Why don't you fill me in on the details?"

"Riley Tatum is an accomplished Virginia state trooper. She's one of the best trackers in the region."

"That's not what caught your eye, is it? It has something to do with this murder scene she responded to yesterday."

Shield moved into Bowman's bare office that had yet to reflect any personality and sat in one of the matching chairs in front of the desk. There were boxes filled with diplomas lined along the wall, two mugs, and a group picture of five men who'd graduated from the Virginia Military Institute with Bowman seventeen years ago. But he'd yet to put anything up. He had been on the move for six years, not settling anywhere since his wife died. Joining Shield Security was a big move for him. It meant learning new patterns. New habits. Accepting that he was home.

"Remember when we worked the Shark case together in the New Orleans bureau twelve years ago?"

Bowman sat. He remembered the case. He had been in New Orleans about eighteen months when bodies of young runaways were discovered strangled with playing cards in their pockets. He and Karen had loved the city and were making a lot of good memories. He and Shield were about six months into the case when Bowman had been relocated to the LA bureau office. A few years later, Karen had gotten sick with pancreatic cancer and he'd transferred to Hostage Rescue Team. The Shark fell off his radar. "How does the Shark relate to Riley Tatum?"

"A buddy of mine at the Virginia State Police sent me a file on a body found yesterday," Shield said. "Young runaway, strangled, with playing cards in her back pocket. Just like the Shark."

Interest stirred in Bowman. "That's an FBI case; I thought you left the bureau behind."

"I left the bureau, but I don't leave any unsolved cases behind. And neither will you."

Bowman tapped an impatient finger on the arm of his chair as he summoned the old case details. "The Shark strangled four girls, as I remember. Five custom playing cards left with each victim. The word *Loser* was written on each card."

"Correct. All the victims were runaways. They had long dark hair, were Caucasian, and wore a yellow dress. After four victims, he went dark. He didn't try to hide the bodies. Simply left them sitting up under trees.

"Later, after you were transferred to LA, I developed an informant for another case completely unrelated. The informant worked in one of the casinos as a singer and sometimes a dealer. She and I got to be close, and one night she told me she heard the girls who had been strangled months earlier were prizes in a high-stakes poker game. The winner had the privilege of choosing if the girls lived or died."

"How'd she know this?"

"She was sleeping with a guy who worked security for several of the gamblers who were the casino's biggest customers. She saw that I was interested and said she'd find more if I helped her beat a cocaine bust. I agreed. Two days later she was found dead. She'd been badly beaten and then shot point-blank in the head."

"How do you know her death was related to the Shark? An informant asking questions can make all kinds of people nervous."

"I didn't associate her death with the Shark until a couple of days after her funeral when I received an envelope in the mail. It contained pictures of the informant plus images of five young girls. Four matched the victims we'd found strangled by the Shark. The fifth girl didn't match any homicides, and we never identified her. We suspected she was also a runaway who he killed, but we just never found the body."

Bowman glanced at the e-mail header. "How does this relate to Riley Tatum? She's a cop who responded to a murder scene."

Shield twisted his 1975 class ring on his finger. In answer, he said, "Have a look at the e-mail attachment. It's the image of the fifth girl."

Bowman opened the attachment and studied the young girl's picture. She had long, thick dark hair, and her face was turned partly away. "You might be right that it's Riley Tatum."

"I am."

"And she just happened to respond to a murder scene that is reminiscent of the Shark."

"You make it sound like a coincidence. And you know this old man doesn't believe in coincidences."

"Has the Shark been active in the last twelve years?"

"Not according to any of my sources."

"And you think he's back? Here?"

Shield grinned. "He's got a perfect mix before him: the victim that got away and the man who's been hunting him—me."

"What about the player who beat him in the game twelve years ago?"

"I've never identified him, but I'd bet money the Shark has kept tabs on him over the years and knows his identity."

Bowman studied the pictures again. "Who gave you the current case details?"

"I've a hit list of ten cold cases I want solved. The Shark is right at the top. I've made inroads with law enforcement all over the country. Without boring you by details, my friend has seen the list and notified me."

Shield had been a master at recruiting informants when he was at the bureau. "Why would this person share?"

"We have a mutual interest in solving cold cases."

"If Riley Tatum was taken, how much do you think she remembers? As I recall, large traces of Rohypnol were found in the victims."

"I don't know. But I find it interesting that she'd made it her mission to work with runaways. Look how motivated she was to catch Jax Carter."

"She's good. I had to hustle to catch up to her. She's smart and would've caught Carter without my help."

"Did you get a good look at her?"

"Sure. In fact, I know Tatum. She and her dog trained at Quantico five years ago."

Shield studied him. "I didn't know that."

"Small world."

Shield removed four pictures from the breast pocket of his suit and laid them out like they were playing cards. Bowman recognized the faces of the four murdered girls in New Orleans. "These are the Shark's confirmed victims."

"Yes." Shield laid down a fifth picture next to the others. "One thing to see this picture of the fifth victim alone, but another to see it next to the other victims. They all look so much alike."

Bowman studied the pictures. "Number five's face is slightly turned." His gut knotted. "It could be a younger version of Tatum."

"That's what I thought when I saw her on television four years ago. She and her canine were featured after they found a crashed helicopter that was carrying key state politicians to a fund-raiser. They were in critical condition when she found them."

Bowman flicked the edge of the paper with his index finger. "Did you ever talk to her?"

"No. But I did some digging. Tatum's originally from New Orleans. She moved to Virginia alone weeks after she turned eighteen. Her stepfather, William Charles, has been known to gamble heavily."

Bowman didn't speak but waited for Shield to continue. "She ran away from home at seventeen," Shield said. "She fell off the radar for a solid month, and then she emerges again working in a restaurant in Ashland. She worked odd jobs and went to community college until she turned twenty-one, then joined the state police. She's sharp and dedicated."

"Why didn't you ever ask her about the Shark?"

"That's your job now. Meet with her. Find out what you can about this murder. Help her find this killer. Keep her safe. She's in deeper waters than she realizes."

"You didn't ask her about the Shark because you didn't want to spook her."

"I always suspected the Shark would come back for her. This killer has an obsession with poker and winning. We know that. And evidence suggests she's the one that got away."

"You've been using her as bait." Annoyance accentuated the last words.

"Is that a problem?"

"I'm not crazy about the idea."

"What would you do in my shoes?"

Bowman slowly shook his head. "It's a logical call."

"She's my only link to this killer."

"And you're hoping she wasn't as juiced as the others and there are some memories?"

"I don't know. But now that there's a new victim, it's time to find out," Shield said.

Bowman dug into his memory. "You never found any of the other gamblers?"

"No. But I did hear of a couple of gamblers that vanished in Las Vegas over a four-month period, months after my informant was murdered. That could have been the Shark cleaning up all loose ends."

"Those gamblers could also have been men who owed money to the wrong men. It's a high-risk business, especially when you're losing."

"You're right. I have nothing linking the dead players to my informant or the girls. But again, I don't believe in coincidences."

Bowman also sensed these random pieces were connected. "If your informant was right, there's one player running the games."

"That's my guess. And I believe the placement of this latest body in Riley's patrol area suggests he knows who she is and he's returned for her."

Bowman again studied the image of the fifth victim. The only thing he was sure of now was that he wanted back in the trooper's life.

"Protect her," Shield said.

"Consider it done."

***

Kevin held the disposable phone in his hand with his thumb hovering over the "Send" button. His stomach remained knotted after the killing, and no matter how much he tried to push the girl's face from his mind, to exorcise the feel of the rope cutting into her neck, to shut out the sound of her last choking breaths, he could not. She haunted him. Chased him in his dreams. He'd thought killing her would be easy. She was a hopeless runaway who was selling her body on the streets. Her death shouldn't have mattered. But it did.

Closing his eyes, he hit "Send" and slowly raised the phone to his ear. The phone rang five times, and he thought for a moment it would simply go unanswered, but then he heard a curt, "Why are you calling?"

Kevin closed his eyes. "I'm turning myself in to the cops."

"You're doing what?"

"I'm going to the cops. I can't do this. I can't live with the guilt of choking that girl to death."

A long pause. "We made a deal. You swore secrecy."

"I never understood why the girl had to die."

"It's important that I won. But it's more important that someone else lost."

Still light-headed from too much booze, Kevin opened his eyes and cleared his throat. He wanted these words to be clear. "I won't bring you into this. I won't tell."

"That's comforting."

"I mean it. I won't tell them about you."

"You also said you would never go to the cops."

"I won't bring you into this. You have my word."

"Why are you telling me this? You could have just gone to the cops."

"To give you fair warning. To give you a chance to flee. I owe you that."

"Why would I have to flee if you don't tell anyone about me?"

"You know how it goes with cops. Some are smart, and events can go sideways. I don't want you caught up in this."

"Sideways. Like now. Like you crumbling. Do you really think talking to the cops is going to give you absolution?"

"I don't know. But I deserve to be punished."

"Did it ever occur to you that you did that girl a favor? Can you imagine what she would look like in five years? Ten years? She's a whore. The streets eat up kids like her."

"She was so young."

"Her beauty was on the verge of fading. It was a mercy killing."

"Mercy killing?"

"You do believe in an afterlife, correct?"

"What does that have to do with her?"

"She's in a better place now. Besides, if the Almighty wanted her to live, then the cards would've turned differently. You would've won and she would still be alive. It wasn't meant to be."

Kevin pinched the bridge of his nose, willing the tightness in his chest to dissipate. "I don't know . . ."

"What're you really asking?"

Unshed tears choked his throat. "I don't know."

"Do you want a second chance?"

"What?"

"A second chance. Another game and another chance to save a poor girl from the streets. You can give her your winnings and a better life. That's part of the reason you took the last one."

"I wanted to help her."

"Don't feed me any of your noble bullshit. You wanted to win. To beat me." The Shark pulled in a deep breath. "You and I aren't that different. We're addicted to the game. Knowing the turn of the cards could mean life or death is too much of a thrill for people like us to pass up."

Kevin rose, glancing at his trembling hand. As much as the idea of killing repelled him, playing again excited him more. Trying to contain his excitement, he said, "Would the same rules apply?"

"They would. You win and I'll see that the girl lives a long, full life. I've let a girl free once before. I can do it again."

Kevin hesitated, disgusted with addiction and fading remorse.

"Think what you can do for that other girl's family. You can help them with some of your winnings. Ease their pain. Your pain."

"I can atone for her death."

"Exactly."

"Okay." A calmness washed over him.

"I'll find the girl this time."

"Where?"

"I have a source."

Kevin was relieved. Trolling for the other girl had created a connection between them. This time it would be more impersonal. It was the edge he needed to beat the Shark. "Okay."

"Meet me at the same place in twenty-four hours. Lady Luck does owe you, doesn't she?"

CHAPTER SEVEN

Thursday, September 15, 4:30 a.m.

Riley rose early, her eyes opening minutes before her alarm. She swung her legs over the side of the bed and willed herself to stand and get moving. After she dressed in running clothes, she passed Hanna's door and peeked inside. She found the girl sprawled on her stomach across her bed, her hair draped over her face and both arms tucked under her pillow.

As she moved into the kitchen, Cooper rose in his crate, his tail thumping. She grabbed his red tracking line and, opening the crate, hooked his collar. "Ready, Coop?"

She strapped on her headlight as the two headed out the back door. Their initial pace was always slow, but it quickly sped up.

After they looped around the track for four miles' worth of laps, she tied his line to a fence and then did a set of fast sprints. By the time she was finished, sweat dripped from her body.

As she collected the dog's leash she stood for a moment, staring at the nearby woods. A sense of unease crept up her spine. Cooper raised his head and sniffed, forcing air from his nose as he did when he picked up a scent. Cooper had also picked up on her tension.

Five years together had taught her to never doubt Cooper. His body, when it tensed, sent a message up the line, vibrating up her sinew and bone. She stared toward the park, wishing now she'd brought her gun.

Feeling exposed, she tugged him. "Let's get out of here, Coop."

The dog barked and glared at the woods for another tense second before turning. They jogged across the lot to the street toward her house. She looked over her shoulder several times, expecting to see trouble, but the area around her remained still. But there was no doubt Cooper had picked up something.

Inside the back door she fed Cooper and then hustled into the shower.

Fifteen minutes later, her still-moist hair was twisted into a bun at the base of her head and she'd dressed in slim brown slacks, a white shirt, and a blazer. She was cooking eggs and toast when she heard Hanna stumble out of her room and into the shower.

"Shake a leg, kid," she shouted as she glanced at the clock on the stove. "Your ride will be here in twenty minutes."

Ten minutes later Hanna sat at the table. "I hate breakfast."

Riley set scrambled eggs in front of her. "Think of it as a late dinner."

Hanna stabbed an egg and ate.

"What's on the docket today?" Riley asked.

"Math test."

"Ready?"

"Yes. School is boring."

"It's the ticket to your future."

"The classes are too easy."

"Maybe you're too smart." The kid was gifted, often outpacing her classmates and some of her teachers.

Hanna's morning frown softened with the compliment.

Fifteen minutes later Hanna was out the door as her ride pulled in the driveway. Hanna tossed Riley a wave and slid into the backseat of the van.

As the van drove off, a car parked a half block away headed toward the house. Eyes narrowed, Riley watched as it pulled into her driveway. Her hand slid to the SIG already on her hip.

Eddie Potter rose out of the car. "Trooper. Looks like I caught you heading out. Figured you'd take it easy on your day off."

"Mr. Potter. You know my schedule and you tracked me to my home." Not illegal but an invasion.

"I understand you identified the girl murdered near here."

She hesitated, wondering if he was telling her the truth. "No comment."

"Her name is Vicky Gilbert," he said.

Her spine stiffened as she wondered who was feeding him information. Barrett? Sharp? And why hadn't she gotten a call? "I can't comment, Mr. Potter. Contact the public information officer for state police."

"I'll be running the story about the girl at the midday and evening news slots. It won't be long. Maybe a minute. If I could interview you, it would get more airtime."

"No."

"I'd like your take on the human trafficking angle. The story might raise awareness."

"Talk to the public information officer. She'll call me with an interview time."

"Can't we cut the red tape?"

"No."

"Does this murder bother you because you once ran away from home?"

"Excuse me?"

"I did a little digging into your past. A friend told me you're from New Orleans and you ran away from home." As her scowl deepened, his grin widened. "Curious by nature. And in today's dicey world of journalism, you need to be willing to hit a nerve."

"How about you give me your friend's name? I'd like to have a chat with him."

"I'm not willing to throw this guy under the bus. Wouldn't be fair. Just doing my job. It's in the DNA."

She wondered what else he'd dug up, but she refused to open that can of worms. Shit. She didn't need anyone digging into her past. "Get off my property."

"If you don't help me write the story, I'll come up with my own angle."

"Good-bye, Mr. Potter."

***

Bowman's drive into Washington, DC, took less than two hours, plus another thirty minutes before he found himself at the end of a cul-de-sac ringed with three old brick homes. He checked the address and parked in the driveway. Out of his car, he tugged on his jacket as a warm wind blew through the thick oaks. The faint scent of boxwoods wafted, hinting of old money and power.

Riley's stepfather, William Charles, was based in New Orleans, but as it turned out, he spent a great deal of time in Washington, DC, as a lobbyist. Charles could trace his roots back to the Revolutionary War, and he attended Columbia, earning a law degree in spite of mediocre grades. He joined his father's law firm and spent most of his career shuttling between New Orleans and DC. Riley's mother had been a newly divorced mother of a two-year-old daughter when she'd joined the Charles law firm as a secretary. She'd quickly caught Charles's eye, and the two were married the following year.

Bowman walked up the front steps and rang the bell.

The faint click of heels echoed in the house and, after a slight hesitation, the door opened. Standing before him was a tall, dark-haired woman in her early thirties. Her build was slim, and she had a look similar to Riley's.

"May I help you?" No hint of warmth in her voice.

"My name is Clay Bowman. I'm with Shield Security and investigating an old criminal case. I'm here to see Mr. Charles."

"Mr. Charles isn't here."

The tech guy at Shield Security, Garrett Andrews, wasn't the easiest to work with, but he was damn good at his job. And according to Andrews's monitoring of Charles's cell phone, the man was here, now. "Tell Mr. Charles this is about his stepdaughter, Riley Tatum."

Manicured fingers curled into a fist. "I don't know her."

"He does. Tell him."

"Look, Mr. Bowman, I don't know what you're selling, but my husband has not seen his stepdaughter in a dozen years."

"Audrey," a deep voice said from a side room. "Show him in."

"Of course, William." Audrey, not happy about being overridden, forced a smile. "Please come in."

He stepped inside and turned toward the sound of the voice. He entered the library as a tall, thin man rose from a seat. He had sharp gray eyes, a nose that hooked like a beak, and neatly cut white hair that thinned at the top. A hand-tailored white shirt with crisp edges matched the creases of his dark trousers. "You're here to tell me about Riley?"

"I'm here to talk about a case that involved a man we came to call the Shark. He killed four girls in New Orleans. Only one victim, his last, escaped."

Charles tugged at starched cuffs. "Again, what does this have to do with me or my stepdaughter?"

"I believe the last victim was your stepdaughter."

The annoyance in his eyes mellowed a fraction. "Riley escaped a serial killer? I never heard about that."

"This attack would've happened twelve years ago, shortly after she ran away from home."

The tension around Charles coiled like a snake. "I don't know what you're talking about. Riley never told me about any kind of attack."

"As I understand, you two didn't have any contact after that point, correct?"

"What're you getting at?"

"I'm trying to find a killer who chooses girls that look very much like Riley." As he spoke he shifted his gaze to Audrey. Her expression reflected a superficial shock.

"I wouldn't know anything about murdered girls," Charles said.

"That would have been the summer your wife died."

"Don't bring my late wife into this."

"She was Riley's mother."

"Yes. They were very close."

"What kind of relationship did you have with Riley?" Bowman asked.

"I became her stepfather when she was nearly three. She was more like a real daughter to me than a stepchild."

"So you two were close?"

"Did she send you to talk to me? What's this about?" Charles countered.

"You are the only link I have to her past in New Orleans."

"I'm not going to talk about her to a rent-a-cop."

Bowman bared his teeth into a grin. "Did you know Riley has lived in Virginia for the past twelve years?"

"You need to leave." Charles shifted under Bowman's hard gaze. "I was always good to her. I treated her like she was my own child. It wasn't my fault that Riley could be difficult to manage and ungrateful."

"Why did she run away?"

"She didn't—"

"I know she ran away."

"*Run away* is a harsh term. It's very dramatic, like her." He stiffened. "Basically, she didn't like the house rules. Her mother and I expected her to accomplish a lot. When her mother died, she stopped caring. And I think if you have any other questions, you may take them up with my attorney."

"I didn't realize there was a need for attorneys."

"I'm not a fool."

"You have a reputation as a gambler. You've had years when you've lost heavily."

"You don't have access to that kind of information."

He didn't, but the man's defensive tone told Bowman he'd been right. "Were you ever in a high-stakes game that involved runaway girls?"

Charles's face whitened. "I don't know what you are talking about. And now I must insist you leave." He moved toward the door.

"If you were losing big and you had a chance to win it all back, would you have staked Riley's life on a bet?"

"Get out."

In no rush to follow orders, Bowman took a moment to survey the room. Noted the large portrait of the woman hanging above the fireplace. Her hair was dark, cascading around her shoulders. Her green eyes held a hint of amusement, as if she knew a secret.

"That's a nice portrait of Riley's mother."

Charles bristled.

"Riley looks just like her."

Charles fisted his fingers but said nothing.

"Nice that you still honor your first wife."

"I loved her very much, and I can't toss the portrait away just because she's gone."

Audrey's body tensed with anger, but she stayed silent.

"I do understand that," Bowman said with real honesty. "How did she pass away?"

"Cancer."

"I'm sorry to hear that. Must have been hard on Riley."

"She was a difficult kid before her mother's death. Afterward, she became impossible. She ran away before I could throw her out. And if she's in trouble, then she brought it on herself."

"Staking her life in a high-stakes game would kill two birds with one stone. Troubled teen gone. Debt wiped free."

"Leave or I'm calling the cops."

"Count on me returning if I have more questions."

"You don't know who you're harassing or you would be afraid."

"I could say the same to you, Mr. Charles."

Bowman stepped outside as Charles slammed the door behind him. Tugging on his white cuffs, he moved down the steps at a leisurely pace.

His relationship with Riley was complicated, and when he would tell her about this visit, it would become contentious. But he was back in her life and he'd do what it took to protect her.

***

"Yes, we did get a hit on Jane Doe's prints. Who told you?" Dakota Sharp's graveled voice rattled over his shoulder at Riley as she raced to catch up to him, crossing the Virginia State Police parking lot toward the building's front entrance.

"Eddie Potter, the reporter," she said. "He has friends in the department, I suppose."

His scowl deepened. "Where did you see him?"

"He came to my house this morning."

Sharp muttered a curse. "That's not good."

"I can take care of Potter and myself. Who's the victim?"

"Her name is Vicky Gilbert."

So Potter was right. "How did you identify her?"

"Isn't this your day off?"

"I can't take days off and do nothing. My kid is in school all day, and I can train Cooper and clean house only so much before I go insane."

A ghost of a smile tugged at his lips. "There must be something else you can be doing other than chasing me."

"Actually, there isn't. This case is under my skin."

He paused and studied her, his expression partly amused but mostly annoyed. "Vicky Gilbert was arrested last year for theft in Chesterfield, Virginia. She and a few friends decided to steal some dresses from a shop in the mall. Her mother paid the store for the stolen items and charges were dropped."

"Charges went away, but the problems did not."

"Exactly." He pried the lid off the to-go coffee cup and sipped. "Could be any number of reasons on the menu: drugs, abuse, the call to adventure. I've heard all the reasons."

Riley pulled off her sunglasses, fingering a worn earpiece. "You said her family is in Chesterfield?"

"Solid middle class from what I can tell."

"And we both know that bad things never happen in solid middle-class families."

He grunted. "You're too young to be cynical, Trooper."

"I see the world for what it is."

"And what's that?"

"Dark and scary. Do you have the address?"

"Yeah. I was planning to pay them a visit as soon as I checked in with my chief."

"I'd like to tag along. I'll have a different perspective than you, Agent Sharp. I work with runaways. I can help you. And maybe if I can find out who killed Vicky, I can put away Carter for the rest of his life." She was like a dog with a bone. "Have you found Darla Johnson? She's Jax Carter's girlfriend."

"We're on the lookout for her."

"Have Vicky's parents called in a missing persons report yet on their daughter?"

"No."

"Don't you find that odd?"

"I learned a long time ago that there're all kinds of dysfunctional families out there."

"They are either glad she's gone or think she'll come back." She calculated the time it would take to cut through the rush-hour traffic. The twenty-mile trip would take an hour tops. "If I come along, I'll drive and you can get some work done."

A sigh shuddered through him, making him look older than his thirty-seven years. "Pull your vehicle around in a half hour."

"See you then." She turned to leave and then snapped her fingers, remembering. "You aren't allergic to dogs, are you?"

"What?"

"Cooper's along for the ride."

He shook his head. "Why not? The more the merrier." Exactly a half hour later Sharp returned and slid into the passenger seat. As she pulled out of the lot, he tensed. Sharp wasn't accustomed to riding shotgun.

As they drove in silence, she thought about the playing cards hidden in her house. A thousand miles and a dozen years separated her and the day someone had given her those cards. She had no forensic evidence or memories she could attach to the cards. And with Hanna's adoption looming, just the suggestion of a link to a serial killer could derail the final judgment. Still, the cards couldn't be ignored.

"Have you considered entering the murder in ViCAP?" she asked.

"The FBI database? Why?"

"The playing cards found with the victim are distinctive. The handwritten word *Loser* on each is a signature."

He cursed under his breath. "Don't make this more than it is."

Gripping the wheel, she pulled herself up a little straighter. "I disagree. They have a distinctive look. I bet they're custom made. It's worth a shot."

"Anything federal amounts to a shit-ton of paperwork."

"I'll do it."

He groaned and rubbed his eyes. "You don't want to deal with the feds."

"You don't like the feds?"

"We've crossed swords before."

"But it's the only hard evidence we have at the moment," she coaxed. "You've got to admit the cards are different."

He tensed as she sped up to merge into highway traffic. "The cards are unique."

"Like I said, I can help."

He glanced at her, eyebrow raised as if searching. "What aren't you telling me?"

If a lead didn't pop with ViCAP, she would tell him the truth. But right now she was betting the database could give him more than she could. "I know the cards are the key."

"I'll look into ViCAP. Right now, I want to talk to the victim's parents."

She loosened her grip on the wheel. "Sure."

Thirty minutes later GPS directed them to a tree-lined street in western Chesterfield County. The acre lots were large for the county and the houses at least three thousand square feet, both indicators that this area was definitely upper middle class.

She parked in front of the tall brick colonial with neatly trimmed hedges in a freshly mulched bed out front. The driveway was aggregate, the landscaping professional.

"Does the dog need walking?"

"He's good for now, but we'll hit a rest stop on the way home."

She left the SUV on, the engine and air-conditioning running. "What do I do?"

He grunted. "When we get inside, don't say a word. Let me do the talking," Sharp said. "No offense, Trooper, but without your uniform we look like 'take your daughter to work' day."

"We don't."

"You do look young."

As they got out, a man dressed in a dark suit stepped out the front door. Grinning, he had a cell phone pressed to his ear and a briefcase in hand. Smooth white teeth flashed as his polished wing tips caught the morning sun. He paused midstride when he saw them approach. The smile vanished as he spoke into the phone before hanging up.

If Dakota Sharp's haircut and stance didn't give him away as a cop, the dark suit did.

Sharp reached for his badge while maintaining eye contact. "Richard Gilbert?"

The man stopped, jangling his car keys in his hand. A thick aftershave scent wafted around him as if he'd just slapped it on his cheeks. "That's right."

"My name is Agent Dakota Sharp, and this is Trooper Riley Tatum. We'd like to talk to you about your daughter, Vicky."

The man studied Sharp's badge. "What has Vicky done? Has she stolen again?" Manicured fingers closed around the keys.

"No, sir, we don't believe she's stolen anything," Sharp said as he hooked the badge back on his belt. "When's the last time you saw her?"

"It's been a month since she took off. She was mad at her mother and me when we grounded her after her last brush with the law. She's living with one of her friends."

"Friend got a name?" Sharp asked.

"I don't remember."

Riley fished her notebook from her back pocket. "By the looks of her, I'd say she's been living on the streets during that time."

Sharp cast a sideways glance toward Riley, but he let the comment slide. Neither mentioned homicide because people usually clammed up when they heard the *h* word.

When Mr. Gilbert did not answer, Sharp reached in his pocket for a stick of gum as if he had all the time in the world. "Is pinning down the date you last saw Vicky a tough question?"

"No. It's not. Let me go inside and get my wife. Bonnie knows our daughter better than I do."

Mr. Gilbert opened the front door, and the three of them entered the foyer. "Bonnie! Can you come downstairs?"

"What do you want?" she shouted back from an unseen room on the second floor.

"There are a couple of cops here who have questions about Vicky."

"Vicky?" Footsteps hurried across the upstairs hallway.

Mrs. Gilbert rounded the corner. Heavyset, she wore jeans and a sweatshirt and her hair pulled up in a ponytail. Despite the puffy contours of her face, there were hints of a resemblance to Vicky.

Bonnie wiped her hands on a rag as she descended the stairs, pausing several steps short of the bottom. "What's this about?"

"Wasn't it last week when we saw her?" Gilbert offered.

Riley's bullshit meter always worked well. Some of the officers in patrol called it her superpower. The human lie detector, others said. But it didn't take a superpower or much police work to know Mr. Gilbert was lying.

Mrs. Gilbert kept wiping her hands as if she would never really be able to get them clean. "Is she okay? I'm worried about her."

"When did Vicky run away?" Sharp asked.

"Hold on," Mr. Gilbert said. "I never used the words *run away*. She became upset with us and moved in with a friend to cool off."

"That's running away, Mr. Gilbert," Riley said.

"You have to be underage to run away," Mr. Gilbert countered. "She turned eighteen a week ago."

"That absolves you of a legal responsibility, but what about a moral obligation?" Riley couldn't hide the annoyance burning under her tone.

Mr. Gilbert advanced a step, but Sharp edged forward, blocking his path. "Mrs. Gilbert, when did Vicky move out?"

"She didn't run away. She went to stay with friends. She texted me several times a week and checked in. I knew where she was staying."

"How long has she been gone?" Sharp asked.

"I'm not sure. But not long."

"You don't know?"

"Not exactly. No."

Sharp studied the slightly frayed tip of his red tie before locking his gaze on her. "Who was she staying with last?"

"I'm not sure," Bonnie said. "She has many friends and it's hard to keep up. But she and Rebecca are very close."

"When did she start staying with friends, Mrs. Gilbert?"

The woman hesitated. "About five weeks ago."

Mr. Gilbert expelled a breath, cursing as he ran a hand through his hair. "Vicky didn't like the house rules. She wanted to do what she wanted. She wasn't interested in school. And then she was arrested for stealing."

"She's a senior in high school?" Riley asked.

"She was supposed to start her senior year, but the first days of school didn't go well," her mother offered.

They were retelling Riley's life, she thought. "Did you only fight about school or the arrest?"

"She was upset," Mrs. Gilbert said, glancing at her husband. Tears welled in her eyes. "She gets very upset sometimes. We took her to doctors, trying to figure out why she became anxious. It was exhausting. When she left, it was nice to have peace in the house."

"Was she on medication?" Riley asked.

"Mood stabilizers," Mr. Gilbert said. "But she never stayed on them long enough for the drugs to really work. She didn't like feeling fuzzy, as she put it."

"Where's my daughter?" Mrs. Gilbert asked. "I want to see her. She's gotten into trouble again, hasn't she?"

Riley glanced at Sharp, and when he nodded she kept her voice steady. "Mrs. Gilbert, your daughter is dead. She was found along I-95 north of here."

Chapped hands rose to the woman's lips as she stifled a cry. "There must be some kind of mistake."

"We identified her using fingerprints on file with the Chesterfield Police Department."

Sharp watched them both carefully, his expression showing no signs of emotion. "There's no mistake."

Mr. Gilbert sucked in a breath like a boxer who'd taken a shot to the gut. "How did she die?"

"You've made a mistake," Mrs. Gilbert said again. She made no move toward her husband. "Vicky isn't dead. She's staying with friends."

As much as Riley believed this murder was connected to a bigger case, she couldn't rule out that someone who knew the girl well had killed her. In over 70 percent of homicide cases involving a female victim, the killer was a loved one.

"We found her about fifty miles north of here," Riley said. In the middle of the night, without traffic, the trip would've taken less than an hour. Maybe her father had a chance to win big money in a poker game. Maybe he was tired of Vicky's outbursts.

"Vicky isn't dead," Mrs. Gilbert said. "I texted her two days ago."

"Two days?" Riley noted the time in her book. Mrs. Gilbert might have received a text from Vicky's phone, but that didn't mean Vicky had sent it.

"Maybe it was four days. But she told me she was fine. She told me she had a lead on a good job."

"What kind of job?"

"In a bar."

"Did she give you a name of the bar, a boss, or a coworker?" Sharp asked.

"No," Mr. Gilbert said. "I think I need to call our attorney."

"Mr. Gilbert, there's no need for an attorney now," Sharp said. "We're simply gathering as many facts as we can so we can solve your daughter's murder. No one is going to get busted today for a kid running away or working in a bar."

Mr. Gilbert's grip tightened on his cell. "I'm calling our lawyer."

"Richard. Please." Mrs. Gilbert's voice cracked. "This is Vicky."

"Who has once again pulled us into a mess." He turned from them all and dialed a number.

As her husband spoke into the phone, Mrs. Gilbert said to Riley, "She said it was good, honest work. I worried about the drinking, but she said that wouldn't be a problem. She said they were sending her to get her hair and nails done. She was going to be a greeter. She was really excited."

Vicky's nails and hair were done, meaning the kid wove the lies with some truth. "Did she say where they were taking her to get fixed up?"

"A beauty salon, I guess. She didn't say where."

"And that was the last time you had contact with her?" Riley asked.

"Yes. That was the last time she responded back to me." Tears welled in her eyes as if the news had finally taken root. "I text her every day. I'm always checking up on her. Sometimes she answers and sometimes she doesn't."

Riley kept her voice soft as if they were two friends having a chat. "What can you tell me about her life? Did the texts give you a clue?"

"She said she and her friends went to parties."

"Friends have names."

"Jo-Jo was one name she mentioned. Another was Cassie. She said they were all pals. Looked out for each other."

Riley glanced at Sharp, who was paying close attention. "Did your daughter have any tattoos?"

"A butterfly and a star." She dropped her voice a notch. "When she showed them to me, I told her not to tell her dad."

"What about the initials *JC* on the back of her neck?"

"She didn't have a tattoo like that." Hope glistened. "Do you think you've made a mistake because my Vicky didn't have a *JC* tattoo on her neck?"

"We have it right, ma'am," she said. "The tattoo is new. Did she have a boyfriend?"

"She dated a boy named Jax. Do you think it was his initials?"

"I think JC was her pimp," Riley said. "I think he marked her as his own."

Mrs. Gilbert wiped away a tear from her cheek as it spilled. "That's not my daughter. She wouldn't have sold herself like that."

"Our daughter," Mr. Gilbert said, shutting off his phone, "was a free spirit. She did as she pleased. If you have questions, you should talk to her *boyfriend.* Jax Carter."

"He works in Richmond tending bar," Mrs. Gilbert said. "I have his phone number." She moved into a side room where she retrieved her phone from her purse. She scrolled through the numbers, and when she found Jax's, she rattled off the number. "He's older than her, but Vicky really liked him. And he wouldn't put her on the streets like you said."

"Is he the friend she was living with?" Sharp asked.

"Sometimes. But not all the time. They fought from time to time."

Sharp's jaw clenched. "How did Vicky break her arm?"

Mrs. Gilbert twisted her fingers around her wrist as she looked at her husband.

"The fracture is a spiral shape," Riley said. "You get those kind of breaks when someone twists your arm."

"I never hurt her," Mr. Gilbert said.

"No one said you did," Sharp countered while continuing to study Mrs. Gilbert's face.

"Ask her boyfriend," Mr. Gilbert said.

"How long have they been dating?" Riley looked at the mother.

She glanced at her husband and then tipped her chin up a notch. "About six months."

"Do you think he did it?"

"He must have."

"Well, this break goes back a few years," Sharp said in a calm tone. "She would've been about fourteen when it occurred."

Mr. Gilbert drew in a breath. Bonnie stood beside him but kept distance between them. "She was an active kid. She fell a lot. That doesn't mean we hurt her. And that's all I'm going to say. We aren't answering any more questions until our attorney calls us back."

Riley closed her book as she glanced at Sharp.

Slowly, Sharp pulled a card from his pocket and held it out to Mr. Gilbert. He didn't take it. Sharp laid it on an entry table. "This is only the beginning, Mr. Gilbert."

"We won't be talking to you again unless our attorney is present," he said.

"Well, sir, that's your choice, but I can promise if I find out you're responsible in any way, I won't be nice next time," Sharp said.

"That a threat?"

"Thanks for your time."

CHAPTER EIGHT

Thursday, September 15, noon

When Bowman was in the bureau, there'd been rules to follow. But now that he was out, the old standard operating procedure didn't apply. His intention wasn't to break the law, but he knew how to bend anything to its breaking point.

Back from Washington, DC, he glanced at the text from Shield's contact in the state police. The female victim had been identified and the connection to his tree-hugging pal, Jax Carter, was established. Bowman made his way along the hospital hallway, already knowing Carter's room number. He wasn't interested in dealing with attorneys or Miranda rights. He simply wanted to have a chat with the man who had last sold Vicky Gilbert.

The room was dark when Bowman entered and Carter was lying on his back, his eyes closed. Sleeping like a baby. Bowman unplugged the call button and settled in the chair next to Jax. For a long moment he simply stared. He wondered if a guy like Jax had lured Riley into the poker game twelve years ago. Had she been drugged and sold as well? He lightly pressed his finger into Carter's wound.

"Jax Carter."

Carter's eyes popped open, his gaze searching wildly. When he saw Bowman in the chair, Jax recoiled like a cat. "Who the fuck are you?"

"I can find you anytime."

Paling at the sound of the familiar voice, Carter reached for the buzzer and pressed it. Nothing happened.

"It's just you and me now," Bowman said, rising.

Carter sat up in bed, trying to put distance between them. "What do you want?"

"I want to know who you sold Vicky Gilbert to."

"I don't know who she is."

Bowman's teeth bared into a very unfriendly smile. He gently laid his hand on Carter's leg. "Sure you do. You've been selling her for the last couple of weeks."

Carter hissed. "I didn't—"

Bowman barely squeezed. "Who did you sell her to last?"

"I didn't hurt that girl. She was alive and well the last time I saw her. Back off!"

Bowman's fingers tightened on Carter's leg. "You sure you don't want to talk?"

Carter's face turned white. "Just let go."

Bowman released his grip but let his hand rest on the leg.

"Not saying that I sold her, but there was a guy. Lewis. Kevin Lewis. He was looking to party with a girl who had Vicky's look."

"What kind of look did he want?"

Carter shifted, trying to move his leg out of Bowman's reach but only managing to scoot over a couple of inches. "Dark hair. Young. Fresh. Like her."

"Why did he want her?"

"I don't ask."

"What happened when he didn't bring her back?"

"I went looking for her. The girl had real potential."

"A moneymaker," he coaxed.

"That's right."

"She'd not worked the streets before?"

"Not really. But she was starting to make serious money."

"Who introduced you to her?"

"My girlfriend."

"Girlfriend?"

Carter didn't hesitate. "Darla Johnson."

Bowman sensed Carter was willing to throw his grandmother to the wolves if it diverted some of the heat off him. "How did Darla meet her?"

"I don't know. Online, I guess."

"You guess?"

"She's always on her phone checking out social media and shit."

"Reaching out to girls like Vicky. Lonely girls. Lost girls."

Carter shifted. "I don't know. Ask Darla."

"What does Darla say to the girls?"

"You'd have to ask her."

"Where can I find her?"

"She moves around."

"In a car? A camper? How does she get around?"

"We have a motor home. We like to stay on the move."

"What's it look like, Jax?"

"White. Midsized."

"Tell me all that you know about Darla."

"She has a rap sheet. Been busted a couple of times for drugs. Five foot four. Round hips. Blond hair."

Bowman's gaze dropped to Carter's thigh. "That knife wound must be hurting now. I hear you took over fifty stitches. That little girl cut you good."

Carter shifted, his eyes darkening. "That's between me and her."

Outside a cart rattled past, reminding him that this was not the time or place. "Not anymore. I'm in the mix now. Leave her alone."

"Or what?"

Bowman squeezed again. "Do you really want to find out?"

Carter hissed in a breath. "No!"

A short knock on the door had Bowman backing away from the bed as a nurse entered. He lowered his voice. "See you soon."

***

Vicky's short, troubled life weighed heavily on Riley as she walked into the small coffee shop near the police station after she dropped off Sharp. A bell overhead jingled as she glanced toward a television behind the bar and spotted Eddie Potter's face. The sound wasn't on, but she could see he was interviewing an older, well-dressed man in the field where Vicky's body had been found. The caption under the old man's face read, *Cain Duncan, festival and concert promoter with Byline Entertainment.*

A young, thin man behind the counter glanced up from the stainless-steel pitcher he was filling with freshly steamed milk. "Riley. Triple espresso?"

"Perfect."

"So, you and Cooper catch any bad guys today?"

"Too many to count," she said.

He grinned. "Coffee's on the house today."

"Why?"

"Appreciate what you do."

"Thanks." She dropped a few bucks in the tip jar. As she settled into a chair, the door opened and she spotted a tall man glancing at the menu above. Though his back was to her, she could see he was fit and radiated an energy that was hard to miss.

Going through the motions, she thought as she tore the sugar packets and dumped both into her coffee. As she savored the combination of bitter and sweet, she glanced a second time at the man ordering a plain black coffee. Short dark hair cut neatly. Nicely dressed. In fact, the jacket was top-of-the-line and fit his broad shoulders well. His eyes remained forward, didn't cut in her direction—but she sensed he knew exactly what was happening around him.

By her guess, he was a fed. Had the look. And they had their share of feds here, so she didn't pay too much attention to them. She thought about the pitch she'd made to Sharp about ViCAP. No way the wheels of progress moved that fast.

She tugged her notebook from her pocket and flipped through the paltry notes from her interview with Vicky's parents. Father was an ass, and she wasn't sure if that was his constant state or if he was overwhelmed and in shock. Mom was in full-blown grief and juggling a load of guilt on top of it. She wasn't sure if Vicky's problems were of her parents' making or stirred up by her own mental health issues. Either way, the kid had landed on the street.

"Thank you." The deep timbre of the man's voice drew her attention as he dropped his change, not just coins but also bills, into the tip jar. He didn't bother with sugar or milk before he turned.

She froze, her cup centimeters below her lips as she looked at him. He wasn't pretty-boy handsome. The profile was too rough around the edges, as if parts had been bruised or broken before. Shit. Clay Bowman.

He took a seat two spaces from her. Long fingers tapped the side of his coffee cup as he fished a cell from his breast pocket.

Riley sipped her coffee, her comfort level plummeting. Clay *f-ing* Bowman. The last guy she needed or wanted to see again.

Hiding was not an option unless she wanted to look like a wuss. She blew out a slow breath, set her cup down. No sense skirting this past mistake.

"Clay Bowman," she said.

His dark gaze rose. "Riley Tatum."

She was actually surprised he remembered her. He'd blasted into her world, made her want too much, and pushed her out of his life.

"So what brings you to my neck of the woods?"

"A case." He allowed his gaze to linger. "You look good. Life must be treating you well."

"Can't complain." His voice struck a chord as familiar words echoed. *Do you have this?* Was he the guy who'd helped her on the side of the mountain?

"Glad to hear it. I always pegged you for greatness." Bowman's presence scraped her nerves and invaded her space as she faced him.

"Did you just arrive in the city?"

He studied her a beat. "Why do you ask?"

The dark paint was gone, but she recognized the wide set of his jaw and angled cheekbones. "I guess I thought we might have crossed paths in the last couple of days."

"I have that kind of face."

"You ever do any hiking?"

"Sometimes."

He answered her questions but gave her nothing extra. He was the guy in the woods. She was sure of it. But he wasn't willing to confirm and she was in no mood to play games.

Sitting around and playing it cool was not her specialty, and she wasn't interested in chatting with a guy she once thought she might have been able to love. Shit. How could she have not recognized him on the mountain?

"It's been a pleasure, Bowman. Glad to see you're doing well."

"You too, Riley."

Waving to Seth, she crossed the coffee shop. "Thanks, Seth."

As she moved, she sensed Clay watching her. Tracking her. Hell, he could be just as surprised to see her here. She kept moving.

Her SUV was already running, AC blasting so Cooper remained cool. When she slid behind the wheel, she shot a quick glance in Cooper's direction. "The universe hates me today."

Cooper looked up, then relaxed back.

Seeking distraction, she grabbed her phone from her pocket. A missed message. Realizing she hadn't turned her ringer back on, she played the message. It was from Bonnie Gilbert, who simply said, "If you want to know more about Vicky, call her friend Rebecca Wayne. Rebecca knew more about my daughter than I did." After rattling off Rebecca's number, she rang off.

Riley dialed Rebecca's phone.

On the third ring she heard, "Hello?"

"Is this Rebecca Wayne?"

"Yes."

"This is Trooper Riley Tatum with the Virginia State Police. I understand you were a friend of Vicky Gilbert."

"Yeah. So?"

"I'd like for us to meet. I want to talk to you about her."

"I'm in school right now. And how do I know you're a cop?"

"We can meet in public. I'll show you my badge."

She was silent for a moment. "I shouldn't be on the phone, but I'm in the girls' locker room."

"When can you talk?"

"School lets out at three and I have tennis practice right after. I can meet you at the courts."

"Great."

Rebecca told her the school's address.

"I'll find it."

***

Bowman sat in Seth's coffee shop watching Riley Tatum through the window as she spoke on her phone. Garrett Andrews had tracked her cell to this location, and though he'd seen her on the mountain and at her home, he wanted to see her up close. She looked better than he remembered.

She noticed him the instant he'd entered the café—good cops knew who was around. Identifying him had brought a wicked frown to her face, and when he spoke, she knew he'd trailed her on the mountain. She'd called him out without giving him away. Savvy. Smart. But that was Riley. Never anyone's fool.

Tall and lean, she carried herself with the straight-backed posture of someone with her sights set on the chief's office one day. Her clothes were nice and crisp, with an edge. One glance suggested she was a gym rat, but she would have to be in good shape to maintain the tracking pace she'd set the other day.

She'd not given any physical indication that his presence bothered her as she rose and left, but he'd sensed her irritation. He shouldn't care one way or the other if seeing him again affected her, but he did.

On his phone, he opened the e-mails from his office that profiled Riley Tatum. At thirty, she'd racked up several citations and a valor award for the rescue two years ago. There'd been talk of her moving to the investigative side, but she'd opted out to stay with her dog. Loyal. As he remembered.

Her arrest of Jax Carter had earned her media attention, which she'd shunned when the reporters surrounded her after the arrest. She did not like the limelight. He couldn't fault her. She was a good cop.

A review of the Shark's victim profiles proved she easily fit the killer's type. Today with her long dark hair draping her shoulders, the similarities were striking. Shave off twelve years and she was a perfect fit.

And now she was connected to the Gilbert case. The killer had been inactive for a dozen years and the previous killings had all happened in

New Orleans, her hometown. He knew she'd crossed paths with this killer and had somehow gotten away.

When he thought back to his visit with Charles this morning, he couldn't picture Riley living the socialite life. Why had Charles called her difficult?

Bowman rose.

Out the door, he strode to his black SUV and slid behind the wheel. He switched on the engine and, certain now that no one could hear, dialed Shield.

He picked up on the second ring. "You made contact?"

"I did."

"What do you think?"

That was a loaded question. "We exchanged a couple of basic pleasantries."

"Did she recognize you from the mountain?"

"She did."

"She's not told anyone about your assist there?"

"I don't think so. I asked for her discretion at the time."

A humorless chuckle leaked over the line. "It's to her advantage not to talk. She gets all the credit."

"True." But she wasn't the type to grab attention. "Her stepfather strikes me as the kind of guy who would willingly gamble her life. He's got a huge portrait of his first wife. She was Riley's mother and they look exactly alike."

There was a long pause. "I wonder if Riley knows how close she came to dying twelve years ago?"

"Hard to tell," Bowman said.

"Whatever you need to get this case solved, consider it done. He's close and we have a real chance of catching the son of a bitch."

"Roger that. She's now my number-one priority."

***

Riley placed a call to Sharp and repeated the conversation she'd had with Rebecca Wayne. He agreed to join her so they could conduct the interview together.

It was minutes before three when Riley and Sharp arrived at the school. Both got out and leaned against the car, enjoying a moment of fresh air and sunshine.

"I ran a background check on Darla Johnson," Sharp said.

Riley leaned forward, her interest keen. "Carter's girlfriend?"

Sunglasses glinted as he tipped his face toward the sun. "She's twenty-three years old and has a list of priors that rivals her boyfriend's. Assault, drug trafficking, and drunk driving make her a perfect fit for Carter. Johnson is a high school dropout and has no primary job. A real piece of work."

"Any idea where she might be now?" Riley asked.

"I've issued a BOLO, but no luck finding her yet."

"Flushing out Darla is not going to be easy."

"I agree."

"Unless we have the right bait."

He tipped his face toward her, his expression unreadable. "What do you have in mind?"

"Her kind often trolls on social media. I could dig out a picture of me when I was nineteen and set up a page and start posting comments about how hard my life is and how no one understands me." She had a picture taken of her at nineteen when her hair flowed around her shoulders. She was smiling in the photo, but her eyes reflected a darkness that showed life had not been a piece of cake. It was perfect.

Sharp remained silent as if mulling the idea.

"The page is only intended to find her. And I'll even use my real name so no lawyer can ever accuse me of using a false identity."

"What name are you using?"

"Elizabeth Riley Tatum. My mother called me Beth."

"Beth Tatum?"

Sensing his interest, she said, "I'll send friend requests to Vicky's high school pals. If a couple accept, I'll look more legit."

He considered her idea. "Set up a page. But if you get any kind of bite, I want to know about it."

"Done."

The afternoon bell rang and as the hundreds of kids poured out of the school, she texted Rebecca. The girl responded back within seconds, and they agreed to meet at the bleachers near the tennis courts.

Riley and Sharp stood in the afternoon sun, soaking up the warmth and the breeze. They watched as the kids assembled by the tennis courts, and when one girl hung back from the crowd, Riley nodded. "I think that's her."

"Okay."

The girl was a tall, leggy blonde wearing a tennis skirt. Her hands trembled as she pretended to adjust the strings on her racket. "Can I make initial contact?"

"Sure."

Both pulled their badges and walked toward the girl with Riley taking the lead. "Rebecca Wayne?"

Rebecca responded to a text on her phone and looked up. "Trooper Tatum?"

"That's right. And this is Agent Sharp. He's also with Virginia State Police." Both held up their badges.

The girl barely glanced at the shields and seemed more worried about making it to practice. "I don't have a whole lot of time. Practice starts in fifteen minutes and the coach gets all bent when I'm late." Rebecca fished a power bar out of the side pocket. "My mom texted me the news about Vicky. Mom is Mrs. Gilbert's friend. I still can't believe she's gone. I saw her about a month ago."

"Any reason why you two haven't seen each other recently?"

"Yeah. Her new boyfriend. Mr. Super Creep."

"His name?" Riley pulled out her notebook and pen.

"Jax Carter."

"How'd they meet?"

"Through his weird sister."

"Sister?" Riley asked.

"Yeah. Darla. She said she was his sister."

It was easier to lure prey as a brother and sister act. "Okay."

"They met us at the mall one day. Vicky and I kind of ditched school a couple of months ago and went shopping."

"You skip school a lot?" Sharp said.

"A few times." She raised the bar to her mouth and hesitated. "You aren't going to tell my parents, are you?"

"Not about skipping school," Riley offered.

She bit into the bar. "Good. That wouldn't go over so well."

"Tell me about Darla and Jax," Riley asked.

"They were hanging out in the food court. She's pretty. He's cute and can be nice. And when they came up to us, it was kind of fun. He started flirting, and we were both thrilled. But I could tell Vicky was into it a lot more than me. She ended up giving him her cell phone number, and within a day, he was calling and texting her all the time. Total mind control."

"Why do you say that?"

"She and I could be hanging out and then he'd text and boom, she was gone. When he snapped his fingers, she jumped like a puppy dog."

"He was good to her?"

"At first. Gave her all kinds of presents. Bracelets, earrings, and a pair of very cool high heels. She was always gushing when she talked about him."

"But you said you didn't like him."

Rebecca swiped a loose strand of hair from her eyes. "She used to play tennis with me. The last time we played was a couple of months ago. She had a wicked bruise on her thigh and when I asked her about it, she blew it off. Said she bumped into the corner of a table. And then in the locker room I saw a bruise on her back. I pressed and she became all defensive and angry. She quit the tennis team the next day."

"You think Carter was hurting her?" Sharp asked.

"Yeah. I told her to tell her parents. Her parents are a pain, but they're okay. They were always trying to help Vicky stay on the path. But she wouldn't tell them."

"What about her mental health?"

"She swung between highs and lows."

"So what was the appeal of Jax Carter?"

"She always liked playing with fire. Which explains why she thought Jax was all that."

"Did you say anything to her parents about Jax?" Sharp asked.

Rebecca glanced at him, nervous. "I told my mom, who said she'd talk to Mrs. Gilbert. I don't know if she ever did."

"When Vicky left home last month, where did she go?"

"She spent a night with me, but my mom started asking questions. Vicky said she was going back home, but I knew that was a lie. She went to live with Jax."

"Where?"

"He has some trailer or motor home. Kinda creepy. She said it felt like home. She'd been talking about running away with him. He kept telling her he loved her and she believed him."

"Have any idea where I can find Darla?"

She folded over the wrapper of her power bar and tucked it back in her bag. "Did you check the mall? I saw her there the other day."

"When you skipped again?"

"Again, you aren't telling my parents, are you?"

"You do it again and I will," Sharp said.

Her face paled even as she squared her shoulders and tried to look tough. "How will you know?"

Riley smiled, but knew it conveyed no warmth. "You really want to test him on this?"

The girl looked away. "No."

"Smart. Do you know where they park the motor home?"

"I know they move around a lot, but where, I don't know. Where's Jax?"

"He's in the hospital. He's under arrest for assault."

"Shit. Did he kill Vicky?"

"No. But he beat up another girl so badly she's in the hospital."

"Did Darla kill Vicky?"

"I don't know who killed Vicky."

A breeze blew the hair back from Rebecca's face, accentuating a sprinkle of freckles across the bridge of her nose. She looked too damn young.

"Ever see another guy hanging out with Jax?" Sharp asked.

"There was a guy once. Dark hair and tanned skin. He sat next to Vicky in the backseat. Jax said he was a friend."

Guys like Jax lured girls like Vicky into prostitution slowly at first. They'd ask them to be nice to a friend. Being nice usually translated into sex. After the first friend, there'd be more until finally sex with strangers was a job. "Was there anyone else she hung out with?" Riley softened her voice, knowing Sharp made the girl nervous.

"After Jax, no. He was it for her."

"When's the last time you had contact with Vicky?"

"She texted me on Friday. Said she'd see me soon."

"Did she say where she was going?" Riley asked.

"A big party."

"That's it?"

"Yeah. She didn't say anything else."

Riley handed a card to Rebecca. "If you think of anything else, will you call me?"

"Yeah, sure." She flicked the edge of the card with her finger. "What was Jax doing with Vicky all this time?"

"He was pimping her out," Sharp said.

"Like a hooker?"

"Exactly like that," he said.

"Damn."

"Don't skip school," Sharp cautioned. "The monsters love the girls that color outside the lines."

Rebecca looked at Riley. "He's intense."

"He's also right," she said.

Riley and Sharp left a shocked Rebecca by the tennis courts and strode back to the car.

"Should we go to the mall?" Sharp asked.

"It's after school so the mall will be full of kids. I'd bet money Darla won't be there. Her kind comes in the middle of the day to troll for the girls who've skipped school. Those girls, more often than not, have some kind of issue and are easy prey."

"So we have a BOLO and social media."

"It's a start."

People stuck to what they knew and criminals were no different. The motor home had been seen at the truck stop shortly before Carter assaulted Jo-Jo. Maybe Darla would double back, and if not, maybe someone knew something about her.

"If you get any leads, Tatum, call me."

"Sure. What about ViCAP?"

"I sent in a report."

"Good. Thanks."

After Riley and Sharp left Rebecca, she dropped him off at the office and drove to the busy truck stop north of the city. She settled back in her seat and watched as a couple of girls milled around the front door of the truck stop's diner. Both wore short skirts and plunging tops. Standing next to them was a tall guy wearing a sleeveless T-shirt. His arms were covered in thick bands of tattoos, and his dark hair was tied back in a slick ponytail. Bringing a cigarette to his lips, he drew in a lungful of smoke and blew it out.

The trio wasn't breaking any laws, but they had the look of street workers. Out of her SUV, she cut across the lot to them. She'd promised Sharp she'd only call if she had something.

The man hesitated and took a step back from the girls. A gap-toothed grin spread across his face. He held up his hands. "Po-Po, what're you doing here? We ain't doing nothing wrong."

She glanced at the girls, who moved closer to him. "You have identification?"

"Why you want to know our names?" he countered.

"You can show me your ID now, or I can call for a patrol car."

"We ain't done nothing wrong," he said.

Testing. They were always testing. "You can explain that to the judge at your bail hearing. Not a big deal but a night of lost wages."

"That's bullshit," the man said.

"Yeah, ain't it?" She reached for her phone.

He held up his hands. "Fine. I got a driver's license." He dug a worn wallet out of his back pocket and plucked out an ID.

She glanced at the name. "Tony Rivers. Mr. Rivers. Ladies," she said, looking at the two girls. "Do you have identification, please?"

Both looked at Tony, clearly waiting for his permission. When he nodded, the shorter of the two said, "I'm Sandy Jones." She dug a driver's license from a small purse and handed it to Riley.

According to the license, she was eighteen and came from Texas.

The other girl shifted her stance, brushed a lock of blond hair from her eyes, and did the same. "I'm Cassie Lawson."

Cassie. "You know a gal named Jo-Jo?"

The girl shoved her hands in her pockets. "I don't know anybody named Jo-Jo."

"Really? I heard you two were friends."

Cassie stole a look at Tony. "I don't know anything."

Riley looked at the ID, knowing with Tony around, the girls would not talk. According to the ID she was eighteen and from out of state. "What are you two ladies doing here?"

Sandy glanced at Tony. "Just standing around. There a law against that?"

"Yes, it's called loitering." She handed Cassie back her license.

She had little reason to detain them, and they had no reason to answer her questions. Trying to make nice, she softened her tone. "I'm looking for a guy. His name is Jax Carter. You know him? I'm guessing he's one of your competitors."

"Ain't never heard of him," Tony said.

"Really? From what I've seen, you two have a lot in common. He had a few girls hanging out with him as well."

"Lucky man," he said.

She smiled, doing her best to look friendly. "You strike me as the kind of guy who's smart. Who knows his competition."

"I know what's going on around me."

"I'm not here to bust you, Tony, or cause trouble. I want Jax and Darla. Tell me about them. You seen them around lately?"

His jaw tightened. "Ain't good for business to talk to the po-po."

Testing again. Her hand shifted to her phone. "I was hoping for a little help, but it looks like I'll now have marked cars following your every move. You won't be able to sneeze without one of my guys seeing it happen. You want that?"

Tony rubbed his chin as he seemed to choose between the lesser of two evils. "I ain't the man's babysitter."

She reached in a back pocket and pulled out a picture of Vicky, which she'd gotten from the Department of Motor Vehicles. Careful not to refer to murder, she said, "Either of you know this girl?"

The girls barely scanned the picture. Each shook their head no and glanced at the ground. Tony leaned over and looked at the image. "She hangs out with Jax. Don't know her name. What happened to her?"

"She's dead. Strangled to death."

He grimaced and his gaze lost what little charm he projected. "I didn't kill nobody."

"I never said you did," Riley said. She stared at the trio. "What can you tell me about the girl? And don't tell me you don't know."

Tony flicked the ash off the edge of his cigarette. "Some of the guys liked the looks of her. Fresh meat. Everyone wanted a taste. Jax had only worked her a couple of weeks when he received an offer on her that was real sweet. The buyer wanted a girl that still looked fresh."

Riley shifted her stance, doing her best to chase away an uncomfortable feeling growing inside of her. "You know who this guy was?"

"Jax knows. Darla knows. I never saw him."

"Tony, you mind if the ladies answer the question?"

Slowly he shook his head. "Fine."

"There was a car I saw," Sandy said, after a moment's hesitation.

"What car?"

"Big black car. Tinted windows. It parked next to their motor home."

"Did anyone get out?"

"No. No one got out," Sandy said. "It was a fancy car, so we were all paying attention. That kind of ride doesn't come here all that often."

"License plates?"

Sandy laughed. "It's never smart to look too hard or to remember. It was nice and fancy. That's all I got."

"Did any of you talk to the driver?"

"Maybe I did," Tony said. "I was getting a feel for what he wanted."

"And?"

"He didn't roll his window down much. He said he didn't like what I had to offer. He wanted a different type of girl. Dark hair."

"Like Vicky?"

"Yeah. Jax saw me talking and came up a few minutes later and talked to the guy," Tony offered. "If he cut a deal, I didn't see it, but he knew there was a buyer looking for a specific type."

"And this would've been last week. What night?"

Tony dropped his cigarette and ground the ash into the concrete with his scuffed boot tip. "Friday or Saturday, maybe. I never saw the car again. And that's all we got to say."

Riley pulled out her business cards, handing one to each girl. "If you ever need a hot meal, Duke's is the place to go. It's safe and he doesn't allow for any shit under his roof."

"But he's always putting people to work," Tony said. "Who wants to sweep floors for minimum wage?"

"Beats working on your back," Riley said.

He shook his head and laughed. Cassie laughed. Sandy did not.

Riley tucked her notebook away as if she were wrapping up the interview when she said, almost as an afterthought, "Any of you hear about any high-stakes poker game?"

Tony scratched his neck, and she noticed a spider tattoo clinging to the skin below his collar. "How high are the stakes?"

"Top level."

Tony shook his head. "Shit. I don't know about that. If the stake is more than a grand, it's over my head."

Looking at him, she believed him. He didn't roll large. "Okay."

She left the three standing silent in the parking lot. Sliding behind the wheel of her SUV, she studied Cassie and Sandy. She exhaled a breath she felt like she'd been holding since she first saw Vicky. The sheriff's words echoed. *She looks a little like you.*

"I don't look like her." As she muttered the words, images reached out from the shadows.

Smoke. The clink of poker chips. Laughter.

"She's pretty," a man said.

"She's your type, right?" a second answered.

Her mind tripped and turned, swirling in a sea of drugs as strong hands gripped her face and twisted it upward. Her eyes fluttered open, but they did not focus.

"Yeah, she's my type. Perfect."

A car horn behind Riley blared, startling her. The light was green. She drove, doing her best to shake it off.

Gripping the wheel, she increased her speed. "I don't look like her."

***

Anxious, Kevin pulled off the main road and wound down the long graveled driveway that cut a mile into the woods and up a small hill to the old building. The structure looked as if it had once been a church, but there were no signs of life around. He checked his watch to make sure he wasn't too early. He was right on time.

This next game would be the turning point in his life. He still had the cash and sensed Lady Luck was with him now.

The building was basic. Well built with white clapboards and yet a broken side window—nothing like the fancy, glittering Vegas casinos. A great thing, if you didn't want to draw attention to an illegal card game.

As he reached for his door handle, a shadow flashed in his side vision. A bullet crashed through the door and tore into his arm. Another ripped into his shoulder. Adrenaline jacked him up as he reached for his gun from the glove box. But before he could open the small door, a hail of shots sliced into his body.

His last thought as blood oozed and his vision blurred was that Lady Luck was a conniving bitch.

CHAPTER NINE

Thursday, September 15, 5:00 p.m.

Bowman was tracking Riley's cell phone signal, and when she and the other agent drove to the high school, he had been on their tail. He watched her drop off the other agent, then drive to the first truck stop. He followed her to three more truck stops, and when she stopped at the gas pump and got out to fill her tank, he decided it was time to know the game plan.

"Riley," he said.

She turned instantly, hand sliding toward her weapon. Her gaze locked on him.

He kept his hands out of his pockets and did his best to keep his face as neutral as possible, except for a small grin. He could scare the devil on a good day and didn't want to put up more roadblocks between them.

Her chest rose as she pulled in a slow, measured breath. "Not polite to stalk, Bowman."

"We need to talk."

"What can I do for you, Bowman?"

"I want to talk to you about the Gilbert case."

She glanced past him at his car, again calculating. He suspected she'd just shove him deeper into the doghouse. "Why?"

"Did you find playing cards with the body?"

Eyes narrowing, she stilled. "Playing cards?"

"We can stand here all day and second-guess each other or we can find a place to talk. I might be able to help you with this case."

"I don't need your help, Mr. Bowman. I'm pretty good at figuring these kinds of things out on my own."

"I was a help in the woods."

"I'll give you that. But this isn't the woods. Nor is it Quantico. We're not a team."

He should have guessed she'd not forgotten a damn thing. "This case is bigger than you think. You're in danger."

"Murder's always pretty big, Bowman."

This close, he was struck by her looks. Thick dark hair that he knew was soft to the touch. Keen green eyes. Cut cheekbones. Beautiful. And she possessed a confidence that still appealed. "Is the case important to you because it hits close to home?"

"There's a dead young girl lying on a slab in the state morgue, Mr. Bowman. That's why it's important to me."

"I know you were a runaway when you were seventeen."

Her eyes narrowed as if he'd jabbed a raw nerve. "You've mixed me up with someone else."

"I haven't."

Hands hitched on her hips, she tapped her finger against her belt. "You're headed down a rabbit hole."

A woman passed by and glanced at the two of them, her gaze alight with curiosity. Bowman, aware he was leaning toward Riley, straightened and tossed the woman a sideways glare, his frown deepening, until she looked away. "I'm not having this conversation here. And I know you don't want to have this chat in your office with your supervisor listening. My guess is that no one knows what happened to you."

Tension vibrated around her.

"There's a restaurant in town. Latrobe's. You know the place?"

"I know it." And with no hint of shame, "It's on your nickel."

"See you there in thirty minutes."

She studied him as he drove off. She didn't like or trust him. That was crystal clear.

When they arrived at the small restaurant, it was past five thirty. Patrons would file in during the next half hour, but for now they had the place mostly to themselves.

He chose a curved booth in the back. As the waiter pulled out the table, Riley gracefully slid into the booth. She smelled of soap, no heavy perfume. No makeup covered her smooth skin. The brief time they'd been together, she never talked about her past, and he had been so wrapped up in his own that he'd never asked. Now he was deeply curious.

He edged into the booth until his back was to the wall. This tactical choice put him a foot from her, but he wasn't worried about invading her space. She could have moved to her left, but like most cops, she wouldn't expose her back to the door.

"How's Cooper?" he asked.

"You didn't bring me here to talk about my dog, did you?"

"No, but I do like Cooper."

"What exactly do you do for Shield Security? How does tracking fugitives and serial killers fit into the job description?"

The waiter returned to fill their water glasses and leave two menus behind. When he was out of earshot, Bowman carefully unrolled his napkin. "Mr. Shield assigns duties on an as-needed basis."

She smoothed a small wrinkle in the tablecloth. "Just like that, he hires you to handle special projects."

"Our families have a history." His tone said he wasn't ready to discuss it further. He scanned the menu and zeroed in on the tenderloin. "I'm starving for a steak. Are you hungry?"

"Sure. I could eat."

When the waiter returned, he took their orders. Riley closed her menu and chose the steak as well.

"I thought women just ate salads," Bowman said.

"Hungry, angry women eat salads." She laid her napkin on her lap. "I also eat real food. Bowman, tell me about Shield Security. Not much press gets out about that company."

"Feel free to call me Clay."

"No."

"We passed being strangers a long time ago."

Slowly, she shook her head. "Let's keep it professional this time."

He nodded. "Shield is based near Quantico. We handle mostly high-end problems that our clients need dealt with quickly and quietly."

"Such as?"

He traced a path through the condensation of his glass. "Discretion is a big part of our appeal. But we generally find missing things or people."

"Nothing illegal."

"Nothing unethical."

She didn't press that point. "I'm guessing Shield Security is doing well judging by the suit."

"It's rewarding. By the way, you dress well."

She arched a brow. "Stop, you're going to make me blush."

A smile tugged at the corner of his mouth. "We appreciate your discretion on the Carter arrest."

"If you hadn't asked for silence, I would've given you credit. You passed up a lot of publicity."

"Which is exactly what we never want."

Small gold earrings dangled from her ears. He remembered she'd been wearing them during their night together five years ago. "So, if you're doing so well and making money hand over fist, what're you doing on my case?"

He sipped his water, allowing the ice-cold liquid to cool his throat. "My boss, Joshua Shield, and I were both with the FBI twelve years ago and assigned to New Orleans. We investigated a series of murders. Four young women were strangled and their bodies left in plain sight in the space of weeks."

Sitting back, she folded her arms. Her expression was blank, as if waiting for the punch line. "Not following."

He realized she didn't know about the four women. "At each murder scene the detectives found five playing cards. They all were hands from a five-card stud poker game. Three were definitely losing hands. One wasn't terrible, but likely not good enough to win. And in handwritten black ink, *Loser* was scrawled on each."

Carefully, she leaned forward and tapped a fingertip on the side of her glass. "Like my victim."

"Exactly."

"Was the handwriting the same on the cards?"

"Same word but each set appeared to be written by a different person."

"You said this guy killed four girls. And let me guess, they all had a similar look. Like Vicky."

"And like you, which you already know."

She didn't respond.

He sat back, tugging on the cuffs of his shirt. "Shield and I spent endless hours poring over evidence looking for this killer."

"What did you find?"

"No forensic data. This killer, who became known as the Shark, is a ghost. He's smart and knows how to cover his tracks. We never released the information about the five cards to anyone outside the case. No one in law enforcement would've picked up on the fact that those cases were connected to the Gilbert case."

"Who says we've connected our case to your cases?"

He tugged the notebook from his breast pocket and carefully flipped through pages until he found the one he wanted. He wasn't ready to play his trump card yet. "You're smart, but your high school grades were average. Cs and Bs. SAT scores placed you in the top 5 percent, yet your schoolwork was lackluster."

"A teenager with a bad attitude about school isn't new or unique."

The waiter arrived with a basket of bread and a small dish of herb butter. Bowman offered the basket to her first and was surprised to see her take a roll. His late wife had never eaten bread. She never ate steak.

Riley tore her roll in half and buttered both sides. She took a bite and Bowman found himself glad to see her eat. He set a roll on his plate but did not touch it. "That kind of disparity between grades and tests always makes me curious. So I did a little more checking on you."

"Must have been a real slow morning for you, Bowman. Most people have better things to do than poke around in my boring life."

Impatience hummed under her words. She wanted him to circle back to the original thread of questioning. But he was in no rush to deliver. Getting this woman to talk or open up would not be easy. Too many layers of ice. "You're not curious about what I found?"

"I lived it, remember?" Again, her expression remained blank and showed no sign of reaction. She should have been a poker player. "Okay, let me have it. What did you find out about me?"

The southern drawl sugarcoated the words, but he suspected underneath lurked a *screw you*. She didn't like him running this show. And though he sensed she itched to tell him to spit it out, she wouldn't. Control was too important to Trooper Tatum.

"You come from a very wealthy family. After high school you moved to Virginia and worked at Duke's diner while taking classes at the community college. When you turned twenty-two, you entered the state police academy. Most would consider that a very unexpected move for a girl who had her debut in New Orleans society."

"I don't worry about what most people think." She bit into the roll, finishing the first half.

"What about your parents? They couldn't have liked your change in direction."

She sat back, carefully dusting the crumbs from her hands as if they were old memories. "The decision was mine."

"Why not go to college and be the sorority girl?"

"How interesting would that have been?" She dabbed her lips with her napkin, a remnant from that old lost life of genteelness that he knew masked something dark. She hesitated before she spoke again. "I thought you checked me out. Are you coming up short?"

He considered telling her about his visit with her stepfather but decided against it. The news would add unnecessary fuel to the fire he suspected was burning behind her calm. "The details of your life before Virginia have been buried. It's as if someone didn't want anyone to know about your early years."

"I think you're being dramatic, Bowman. I was understandably upset after my mother's passing, so I moved and switched schools. Very cut-and-dried." A grin, which didn't reach her eyes, curled her lips. "I enjoy being independent."

"I'll give you that." Absently, he picked up the knife in the place setting and turned it over a couple of times. "At the police academy your scores were tops in academics, physical fitness, and marksmanship. You made dean's list in college."

"I'm a late bloomer. Get to the good stuff."

Riley pushed the bread plate aside as the salad arrived. They ate in silence for a moment and he was glad for the interlude. If he thought he'd rattled her by showing up and telling her what he knew about her past, he was wrong.

Finally, when the steaks arrived, she said, "Make your point."

He cut into his rare steak but then set his fork and knife down. "After I was transferred out of the New Orleans office, Shield received an envelope. No return address. Inside were five pictures of young girls. Four matched the Shark's victims, but Shield never found a match for the fifth."

Riley focused on eating her tenderloin, seemingly more worried about her food than him. "Okay."

"I had my IT guy pull your high school photo for confirmation."

Her fingers tightened slightly around her utensils.

Bowman reached in his pocket and pulled out her old picture. In that image, she wore her hair loose around her shoulders. Her smile was wide, her eyes bright. Showing no emotion, he removed a second picture, holding it up like a gambler did a winning card. "This is the picture of the girl we could never find." He placed it beside her high school picture.

Riley's silverware clanged against the plate. "It's not a match."

"Don't lie to me or yourself."

"Do you know how many people have brown hair and brown eyes, Mr. Bowman? Billions. I might have the same hair color as the victim's, but I'm *nobody's* victim and I've nothing to hide from you or anyone else."

"I don't buy it, Riley. I don't. I think you were the one that escaped. I think the fact that Vicky Gilbert was killed and dumped in your area isn't coincidence. The Shark is back, and he's in Virginia for a reason." Taking a breath, he softened the edges of his tone. "He's coming for you."

Very deliberately, she set her napkin to the side of her plate. "Thank you for the early dinner, but this fantasy story you've concocted is now boring me. I've work to do. Good luck with your case."

He placed his hand on hers, stopping her from sliding out of the booth. Tension radiated from under her skin. "We can help each other, Riley."

She glanced at his hand, as if she expected him to remove it. When he didn't, she pulled it free. "I can solve this case by myself."

"You won't. Not because you aren't smart but because this guy has been at it a long time and he's stayed a few steps ahead of everyone."

"You underestimate me."

"I might," he said, pulling his hand back. "I thought you were a police officer willing to do whatever it took to find her killer."

"I am."

"You'll play ball as long as you can keep your secrets."

"I don't have secrets, Mr. Bowman." Her clenched teeth practically ground the words to pulp.

"I'm not your enemy, Riley. I'm trying to save your life. If you can forget our history—"

"Mr. Bowman, I barely remember our history, so that's not a factor. I don't really know you or your agenda. You insinuate yourself into the search for Carter and now this case. I didn't ask for your help last time, and I'm not asking now."

"What more do you want to know about me?"

Slowly, she shook her head. "I don't want to know anything more about you."

"Feel free to check up on me, but do it quickly."

"I suspect if I bothered to check, I'd find a few facts that don't amount to much. For all I know, the Shark could be your client and this is one of the messes you've been hired to clean up."

"We don't take those kind of clients at Shield."

"So you say."

He was trying to help her. Instead, she was cool as a cucumber and he was getting annoyed. He didn't appreciate the knock on his integrity. "There're going to be more bodies, Trooper. In his killing year there were four bodies." He balled up his napkin and placed it on the table. "It's too bad that another girl will have to die before you see the light and tell me what you know." He reached in his breast pocket and pulled out a business card. "If you change your mind, please call me."

Her chest rose and fell. She glared at him while sliding out of the booth and grabbed her purse. She left his card behind. She moved with a steady precision that had him watching the sway of her hips. "I know you're the one, Riley. I know it."

***

When Riley slid into her SUV, the seat's warmth seeped into her skin but didn't quite chase the chill from her body. She didn't have any real memory of what had happened to her in New Orleans, but Bowman was right, she needed to tell.

With a trembling hand, she checked her messages and realized Dr. Kincaid had called. En route home to walk Cooper and check in on Hanna, she called the medical examiner and was sent to voice mail. "Dr. Kincaid, this is Trooper Tatum calling you back."

As she hung up the phone, it rang, displaying Dakota Sharp's name. "Agent Sharp."

"Where are you?"

"About home. What's up?"

"I've a body that might be of interest to you."

Her breath stilled. "Why's that?"

"He has poker chips in his pockets, and his suit reminds me of a fancy gambler."

"Give me the address."

When he shared the location, she didn't need to plug it into her GPS. It was five miles from her home and close to where they'd found Vicky. She drove fifteen miles north and took the exit she took every night to go home. She wound along the back road until she spotted the flash of cop car lights in the distance. Parking behind Dakota's vehicle,

Riley stepped out and moved toward the tape where Agent Sharp and Sheriff Barrett stood.

"Had an interesting visitor. From Shield Security," she said.

"I've heard of them," Barrett said. "Firm near Quantico."

"What're they doing here?" Sharp asked.

She held his gaze. She knew Sharp was a straight shooter, and at this point she had to trust someone. "The Gilbert case landed on Shield's radar."

"Okay."

"Joshua Shield, the firm's CEO, used to be FBI. When he was with the bureau, he investigated a string of cases similar to our murder. They called the killer the Shark."

Sharp didn't speak for a moment, as if choosing his words carefully. "Shield sends a guy. Why go to you?"

"Lucky, I guess. The guy who paid me a visit is Clay Bowman. He was picking my brain on the case." She held up her hand as he readied to argue. "And I didn't give him anything on Vicky Gilbert. This is your active investigation, and I'm not that green."

Sharp looked dubious. "Did he offer up any help?"

"He did. I refused it."

"Why'd you say no?"

"Nothing's free." She shielded her eyes against the setting sun as she stared over the billowing yellow crime scene tape toward the technicians photographing the body next to a dumpster. "This killer, the Shark, is apparently a ghost. Blew into New Orleans, killed four girls, and was gone within a couple of weeks."

"They call him the Shark? As in a high-stakes card player?" Sharp confirmed.

"Yep."

"What the hell is he doing here?" Sharp asked. "We aren't exactly a hotbed of gambling."

"Private games aren't just in Las Vegas and Atlantic City," Riley said.

"What aren't you telling me?"

Her chest tightened. "I'm from New Orleans. When I was a teen-ager, it wasn't good in my home. I ran away."

Silent at first, he stared at her. "What are you saying?"

"Bowman said we'd see more bodies in the next few weeks if we don't catch this guy," she said. Bowman's words weighed heavily on her shoulders. She had been glib with him, but to think she was the reason that young girl had died made her sick.

"Keep talking."

It was confession time, so better to spit it all out. "I have a gap of several missing days while I was in New Orleans. When I woke up I was in Virginia, and shoved in my back pocket was a set of cards like the one we found on Vicky. My hand was a royal flush and nothing was written on them."

Sharp sighed. "Why didn't you tell me this before?"

"I didn't want to be associated with the victim. I'm days away from finalizing Hanna's adoption."

"Where are the cards?"

"At my house."

"I want them."

"Right. Of course." She looked at him. "If I could recall any detail I thought would really help, I'd have told you sooner."

"Get me the cards by tomorrow morning."

"Please, don't pull me off the case."

A muscle pulsed in Sharp's jaw. Without giving her an answer, he nodded toward the yellow tape. "According to this victim's driver's license, his name is Kevin Lewis."

"Kevin?"

"He has a couple of hundred dollars shoved in his wallet and a diamond ring on his hand."

"So not a robbery."

Sharp pulled his sunglasses off and bit on the end of an earpiece that looked half-eaten with worry. "If it were, the killer was after something entirely different. The ring and cash might have been small change in comparison."

"Can I have a look?" She half expected him to say no.

"Suit yourself."

Riley accepted latex gloves from Sharp, and tugging them on, ducked under the tape to move closer as he trailed behind her. Martin, the forensic investigator, was sketching out the scene on a large white pad of paper. "Martin, what do you have?"

Martin labeled something on his sketch before he looked up. "Kevin Lewis. Fifty-one years old and from Las Vegas. I count at least a half-dozen bullet wounds."

She knelt by the body. Lifting his hand, she noted it was just stiffening with rigor mortis. The nails were buffed, but the tips on his right hand were stained with nicotine. The diamond in the ring was at least a carat. "He's not been dead all that long."

"Less than six hours."

His face was ghost white under three or four days' worth of beard. Streaks of silver hair feathered around his temples. Hints of an expensive aftershave still lingered on his clothes. An old scar etched his left cheek. A gold earring winked from his left earlobe.

His black pants were tailored and made to fit the guy's toned frame. The belt with a stylish silver buckle looked expensive, as did the white shirt now stained with multiple blooms of blood in the center of his chest. She could imagine him sitting at a poker table, a cigar or cigarette hanging from his mouth as he fanned his cards.

"Martin, can I move the victim?" Riley asked.

"He's clear, have at it."

She rolled him on his side and noted the bullets didn't exit his back. Likely a .22 caliber using hollow-point bullets. Nasty bullets create maximum damage.

Pulling up his shirt from his waistband, she studied the skin on his back. Clean. She rolled him back and looked at his belly. Clean. She lifted his pants leg. His ankle and foot were blue, like they were bruised.

"He wasn't killed here."

She ran her hands through his hair and found no blood or signs of trauma. Garden-variety shooting. This kind of thing happened to gamblers when they ended up on the wrong side of a bet they couldn't pay back.

Agent Sharp watched as she began checking his pockets. But other than a half-chewed pack of gum and a rubber band, his back pockets were clean.

"You have his wallet, you said?"

Sharp handed the now-bagged wallet to her. "Nothing remarkable."

She accepted the bag and held it up. The wallet was fine leather, likely Italian. This guy knew how to dress the part of success. "I can run a background check."

"Isn't this your day off?"

"I want this case solved."

"Thanks, but I got it from here. Your job is to get me those cards."

"Right."

"By the way, I received a call from Carter's attorney today. He has a bail hearing tomorrow, and there's a good chance he'll post it."

"What about Jo-Jo, the girl Jax beat up? She's still in bad shape. She can't defend herself if he decides to make trouble."

"She's in a lockdown ward at the hospital with a no-visitor mandate."

"But no armed guard."

"No."

"Damn it."

Riley now reached in the victim's front left pocket and pulled out a rabbit's foot. "Gamblers do like their good-luck charms."

"Even the best ones have their quirks."

Martin handed Riley an evidence bag. "Put it in there and I'll mark it."

Riley dropped the rabbit's foot in the bag and handed it over. She searched the front right pocket and found a gold money clip holding several twenty-dollar bills and a pack of matches that read *Casino*.

"These pants set him back at least a grand." She ran a gloved finger along the stitching. "This is some nice work. Hand tailored."

"You're the first trooper I met who knows hand tailoring," Sharp said.

"I do have my talents."

"Don't tell me you grew up with a silver spoon?"

"I had a stepfather who liked to dress well."

"Today is the first time you've mentioned family."

"We aren't family." She'd seen Lewis's kind in New Orleans coming in and out of the casinos. "Kevin here thought of himself as a high roller."

"Lady Luck didn't agree."

"We find a victim with playing cards on her body and a guy who looks like a high-stakes gambler. Not a coincidence," she said.

"Shield's theory of the Shark fits a little too well into this scenario," Sharp said.

"Yeah." Tension knotted her chest. She did not want Bowman or Shield to be right. She did not want to be connected to this case.

Sharp pulled a stick of gum from his pocket. "A down-on-his-luck gambler will do whatever it takes to get back on top. He has his lucky rabbit's foot and believes he can beat a high roller like the Shark, win big, and then what? Release the girl and scoop up the cash? Or just another creep playing with someone's life for his own ego?"

The theory struck too close to home for Riley. "Both are viable theories."

Sharp stared at the body, a faint look of disgust darkening his eyes. "If Bowman offers any more words of wisdom, be sure to share. I'm territorial, but I'll take whatever information I can get if it means no more dead girls in my jurisdiction."

"I'll keep looking for Darla."

"Bring me those cards in the morning."

CHAPTER TEN

Friday, September 16, 7:00 a.m.

If anyone ever made it past the first checkpoint of Shield Security or the second guard station positioned at the end of the long access road, they'd find a three-story nondescript building. Its rectangular shape was nothing remarkable and could have been the headquarters of Any Company USA. Glass reflective windows allowed no one to see inside and there were no shrubs or trees around the building, negating possible hiding places. An entrance in the front required the swipe of a security card.

Bowman entered the offices, showing his identification to the guard at the front desk and riding the sleek elevators to the top floor. He made his way to his office, glancing toward the unpacked boxes and pictures yet to be hung.

He'd officially been here five days, signed a two-year contract—but he still hesitated to make any permanent claim on the office space. In the bureau, he'd moved around a lot, assigned to a new field office every couple of years. And for most of that time, he was working a case, sometimes weeks at a time while living out of a suitcase.

His wife, Karen, had been the anchor in his life. She took it all in stride. An artist, she always found a way to make their newest apartment a home. Since her death, he'd not been able to attach permanence to any subsequent place in which he stayed.

As he walked into his office and switched on the light, he glanced at the box of photos to his left. He'd moved the box from office to office over the last six years but never unpacked it.

Now, for some unknown reason, he reached into the box and pulled out two pictures. One was of Karen taken on the beach at sunset right after they met. The other was of him and his roommates at the Virginia Military Institute nearly two decades ago. The image captured the four young graduates standing in front of Jackson Arch. Their arms were linked and all were grinning, knowing they had bright futures. Bowman was headed to the FBI training facility in Quantico. The tall, thin guy on the right, Jacob Taggart, was a commissioned army officer. The guy on his immediate left, a sturdy Texan named Rafe Murdock, was slated to take his marine commission. And the last guy, Gavin Loch, chose medical school.

He dusted each frame off with his fingers and set them on the credenza behind his desk. Hardly staking a claim on this place, but it was a start.

On the pile of papers in an in-box that grew by the hour was a memo detailing a trip to Houston where he was set to review security for an oil company. Another memo mentioned a trip to Kansas City. More security and a threat assessment. The billable hours on both cases would ultimately earn the company close to a quarter of a million dollars, yet Shield had pulled him off them to catch the Shark.

A knock on his door had him turning. Shield moved into the office, his gait slightly uneven as if his back bothered him. "I'll have someone in maintenance hang up those pictures."

"No need. I'll get around to it."

"I remember your last field office in Kansas City. Not a picture up on the wall."

"Never made sense. Why mark up a wall when I wasn't staying long?"

"Kansas City was a temporary assignment, but this time you aren't moving on. This is your last stop. I expect you to be running this show one day."

He'd committed to work for Shield for two years. To anchor himself beyond that would take serious soul searching.

"So how did it go with Tatum?" Shield asked.

"She knows more than she's saying, that's clear. When I mentioned the playing cards, I hit a nerve." He'd learned the best intelligence didn't always come from what people said, but what they didn't say. "The latest victim was identified. Vicky Gilbert. The girl hooked up with a guy named Jax Carter, and he sold her to one of the gamblers."

"Word arrived that another body was found near the Gilbert body. A male. His wallet identified him as Kevin Lewis."

Bowman tilted his head toward the older man and grinned. "You haven't lost a step."

"Pays to have friends. What do you think of Tatum?"

"She's sharp. Wants this case solved. She's driven, just like she was at Quantico."

Shield never showed surprise, making it hard to gauge his reactions. "So what do you suggest, Clay? The cops won't catch him."

"You sound sure."

"I'm one of the best and I've never caught him even after he sent me his trophy pictures."

"How do you know he sent them?"

"The Shark is a guy who loves high-stakes games. If he thinks he's getting too far ahead of me, what better way to keep the juices going than to send me the pictures."

"But the Shark is not perfect. Serial killers kill again when there are stressors in their life. Bad health. Money. Death in the family. Job loss. All are hard to deal with for a normal person, but for a guy like the Shark, it's the perfect trigger for murder."

"Logical, or it simply bothered him that Riley slipped through his fingers."

"Maybe."

"Whatever the Shark's reason, stay close to her. She's the key."

"I see a couple of memos on my desk from Houston."

"It can wait. All of them can wait. This case has stuck in my craw for twelve years and now I have a chance to nail him. Solve this case and I'll give you the whole damn company tomorrow."

***

Riley delivered the cards to Sharp, oddly grateful to turn them over to someone else.

"This is all you have?" he asked.

"Just the cards. I can't tell you how I got them or who gave them to me. I just know they were in my pocket when I got to Richmond."

"And you have no memories?"

"Sometimes the scent of cigars makes me feel tense. Occasionally dreams. But there is nothing I can grab on to, and believe me, I've tried."

"I'll have these dusted."

"I did that eight years ago. They were wiped clean."

"So all we know right now is that your cards look like the ones in Gilbert's backpack."

"Yes."

"All right."

"What do you want me to do?"

"I'll call you if anything comes up."

***

Bowman went to the parole board offices after he left Shield headquarters. Fluorescent lights buzzed as he moved down the building's main hallway to the door at the end. He knocked.

A heavyset man with gray hair looked up from an outdated computer. "Yes."

"Ken Trice?"

"Yes."

"I'm Clay Bowman with Shield Security. My boss, Joshua Shield, called about Darla."

"Right." He clicked a couple of computer keys and read the screen. "A nasty lady, if I do say so myself. Why are you looking for her?"

"She and her boyfriend are believed to be selling girls."

"Is this about the girl strangled and dumped north of the city?"

"She's the one. I think Darla and Carter recruited the victim and then sold her to another guy."

"Nothing surprises me anymore."

"Any idea where I can find her?"

"She lists her mother's address as her residence." He rattled off an address south of the city. "You know the place?"

"I can find it."

Bowman left his card with the man and made his way back to his SUV. He dialed Riley's number. She picked up on the second ring.

"Bowman, why are you calling me?"

The snap of annoyance in her voice was about what he expected. "How would you like to go on a little field trip with me?"

"What kind of field trip?" she said carefully.

"I have the address of Darla Johnson's mother. Want to tag along?"

She didn't hesitate. "Yes."

"Where are you?"

"Leaving the state police offices now."

"Stay there and I'll pick you up in twenty minutes."

"You can just give me her address."

Seconds ticked as she waited for his response. Finally she yielded. "Fine. I'll wait."

Twenty minutes later Bowman found Riley and Cooper in her SUV. He parked and as he approached her vehicle, she unlocked the doors. He slid into the passenger seat. As he read off the address for her to plug into the GPS, she tossed him a curious look.

Checking her rearview mirror at an alert Cooper, she pulled into traffic and headed south. "Why are you including me?"

"Because we are a team."

"We are not a team."

"Yes, we are. You just haven't accepted it yet."

"Right."

He studied her profile. "You seem tense."

"I'm always tense."

"More so than usual."

"A lot on my mind."

"Care to share?"

She looked over at him and he thought for a moment she'd tell him, but she only shrugged. "Nothing important."

Fifteen minutes later they found themselves in front of a small brick rancher. The front lawn could have used a mowing a month ago, but the house itself looked fairly well kept. Riley left the AC running and stepped out, waiting for Bowman to join her. Locking the door, she laid her hand on her gun as they moved to the front door decorated with a welcome wreath. Glancing in the bushes on his left and right, Bowman rang the bell and stepped aside. Inside, a television buzzed.

The front door jerked opened to a short, stout woman who wore jeans and a green collared shirt from one of the local grocery store chains. Her narrowing gaze darted between the two of them as she folded her arms. It was obvious she had been through this before. "Darla ain't here. I haven't seen her in a couple of weeks."

"Why do you think we're looking for Darla?" Bowman asked.

Her nose wrinkled. "You two are cops. Why else would you be here?"

"Your name is Betsy Smith and you're Darla Johnson's mother?" he asked.

"That's right. But I ain't seen her."

"Has she called, texted, or e-mailed?"

"Nothing from her. But she owes me money, so I'm not surprised. She won't surface until she or that damn Jax needs a meal or a place to crash."

"The last time you saw Darla, was anyone with her?" Riley asked.

"Other than Jax? Yeah, there was another girl with them. A young girl, a pretty little thing."

Riley scrolled through her phone and found the picture of Vicky. "This her?"

The heavy scent of cigarettes radiated from Ms. Smith as she leaned forward. "That's her."

"What can you tell me about her?" Bowman said.

"She never got out of the car. Darla said she was shy. I didn't buy that, but I wasn't in the mood for an argument. Darla has a temper."

"You get a name?" Bowman asked.

"I didn't care enough to ask. I was more anxious to see Darla and Jax get off my property. I didn't need trouble."

"When was this?" Bowman asked.

"About two weeks ago."

"How'd the girl appear to you?" Riley asked.

"Fine, I guess." She rubbed her hand along her arm. "I could see the kid didn't have a clue about those two. I wanted to tell her to get as far away from Darla and Jax as she could, but Darla never let me get close. That girl all right?"

"No, ma'am, she's dead," Riley said.

The lines on her face deepened. "I'm sorry to hear it. Darla do it?"

"Why do you say that?" Bowman asked.

She laughed. "She can be jealous. My girl don't like sharing nothing with nobody. I could see Jax had eyes for that pretty girl. Kept touching her and kissing her when Darla wasn't looking."

"Did Darla leave any of her possessions here?" he asked.

"No. Moved them all to Jax's trailer, but I couldn't tell you where that's parked these days."

Riley pulled a card from her pocket. "If you hear from her, will you give me a call?"

"Sure. I'll call, if you promise to lock Darla away. She's my own flesh and blood, but she's mean as a snake."

"Thanks."

Bowman followed Riley to the car. He could see she was frustrated. "We'll find her."

"She's slithered under a rock and she might not ever come out."

"We'll find her and the man who bought Vicky from her."

She paused at the car and her shoulders slumped a fraction. "You sound so sure."

"I am." A part of him wanted to pull her into his arms and tell her he'd keep her safe. But she didn't really believe he was here to stay yet. But she would.

***

Darla's phone rang as she sat in a borrowed blue Chevy truck, staring up at the two women standing outside the diner. She knew them both. Sandy and Cassie. They worked for Tony.

"Yo," she said into the phone. "What do you need?"

"I'm looking for a girl." The deep voice sounded raspy.

The man's voice was new to her but that didn't mean much. She'd put up new ads on the Internet last week before Vicky got herself killed and Jax messed up Jo-Jo. "What kind?"

"Young. Dark hair."

"When do you need her?" She didn't have any girls now, but there was always a girl to be found on the street. She could be nice when it suited, and if the girl needed drugs or a meal, then convincing her to work could be easy.

"Tomorrow. I'm having an overnight party."

"Overnight will cost you a grand."

"That's a lot."

"If you can't afford it, stop wasting my time."

"All right, a grand. But she's mine for the night. And she has to have dark hair and wear a yellow dress."

She never questioned a john's special request. Her job was to find him what he wanted. "Sure. No problem."

They agreed to meet and she hung up.

As if Jax were sitting beside Darla, caution whispered in her ear. That damn Vicky had gotten herself killed and the cops were swarming around. Selling another girl now was asking for trouble. But a grand was enough money to get her and Jax out of the state as soon as he made bail and they took care of that bitch cop and Jo-Jo.

She sniffed and took another drag before tossing her cigarette out the window. She glanced in the mirror and practiced her smile. The girl by the diner, Cassie, was a blonde, but that was easily fixed. She also belonged to Tony, but he would cut a deal with her if the money was right.

***

Shuffle of poker chips. Cigar smoke. Plush velvet. She lay on the soft couch, her brain addled with drugs. She had discovered too late the water she drank was laced with something. Who had drugged her? And why?

As much as she struggled to study the faces of the people around her, their features faded into a haze of blurred beige ovals.

The hum of male conversation pulled her attention toward her left. They were fuzzy, distant shapes. There were two, maybe three men. She couldn't tell. Couldn't see well enough to figure anything out.

"She's waking up."

"Give her more," one of the men said. "We don't need trouble."

"Where am I?" she whispered. She was rolled onto her back and her sleeve shoved up past her elbow. Eyes narrowing, she stared into the featureless face looming over her.

Dark eyes. Pale skin. She was looking at the face of a ghost.

"Help me," she whispered.

"This is the best help for you," the ghost said. "It'll keep you out of trouble and maybe, if you're really lucky, alive." A needle pricked her arm, its sharp point plunging below the surface. Only seconds passed before her mind fogged and her thoughts became disjointed. Her vision went black.

Riley sat up in bed, swallowing a scream. Shoving her hand through her dark hair, she gulped in air and stared at the shadows dancing across her small bedroom. Gripping the sheets, she clung to the familiar. The chair covered in a dark-blue pattern, the quilt neatly folded and draped over it. A few pieces of jewelry from her grandmother lined along her dresser.

She glanced at her trembling hands. For an instant she felt helpless. Lost. It took a few seconds before the haze of sleep passed and her thoughts sharpened.

A knock on her door had her sitting a little straighter. "Riley?" Hanna said.

She cleared her throat. "Yes?"

"You all right?"

"I'm fine." She looked at the time displayed on her phone. It was minutes after two in the morning.

Hanna cracked the door, letting light from the hallway spill into the room. "I heard you cry out."

Running her hand through her hair, she mustered a half smile. "I had a dream. You know how I'm always chasing bad guys, and sometimes I relive it during the night. Nothing to be worried about."

The light behind Hanna cast a warm glow and helped settle her. "You've never done that before."

"There's always a first time." Realizing her explanation wasn't dispelling Hanna's worry, she added, "I get worked up when I'm in a foot pursuit. And in my dreams I was chasing three guys."

"Three? Really?"

"It was a dream, but they were armed. They were ready to shoot. I had to choose which one to go after first."

"Okay. That's too much of a riddle for me at two a.m. See you in the morning."

The door closed but Riley didn't lie back on her pillow. Instead she waited, listening for Hanna's footsteps and the light under her door to click off.

Years had passed since she'd had that dream. Vicky's death and Bowman's reappearance had jostled loose too many skeletons from the shadows. She'd dearly love to shove them all out of sight but knew it wouldn't happen tonight.

She tossed off her blankets and crossed to a small desk where she kept her laptop. She opened it. There'd been no time to research Bowman today. Too much happening.

In the search engine she typed: Clay Bowman. Shield Security. FBI. Hostage Rescue Team.

A second passed before several listings on Shield Security materialized, but nothing on Bowman. That didn't surprise her.

When he had been a part of the training team at Quantico, he was the quietest of all her instructors. He would stand, arms crossed, watching and speaking only when someone needed assistance. She learned through the class grapevine that his wife had died, and that softened her heart toward him and made her want to help. She had been naive enough to think she could make an immediate difference in his life. But his wounds ran bone deep and she'd learned the hard way that they were far from healed.

When she'd gone to his motel room, she knew she was throwing common sense to the wind but sensed he was as drawn to her as she was to him. So when she knocked and he opened the door, she stood her ground as he glared down at her. It had taken all her courage to kiss him. Bowman said nothing, but she felt his response. For a split second she thought he'd send her packing, when suddenly he pulled her into the room and kissed her back.

His touch unleashed a passion that made her knees weak. When he turned her to face the bureau mirror, she'd never wanted anyone more in her life.

As his calloused hands slid up under her shirt and cupped her breasts, he teased her nipple through the sheer fabric of her bra. Teeth nipped at the skin on the side of her neck. When she reached for the snap on her pants, she felt the energy and urgency in his touch as he slid his hands over her hips. He pushed her pants and panties down and slowly entered her. Their gazes locked in the mirror.

"Are you okay?" he whispered.

"Yes."

He thrust inside her with an intensity that shattered the walls she'd built around herself.

Only later when she relived the moment, trying to understand why he'd asked her to leave, did she realize he'd never spoken her name. She shook off the memory.

She checked the time. Several more hours to go before the alarm went off at seven and she would have to drag Hanna out of bed for her track practice. Wide-awake and with no hope of getting back to sleep, she rose, shrugged off her nightgown, and tugged on her gym clothes. Cooper glanced up from his crate, but when she didn't signal they have to work, he curled back up to sleep. She carried her running shoes and laptop into the kitchen and fired up the coffeemaker.

While toasting a frozen bagel, Riley thought about last night's meal she'd shared with Bowman. She hated leaving good food on the table. No matter how many years had passed, she never forgot the raw gnawing of hunger dished out to her by the streets. Since those days, she never wasted food. God, the steak on her plate had been so tender she could have cut it with a blunt knife. And she'd left most of it. Damn.

Finishing the last of the bagel, she moved to her computer. She typed: *serial killer*, *New Orleans*, and *strangled girls*. Everything and nothing popped up, so she added the date from twelve years ago. A few references hit that briefly mentioned four girls, all minors, found dead. Strangled. Because the girls were underage, their names were never released. The bodies were all displayed in places where they could be easily found. There were no follow-up stories.

All victims matched a similar description. Dark hair, dark eyes, between sixteen and seventeen, and all runaways. Just like her.

None of the articles mentioned playing cards discovered at any of the crime scenes. That made sense. Always a smart idea for cops to keep a few facts undisclosed that only the killer knew.

Absently, her fingertips now went to her neck. There'd been no sign of bruising on her neck. The needle marks had healed on her arm. Now, she almost doubted it had happened. But the playing cards didn't lie. They were the evidence that she'd been taken.

She opened the bogus social media page she'd created to see if Darla had reached out. Four more of her friend requests had been accepted but nothing from Darla.

The alarm on her phone sounded, startling her back to the present. She went into Hanna's room. "Rise and shine. It's time to get up."

"It's Saturday."

"You said you wanted up early for the run practice."

Hanna groaned and turned on her side. "Five more minutes."

"It doesn't work that way. Five more minutes always leads to five more, and besides, you never really fall back to sleep. It just prolongs the inevitable."

Hanna pulled the blanket over her head. "Stop making sense."

"I'll make you a coffee. Want a bagel?"

"With extra cream cheese."

Hanna's pouty voice made Riley smile. She sounded like a regular teenager, which was a good thing. "Coming up."

Fifteen minutes later, Hanna emerged from her shower. She was dressed and her hair was pulled back. She sat at the table and took several sips of the hot coffee. "So how many more days do you have off?"

"Three."

She bit into the bagel. "Are you actually taking time off?"

"Sorta."

"Meaning no." She took another bite and chewed. "I read about that strangled girl. Did you see her?"

Riley rinsed out her cup and put it in the strainer by the sink. "I did."

"Was it awful?"

"It was. In a nutshell, don't talk to strangers."

"You say that all the time."

"I mean it. Is Mrs. Taylor picking you up today?"

"No. Julia is skipping practice."

"So you're driving yourself? Do you have enough gas in your car?"

She took another mouthful of bagel. "Put ten dollars' worth in yesterday."

"Chew and then speak."

Hanna rolled her eyes, chewed, and made a show of swallowing.

"I'll see you this afternoon."

Hanna saluted. "Roger that."

Riley gave Hanna a quick hug as she passed. She was a step from her room when her phone chimed the arrival of a text. She glanced at it. Clay Bowman. "Damn it."

"What?" Hanna called.

"It's a guy who is proving to be a big pain in my ass."

CHAPTER ELEVEN

Saturday, September 17, 9:00 a.m.

Bowman arrived in front of the medical examiner's office first thing in the morning. Shield had called in favors and gotten him this weekend interview with the pathologist who'd performed Vicky Gilbert's autopsy.

Riley pulled up in her SUV. Out of the vehicle, her jacket flapped open as her heeled boots landed with hard, determined strides across the parking lot. Annoyance sharpened her dark eyes as her gaze speared him. "Mr. Bowman."

"Riley."

They each showed their IDs to the guard and moved toward the elevators. Riley kept pace, double-timing it to match his long strides across the lobby. When the elevator doors closed behind them, Bowman hit the "Stop" button, freezing the car in place. Her eyes bored into him, oblivious to the limited personal space in the elevator.

"We're on the same side, Riley. I need your help."

"Right."

"I'm here to help."

"Or to impede?"

"Careful," he warned. He released the button and the elevator descended, the doors opening to the cool antiseptic air of the medical examiner's offices and Joshua Shield.

Shield was dressed in his trademark dark suit with his shock of white hair combed off his angled face. He strode straight to them, his attention riveted on Riley. Dark eyes collected and inventoried details quickly. "Trooper Tatum. I'm Joshua Shield."

"I recognize you from your press pictures."

Bowman noticed that most people were intimidated by Shield. They dropped gazes, shuffled feet, or fidgeted in some way. Not Riley. She glared at him as if he were a rookie intern late for his first briefing.

Shield extended his hand to her. "Nice to finally meet you," he said. "Mr. Bowman speaks well of you."

Clasping hard, she held his gaze.

"Solving this case is a team effort," Shield said.

Smiling, she shook her head. "We'll see."

Bowman gave her props for not pulling punches.

"Consider the advantages of my expertise," Shield said. "My company resources helped you in the past."

"You were an uninvited guest that I could have managed without."

He grinned as if enjoying the sparring.

Before he could respond, Dr. Kincaid appeared. She wore a lab coat and glasses that covered slightly bloodshot eyes.

"Dr. Kincaid," Bowman said. "We appreciate you meeting us. Sorry to get you out of bed so early on a Saturday morning."

"Mr. Bowman, Mr. Shield, you gentlemen have friends in powerful places." Calm and unruffled, she extended her hand to both.

Shield shook her hand. "We help each other out when we can."

Dr. Kincaid glanced at Riley. "I'm assuming Agent Sharp called you."

"No, it was Mr. Bowman. But I contacted Agent Sharp."

"Good," Dr. Kincaid said. "Follow me." She led them down the long hallway and pushed through a set of double doors. "I understand you also want to see Vicky Gilbert's body."

"Correct," Shield said.

"Your timing is fortuitous. The funeral home is picking up her remains in a couple of hours. Her mother opted for cremation."

"And you've done a complete exam?" Shield asked.

"I have. I've collected enough samples so that we can run any kind of test conceivable in the future if necessary. The Gilbert family is anxious to have a memorial service."

"Their daughter ran away from home over a month ago and they didn't call the police or try to find her," Riley said. "What's the big rush now?"

A slight shift in Riley's tone could have made her sound bitter. But she kept her voice monotone, effectively hiding any potential anger or resentment.

Bowman reached in his pocket and removed a slip of paper. "Dr. Kincaid, I'd like you to test for this sedative."

"Propofol? That's a very powerful narcotic and I don't see it often."

"If we're dealing with the man we suspect is the killer, this is likely the drug he used on his first four victims. This killer is a creature of habit. The sedative is one of his signatures."

Dr. Kincaid folded the note and tucked it in her lab coat pocket. "I'm already testing for Rohypnol thanks to Trooper Tatum's suggestion."

"You suggested it?" Bowman asked.

Riley met his gaze. "It made sense to test for drugs, including this particular one, which is common with sex offenders."

Dr. Kincaid crossed to a bank of square refrigerator cubbies and opened the second one from the left. She pulled a long tray containing a sheet-draped body.

Riley moved toward the body, traces of sadness tugging at her cool facade.

Dr. Kincaid pulled back the sheet and revealed the pale, expressionless face of Vicky Gilbert.

Bowman's anger sparked as he remembered the bodies he'd seen in New Orleans twelve years ago.

"The victim was eighteen," Riley said. "By two days."

"I can tell you from the autopsy that she was in good general health at the time of her death," Dr. Kincaid added.

"Most of the Shark's victims experienced some form of abuse before they ran away," Bowman said. "Young girls like Vicky Gilbert are often the most vulnerable."

Riley grew so still she wasn't sure if she was breathing as Dr. Kincaid reviewed the autopsy summary.

"I've read about the New Orleans cases," Riley said, her voice professional. "Many of the girls were missing for days if not weeks before their bodies were found. Mr. Bowman, you might know better than most what he does with them in the interim."

Bowman pulled back the sheet a little farther, revealing the victim's neck and the very top portion of the stitched Y incision on her chest. He was including her as much as possible because he wanted her to trust him. "We don't know. But holding the victims for three days up to two weeks was consistent from case to case."

Shield folded his arms, his gaze not wavering from the body.

"Was there any sign of sexual abuse in past victims?" Riley asked.

"In several cases it was clear the victims had engaged in intercourse, but there was no bruising. We ran DNA on all the samples and each originated from different persons."

Riley tapped an index finger against the tray. "That profile fits with this victim, correct, Doctor?"

"That's right," Dr. Kincaid said.

"Vicky Gilbert was only missing a couple of days. Her friend Rebecca Wayne was in contact with her via phone two days before her body was found."

"It appears the Shark is not as patient as he used to be." Bowman stared at the deep bruising around the victim's pale neck. How close had Riley come to dying? She wouldn't like him protecting her. But until this psychopath was caught, Bowman was keeping close tabs on her.

"Did you come across the body of a white male in his early fifties? His name would've been Kevin Lewis," Bowman said.

Dr. Kincaid glanced at Riley. "He came in yesterday."

Riley stared at Bowman. "We haven't released his name. How would you know about this?"

"I have it on good information that Mr. Lewis bought Vicky from Jax. I assumed the Shark killed him."

"Really? Who told you about Lewis?" Riley challenged.

"Jax Carter."

"He told you?"

"He did."

Riley muttered an oath. "We found Kevin Lewis yesterday afternoon."

"Where?" Shield asked.

"About a mile from where we found Vicky Gilbert."

"How did he die?" Shield asked.

"He was shot," Riley said. "Agent Sharp is getting a warrant to search his hotel room. It'll be ready later this morning."

"I'd like to be present when you do his autopsy," Bowman said.

The doctor covered Vicky Gilbert's body and pushed it into the cold cubicle. "That's up to Agent Sharp."

"Were there any men found around the time of the New Orleans victims?" Riley asked.

"Never," Shield said. "We only found the girls. But several gamblers vanished in the Vegas area the summer after the New Orleans cases."

"These gamblers ran with a rough crowd, but there is no loyalty. It's understandable that when one disappears, it isn't always noticed immediately," Bowman said.

"Nothing guarantees silence like death," Riley said.

"Please test Mr. Lewis's DNA for any trace evidence of Vicky Gilbert," Shield said. "I'd bet money he's the one who strangled her."

Dr. Kincaid moved three spaces over and opened another drawer. She pulled out the tray and drew back the sheet. They stared at the pale angled face of a man with neatly cropped hair. "Agent Sharp already ordered DNA on Mr. Lewis to be cross matched with Gilbert."

"How did he know to look?" Shield asked.

"Lewis was a card player dumped near a dead girl with cards in her pocket," Riley said. "He doesn't believe in coincidence."

Shield's nod to Bowman conveyed his approval.

"I haven't autopsied him yet," Dr. Kincaid said. "I was planning to do that when Agent Sharp arrives shortly."

Riley pulled out her phone. "I'll call him to give a heads-up that Bowman will be attending."

Shield checked his watch. "I'm headed back to the office. Clay, call me if you need anything."

"Will do."

Shield turned to Riley, extending his hand. "Been a pleasure."

She grasped his hand, studying his face as if she were trying to peer behind his neutral expression. "Yes, sir."

"If it'll help," Shield said, "I can offer you and Agent Sharp a briefing of my case notes on the Shark."

"I'll mention it to Agent Sharp."

"I'm at your disposal."

He released her hand and pushed through the swinging doors.

"I need to call Agent Sharp," Riley said before turning and moving through the doors.

In the hallway, Bowman watched Riley raise the cell to her ear and pinch the bridge of her nose as she spoke quietly. She shot him an annoyed glance, a sign that Sharp was telling her to cooperate. Shield was already making calls and reeling in favors as he drove north.

Afterward, she looked at him with resignation. Bowman hadn't expected to be greeted with open arms, but she didn't attempt friendly.

"The conversation didn't go well?" he asked.

"Agent Sharp reminded me I can only be a part of this investigation if I play by his rules. And the rules are now that I have to make nice with you."

"Buy you a cup of coffee?" he asked. "Just don't throw it on me."

"Melanie's Diner has the best."

"Lead the way."

A steady rise and fall of her chest tempered some of the tension in her face. "Right."

He followed her to the elevator.

"The place I'm thinking of is a few miles from here. It'll be quicker if I drive."

"Sure."

Outside, she led him to her SUV. When they sat in the front seat, the smell of rug cleaner and Armor All didn't mask the scent of Cooper.

"Where's Cooper?"

"At home. I'll get him midday. And if I'm running late, Hanna will let him out." She started the engine.

"He's one hell of a dog."

Mention of Cooper softened her tone a bit more. "He's the best."

"How often do you train with him?"

"We run through tracking skills at least weekly. We work out together daily."

This close he noticed the scent of her soap and saw the faint wisps of damp hair by her ear. His text this morning about the autopsy had caught her off guard.

"Your training showed on the mountain. You both are in top form."

"Thanks."

He clicked on his seat belt, wondering how she'd put a thousand miles between herself and New Orleans and rebooted her life after she escaped the Shark.

"What else can you tell me about the Shark?" she asked. "How did you and Shield first come across him?"

"We were both working in the New Orleans FBI office when Joshua read about two young girls who were strangled in a one-week period. Both runaways found with playing cards in their pockets."

"Dead runaways don't warrant FBI interventions." Her knuckles whitened as she gripped the wheel.

"He had a daughter once. She went missing when she was a young child. He was never the same after."

"And when did his interest in the New Orleans case become official?"

"We were called in when the third and fourth girls were found. Again, cards in the pocket."

Riley's jaw tightened a fraction. "I did a search on the case. The media picked up the story. It was sensational enough to get some airtime but faded quickly. Has he struck again?"

"No. He's been dark for twelve years."

"Until now."

Until you.

She pulled into the parking lot of an old diner that he'd never have considered as a place that made great coffee.

As if reading his thoughts she said, "Don't let the looks of the place fool you. It'll be the best coffee you've ever had. And if you aren't worried about your figure, go for one of the doughnuts. Homemade each morning."

"Cops and doughnuts. The cliché doesn't bother you?"

"Not even a little."

Bells jingled above as they entered the crowded diner. Booths lined the walls and bar stools circled a counter. Each seat was occupied. Riley waved to a hostess and moved to the takeout sign. She ordered two coffees and a doughnut for herself as she drew a slim wallet from her coat pocket. "Is that a yes or a no to the doughnut?"

"Pass."

"Your loss." She dropped five bucks on the counter and accepted the two cups. "Cream?"

"Black."

"Right." She dumped a sugar packet into her coffee and added a splash of cream. She sipped, closing her eyes and savoring the flavor before moving to a booth that faced out toward the door.

One taste of coffee and Bowman had to admit she'd been right. Damn good. He sat across from her in the booth, watching her bite into the doughnut and clearly enjoy it.

"Do you remember hearing anything about the New Orleans girls when you lived there?" Bowman asked.

She plucked two napkins from the dispenser. "No. I had my hands full with personal matters." She glanced at him, her gaze darkening with annoyance. "Why do you keep pressing a connection to me and this case?"

"The fact that you were a victim of a crime does not take away from your accomplishments."

A mirthless smile tugged at her lips. "In my line of work, I can't afford to be a victim. Not once. Not ever."

He dug between the lines and extracted the meaning lurking in the dark. "What happened to you?"

"Stirring the pot won't help you at all, and it'll hurt me a lot. I've got a career. A kid. An adoption pending."

"Why'd you leave New Orleans?"

"Things weren't good at home. My mother died and my stepfather wasn't *Father Knows Best*. I figured out pretty quickly it was better for me to get out of town."

"You were underage."

She was reaching for the doughnut again but stopped at his words. "Desperation knows no age."

"Your stepfather didn't try to bring you back home?"

"He wanted me back. Came looking for me. Almost found me in a coffee shop the day after I left, but I ducked out." She shook her head. "I still remember his face when I saw him crossing the street toward the shop. He was pissed."

"Not concerned?"

"No, definitely angry. I threw one hard punch that last night I was in his home. Connected with his face so hard I thought I broke my hand. His broken nose told me he was hurting."

"Why'd you hit him?"

She pushed aside the remains of her doughnut. "He wanted to play house."

He'd suspected as much but hearing her say it triggered cold, deadly contempt. "Did he?"

"No. But he tried and I clocked him."

"Good for you."

She flexed the fingers of her right hand, glancing at an index finger that was slightly bent. "I was sorry I didn't hit him with something harder."

"What about your biological father?"

"Left when I was two. Haven't seen him since. His parents are dead. No extended family except for my mother's great-aunt, but she was old when I was born. I think a lack of extended family was one of the things that appealed to William when he met my mother."

"Do you have any siblings?"

"No. William was never able to produce a male heir, which always bothered him. In fact, the more years that passed and he didn't get his son, the more he resented me." She shook her head as if brushing off a memory.

"So you picked Virginia just like that?"

"Nothing strategic. This is where the bus money ran out."

"And from there?"

"There's a man in the area named Duke Spence. He helps runaways. I was lucky. He and his volunteers were at the bus station the day I arrived. He gave me a place to stay and told me to get into school. I did and from there, I took it one step at a time."

"You mentioned a kid and an adoption. Is that Hanna?"

"She's seventeen. She was in a dark place when I found her several years ago. I'm offering her a hand like Duke did for me."

"You're taking it a step further with an adoption."

"It means a lot to her. To me."

In the last five years, he'd thought about Riley several times. He'd never pictured her with a child. A teenager explained the second car in the driveway. "She's lucky."

A hint of color warmed her cheeks. "The luck cuts both ways. She's a great kid." She reached for her coffee. "Better get back. Dr. Kincaid and Agent Sharp wait for no one."

"Understood."

Ten minutes later, she parked in front of the medical examiner's office. Hands on the steering wheel, she drew in a breath, studied the building, as if she were mulling over a question.

Out of the car, she didn't hurry inside but stood stiff, staring ahead, her dark glasses obscuring her eyes.

He opened his door and paused, knowing there were moments in the job when silence and patience were critical. "My sole motive is to catch this guy, Riley. I don't want the Shark to hurt anyone else. Anyone like you or Hanna. You're a cop. You know how important witnesses are to an investigation."

"If I had any information, I'd share it."

Did that mean she was talking? "You can trust me."

She didn't speak for a long moment as she absently tightened her grip on her keys. "People get burned in police investigations all the time. We don't always mean for it to happen, but it does."

Traffic buzzed past on the busy street, but he sensed she didn't notice any of it as she glanced up at the building.

"Talk to me, Riley. None of us wants to see another girl like Vicky get killed."

She flinched as if he'd struck a nerve. "I don't know you. There was a time I thought I did, but I was wrong."

"You knew me better than I did myself."

She moistened her lips while shaking her head. "You were very clear."

"I was wrong."

"It's not that easy."

"No, it's not."

For a long moment she was silent again. "After I ditched my stepfather, I ran to the back of an alley and hid for hours. I wandered for a couple of weeks, trying to stay away from trouble and the cops." She sighed. "The little money I had ran out, and I remember being so hungry I thought my stomach was going to eat itself. There were offers for me to make money, but I wasn't taking that road willingly."

He marveled at her strength. She took it for granted, but it was a rare thing in this world.

"I was drinking a bottled water one minute and the next my vision was blurring. The next thing I knew, I woke up in this fancy room." Her voice was a ragged whisper, as if speaking each word hurt.

"You were out the entire time?"

"I came around twice. First time there was someone there who seemed to notice I was awake and shoved a needle in my arm. I went right out. The second time I remember the sound of poker chips. A man cursing and then someone grabbing me by the hair and calling me 'one lucky bitch.' I passed out and woke up a thousand miles north in a bus station in Richmond, Virginia. There was a bus ticket crammed in my back pocket with the playing cards."

"What about the bus ride?"

"I stumbled off the bus and like I said, Duke was there. He noticed me and took care of me. If not for him, well, I don't know what would've happened."

"The Shark never made contact with you?"

"Not one time. Never a note or a call or anything. It was like the whole thing never happened. To keep my sanity, I convinced myself it was a bad dream. The dreams stopped. Life moved on. I thought it was over until I saw Vicky lying in the grass. When I saw the cards in her backpack, the twelve years vanished."

"What about the yellow dress? Were you wearing one?"

"No. I never saw a yellow dress, but there is so much I don't remember. All I know is I had cards in my back pocket."

"Where are they?"

"I told Agent Sharp about the cards and gave them to him. He's having the forensic lab look at them, but I can tell you like I told Sharp, they were wiped clean. If not for the cards, I have no proof it ever happened."

"What were the cards?"

"A royal flush. Diamonds."

He shoved his hands in his pockets and fingered the loose change against a small pocketknife. "Doesn't get much better than that."

"No, it doesn't." She studied him. "What's the point of the card game?"

"Shield's contact said this killer isn't motivated by money. He uses it to leverage the other players into finding human poker chips to stake the game."

"And all these dead girls died because of a turn of the cards."

"I think so."

"Damn."

"Is there anything you remember about the room where you were held?"

"Red and gold colors. Thinking back, I always sensed it must have been a hotel room. I assumed it was going to be about sexual exploitation, but I don't think that ever happened. Duke had me see a doctor after I arrived at the shelter. Her examination revealed no traces of assault."

"You never called the cops?"

A wry smile tipped the edge of her lips. "I wasn't eighteen when I stumbled into town. I was terrified they'd send me back to New Orleans and my stepfather, so no, I didn't call the cops."

"What did you do?"

"Whatever happened scared the shit out of me. I realized if I didn't do something, I would get swallowed up by the streets. Duke offered me a job at his restaurant and I took it. I worked hard and graduated high school. Won a partial scholarship to community college. I juggled school and work until I graduated. There was an opening at the police academy and I jumped at it."

"That's an odd choice."

"How so? The way I saw it, the job had good benefits and I'd be a part of a group that would teach me how to shoot and take care of myself."

"You've done well."

"I've worked my ass off." She shook her head. "I don't want to lose the life I've created."

"We'll catch him."

She ran a hand over her hair, tossing him a worried look. "Dr. Kincaid is waiting, and I think Kevin Lewis may shed some light."

***

Doubt spiked in Riley, jabbing adrenaline through her muscles. After all these years of silence, she thought she'd feel some kind of cathartic relief in telling her story. But she didn't feel relieved. She felt exposed. As she reminded herself a thousand times before, her past was nothing to be ashamed of, but dragging it back into the light in front of Bowman made it seem pathetic.

Without any more conversation, they made their way inside to the elevators. He stood beside her, his hands clasped in front of him. Though she stared ahead, she sensed his gaze on her.

The doors opened and she kept her sights on the medical examiner's entryway, hoping this time when the doctor cracked open the victim, she would keep her shit wrapped tighter. Bowman already had her pegged as a victim, a view she found untenable.

They both gowned up and moved into the exam room.

"How many of these have you seen, Riley?" Bowman asked.

A challenge hummed under the question like a rattler ready to strike. "Enough."

Dr. Kincaid threaded her gloved fingers together, working the latex into a tight fit. "Trooper Tatum is an old pro at this," she said. "You worry about yourself."

Old pro. Riley appreciated the doctor's good word. She hoped the doc was right.

Ken Matthews assisted Dr. Kincaid and pulled back the sheet to reveal Kevin Lewis's long, lean, and very pale body. Multiple bullet holes stitched along his left side. Her stomach knotted as the scent of decay wafted. Standing a little straighter, she refused to look away, even trying to look a little bored as if she'd seen a thousand of these cadavers.

"Agent Sharp called me," Dr. Kincaid said. "He's running late. Said to start without him." She began with an external exam, detailing the victim's tattoos: a queen of hearts on his left bicep with the name *Susie* worked into the design, a snake on his right calf, and in the center of his back, two hands pressed together and pointed upward in prayer.

"Sharp is expecting a search warrant for his hotel room," Riley said. "Hopefully, he'll find something."

"What about Lewis's financials?" Bowman asked.

"You'll have to ask Agent Sharp about that. Technically, I'm not a part of this investigation."

Bowman didn't seem concerned.

Dr. Kincaid noted dark bruises on the man's back and ribs. "I'd say he took a beating within a week prior of his death."

"Broken bones?" Riley asked as her stomach tightened.

"Three cracked ribs on the X-rays."

"It would hurt like hell, but it didn't kill him," Bowman said. "That kind of beating was sending a message to pay up."

"Maybe the Shark beat him up," Riley said. "Gave him an ultimatum."

"Or the beating was the reason for Lewis to risk it all with the Shark."

Dr. Kincaid concluded the external exam and reached for her scalpel. As she began to cut, Agent Sharp entered.

His frown deepening, he said, "It's always a party in here."

Bowman extended his hand. "Clay Bowman."

Sharp accepted the hand, gripping hard. "My commander told me about you. Said you'd be offering an assist. Worked a similar case with the FBI?"

"Twelve years ago," Bowman said.

Sharp accepted a set of latex gloves from Matthews along with a gown. The agent wasn't happy about it but was smart enough to know when his options were limited.

"Mr. Bowman was asking about the victim's financials," Riley said.

"Will have something by lunch. Dr. Kincaid, don't let me hold you up any longer."

Dr. Kincaid pressed the tip of the scalpel into the victim's pale skin, and as she sliced, Riley did not have to turn away or catch her breath this time.

By the time the autopsy was completed, they'd confirmed that six bullets had shredded the heart. His lungs had considerable damage from smoking, and his liver was enlarged from alcohol. He was fifty-one, but he had the organs of an old man.

After the autopsy Riley stepped outside and stripped off her gown. Rolling her head from side to side to relieve tension, she glanced at the clock. It was after eleven and she was starting to feel fatigue settling in. When she heard Sharp push open the doors behind her, she drew in a breath, knowing she'd find a second wind somehow.

"Tatum," Sharp said. "You don't look as green as the last time."

The doors opened to Bowman and she shelved whatever ribbing she had readied to fire back. "Thanks again, Agent Sharp."

"Appreciate the input." Sharp shifted his attention to Bowman. "Any insights? You think he might be your killer from New Orleans?"

He shook his head, his gaze on Riley. "No. It's all too easy and too convenient."

***

Riley arrived at the forensic department before lunch to find Martin hunched over the clothes that she recognized as Vicky Gilbert's. With tweezers in hand, the assistant plucked a hair fiber from the fabric and dropped it into a plastic bag.

"I don't suppose you found a smoking gun yet, Martin?" she asked.

"Not so far, but you never know what kind of gems are waiting for me." He reached for a legal pad and glanced at his scrawled handwriting. "Medical examiner sent over the semen sample from the Gilbert autopsy. It's been sent off for testing. And as you know, DNA testing is a beautiful thing, when it gets processed quickly. But with the backlog at the state lab, I doubt I'll see results until next month."

"There's a private security guy who is throwing his weight around, and something tells me you're going to get your results much sooner."

"Shield?"

"Yeah. How'd you know?"

"Sharp said to cooperate fully with Mr. Shield and his man, Bowman. You know anything about these guys?"

"Mr. Shield? The man has influence. His right-hand man, Bowman, is just as capable." She shifted, rolling her head from side to side. "Anything that caught your eye that I can run down?"

"Gilbert's clothes were older and well worn. But in the yellow dress I found a clear plastic thread used to attach a price tag to a garment. Someone must have missed it."

"But no tag?" Riley asked.

"No, but I searched the clothing label online. It's high-end. There can't be many shops in the area that carry it. It wouldn't hurt to check their sales records and see if any of them have security cameras or credit card receipts."

"I could start checking security footage. Maybe something will pop up."

"Hell of a coup if we caught this guy," Martin said.

"So they tell me. Thanks again."

Riley left Martin in the lab and returned to her car, where she did a search on her computer. She discovered only one shop in a fifty-mile radius that carried this designer. The store was in a high-end hotel in Richmond. She checked her watch. If she discovered information that linked to the investigation, she'd call Sharp.

Thirty minutes later, she parked in front of the tony hotel. It was an older grand hotel with a marble facade and a stone circular drive where valets parked expensive cars. She realized immediately that she was underdressed. She could tell she'd stick out as someone who didn't belong as she glanced in her mirror. The plain clothes made her look like a cop.

She reached for the pins in the back of her bun and pulled them out, combing her fingers through her long hair until it draped her shoulders. She unfastened the top button of her shirt and moistened her lips. She still didn't fit, but the look was a bit less formidable.

She walked into the hotel, shoulders back as if she had purpose. A glimpse around the lobby and she spotted the dress shop. Her booted heels clicked on the marble foyer. In the shop she was greeted by floral scents and gentle classical music. The clothes weren't packed in together as they were in the thrift stores but displayed like fine works of art.

The last time she'd been shopping with her mother, it had been in a shop like this. The clerks had rushed to help them and they'd been served tea. Her mother never once looked at a price tag or wondered if an item was on sale. She simply chose what she liked and pulled out her husband's credit card. Looking back, Riley saw that spending money was a way for her mother to get back at her stepfather. Judging by the light in the salesclerk's eyes as she rang up the final tab, her mother must have been furious that day.

Today, the clerk was a man and dressed in a sleek dark suit. When he raised his gaze to her, his smile froze for a split second but he recovered. Smart clerks understood that patrons with money came in all shapes and sizes; he'd play along until he figured out there was no commission in it for him.

"I'm Mr. Delany," he said. "May I help you?"

She smiled as her mother had once taught her. Polite, but not too friendly. "A friend of mine bought a beautiful dress here and I loved it. I was hoping you might have something similar."

"Most of our items are one of a kind. And very expensive."

She held her ground and reached for her phone. "Maybe if I showed you a picture."

"Of course."

"The dress is yellow. The skirt is covered in lace. Very delicate." She glanced at her fingers. Her nails were short, shorn to a practical length, but not the manicured look ideal for this environment.

"I know the dress. I sold the only three we had in stock."

"You did?"

"To one customer."

"Does this customer have a name?"

He studied her, catching a hardening edge in her tone. "Why does that matter?"

"You're out of stock. He has three. Maybe he'll sell me one."

Carefully, he shook his head. "Maybe you should speak to our head of security."

"Why? Does he manage your dress inventory?"

"No, he deals with the police."

"What makes you think I'm police?"

A brow arched as he pressed a button by the register. "I wasn't born yesterday."

"While we wait, can you tell me about the dress?"

"When security arrives."

Seconds later a tall, broad-shouldered man came into the shop. He looked as out of place as Riley did around the fine, frilly pieces.

The security guard took one look at her and asked, "Officer, what can I do for you?"

Riley smiled and pulled the picture of Kevin Lewis. She showed it to the guard. "Has this gentleman been in to buy a yellow dress?"

The guard shifted his gaze to the image. "We guard the privacy of our customers closely."

"This gentleman is on a slab at the morgue now. He's a suspect in a murder investigation."

"I haven't seen him." The guard nodded to Mr. Delany, who then leaned forward and peeked at the picture. "I remember him."

"He must have bought the dress here," Riley said. "This is the only store in a hundred miles that sells this label."

The guard nodded again to Mr. Delany.

Mr. Delany knitted his fingers. Buffed nails glistened in the soft light. "The gentleman was very specific about the color. He also said the dress had to be the best."

"How did he pay for it?"

"Cash. That's part of the reason he stuck in my mind. We see cash when someone wants to hide a purchase."

"Did he say who the dress was for?"

"Said it was for his daughter. She had a big party. He wasn't sure about her size, so he purchased all three. We didn't talk much. He saw the three dresses, asked me to box them up, and paid for his purchase. He was here ten minutes." He glanced at the guard. "I'd bet a month's commission the dress was not for his daughter."

"What day was this?"

"Last Friday. Right before closing."

"Was anyone with him?"

"He was alone."

"Has anyone else ordered a similar dress?"

"No."

CHAPTER TWELVE

Saturday, September 17, 3:15 p.m.

Bowman sat in his SUV across from the youth emergency shelter, waiting for Duke Spence to arrive. According to a call to the man's office, he would return to the shelter around three. He checked his watch. A red truck, beat up and dented, pulled into a parking space and an older man got out. He had shoulder-length gray hair tied at the nape of his neck and wore a dark T-shirt that tightened around strong, still-taut, tattooed arms. Faded jeans had seen better days, as had the scuffed brown boots.

After hearing Riley's story today, Bowman had dug into Duke's past. It might have been a coincidence that she'd landed in this man's backyard, but he never assumed. Serendipity was for fairy tales and fools.

Duke Spence had a checkered past, starting his career as a gambler in Vegas. He'd spent the better part of his twenties and thirties winning some and losing more until he'd ended up owing too much to the wrong guy. He had the piss beaten out of him on a side street in Las Vegas. Call it the fear of God, but that beating by all accounts had turned him around. Twenty years ago he married a cocktail waitress and they moved to Virginia. A year later they opened the shelter. He'd stayed clean since. He and his wife were model citizens, giving back to the community.

Bowman stepped out of his SUV. "Mr. Spence."

Duke paused and turned at the sound of the baritone voice. His head cocked. "Do I know you?"

Bowman pulled off his sunglasses. "Clay Bowman. I'm with Shield Security."

"You look like a fed."

"I was. Retired now."

Duke squared up and took a step toward Bowman. Not intimidated, he said, "What can I do for you, Mr. Bowman?"

"I have a few questions about Riley Tatum."

Duke's jaw tightened. "If you have questions about Riley, ask Riley."

"I've talked to Riley, and now I'm talking to you. This is about a recent murder she responded to."

"The dead girl."

"That's right."

"What does that have to do with me?"

"You were the first person who saw Riley when she arrived here twelve years ago."

"Barking up the wrong tree, pal. Talk to Riley." He turned and walked toward the restaurant.

Without raising his voice, Bowman said, "I believe someone tried to kill Riley in New Orleans and now he's back."

Duke paused, hesitating before he turned. "Riley would have told me if anything like that happened to her."

"There was a case I worked when I was with the bureau. We called him the Shark. Killed four girls."

"Riley never said anything about anyone trying to kill her. Ever."

"I believe she was drugged. Her memory was nearly wiped. But she knew something bad had happened."

"She tell you that?"

"The memories are stirring," he offered, much like a fisherman dangling bait in the water.

Duke, flexing his fingers, approached Bowman. "I don't know what the hell you're talking about. If Riley was having any bad memories and going to talk to anyone about it, she would be talking to me. I'm family. She's like a daughter to me."

The intensity behind Duke's tone suggested the truth. But Duke had been a gambler and the smart ones could bluff with the best. "Then help me protect her."

Duke shook his head. "I don't know you. You show up out of nowhere and ask me about a person I care about? I'm not telling you squat."

Was this righteous loyalty to Riley for real or for show? "This killer strangled four young girls who looked like Riley. He's killed a young girl in Virginia days ago."

"I saw it in the news, but they barely gave the story more than a thirty-second spot. How do you know Riley is connected?"

"The body was staged in Riley's patrol area. She was the officer on duty who responded to the call. The dead girl looks like the other victims, who all look like Riley."

"Her looks aren't that distinctive, Mr. Bowman. And she's dealt with all kinds of nastiness on the road. She's a cop."

"There were playing cards in this victim's back pocket just as there were in the New Orleans victims' pockets."

"Okay." Duke drew out the word. "Still not convinced of a connection. You're reaching."

Instead of answering, Bowman shifted tactics. He wasn't ready to share everything yet. "You used to gamble."

"Is that what this is about? I gambled, so now I'm connected to a killer who has a thing for sticking cards in dead girls' pockets?"

"You were a gambler for a couple of decades. That's a dark world and a lot of bad things happen in it."

"They do. And I saw a lot of it. Hell, there were things I did in those days that I'm not proud of and don't want my wife to ever find out about. But it's behind me. Has been for twenty years."

"You consider yourself an addict?"

"I sure do. That's why I stay the hell away from anything like gambling. No bet is a good bet for me."

"Ever hear of a gambler—a whale—that required a human stake to get in his game?"

Duke met Bowman's gaze as if he held the winning hand. "Hell, no. I lost a lot of money, but I never played for anybody's life."

Winners knew how to bluff with a losing hand. "A winner would've received a huge payout."

"Like I said, I haven't played in over twenty years. Not even a scratch card."

"Know anyone I could talk to that does know that world?"

"I got nothing. No contacts. No ties. Now, do me a favor and get the hell out of here."

Bowman's gaze didn't waver. "If I find out you're lying to me, I'll bury you."

***

It was six thirty when Riley pushed through the front door. She'd been on her feet for nearly fifteen hours. That was nowhere near a first in her career, but that didn't stop her from feeling dog-ass tired.

Before she could examine the package on the kitchen table, Cooper barked in his crate and she opened the door. He barked again, demanding she rub his ears. As she dropped her purse and hooked his leash, she saw the note.

*Hound walked one hour ago. I'm at triathlon practice.
(Swimming, yuck.) Home by seven or eight.*
Hanna
P.S. A package arrived for you.

With Cooper tugging on the line, she kicked off her work shoes and slid her feet into her running shoes. Cooper's walk took less than fifteen minutes before they were back inside, and her attention turned to the package Hanna had mentioned in her note.

The box was the size of a shoe box and wrapped in brown paper. There was no postage or any shipping company information. And Hanna's quick note did nothing to help with the mystery. She reached in her back pocket and texted Hanna, confirming her ETA.

Seconds later: Twenty minutes.

Who sent the package?

Don't know. Was sitting on front porch when I came by the house.

She stared at the box, frowning. She didn't like surprises. Thanks. See you in twenty.

She moved to the fridge and grabbed a diet soda. Popping the top, she turned back toward the box. She unclipped her gun and set it in a lockbox on top of the refrigerator.

Picking up the package, she shook it gently. It wasn't her birthday. Duke would have texted her if he were sending over something. And seeing as her dating skills had atrophied, it wasn't from any secret admirer. Or Bowman.

As Cooper settled on his dog bed by the couch, she sat and dug her fingernail under the tape securing the end. She ripped open the tape and pulled the paper apart, revealing a simple brown box. No label. Plain. She hesitated. It was likely nothing special. Still, she retrieved latex gloves and slipped them on her hands.

Lifting the lid, she moved slowly as if she half expected a snake to jump out. Instead, she found a DVD in a case nestled in a bed of white tissue.

She lifted the DVD and removed it from its case. The disk was neatly marked with a white label reading "Round Five."

Holding up the DVD, she checked the back for any identification, but there was none. She moved to a small TV. She didn't have cable, and on the rare times she watched television, she streamed it live through her computer. But inserting a strange DVD into her computer was not an option, so she popped it into the old DVD player and switched on the television. The image was gray and grainy, and for a ten-second count she saw nothing. She leaned forward, ready to switch off the television, when the image of a room came into focus. It was a nice room. Thick, lush carpet, cream drapes in the background that pooled at the bottom. The camera panned toward a chair. Slowly the cameraman moved around it.

She hit "Pause," her heart hammering so hard she thought it would crack her sternum. Memories, distant and forgotten, moved and stretched as if they had slumbered for too long a time.

Sitting straighter, she hit "Play" and watched as the image slid around the tall chair. From this angle, the cameraman shot from above, enough to see that someone sat in it. Long brown hair. Female. The photographer panned around the room, lowered the camera, and shot directly toward the girl, whose head slumped, dark hair draped over her face.

Riley turned up the volume and leaned closer. She glanced behind her at the clock and noted that Hanna would be home soon. Whatever was on this disc was not good. Hanna would never see it.

She leaned toward the image, studying every detail. The female's wrists were bound to the arms of the chair. Vicky too had marks on her wrists. This girl on the television wore a lovely yellow dress that hugged her narrow waist and skimmed her calves. Like Vicky. She wore a gold locket around her neck. Like Vicky.

She then remembered the car she'd spotted while she was running the other day. Was the driver Vicky's killer and had he sent this to her?

On the video, a man's hand entered the right side of the screen. His fingers were long, the nails buffed, but rough skin and deep veins suggested he was older. He traced a finger slowly along the girl's hair, and then reached for her chin. Gently, he lifted her head back until the hair fell away from her pale, angled face.

The girl in the chair wasn't Vicky.

"Shit! It's me."

Blood rushed from her head and her heart pounded. *Oh my God!* Tears burned her eyes, and she thought about the cards and the missing days from her life. Seconds ticked as she stared until the image ended and there was gray static.

A car pulled in the driveway as she tried to process what she saw. A car door slammed.

Wiping away a tear, Riley shut off the television. She ejected the disc and with trembling hands, replaced it in the case and shoved it in her purse. Moving fast, she scooped up the box, hurried to her room and laid it on the floor under her bed. She stripped off her gloves and threw them beside the box. Later, she'd dust the box for prints.

Standing, she smoothed her hands over her jeans, dug deep, and pulled up a smile that she hoped warmed her face. "Hanna!"

"How was your day in investigator land?" She dropped her gym bag to the floor and kicked off her shoes.

"I'm not an investigator."

"Bet that didn't stop you from asking questions."

"True." Riley moved into the kitchen and retrieved her cell out of her back pocket. Fingers poised over the keypad, she was grateful her hands had stopped trembling. "How about pizza? I can order it right now."

"That would be great. I ate at Duke's, but that was around four."

"No worries. I could use a few slices myself." Her brain on automatic, she called in the pizza, pepperoni with extra cheese. Not Riley's favorite, but Hanna loved it and it was easy enough for her to pick off the pepperoni and scrape off most of the cheese.

She reached in the fridge and handed Hanna a flavored water.

"You okay?" Hanna asked.

"Just a little tired. Wondering why you like this water. If you were going for chemicals, go all out and get the diet soda."

Hanna rolled her eyes. "It's more healthy because it has vitamins in it."

"As long as you like it." The flavored water was one of the few things she could do to spoil the kid, so she picked up a couple of cases whenever they were on sale.

"Catch any bad guys?" Hanna asked.

Riley laughed, doing her best not to look upset. "At least eight."

"Only eight? Ahh, don't feel too bad."

Her heart slowed, but her nerves were on edge. "Better luck tomorrow."

"When do you get back on patrol?"

"Tuesday."

Hanna held up her vitamin water. "Here's to catching bad guys."

Riley's poker-face grin hid her swirling thoughts, which shifted back to the image of her own seventeen-year-old face. Eyes barely open, her mouth pouty and slack-jawed, her long hair threaded through the hands of a stranger. The DVD was a link to the missing days of her life and a calling card from the Shark.

She nodded as Hanna prattled on about her day. They talked about the college applications over pizza. All normal. And yet the images burned in her mind. The past was not dead and buried as she had hoped.

It was past ten when she took Cooper on his final walk, crated him, and fell into bed. As much as she needed sleep, she couldn't erase the DVD images from her mind. Quietly, she got up and shoved the DVD into her computer. With earbuds jammed in her ears, she watched the images again.

The man shooting the video was also the one who'd held her face and tipped it up to the camera. He murmured something softly in the background, but it wasn't loud enough for her to understand, even after she cranked up the volume. In the background she detected the sound of a guitar playing softly. Behind her image, the cream-colored curtains opened onto a clear night sky, and if she wasn't mistaken, she could see the view from the big casino that overlooked New Orleans. By the fourth time through the images, she didn't flinch when the man took her face in his hands and tipped her head back. She knew he wouldn't do anything more to her. She knew the recording would run out and there'd be no video image of what had happened next.

By one in the morning, she shut off the computer. Four hours of sleep last night was manageable, but compound that with another short night and it would all soon catch up with her. She needed to stay sharp. Especially now that the Shark was coming for her.

She thought of taking this DVD to Agent Sharp, but it was one thing to give him five playing cards and another to hand over video evidence of a helpless Riley. God only knew how many investigators would gawk at it. But she couldn't just sit on this evidence.

Thoughts skittered to Bowman and Shield, who'd been linked to this case for as long as she had. All she knew about Shield Security was what Bowman had told her, and that wasn't saying much.

However, both men would do whatever it took to catch the Shark.

***

Bowman had also traced the dress found in Vicky Gilbert's backpack to the posh Richmond hotel. Calling in a few favors, he soon found himself standing in the security office viewing twenty-plus monitors of the marble lobby.

"What days of footage do you want?" the young man asked.

"Pull last week."

"You want the cameras in the lobby?"

"I'm interested in the cameras covering the dress shop."

"We had a cop in here today asking the same question. What's with the shop?"

He checked his own surprise. "Pull up the footage of the cop."

A tap of several keys and he was watching Riley entering the dress shop, her hair loose around her shoulders. She moved with a straight-backed posture that telegraphed purpose. She'd barely spoken to the counter clerk when a thick-necked guy wearing a security jacket entered the store. Her tight expression was directed toward the security guard and conveyed annoyance. No doubt the guard had been dispatched to keep her on a short leash.

Bowman watched the security guard move to the front desk, where he stood staring at her ass as she left. He'd done some of that himself. But as he watched this guy ogle Riley, annoyance flared. "Send me copies of the last three weeks."

Tapping keys clicked behind him and when he heard, "Mr. Bowman," he turned to find the young guy holding out a flash drive for him. "I can't send it to you without leaving a trail. No one is likely to notice this copy."

Bowman pocketed the drive. "Thanks."

The guy slid nervous hands into his pockets, chewing on his lip as he glanced toward the door. "This makes me even with Shield?"

"Yes, it does."

Relief relaxed his shoulders. "Thanks."

Bowman left the security office and made his way out the back service exit. In his SUV he started the engine, knowing full damn well that this video would not be admissible in a court of law. But he wasn't worried about the court system anymore. He didn't care about paperwork, or the right channels or procedure. This was about seeing justice done. No more playing by the rules.

Bowman drove back to his house, on the eastern edge of King George County. Away from the congestion near I-95, the strip malls, and the subdivisions, the rolling land was lush and green. The two-story white antebellum house had been built over 150 years ago at the dawn of the Civil War. There was a lone rocking chair on the wide front porch supported by thick round columns. Tall windows, flanking the wide front door, stretched from the porch floor to the ceiling. There was a huge oak tree towering to the right with long-reaching branches covering the roofline. The realtor who'd sold him the property said Union soldiers had been hung from that tree and their ghosts now haunted the house. The idea of a few ghosts appealed to him.

The last major renovation had been in the seventies, and now he was tackling the job of bringing it into the twenty-first century. During the long stakeouts when there had been a sleeping bag for a bed and MREs, he said when he finally settled he'd remodel an old house. Well, now he was about to put his money where his mouth was.

Tugging off his tie, he flipped on lights. He shrugged off his jacket and hung it over the back of a chair in the kitchen. From the counter he grabbed a glass and a bottle of scotch. Filling three fingers' worth, he sipped as he opened the laptop on the table.

A full moon hung over the fields, casting a soft glow. The night was always his favorite time, when the clatter of the day was silent and he could think uninterrupted. His wife had been a night owl, and she would often wait up for him. They'd laugh. Talk. Make love. This had been their time. He closed his eyes and tried to picture Karen. He was able to capture the soft outline of her face and the way her blond hair skimmed her shoulders, but he couldn't see the smaller details of her features anymore. Time was stealing them bit by bit. He tried to concentrate on his late wife's smile, but instead of seeing Karen, he saw Riley. No soft lines on her. No easy smiles. She was all gristle and grit. Karen had been easy to love. But not Riley. She would make any man in her life fight for every bit of ground.

The first time with Riley hadn't been polite or tentative. In his motel room, he had turned her toward a bureau and shoved her hips toward him. He remembered how she glanced up, surprise flickering in her eyes as she stared back at him in the mirror. Then she smiled and unfastened the snap on her pants. He ran his hands over her smooth hips. A dozen sensations he'd thought dead forever had fired to life. He kissed her on the back of her neck, inhaling her scent as his hand cupped her breast and teased her nipple to a hard peak. She hissed in a breath and dropped her head back toward him, her long soft hair brushing his cheek. Hard and ready, he unzipped his pants, positioned himself at her moist entrance, and rubbed against her. She moaned. Unable to hold back anymore, he pushed into her.

She was tense, so tight, and for a moment didn't move.

He raised his gaze to the mirror and met hers. "Are you okay?"

"It's been a while."

He felt her relax and he slowly moved inside her. When she grew wetter, he pushed deeper. She arched back and for a moment he forgot about everything but her.

Now, turning from the window, he moved toward a couch, which was the lone piece of furniture he'd ordered. No sense furnishing a house that would soon see construction crews.

When his wife died, he'd not kept any of the furniture they shared, unable to deal with the grief he attached to everything she'd collected over the years. So he'd given it all away and moved into a furnished studio apartment until his next assignment. He'd lived out of a suitcase for the next few years.

Fatigue tightening his muscles, he moved back to the computer and opened the file marked *Elizabeth Riley Tatum*. Sipping scotch, he picked up the picture taken of her when she was a junior in high school. She stared directly into the camera, forcing a smile, her long dark hair flowing around her shoulders. In the next image she wore a fancy dress and held a bouquet of flowers. The dress fit her body well and clearly a lot of time had gone into making it, but it didn't look like something she would have picked for herself. When he studied her face, he could see that she was uncomfortable. She reminded him of a fashion model with no expression. Like the dress, the name *Elizabeth* didn't suit her well. Too proper. Too fussy. *Riley* fit her better.

She'd done substandard work in high school, making Cs and some Bs. She had been on the tennis team and played local tournaments. By all appearances, she was the perfect society girl. Then her mother died, and within a week she ran away from home, vanished for seven days, and found herself in Virginia. There were no police records of her leaving home. But a stepfather like Riley's wouldn't want the world knowing what had happened in his house.

He tapped his finger on the side of the glass and flipped through the files until he had her stepfather's profile in front of him. He'd instantly disliked William Charles and knew he was hiding secrets. Shield said he was a gambler, but Bowman sensed there was more. So he started digging.

William Charles, age sixty-five, had come from old money and worked as a lawyer in New Orleans. He enjoyed a thriving practice and a solid reputation as a corporate attorney, splitting his time between New Orleans and Washington, DC. Eight years ago he married a woman twenty-five years his junior. The lovely look-alike of his first wife.

Bowman had to excavate deep into the computer files before he found a New Orleans police report for Charles, who had been picked up for solicitation fifteen years ago.

He reached for his phone. It took three calls and a promise of a big favor before he finally got through to the officer who'd arrested William Charles.

"Who is this?" The officer's graveled voice fired the question as if he faced an assailant.

"This is Clay Bowman. I work with Shield Security in Virginia."

"That supposed to mean something?"

"It means enough to your boss, Lieutenant Randy Mills. He gave me this number."

In the background he heard the click of a light. "Okay, Mr. Bowman. What do you want?"

"I'm digging into an arrest you made fifteen years ago."

The officer chuckled. "That's a hell of a long time ago."

"I know. But this guy was fairly prominent. His name is William Charles."

A long pause followed. "I remember him. Bigwig. A real charmer."

"I'm interested in his history."

Silence.

"And?" Bowman prompted.

"He was picked up in a sting operation. The powers that be at the time were going after the johns. The program didn't last very long. They scooped up a few too many big fish in their nets."

"Including Charles."

"He was one of several that were caught with an underage prostitute."

"No charges were filed."

"None. And the girl in question vanished a few days after the incident. Some say he paid her off, whereas others think maybe she's at the bottom of Lake Pontchartrain. No proof either way."

Fifteen years ago, Charles's wife would have been ill and Riley close to sixteen. "No one ever took a statement from the prostitute?"

"If they did, the report vanished along with her," the officer continued. "Word is he was a regular. He liked the younger girls. He was particular about what he wanted. Dark hair, I recall."

Like his wife. Like Riley. "Any other reports against him?"

"None. As far as his records are concerned, he was a choirboy who had a minor fall from grace."

"Right."

A chair squeaked as if he leaned forward. "But don't let that fool you. Guys like him don't quit. They adapt."

CHAPTER THIRTEEN

Sunday, September 18, 7:15 a.m.

Riley had slept very little last night. Her head buzzed with images from the video as she paced her kitchen and waited for the sun to rise. As soon as Hanna was off to her morning training run, she would contact Bowman.

He picked up on the first ring. "Riley."

"We need to talk."

"Okay. I can meet you." He sounded alert, focused.

"How about Duke's?"

"When?"

"An hour?"

"Done. Are you okay?"

"Just be on time."

She grabbed Cooper's leash and took him for a quick walk. As they moved toward the street, a dark-blue car was parked in front of her house. She slowed her pace, absently checking the gun holstered on her hip under her shirt. When the back car door opened, she unsnapped the holster's guard and settled her hand on the gun's grip.

An older, thin man rose out of the car, tugging off sunglasses as he turned. She took a step back, releasing the gun as her heart hammered in her chest.

"William?"

He stopped and studied her. "You look well, Riley."

"What do you want?" She thought about the video. Was he playing a game with her?

"Curious about you."

"Well, as you can see, I'm alive and well. Now leave."

His eyes narrowed. "Who is Clay Bowman?"

"Excuse me?"

"He came to see me. Asked questions about you."

She refused to let him see her surprise or anger. "And what did you tell him?"

"The truth. You were a difficult child."

Riley flexed her fingers, her annoyance at Bowman consumed by old angers toward this old man. She took a step toward him. "Did you also tell him how you made a move on me? How you wanted to play house?"

He raised his chin. "You clearly do not remember what was the truth."

"And that was what? That you were the noble stepfather who only had my best interests at heart?"

"That is true, Riley. I only wanted the best for you."

She could rail and shout and call him a liar, but what difference would it make? He was a creep. Always would be. And nothing she said would change that. "There was a car following me a few days ago. Was it you?"

Confusion glistened in his eyes. "What are you talking about?"

"You've been to my house before," she pressed.

"No."

He'd always been a bad liar, but at this point she couldn't tell. "Get off my property, William."

He turned to the car and hesitated. "I hear you're about to adopt a kid. That's a surprise. Maybe we'll meet again."

She closed the gap between them in seconds. In a low voice so only he could hear, she said, "If you come within a mile of my kid, I will kill you."

"Is that a threat?"

"Absolutely, William."

He held her gaze for a moment, but whatever bravado he'd mustered had vanished. He slid back into the car, and she stood in the same spot, fists clenched until the car vanished from sight.

Bowman had gone to William behind her back. Damn it!

She tipped her head back, wondering if she should trust this guy. Like his boss, the man was impossible to read and she'd already misjudged him badly five years ago.

***

Riley's stomach was in knots as she pushed through the front doors of Duke's. When she smelled the eggs cooking, her stomach should have churned with hunger, but she was too worried to eat. She paused at the waitress station when she spotted Maria.

The woman had tied her unruly dark hair up into a topknot that trickled ringlets around her round face. "My goodness, you looked loaded for bear."

"I have a meeting."

Maria was Duke's wife, and as he said more than once, his saving grace. They'd married twenty years ago, and though the two never had children, they were devoted to each other. To hear Duke tell it, Maria had yanked him off the streets, sobered him up, and convinced him that gambling was no way for a good man to earn a living. They'd opened this diner, and a year later, the shelter. Maria had saved Duke's life and he in turn had saved Riley's along with countless other runaways. Paying it forward.

"So what marathon workout was it this morning?" Bracelets jangled on her wrists as she reached for silverware and a menu for Riley.

"I skipped my workout today."

"That's a first. Everything all right with you and Hanna?"

"Yeah, we're fine."

"When is the court date for the adoption?"

"Nine days."

"You've got to be excited."

"I'll be glad when the papers are signed."

Maria's expression sobered. "I heard about that murdered kid. It was on the news again last night. Any closer to finding her killer?"

"I'm meeting someone here to talk about it."

"Must be the man who sat down a few minutes ago. He asked if you were here. Tall, scary dude." She leaned forward, whispering, "Looks like a fed."

"Close. Where is he sitting?"

"Table six. He wanted a table in the back. Should have known it?"

"Something like that."

"Thanks. I'll catch up with you soon."

"Sure."

Riley cut through the crowded restaurant. With each step her body tightened with tension. She was a coiled spring ready to unload. Bowman saw her, and holding his tie back, he rose.

"Bowman."

"Good morning, Riley."

She pulled out a chair. A coffeepot and two mugs were in the center of the round table. She waved him down and sat. "You went to see William."

He didn't hesitate. "I did."

"Why?"

"I'm searching for the Shark. He fits the killer's profile."

"William is a coward," she said, teeth clenched.

"So is the Shark. He works in the shadows and kills girls."

"Why did you go behind my back?"

"I didn't see it that way. I needed to see him for myself. And to have you along would have biased his response."

He was right. Her presence would have changed William's answers. "And what did you find? Do you think he's the Shark?"

"I don't know yet."

Maria showed up at their table with a couple of menus and set them in front of Riley and Bowman. This wasn't Maria's table. She was checking up on Riley.

"Would you like to hear the specials?" Maria asked.

"No thanks, Maria. Coffee is fine."

Maria rolled her eyes. "No starvation diet for you. I'll get you the number six." She smiled at Bowman. "I'm Maria Spence."

He rose and extended his hand. "Clay Bowman. Good to meet you, Maria."

The woman lingered, clearly curious.

Riley shifted. "I think you have folks at your station, Maria."

Maria tossed Riley a questioning look. "Right. Thanks."

Bowman watched the woman stop at a table and hand menus out to a couple of guys. "She's looking out for you."

"She is."

"She had me in her sights the moment I asked for you. She's very protective. I admire that."

She wasn't sure how to take his keen interest. "You're a wild card and she doesn't take kindly to those."

He turned the handle of his coffee cup and raised it to his lips. "Sounds like you."

"Maybe."

Their waitress arrived. "Maria has already ordered you the number six, Riley."

"I'll take the same," Bowman said, looking amused.

"Good choice," the waitress said.

After she was gone, Riley said, "Now that we are a team, I'd like to see your case files on the Shark."

He sipped his coffee. "You always talk about work?"

"It's the cornerstone of our relationship." And she needed time to screw up the courage to tell him about the DVD.

He tapped his finger against the mug. "How was your workout this morning?"

"Why do you ask?"

"It's called conversation."

Shaking her head, she reached for her coffee cup. "I skipped it. When can I see the files?"

"Why'd you skip? Is something wrong?"

The waitress returned with two hot plates of food. The number six came with a couple of scrambled eggs, pancakes, and bacon.

Bowman reached for his fork. "They don't mess around with the portions here."

"It's good." Absently, Riley poured syrup on her pancakes.

"How is Hanna?"

She hesitated, trying to decide if she wanted to attempt conversation. Then, remembering the video, she dialed it back a notch. Needing his help didn't make it any easier for her to ask for it. "Excited about her trip to Atlanta."

"You said triathlon, right?"

"Yes."

He sat back. "What's eating you?"

"This case. That there might be a killer after me."

A cold chill seeped through her bones. Dying scared her, of course. But the idea of leaving Hanna behind terrified her. She'd been so sure about telling him about the video this morning, and then she found out he'd gone behind her back and spoken to William. Would he have told her if she'd not confronted him?

He dropped his gaze to his pancakes and cut a large piece dripping with syrup. "You have no security at your house, correct?"

Her appetite vanished as she stared at the half-eaten pancakes. "Good locks on the doors."

"That's not enough."

"What do you suggest?"

"The company understands security better than anyone. Let us install an alarm system." He sat back as if sensing he had her attention. "The cost is on us. We have a vested interest in keeping you safe."

"I don't know."

"Don't think of it for yourself. It's for Hanna."

"Do you ever play fair?"

"When I can. When I can't, I don't."

She swallowed a retort. It wasn't about her anymore. There was Hanna. "Okay. But this isn't for me. It's for Hanna."

"Understood."

The video loomed. She needed someone's help. Specifically, Bowman's. She drew in a breath. "Hanna is at practice this morning, but this afternoon she is going on her trip to Atlanta."

He watched her.

"The team will be back Friday."

Again, he said nothing, sensing she needed something.

"And honestly, right now that's a good thing. I want her out of town now."

Bowman let the comment sit.

"Someone sent me a video."

"What kind?"

A waitress moved up to their table and refilled their coffee cups. Riley sat back, tapping her index finger on the table as she waited for the woman to move on. When they were alone again, she said, "Not here. Someplace private."

"My place," he said.

"I have to drop Hanna off at eleven."

"I'll text you the address. Come directly to my house."

"Okay."

***

After she walked Bowman out the door, Riley doubled back to Duke's office. She knocked on the door.

"What?"

"On a scale of one to ten, that's an eleven on the not-too-happy meter," she said.

Duke glanced up, a reluctant grin curling his lips. "So what's the deal with the suit?"

"He's with Shield Security. When he was with the FBI he worked on a string of murders in New Orleans."

Duke sat back in his chair. "What does he want with you?"

She trusted Duke with nearly all her secrets, but this case reached too deep for her to share it with anyone else now. "He thinks the murder case I'm working on reminds him of the New Orleans murders."

"He dig up any suspects?"

She leaned against the doorjamb, not sure if she wanted to open up an old wound. "Nothing yet."

"It's not like you to sound glum."

"The case, the victim, reminds me a little of me back in the day. Remember when you found me, Duke? When I first came to town on the bus."

His expression sobered. "Yeah, I remember."

"What was I like?"

"Doped up. Too thin. Pale."

Hazy images of the Greyhound bus flashed in her mind. The seats were rough against her cheek, and she smelled the strong scent of corned beef. Someone near her was eating a sandwich and the smell made her sick to her stomach. "Did I say anything that you remember? Did I give you any clue about what happened to me?"

He pulled off his glasses and leaned back in his chair, his expression unreadable. "You could barely stand, let alone form sentences. Why?"

She shrugged. "I wonder about those days from time to time."

"Why?" He got up, pushing up his sleeves and exposing tattooed forearms. "That was a lifetime ago. You're a different person now."

"Sometimes it feels like yesterday."

She had never pieced together the details of that first day in town, but she also had never really wanted to until now. "Why were you at the bus station?"

"My volunteers were working the station that day. We were trying out a program of meeting runaways before they landed into real trouble."

"Was Maria there?"

"Yeah, I suppose. The bus station outreach was her idea. She wanted to get to the kids before the street did."

"You don't go to the bus station as often as you did then."

"The kids seem to find rides by hitchhiking. That's why we have the youth shelter."

"How many people have you saved?"

"Not enough. Out of every hundred kids we make contact with, three or four might hang around here for more than a meal, and of those, maybe two a year turn their life around."

"Why did I trust you?"

"Can't say that you did. You were spitting mad. You tried to slug me."

"I did?"

"Kid, you were such a mess. But there was something about you. If not for Maria and me, you wouldn't have made it five steps on the streets without someone taking advantage." He rubbed the back of his neck with his hand. "What do you remember?"

"Not much. I lost seven days and all I can say is that cigar smoke still makes me sick to my stomach."

He shook his head as if chasing away a memory. "Whatever you took, you were really high."

"I've never taken drugs. Not once in my life. Someone did that to me."

"I took you to a doctor. He said there were no signs of abuse."

"I remember that." Riley had recoiled at the doctor's touch. She was terrified. But the doctor was nice and patient, and finally she allowed the pelvic exam.

A sigh shuddered through him. "When I drank, I lost lots of days. Too many days. It's not a good feeling not knowing what you did or didn't do. But you have to decide to let it go."

"I know you're right." Riley shook her head and grinned. "I have no idea why I'm letting this case get to me."

"It's not like you."

"You're right. It's stupid. I'm fine." But it was all lies. She wasn't fine. Someone had left a video documenting her trip to the abyss.

"Maria and I are always here, if you need us."

"I know. Thanks."

* * *

Cassie's skin felt like it was two sizes too small as she watched Darla unlock the motel room. Sniffing, she scratched her arm, craving the crack she'd had yesterday. She'd heard it was addictive but figured she could handle it. She was tough, or so she thought. Gristle and bone, her mother used to say.

But living on the streets this last month had tested her each day. Yesterday, the weight of living out here had grown heavy. She was tired of scrounging for food, selling her body, and searching for a decent place to sleep. The nights had been really bad. First there'd been word about Vicky dying, and then Darla had convinced Tony to let Cassie work for one of Jax's clients. Tony was happy, making $500. He told her to be nice.

Darla flipped on the lights and dropped a plastic drugstore bag on the bed. "You need to hit the shower and wash your hair. I bought hair dye."

"What's wrong with my hair?"

"It's fine, but the client likes dark hair."

"Most of Tony's clients like blondes."

Darla shoved her hard toward the bathroom. "Get in the damn shower."

Cassie took a step but stopped. "You promised me a taste."

Darla rustled in the bag for the box of hair dye. "Get cleaned up first. Then I'll give you a little treat."

Cassie didn't like Darla. The woman was all smiles to the clients, but Vicky said more than once she could be meaner than a snake. "I want my taste now."

Darla lifted her darkening gaze. She fished a knife from her pocket and crossed the room in a split second. The knife pressed against Cassie's neck, pricking the delicate skin until it bled. "Get in the shower."

Cassie backed up a step, knowing the woman was crazy enough to slice her throat from ear to ear. "Okay."

She turned on the shower and washed the sweat, dirt, and stench of men from her body. It had been days since she'd taken a hot shower. God, it felt good.

A fist pounding against wood startled her. "Get out of there now. I need to color your hair."

Cassie shut off the water and grabbed a couple of towels. One she wrapped around her body and the other, her hair. She stepped out and Darla stood by the sink, gloves on her hands and the foam hair dye at the ready.

The coloring took a half hour, and the next time Cassie looked in the mirror her hair was dark. The darker shade made her look sickly. She didn't recognize herself.

Darla stared at her, smiling. She fisted a few pills from her pocket and handed them to Cassie. "Here's your treat."

"What's this?"

"Oxy."

Cassie swallowed the pills and soon her worries faded. She slipped on a yellow dress and a pair of high heels. As she moved around the room, she twirled. She felt like she could do anything. Hell, even the colors looked brighter. For the first time in weeks, she was happy.

Darla hovered by the window peering out, taking a big pull from her cigarette. When the john's car pulled up, she stepped back and put out her cigarette. She moistened her lips and opened the door to a tall man wearing a real nice suit. Three gold rings winked from his thick fingers. The letters embossed on his neatly starched shirt cuffs told everyone he had class.

Darla pulled Cassie forward by her elbow. "Smile."

Running her tongue over her teeth, Cassie flipped her hair out of her eyes. She smiled like Tony had told her. "You want a date?"

The man studied her closely. "Run your hands through your hair."

"My hair?"

"It's dark, like you requested," Darla said. "Show him your hair."

With trembling fingers, Cassie carefully brushed her dark hair over her shoulder. "You like it?"

More silence, and then, "It'll do."

"I want five hundred more," Darla said. "Cost me money to get her ready."

"We agreed on one grand."

Darla didn't flinch. "Five hundred more."

The man hesitated, then reached in his pocket and peeled off five one-hundred-dollar bills. He handed them to Darla, squeezing her hand when she reached for the money. "For twenty-four hours," the man said. "And if you go to the cops, you're dead."

Cassie looked at Darla. "You said an hour."

Darla gently brushed the wisps of hair from Cassie's eyes like she was sending off her daughter to the prom. "It'll be the best twenty-four hours of your life. All champagne and caviar."

She'd never eaten caviar and didn't want to try it. She wanted a hit. Twenty-four hours. "Yeah, sure."

He took Cassie by the elbow and led her to a dark, shiny car with tinted windows. He opened the front passenger-side door for her, and she slid onto the soft leather seats. When he closed the door, she flinched. Seconds afterward, the locks fastened with finality.

Her stomach churned as she became aware of the faint scent of aftershave mingling with cinnamon. *An odd combination,* she thought as he drove, in no rush. A glance in the side mirror caught Darla standing by the open motel room door, shoving the money in her pocket and turning away as if she'd forgotten all about Cassie.

The girl squirmed. A bad feeling knotted in the pit of her stomach. "Where are we going?"

"To a party."

"A party?" She tamped down the rising panic. She'd been to a lot of parties. "You have a name?"

He tapped a ringed index finger on the steering wheel. "Lenny."

"Lenny. That's a nice name." Sometimes the johns were nicer if you used their names. "I'm Cassie, Lenny."

"Cassie."

The lights of the city began to move faster and faster past the window as the car picked up speed, heading out of town. "Where's this party?"

"In a private place."

She hitched her chin up a notch. "You paid Darla for twenty-four hours. That includes transport." Always good to watch the time carefully. Johns were always trying to squeeze a little extra for free.

"We aren't going far, Cassie."

She shifted in her seat, her fingers absently running over the door handle.

"It's a nice place," he added. "You'll like it."

The good thing about a cheap motel was that there were lots of people who could hear her scream if necessary. But where they were going, Cassie wouldn't be heard. *Oh shit, this can't be good.*

***

Riley arrived home to the shower running and the radio in Hanna's room blaring.

"Hanna, you need to hurry. We have to get to school. The bus leaves in an hour."

"I'm almost ready," she shouted back.

Riley retrieved the DVD from her room and shoved it deep in her purse just as Hanna came out of the bedroom hauling a large suitcase.

"I might have packed too much," Hanna said.

"Don't worry about it. Better to have too much than not enough." She checked her watch. "Ready?"

"Yeah. You look tense. You okay?"

"It's the case. Sorry."

"You'll solve it. You're good at that kind of thing."

Was she? "Thanks."

Hanna opened her bag to double-check a few items. "What was in the package that came yesterday?"

Riley's breath stilled. "Nothing important."

"You looked a little upset."

"I wasn't upset."

Hanna shook her head. "Bull."

"I wasn't upset. And there was nothing that important in the package." Truly, at this point she liked the idea of Hanna leaving for a few days and being away from all of this. Whoever was out there knew about Hanna.

"All packed and ready to go."

As they moved to the car, Riley asked, "Tell me again, when does the bus arrive in Atlanta?"

Hanna rolled her eyes. "We've been through this a million times."

"Try a million and one."

"It's a twelve-hour drive. We arrive after dinner. Check into the hotel and then our meet starts the next day." Hanna dumped her bag in the backseat.

"You're going to have fun." She dug in her back pocket and handed Hanna $200 in cash. "Take this."

"I have money."

"I know. It's in case of emergency or if you see something fun."

Hanna glanced at the money as if she didn't feel she deserved it. "You don't have to do this."

"I know. I want to. This is going to be a good time for you, and I don't want you counting pennies."

Hanna hugged Riley. "You're the best."

Riley held her tight. "Be careful."

CHAPTER FOURTEEN

Sunday, September 18, 10:45 a.m.

Riley drove deeper into the countryside, barely noticing the clear sky. On a good day she admired the gently rolling land and the lush green fields. But today, as she traveled into the country toward Bowman's house, the remoteness reminded her of vulnerability and isolation.

She found twin brick pillars that marked a driveway cut into a stand of old oaks. She made her way under the canopy of thick trees, which opened to a field with an old plantation-style home in the center.

She double-checked her address, trying to reconcile the man with the house. Out of the SUV, she leashed Cooper and he climbed out. They climbed the wide front steps and crossed the ten-foot-deep front porch. To her left and right were stacks of drywall.

When she raised her hand to knock, she heard determined footsteps moving toward the door. He knew she was here, but she knocked anyway. The door snapped open to Bowman. He'd changed out of his suit and now wore a clean white shirt and pants, but no tie.

He studied the dog and then rubbed him behind the ear. "Did you have any trouble finding the place?"

"No. GPS did the trick. Kinda off the main road, aren't you?"

"Never had a chance to put down roots and now that I do, I'm going for it." He stepped aside so she could enter.

"Looks like you bought some real history. Let's hope it isn't a money pit."

"I think of this as a challenge."

"Your carpentry skills on par with your tracking skills?"

A massive banister curled at the base of a sweeping staircase. Over the foyer hung a large lantern-style fixture, more quaint than functional. It cast a light onto the hallway that ran through the center of the house separating the two rooms on the east side from the two on the west. The room on her right was set up like an office, but judging by the boxes, he'd done little unpacking.

"Impressive," she said.

"Go big or go home."

"Right."

"Come on back to the kitchen. I've coffee and bagels."

"You're okay with the dog?"

"Of course."

"Thanks. Coffee sounds great."

"You don't eat?"

"Not when I'm wound up."

Neither spoke as they moved into the kitchen that dated back to the seventies. An inspection of appliances told her this room would also need massive work. But there was the morning light and a tremendous view of rolling green fields.

She walked to a large picture window that offered a stunning view of the river. This alone would be reason enough to buy the house. "How'd you find this place?"

"Out driving one day and saw the 'For Sale' sign."

"I suppose it fits. You strike me as a traditional kind of guy."

Lines at the corners of his eyes creased when he smiled. "And you're not traditional?"

"I might have been born into it, but it didn't take." Despite her upbringing, she'd never imagined herself living in a house like this one. She reached in her bag and pulled the DVD out. "I'm not sure why I'm trusting you with this."

"Why are you?" His body was relaxed, but tension hummed behind the words.

"You might be my best chance to solve this."

She handed him the DVD, which she'd dropped into a zip-top bag. His fingers barely brushed hers as he accepted it.

He hesitated before he touched the disc. "Should I wear gloves?"

"My prints are all over the exterior package, but I put on gloves before I touched the DVD case and disc."

He put on latex gloves without a word, moved to a DVD player, carefully inserted the video, and hit "Play." Slowly he stepped back and stood next to Riley.

Instinctively, she tensed, bracing for the image and his reaction. She feared he'd see her as a victim. She feared he'd treat her differently. And she wanted no one's pity. Especially Bowman's.

Her image appeared. Behind her were the cream-colored drapes, thick carpet, and a Queen Anne table overlooking a glittering skyline. Music played soft and delicate in the background.

Folding her arms over her chest, Riley forced herself to breathe as she watched Bowman's jaw clench. He flexed the fingers on his right hand as if he wanted to punch the screen.

He hit "Replay" and watched the recording again.

When the camera moved closer to the chair and focused on her tied hands, Bowman looked away from the screen and studied her reaction. "When did this arrive?"

"Last night." She nodded. "Watch."

Old hands reached for the girl's chin; her dark hair fell back, and looking at the camera was a seventeen-year-old Riley.

He paused the frame and stepped closer to the screen. For a long moment he said nothing.

Riley chewed the inside of her cheek, clamping down the rise of fear and nausea that rushed her each time she saw this. The young girl in the video moaned. She forced herself not to hear. Her throat tightened.

"How did you receive this?" Bowman demanded.

"It was waiting on the front porch of my home."

"You found it?"

"No, Hanna did yesterday."

"Did Hanna open the package?"

"No. She left it on the kitchen table for me with a note."

"You're sure she didn't see the video?"

"Yes. The package was undisturbed, and when she came home, she was her normal self. Nothing out of the ordinary for a teenage girl."

"Do any of your neighbors have security cameras around their houses?"

"Not that kind of neighborhood. Working-class folks don't have that kind of money. But I made a point to check for cameras along the block this morning when I walked Cooper."

"Did you talk to your neighbors? Did anyone see anything?"

"No. But I can follow up today."

"I'll do that."

"But these are my neighbors."

"I'm impartial. Better from me. I'll find a way to leave you out of it. Any memories of how you landed in that room?"

"I have no idea. I have seven missing days. I was accepting something to drink one minute, and the next I was stumbling off the bus in Richmond a thousand miles away."

"And you gave the cards to Sharp?"

"Yes. But I took pictures of them." She scrolled through her phone and showed him the spread.

"A royal flush? There are four possible royal flushes out of 2.6 million possible hands. To say you were lucky would be a huge understatement."

"I knew it was good. Didn't know it was that rare."

He studied the photos she'd taken of the back of the cards. "Just like the ones we found on the victims in New Orleans, except no writing on yours."

"Like the ones I found in Vicky Gilbert's backpack." She tumbled through the facts of the Gilbert case as Bowman viewed the pictures. "Vicky and I share similarities. Runaways, but neither of us had been on the streets long. We do look alike. I didn't realize how much until I saw the video. I'd forgotten how long my hair used to be."

"You haven't changed that much."

Riley rolled her eyes. "Please don't say that in public. Looking like a teenager doesn't help my badass image unless I'm going undercover at the local high school."

"Understood."

Energy buzzed in her body, creating a wave of panic. "I thought it was all behind me. But the Shark is circling back, isn't he?"

"You're not alone in this, Riley."

Her gaze shot up, searching for some kind of resolution. "It's ironic I track fugitives and now I'm on the receiving end."

"You aren't prey."

Tears threatened, which only stoked her anger. "The hell I'm not."

He closed the gap and laid a hand on her arm. More energy surged up, but this time it didn't snap and burn. It tingled. In a good way.

Slowly, she pulled her arm away, knowing she didn't need to complicate what was already pretty damn complicated. Though she'd broken the connection, he didn't back away.

Her phone hummed so she checked the screen, grateful for the interruption.

Sandy had sent her a text.

Cassie is missing.

Riley typed: How long?

Since last night. She texts me every hour.

Frowning, she pictured the young runaway girl she'd met at the truck stop a few days ago. She looked up from the phone and found Bowman's gaze full of questions.

"Homicide?"

"I hope not. I interviewed a couple of the runaways when I was looking for Darla. Sandy and Cassie. Sandy says Cassie is missing."

"Does she fit the profile?"

"No. She has blond hair. Small. ID says eighteen but I doubt it." She texted Sandy for details. "Sandy says that Darla cut a deal with Tony for the girl."

His chest rose and fell with a sigh. "She's blond."

"That's fixed with a bottle of hair dye," she said. "Darla already had a connection to this network. I need to find Sandy and find out what's going on."

"I'll back you up."

She shook her head. "No thanks, I have this."

"Did you note the lack of a question mark at the end of my statement?"

"Jesus, Bowman, you helped me out on the mountain. And now, on the streets?"

"Technically, it's your day off. If anyone were wondering, we could simply say we were out for a stroll."

That prompted a laugh. "That's the last thing anyone would picture us doing."

"I can't control what they believe." He tapped his finger on the DVD case. "Can I keep this? I have a tech guy who can analyze it. He can separate out background sounds, reflected images, and do things you and I couldn't imagine."

She'd laid bare her darkest secret to him without knowing much about him. It wasn't like her to be open, but urgency tilting toward desperation had forced her hand. The frozen image of her drugged face stared back. "That cannot go public. None of your buddies at the FBI, CIA, or anywhere else can see it."

"Just my people will see it. They are always discreet."

She cringed. "I might regret this, but fine. Keep it. But if you find anything that will help Sharp's murder investigation, I want you to give it to him."

"Of course."

Rising, she drew in a breath. Cooper stood, looking up at her and waiting for his next order. She took a small step back, folding her arms. "I don't like having it in my house anyway."

Bowman followed her to the door, opening it for her. "Payback for this killer is coming, Riley. Just a little more time."

"I hope so."

Floorboards creaked as he shifted his weight. "I'll be there."

She looked up at him. "I'm betting a lot on that."

"Where are you going to meet Sandy?"

"There's a truck stop off the interstate where a lot of the girls are working now." She gave Bowman the location.

"I'm five minutes behind you."

"You were an hour behind me in the woods and caught up. How'd you do that?"

"I was motivated."

"Why were you there at all?"

A smile tugged the edge of his lips. "Civic duty."

"Does Shield Security do these things often?"

"From time to time."

"Why this case?" she asked.

"Lucky for you, I suppose."

"Luck?" She opened the door. "No such thing. How long has Shield known about me?"

He hesitated, considered her. "He saw you on the news a couple of years ago. He thought you were the fifth victim. He did a little digging and found out you were from New Orleans. He's kept an eye on you ever since."

"My guardian angel."

Bowman's mouth flattened into a grim line. "He's determined to solve this case, and you're a part of it."

The notion that Mr. Shield had been watching her like the Shark was unsettling. "I need to get back into town."

"After you."

She got in her SUV, glanced back at Cooper, and headed toward town. Several times during the half-hour drive, she looked in the rear-view mirror expecting to see him trailing behind her, but when she looked he was never there.

When she pulled up to the diner near the bus station, she spotted Sandy. She was leaning against a van, her hands hovering close to a warm cup of coffee, clearly waiting for her next date. There was no sign of Darla, but people like her didn't need to be physically close to control their girls. The pimps were good at manipulating their prostitutes with drugs, threats to their families, beatings, and sleep deprivation. Most girls simply followed orders sent via text without question.

The girl shoved her hands in her pockets and stomped her feet as if trying to stay awake. No doubt she'd not slept well in a while.

"Be right back, Coop." Out of the car, Riley crossed the graveled lot in long strides.

Sandy looked up, her face a mask of composure. "I wasn't sure if you'd make it."

"Sorry. Traffic."

The girl looked around, then pushed away from the van. "Feels good to rest. My feet are killing me."

"Want to go inside? I'll buy you a meal and you can sit."

"Tempting, but that wouldn't be the smartest move."

"When is the last time you ate a real meal?"

"I don't know."

"Is Tony around?"

She grabbed her cell phone from her pocket. "He's always texting."

"Can you eat and respond to texts?"

"Sure."

"So take fifteen minutes."

"Okay. Let's go inside. Can I have eggs and pancakes?"

"You bet." A glance toward her vehicle showed a dark SUV parked beside her. A shadow passed across the front windshield, making it hard to see inside, but she knew it was Bowman because the hair on the back of her neck was standing up.

Riley and Sandy crossed the lot into the small diner that smelled of fried eggs, bacon, and grease. The floors dated back fifty years and the counter was a throwback to *Happy Days*. A guy slinging hash at a well-seasoned grill turned, glanced at Riley, and nodded to the "Seat Yourself" sign. She chose a booth close to the back and sat in the seat against the wall. Sandy slid in across from her.

The dude behind the counter raised his spatula. "You can't sit and just drink hot water."

Riley raised her hand. "I'm buying."

The cook glared at Sandy. "No hot water."

Sandy hunkered lower in her jacket as the few people in the diner stared while a heavyset waitress with a coffeepot turned over the two stoneware mugs and filled each with fresh brew.

Sandy didn't glance at the menu. "The number one."

The waitress arched a painted-on brow. "That's a lot of food."

"I'll eat it." Bracelets rattled on Sandy's wrist as she reached for the sugar and dumped in a few teaspoons before she splashed in milk.

Riley realized the kid had ordered a stack of pancakes as well as bacon and three scrambled eggs with toast. "I'll have a bagel."

"Sure."

When the waitress left, Sandy leaned forward. "The cook can be a jerk, but he makes great eggs. Whenever I have extra change I eat here. Coffee is unlimited. Amazing how long you can go on coffee."

"And hot water."

"With ketchup, it's a soup." She drummed her fingers on the greasy table and snuck a glance toward the waitress. "You can play that card once here. Nico, the cook, doesn't like it."

"I'll bet." She traced the edge of her cup. "What's going on with Cassie?"

"I haven't seen her in over a day."

"Is that unusual?"

"For her, yes. She likes to check in with me. And Tony is freaking out. He's looking for Darla now. Wants to know where Darla took his merchandise."

"No sign of Darla?" Riley asked.

"No. She's hiding out."

"Do you have any pictures of Cassie?"

"No."

"This guy I'm looking for likes dark hair."

Sandy's eyes narrowed. "Cassie said Darla wanted to color her hair dark."

From what she'd heard about Darla, the woman was resourceful. If a buyer wanted a brunette and she didn't have a girl that fit the bill, she'd make one. "Did she say who the john was?"

"I asked Tony. He said the guy was rich and would show her a good time. Said not to worry." She shook her head. "When Tony says not to worry, I do."

The waitress arrived with Riley's bagel. "The other gal's order will be right up."

"Thanks." Riley looked at the girl's gaunt face. She pushed the bagel toward Sandy. "I'm not hungry. Why don't you snack on this while you wait for your meal."

"I won't say no." Sandy bit into half of the bagel and shoved the other half in her pocket.

"Where's Cassie from?"

"Western part of the state, I think. Some little hick town. Figured she'd come to the big city, get a job, and her life would get on track."

"That didn't work out well, did it?"

"No."

"Drugs?"

"She didn't want to at first, but Tony kept pushing. It's not out of control, but . . . close." Sandy sniffed. "She can't handle the drugs or streets like me."

Riley studied the dark circles under the girl's sunken eyes. She wasn't really handling it either. This life was simply killing her more slowly. "How much longer can you handle it?"

The waitress arrived at the table with Sandy's food, and she didn't speak for several minutes while she inhaled the feast.

"Darla drives a motor home," Sandy said.

"Know any places she likes to park it?"

"There's an old motel about twenty miles east. Has lots of rooms not connected."

"Cottage-style?"

"Yeah."

"Okay." Riley glanced out the window and saw Bowman standing by his car. Even from this distance, she could see him watching them.

"No one will testify against him or Darla. They're too afraid."

"What about you?"

"I'm not planning on sticking around. I don't want to end up dead."

"They won't let you leave."

"I'm not going to ask for permission." She looked toward the door as if she suddenly thought Tony might be watching.

"If you want to get out, I can help."

"I've pushed luck enough as it is." Sandy mopped up the syrup on her plate with the last bit of pancake and ate it. As she swallowed, her phone buzzed and she tugged it from her pocket before the second ring. "I need to go."

"I can help you, Sandy."

"Don't worry about me," she said, sliding from the booth. "Just find Cassie. She has a chance to get out."

Riley slid to the edge of the booth, pulled another business card from her back pocket, and pressed it into Sandy's hand. "Just in case."

"I have your number."

"Then give it to another girl who needs help."

"You lived on the streets, didn't you?"

Riley dug a twenty out of her pocket, set it on the table, and placed her untouched coffee cup on top of it. "What makes you say that?"

"A vibe. Like you get what it's like. No judgment in your eyes."

"I've been a cop for eight years. I've seen my share."

"A lot of cops see." She texted a message on her cell phone. "Few understand."

"Lucky, I guess."

"See you around, Lucky."

Riley watched the girl push through the front door and cross the lot outside. She moved toward a dark truck, spoke to the driver, and climbed inside the cab.

Never in Riley's career had she wanted to see two people behind bars more than she did Darla and Jax. Jo-Jo might not ever testify against Jax, but he'd broken enough laws, including evading the police and possession of drugs in his car, to get him some time in prison. A prison sentence would give her the time to build a human trafficking case against him.

Outside, she walked toward the parking lot, watching as Bowman stepped away from his vehicle. He wore a dark sports coat over his white shirt and dark pants, but when a flap of wind caught the edges of the jacket, she glimpsed the weapon at his side.

"What did she say?" he asked.

"There's a motel about twenty miles east of here."

"You want to check it out?"

"I do. If we don't find Cassie, I'll call Sharp."

"Let's go."

The first forty-eight hours in a missing persons case were the most critical. Didn't seem like a case could go cold so fast, but the best leads vanished with the ticking clock. She didn't want to rely on Bowman, but she wanted to stack the odds in her favor. She didn't want to lose this hand. "Okay."

"I'll be right behind you. If we get separated, wait for me."

"Understood."

CHAPTER FIFTEEN

Sunday, September 18, 2:15 p.m.

Two players sat at the mahogany table covered in fine green velvet. They'd been at the table for six hours. The younger of the two, Lenny Vincent, had come to the table with a belly full of bravado, brains, and luck. Like the best players, he believed he could take the Shark. It had been done once before—it could be done again.

The Shark wasn't looking good. His skin was pasty white; it hung on his bones like melting wax. When he sat at the table, he moved slowly as if every muscle in his body ached. The Shark might have been king of the game, but his time had passed. It was Lenny's turn now to ascend the throne.

However, the easy win Lenny expected hadn't materialized. After six hours of play, he realized the old man might lack physical stamina, but his mind remained sharper than ever. Lenny's stash of poker chips was slowly deserting him.

Now, as the Shark laid out the final card on the table, Lenny leaned back in his chair, resisting a clawing wave of panic. The old man's tie remained in place, a tight Windsor knot twisted as taut as Lenny's gut.

"Show me your cards," the Shark whispered.

Lenny's hand was decent enough—two of a kind, aces high—and it could win if the Shark's luck turned. Damn. How many times had he said that to himself in the last few hours? A half dozen? The pile of chips in the center of the table was the largest pot tonight. He was all in. This was the make-or-break moment.

Lenny carefully fanned out his cards on the table.

The old man's eyes shimmered with satisfaction in a way that promised ruin for the younger man.

Lenny's fluttering hopes of a win vanished. The tide would not turn for him. Shit.

A sly, contented grin tipped the edges of the Shark's face. "You're good. Very good."

Even as Lenny watched his opponent's corpse-like hands slide the winnings to his side of the table, he still believed he could pull this off. One more chance.

He imagined Lady Luck standing beside him, smiling. She was a fickle beauty who enjoyed his suffering. She wanted to see him crack and break. Well, she could keep waiting.

Lenny reached for his scotch, now watered by the melted ice, and sipped it. "So this is it."

The old man studied the paper marker written in a bold handwriting when the game began. "Yes."

Lenny rose and moved to a side bar where a collection of crystal decanters sat. He removed the top of one and filled his glass. The scotch was top-shelf, some of the best he'd ever had. Why not enjoy it. He'd need it to do what came next.

The old man smiled. "Get her."

Lenny swallowed the last of the scotch. His heart kick-started into high gear as consequences crowded around him. "Why don't you play for money?"

The Shark held up his glass, studying the spectrum of light in the crystal carvings. "I stopped caring about money a long time ago. There's no juice in it. But if I can take a damaged girl and set her free from this life, well, that has value."

"But why the girls? They're nobodies from the streets. No one cares."

"But I care, and that's all that matters."

"They aren't worth the specialty cards on this table."

The Shark sipped his scotch. "Enough talk. Let's do this."

Lenny moved to the large door and opened it. On the other side sat the girl, Cassie, in a red chair, her head slumped forward. He gently tipped her head back so she looked up at him with glassy eyes. He let go and her chin fell back to her chest.

The Shark stood silent, his attention laser sharp as always.

Cassie raised her head slightly, trying to focus. A tentative smile teased her lips. "Is it time to go yet, Lenny?"

The Shark pushed her chin up further and studied her face. He frowned.

"Will she do? She meets all the items on the list."

The old man with dead eyes frowned. "Her face is too wide and her eyes are too dark."

"You accepted her at the beginning of the game."

"I can see now her hair is also wrong."

"You said you wanted brown," Lenny said. "Her hair is brown."

The Shark traced his cold hand over her hair. "It's too dark," he said, letting her chin slip from his grasp. Releasing her face, he stepped back and pulled a handkerchief from his pocket. Carefully, he wiped his hands.

"I can change her hair. Her makeup."

"She's not the right one."

Lenny brushed the hair from Cassie's eyes. "Don't be hasty with this one. I bet you like her as much as any of them."

As the Shark studied the girl's droopy lids, his mouth thinned. His gaze dropped to her thin white neck. "Where did you get her?"

"From Darla, the lady you told me to use." When the old man didn't appear impressed, he added, "Darla's boyfriend wasn't around. He was arrested by that lady cop."

"I saw the story on the news. She tracked him into the woods."

"I hear Jax and Darla are both furious with the cop. My money is on them killing the cop in the next day or two."

"No, no one touches the cop. She's all mine. Is that clear?"

"Sure. You like the cop?"

"Like? Let's say she's got the kind of looks I like." He motioned to the corded silk rope lying on the poker table. "Finish her. I'm already bored and ready to move on to the next game."

Without hesitating, Lenny picked up the rope and tightened it around the girl's neck. She coughed, reached for his hands, but he was strong and knew it was either her or him. He had too much at stake to back down now.

He felt no remorse as he twisted the rope tighter, and her eyes closed. When her breathing stopped, he didn't let go of the rope, holding on longer for fear she might spontaneously breathe again. When he was sure she was dead, he let her go and watched her body fall limp to the floor.

Lenny pulled a handkerchief from his pocket and wiped his hands. He'd not made the fortune he'd hoped, but there would be other games. He'd find a way out of this hole somehow. "That's it. She's dead, and I'm done?"

The Shark turned a poker chip over and over in his hand. "Not quite."

"What else?"

"You have a wife and two children. Brenda. And your children are Francis and Patricia."

Lenny glanced at the girl. He felt no emotion for the dead girl, but he loved his family. They meant the world to him. "How do you know about my family?"

"You love them. You want to keep them safe."

Lenny's grip tightened around the handkerchief. When Lenny had made a deal with the Shark, he should have expected the old man to keep a card up his sleeve. "I would do anything for them."

"Good." He turned to the poker table and picked up the losing hand as well as another single card. He handed the five cards to Lenny along with a pen, watching closely as Lenny wrote *Loser* on each one.

"After you get rid of her and leave the cards in her pocket, I have one more job for you."

"What kind of job?"

"The kind of job that will ensure your family doesn't die."

***

Riley found the old motel twenty miles east of the interstate as Sandy had described. There were six cottages close together. Once painted white, they'd washed out to a dull gray color. Each had a black door with a small window, and all looked battered by time. The grass was long worn away, leaving a clay-packed yard and a handful of weeds.

Parked in front of it all was the twenty-five-foot motor home.

Riley's seat creaked as she leaned back. She studied the collection of buildings and the courtyard, knowing this was the perfect place for an ambush. It wasn't lost on her that Sandy could be loyal to Darla and Jax and this was a trap.

Drawing in a breath, she glanced in her side mirror and saw Bowman approaching. He'd drawn his gun, holding it close to his side. She unclipped her holster and reached for Cooper's tracking line.

Without a word she was out of the car. She quickly leashed the dog and moved toward Bowman.

"Tell me you would not have come here alone." Bowman wasn't looking at her. Instead, his gaze swept the building and the motor home at a methodical pace.

"Under normal circumstances, no."

"*Never* was the right answer." He raised his weapon. "Stay."

"What? Like Cooper?"

He shot her a look that silenced her next comment. He moved to the first building, doing a careful sweep of the structure. Then he moved to the second and the third and so on. When he returned to her side, he nodded toward the motor home. "Any movement?"

"Nothing."

The motor home curtains were drawn, and out front stood a trio of lawn chairs, which she supposed served as a waiting room when the place was operational.

He carefully pulled off dark glasses and tucked them in his pocket. "You think Darla is here?"

"I don't know."

"Has Carter made bail?" he asked.

"He wasn't scheduled to be in court until tomorrow, but that doesn't mean he didn't get an earlier date."

"Do you think they would have taken off?"

"Not while Jo-Jo is still alive. They'll wait for her to be released from the hospital. In their minds, she belongs to them."

She stared at the dingy motor home. She'd never turned a trick on the streets. Never used. But her time on the streets had amounted to only a few weeks. If it had been months, and she was hungry enough . . . desperation could easily have led her here.

A muscle ticked in Bowman's jaw. He moved to the motor home and banged on the door with his fist. Both stood in silence, waiting. He reached for the door handle.

"Last I checked, you're a civilian now," she said.

The edge of his mouth ticked up. "That's amusing."

"I'm police. You're not. You get shot and it's my ass."

"I'm not going to get shot."

"If you do find anything, it won't be admissible in court."

A curtain in the trailer fluttered, and his gaze caught it at the exact moment Riley did. He motioned for her to stand to his left, away from the front door. He banged on the door again with his fist.

She shouted, "Police. Trooper Tatum. I'm here for Darla."

Silence. Then steady, controlled footsteps. No rush. No worry. She guessed Darla had encountered police enough to see them as an annoyance rather than a real threat.

The doorknob rattled, turned, and the door opened—to Jax. Bowman raised his gun, and Riley held her ground with Cooper alert at her side.

She was struck by Carter's muscled build. In the woods, he'd been sitting against the tree, but now he loomed tall. A gold-capped incisor matched a thick necklace hanging around his neck. Dark running suit, metallic T-shirt, and expensive athletic shoes—he'd mastered the style of the pimp as if he'd been born to the job. A cigarette dangled from his fingers.

"Jax Carter," she said. "So you did make bail early."

"Trooper Tatum." His grin widened until it swept right and landed on Bowman. Straightening, he sniffed. "Nice of you to pay me a visit." He lifted up the hem of his pant leg to reveal an ankle bracelet. "As you can see, I'm not going anywhere. Playing by the rules like a good boy."

"We're looking for Cassie," Riley said.

Carter leaned his forearm on the doorframe. The thick scent of body odor mingled with cheap aftershave. "Do I look like a halfway house?"

Bowman didn't speak, but a controlled ferocity radiated from him, much as it would from a guard dog.

"Is the girl with you?" she asked.

He couldn't suppress a smile. "I don't know a Cassie."

"Darla does."

Carter held his hands chest level and stepped out of the motor home. "You'd have to ask Darla. I was in lockup until late Friday."

Bowman shifted. "Where's Darla?"

Carter sighed, and turning his head slightly, shouted, "Darla, get your ass out here. Police want to have a word."

Footsteps slightly rocked the motor home before she appeared in the doorway. Greasy dark hair hung around her round face. Thick eye shadow accentuated her wide-set eyes, and smudged lipstick drew attention to full lips. She wore a tank top and faded jeans that hugged full hips.

"Jax, who's this?"

"This is Trooper Tatum," Carter said. "She's looking for you."

Darla folded her arms. "What do you want, Trooper Tatum?"

"Where's Cassie?" Riley asked.

"I don't know a Cassie," Darla said.

"That's not what I heard. I know Tony is hunting you," she said. "He wants his girl back."

Darla's muscles tightened, drawing attention to a rose tattoo on her arm. "I don't know a Cassie."

"Where've you been the last couple of days?" Riley asked.

"Here at the trailer, waiting for my baby," Darla said.

"You have ID?" Riley asked.

"Yeah, somewhere." She patted her pockets but only found a half stick of gum. "I don't know where it is. And I don't have to give it to you. I know the law."

Always testing. Riley reached for her phone. "I bet Jax has something in that trailer that's violating the terms of his bail."

"I have your ID, baby," Carter said.

Darla smoothed long fingers over a bruise on her forearm. "You don't have to show her."

His grin widened. "We don't want trouble."

Cooper was silently watching, but his tension radiated up his tracking line into her arm. Carter handed her the ID, and she studied it. Darla was twenty-three.

Riley held on to the license as she spoke. "I know Kevin Lewis bought Vicky. Who bought Cassie?"

Darla rubbed the underside of her nose with her index finger. "I don't know Cassie. And girls like her take off all the time."

"She didn't take off. You sold her," Riley said.

Darla's bloodshot eyes sharpened. "I don't know anything about that."

"What did you do with the money the john paid for Cassie? Did you tell Jax about it?"

"Of course I told Jax," Darla said.

Carter glared at his girlfriend. "Shut your mouth. They're fishing. They ain't got nothing on us."

Darla fingered a gold hoop earring. "This is harassment."

Bowman was silent, but he didn't miss a detail. His hand wasn't on his weapon, but it was close. At Quantico, his draw was one of the fastest.

"Are you gonna arrest us or not?" Carter asked.

"Not," Riley said as she handed the ID to Darla.

"But we'll let Tony know that Darla is with you," Bowman said.

Carter shook his head. "What the hell? Don't go spreading lies to Tony."

"The real sharks are swimming on the outside of the tank, aren't they, Jax? But you already know that," Bowman said.

"Little fish like you don't have a chance against the sharks," Riley said.

"Fuck you," Carter responded.

Deflecting the comment, Bowman said, "If I were you, I'd get in that trailer and start driving. In about thirty minutes, this won't be a safe place for you anymore."

Darla chewed her bottom lip. "I do know a girl named Cassie, but I didn't sell her to nobody. She drove off with a guy named Lenny. Tony was cool with it."

"Tony's not going to be cool when she doesn't come back."

"I don't know anything about when she's getting back."

"What's his last name?" Riley asked.

"I don't ask for last names," Darla said.

"Shut up," Carter said.

"Why did he want her?" Riley asked.

"The usual, I guess." Darla shook her head. "Tell Tony he needs to find Lenny."

"I'll bet it's easier for Tony to find you," Riley said.

Carter cursed, flicking his cigarette to the dirt and crushing it with his boot.

"Did you dye her hair?" Riley asked.

"Yeah. Lenny said he liked dark hair."

"It ain't Darla's fault you got a missing hooker," Carter said. "And for all you know, she'll stumble back into town any minute with cash in her pocket."

Riley reached for her phone and took a picture of the two. "Texting Tony your location now. Nice picture, by the way."

Carter cursed as he pushed Darla inside and slammed the door. Seconds later the engine roared to life and rumbled from the tired lot.

After they drove off, Riley opened the back door of her SUV and watched as Cooper jumped inside. "Thanks. I wish the trip had been more productive."

Bowman grimaced. "This case has been full of blind alleys."

She shook her head. "You sound old when you say it that way."

"I do feel old right now."

"How old are you?"

"Thirty-nine."

"When I get to be your age, I hope I'm more optimistic."

Her wisecrack coaxed a grin as he slowly shook his head. "Right."

She shifted to an uncomfortable subject. "When will your people know anything about the video?"

"In a day or two."

The idea of a whole bunch of strangers watching her like that stoked her shame.

As if reading her thoughts he said, "Remember, we're *private* security. We don't share information."

"Still, more people in the loop."

"You didn't do anything wrong."

The thought that anyone would pity her like she pitied Sandy or Cassie sickened her. "And you think that logic is going to wash away the emotion? The lone detail that separates me from Vicky and the others is a winning hand of cards."

"You're the lucky one."

"Right."

***

Despite a dozen years, the Shark could still play back the video of that last girl and feel the bitter disappointment of losing her. By the final round of games that year, he'd been on such a winning streak that he never considered losing as a possibility. The old man believed he was invincible and didn't need Lady Luck. He would play and kill for as long as he wanted. And then, the other player laid down his winning hand of cards. The odds of a royal flush were so distant that he thought at first it was a trick of his mind or cheating. But he regulated the cards and the games carefully and knew the other player hadn't cheated. Lady Luck had allowed him to rise to the top, and then she sent him crashing to the earth with the turn of a few cards.

The other player, instead of looking elated, was clearly relieved.

The Shark raised a trembling hand to his gray hair and, nodding, said, "The girl lives."

He could have killed them both. He had the power. No one would have known. But the rules were the rules. Lady Luck determined which girls he could kill and which he could not. And if a man didn't honor his personal creed, what was he worth? So the girl and the gambler left.

Days after their release, he returned to the tables in a legal casino, determined to test his luck and Lady Luck's devotion. But when he sat at the table, he was on edge, thinking and rethinking every hand, actually fearful he would lose again. He folded the hand. Walked away. The next game was the same. And the next.

He'd lost his edge.

Lady Luck had turned her back on him.

Then the docs told him that his heart had turned to shit. They told him to give up his cigars and the booze and maybe he'd have a few crappy years of watching his strength fade away.

But the craving to kill burned inside him just as it had when he was a young man, and he was determined to savor these last games. Now that his days on this earth were dwindling, he had nothing really to lose and everything to gain.

The Shark sat back in his chair, staring at the lights of the city below. He'd lived most of his childhood on the streets, fighting and scrapping for every bite of bread. The streets had pounded him, bloodied him, and done their best to destroy him, but he had climbed up out of the hole.

He'd muscled his way out of so many scrapes, but he wouldn't escape death. It was coming. But he'd be damned if he'd waste away in a chair, cowering. He'd spent too many years living on the edge, risking and winning.

It wasn't enough to play more games and kill more women. He needed more risk. That's why he'd sent Riley the video. He knew she'd take it to Shield or the cops and that the search for him would intensify. His heartbeat jacked up a notch.

The first two girls were little more than bread crumbs in a trail that would lead Riley to him. Now it was Lenny's turn to play his last part.

CHAPTER SIXTEEN

Monday, September 19, 9:00 a.m.

Riley pushed through the front doors of the hospital, tensing the moment the antiseptic smell hit her nose. She'd been to the emergency room enough times to take statements from victims. Eight years on the force should have made it easier, but it didn't. The smells of the hospital always reminded her of her mother's last days and the long, difficult visits she and her stepfather had made to her bedside.

"Please, Mom, don't leave me," she whispered once in her mother's ear. *"Don't leave me alone with him. Fight for your life."*

But her mother simply smiled and brushed the hair from her eyes. "You'll be fine. He's a good man."

"He's not good. He's sick."

Her mother closed her eyes. "You're wrong about him."

Riley rode the elevator to the seventh floor and paused at the nurses' station to show her badge. "I'm here to see Jo-Jo. How's she doing?"

"Awake, but moving slow. She was watching television a few minutes ago."

"Thanks," Riley said. "Do you have any update on her family?"

"No. She gave us a number, but no one answered. I'm not sure it's legit. She's barely said a dozen words."

"Okay." Down the hallway, she pushed into the room to find the girl sitting in her bed, remote in one hand, a cast on the other. She stared at the television, switching channels as if nothing really mattered. The plate of food was at least half-eaten. A good sign.

"Jo-Jo."

The girl looked over with a left eye black-and-blue and swollen shut. Her lip was split, and there was a nasty cut across her neck. "I'm Riley Tatum. I came to see you a few days ago, but you were out of it."

"You're a cop?"

"That's right." She moved toward the bed, pulled up a chair, and sat. "How did you know that?"

"I've seen you around talking to the girls." Jo-Jo shut off the television. "I know what happened to Vicky. I saw it on the news. They didn't say much, but I knew it was her."

"She was a good friend?"

"Sorta."

"Why did Jax Carter go ballistic on you? What happened?"

She smoothed her hand over the rumpled fabric as if erasing the wrinkles would bring order to her screwed-up life. Her tone was laced with anger as she said, "Why don't you ask him?"

"I have. But you know Jax. He's not a chatty guy."

Jo-Jo studied her for a long moment. "Where is he?"

"He's out on bail. But don't worry. You're in a lockdown ward. He can't get you in here."

"He's going to be looking for me. He'll finish what he started when I get out."

"He won't. I'll see to it."

Jo-Jo shook her head, absently plucking at her blanket.

"Are you willing to press charges against him?"

Jo-Jo rolled her eyes. "No."

"We've charged him with a half-dozen crimes that have nothing to do with you. But that won't hold him long."

Absently, she scratched the bandage holding her IV in place. "You're the one that chased him into the woods, aren't you?"

"That's me."

"Why would you do that? Nobody chases Jax."

"That would explain the shocked look on his face when he saw me coming over the crest of the hill. He's used to getting his way, but so am I."

"But why did you do it?"

"I saw the surveillance camera footage of him beating you. Nobody deserves that."

Her brow knotted. "You went after him because of what he did to me?"

"Aren't you worth it?"

"That was stupid. I'm nobody."

"When I watched that video, I saw a kid. A kid that could be anything she wanted to be if she had a chance."

"A chance? I've about as much chance of getting out of this life as I do winning a million dollars."

"I can't get you a million dollars, but I've a few chances up my sleeve for a better life."

Tears glistened. "How can I have a chance? I don't have family and the one guy that was nice to me just about beat me to death."

"I know places where you can go. Good people who can take care of you. It's not hopeless."

"You make it sound easy."

"You and I both know it's not easy, Jo-Jo." She sat back. "What's your real name?"

"Everyone calls me Jo-Jo."

"I didn't ask you what everyone calls you. What's your real name?"

She plucked at a stray thread on the sheet. "It's Melanie."

"Melanie. That's pretty. Melanie, what's your last name?"

"Don't call me that name. She's not me anymore." She shook her head. "I can't have you calling my family. With them, it's worse than Jax."

"So the number you gave the hospital is false?"

"Maybe."

"No judgment. Be nice if I can tell the nurse she can stop calling. I'm not calling anyone. I just want to know who I'm talking to."

"Melanie Lawrence."

"How old are you? And let's not start with eighteen."

She lifted her chin a notch. "Fifteen."

"Okay," Riley leaned forward, "Jo-Jo, how did you know Vicky was the murdered girl?"

"Because Jax and Darla sold her to this weird guy."

"Weird how?"

"Most guys don't want the girls for more than an hour. But this guy insisted he have Vicky for the weekend. And he kept harping on her brown hair and how her look was perfect."

"Her look?"

"This guy, Kevin, wanted a girl with brown hair. Jax brought us both to show, but Kevin said I was too skinny. Too hard looking. Too blond."

"Vicky was new to the streets?"

"Yeah. She'd only been working a few weeks. Did Kevin kill Vicky?"

"We're waiting on the DNA tests, but that's my bet."

"When she didn't come back, I told Jax he had to do something. He got pissed. That's when he started whaling on me."

"And then you stabbed him?"

"I didn't want to die."

"I get it. And that wound slowed him enough so I could catch him."

"Good."

"Did Kevin say where he was going with Vicky?"

"He said it wasn't far. Said there was a party about twenty miles west of the city."

"What kind of party?"

"Said he was playing poker and always did better when he had Lady Luck with him."

"He said Lady Luck?"

"Yeah. I thought it was weird."

"Anything else?"

"Is that why Kevin killed Vicky? Did he run out of luck and get mad at her?"

"It had something to do with that, but I don't have all the pieces yet."

Tears welled in her eyes and when one spilled, she wiped it away. "Jax convinced Vicky to run away with him about four weeks ago. He said he loved her." Swollen lips twitched into a wry smile. "He said the same thing to me as well as Darla."

Riley sat silent for a moment, knowing there was nothing she could say to the girl right now. "I saw Sandy."

"Is she okay?"

"She's worried about Cassie. She's been gone for a couple of days."

Jo-Jo pushed back a strand of dirty blond hair. "Shit. And she's new. Not as new as Vicky, but Darla would've fixed her up. Did Kevin come back for her?"

"Kevin is dead," Riley said. "Someone shot him."

Her brow wrinkled in a frown. "Good. If he killed Vicky, then I'm glad he's dead. But who took Cassie?"

"Do you remember anything else about Kevin? Did he have friends?"

"Kevin told Jax there was a tournament," Jo-Jo said. "He said they might need more girls. He wanted to pass Jax's name along to the others. Jax was thrilled."

"Did Kevin say where the other players were coming from?"

"All over. They all wanted to challenge the old man."

"Any names?"

She shook her head. "No."

Riley drew a slow breath.

"Where's Jax?" Jo-Jo asked.

"Right now, he's hiding out in his motor home with Darla. A friend of mine put the fear of God in him, so he's gone underground."

A smile teased the edges of her lips. "That must be some friend."

"He's not someone to mess around with."

She tugged at the sheet's coarse cotton. "Jax won't stay afraid long. He's mean, but not always smart."

Right now Carter was trying to stay out of sight and alive. "You're supposed to get out of here tomorrow, right?"

Panic flared in her eyes. "I don't think I'm ready to leave."

"I know. It's safe here. But I know a place. It's a house run by a nice couple. I can call them for you."

Annoyance flashed across her bruised face. "You can't make me go anywhere."

Riley's phone pinged with a text from Duke. She read it and texted back. "I'm not going to make you go anywhere," she told Jo-Jo.

There was a knock at the door and the girl stiffened, sitting straighter in her bed. "Who's that?"

"A friend."

"The scary one?"

"No, though he looks meaner than a snake. Don't let the ink scare you. He's about the most gentle guy you'll ever meet." She moved to the door and opened it to let Duke into the room.

Jo-Jo studied him closely, her body as tense as a taut rubber band. "Who's this, your grandfather?"

Laughing, Duke rubbed the back of his neck with his hands, showing off an arm covered in tattoos. "Hey, I might be old enough to be her dad, but not her granddad. I'm not that broken down, kid."

Jo-Jo shook her head. "You're up there, Pops."

Duke looked at Riley, amused. "Tough crowd."

"They all are at this stage. Didn't you say I took a swing at you?"

He rubbed his chin. "Barely missed."

Another knock on the door and Maria entered. She was grinning and had a large grocery bag full of clothes. "Sorry, I stopped at the nurse's station. I know one of the gals from church." She smiled at the young girl. "So you must be Jo-Jo. I'm Maria and this is Duke, my husband. We run a restaurant and we shelter kids. And in this bag are clothes. I had to guess your size, so there're all kinds."

"Her real name is Melanie Lawrence," Riley said.

"Melanie," Maria said, smiling. "I like that. Very pretty."

"My name is Jo-Jo," the girl insisted.

"Okay." Maria nodded as if knowing the kid clung to the name because she was afraid.

"Are you, like, foster parents?" Jo-Jo asked. "I've done foster care and it sucks."

Duke slid a ringed hand into his front pocket. "We work with social services, but we don't take government money. Our place is all donation based. And it's not foster care. We offer a safe harbor until you figure out what's next."

"So what's the catch?" Jo-Jo asked.

"You agree to come with us, and I'll talk to social services. Then you got to go to school," Duke said without hesitation. "Education will get you out of this life."

"School." She laughed. "Right."

Riley pulled a card from her pocket and handed it to Jo-Jo. "The decision is yours. I can't make you go. Neither can Duke or Maria."

Jo-Jo flicked the edge of the card, not bothering to look at it.

"They gave me a second chance, and I took it. If not for them, I don't know where I'd be now. Play it smart, and take the offer. You won't get another one."

***

After Jo-Jo's sullen acceptance of Duke's offer, Riley left the hospital, not convinced the kid would have her happy ending. The road ahead would be tough for a girl who'd seen too much in her fifteen years.

As she opened her car door, her phone buzzed. Agent Sharp's name popped up on the display. "To what do I owe the pleasure?"

"We found Lewis's hotel, and I now have a search warrant. Want to play agent one more time before you put the uniform back on?"

"I do."

"I'll text you the address."

She arrived at the hotel a half hour later. It was decent but not plush like the casino hotels in the big cities. A black SUV was waiting for her as she crossed the lot. Bowman got out, his dark suit and glasses making him look like a fed. If he really was retired, you'd never know it looking at him.

"What're you doing here?" she asked.

"Agent Sharp called me."

"So I'm not the only one he called to the party. My feelings are hurt."

Bowman tipped his head toward her. "Given the choice, he'd pick you over me any day. I would."

The deep timbre of his voice triggered a rush of heat in her body. She cleared her throat and looked at the hotel. "Wonder if Kevin was on his way up the ladder of success or down it?"

"If I had to guess, I'd say down. My guess is that he owed money, and that's what got him killed."

"Makes sense."

She approached the front desk and waited until the clerk looked up from her computer screen before she raised her badge. The midtwenties woman wore her dark hair pulled into a tight ponytail, chic glasses, and a navy-blue suit that didn't quite fit. "Yes?"

"I'm Trooper Tatum, and this is Mr. Bowman. Agent Sharp called earlier."

"He's upstairs." She lowered her voice. "In that dead man's room."

"Right."

The clerk coded a new plastic key and handed one to Riley. "Room 202. The elevators are around the corner."

"Thanks."

They made their way to the bank of elevators and Bowman punched 2. As the doors closed, two young girls about the age of twelve scrambled into the car. They both wore wet bathing suits wrapped in towels and dripping with water. The girls glanced at Bowman and Riley, making no effort to hide their curiosity.

One whispered something to the other, and they both giggled. Riley couldn't remember a time when she ran free or kicked around with a friend. Her mother and stepfather had kept a tight rein on her, believing if they gave her too much time to herself, she'd find trouble. *Monsters live on the streets*, her mother used to say. They also lived in the house, though her mother never would admit it.

The doors dinged open and Riley and Bowman exited, finding their way to room 202. They both pulled on latex gloves. A swipe of the key and they were inside. Cigar smoke. The scent permeated the room.

Riley doubled back and checked the room door. "It's a nonsmoking room."

Bowman sniffed. "Surprised he'd break that rule?"

Sharp and Martin were in the room. While Sharp searched a drawer, Martin dusted a doorknob for prints. A "Do Not Disturb" sign hung on the doorknob.

Martin looked up, his gaze settling on Bowman. "I need you both to sign my log so I know who was at my crime scene. Don't want it turning into a circus."

Bowman picked up the clipboard holding the sheet and signed his name and phone number. His bold handwriting bored into the paper.

He handed the pen and paper to Riley, who quickly signed her name under his.

A scan of the room didn't reveal much at first glance. The bed was made, the curtains drawn. In the bathroom, the toothbrush, toothpaste, and other toiletries were lined up in a neat row.

"I noticed a "Do Not Disturb" tag on the door," Riley said.

Sharp straightened. "He didn't want the maid in his room. He wasn't scheduled to check out for another three days, so the staff left the room alone."

"Can't blame the guy for no maid," Bowman said. "I traveled a great deal and always declined the cleaning service. Never liked strangers in my space."

Riley's budget had never allowed for much travel. All her extra money went first to her college education, then the house, and now Hanna. "I guess you've seen about all the world there is to see."

"Basically. What about you?"

"I've seen New Orleans and Virginia."

"You're still young."

But Riley's budget would be tight until Hanna graduated college. "That's true."

"He didn't spend much time here," Bowman said, looking in the closet where a dark suit and three dress shirts hung. On the floor by the bed sat a pair of shiny Italian loafers.

"Those shoes set him back a grand and the suits twice that," she said.

"How do you know?" Agent Sharp asked.

She touched the soft fabric and glanced at the label. Armani. "Take my word. When we found him, he was wearing gold cuff links, a gold chain around his neck, and a diamond pinky ring."

"Guy rolls large," Sharp said.

"Part of the image," Bowman added.

She moved toward the windows and opened the curtains. It was a view of the parking lot. Not exciting.

"We found a rental car receipt in his pocket," Sharp said. "I called the company, and they're going to track its location via GPS. When they find the car, they'll contact me." His phone rang, and frowning, he said, "I have to take this. Be right back."

Riley moved to the desk, where she spotted a hotel writing pad. The imprint of letters caught in the light prompted her to grab a pencil and shadow the page. The words *Round Six* appeared. *Round Six*. The DVD sent to her had said *Round Five*.

With her phone she snapped a picture of the pad and asked Martin to bag it in a plastic evidence bag. She moved to the nightstand, opened the drawer, and found a Bible. She lifted the Bible and thumbed through the pages, knowing if she were a gambler, this would be the spot where she'd hide something. Finding nothing, she moved to a black leather bag. In one side pocket she found a few zip-top plastic bags, and in another a few rumpled tissues. If this guy had anything of value, he was wearing it when he died.

"Lewis has a record," Bowman said. "No surprise there. Embezzlement and a couple of domestic abuse charges."

"How do you know this?" Riley asked.

"Our computer guy at Shield."

"Of course," Riley said. "Who filed the abuse complaints?"

"His ex-girlfriend. In her statement she claimed he tried to kill her. But when it came down to it, she wouldn't actually file the charges."

"Where was this?" Riley asked.

"Las Vegas. The ex-girlfriend worked as a dealer in one of the big casinos. That was three years ago, and since then he got married and his record has been clean."

"Or he's smarter," Riley said.

Bowman nodded. "Once you get a warrant and have a look at his financials, you'll find he had a lot of debt."

"Computer guy whisper that fact in your ear?" she asked.

Bowman shrugged. "You'll find out when you see the records."

Riley knew she'd be back in uniform tomorrow and her active time in this investigation would be limited. Pushing aside regret, she looked under the bed and behind the curtains. Finding nothing, she moved to the bathroom. Her first stop was the toilet, where she lifted the tank lid. Taped to the underside of the lid was a zip-top bag crammed with cash. "Who says those stings with vice never taught me anything."

"You worked vice?"

"In a miniskirt, halter top, and thigh-high boots. I stood on the street corner in April and lured johns to a hotel room. Loved the look on their faces when the deputies came busting out of the bathroom."

Bowman stared at her as if trying to picture the image. Interest sparked.

She arched a brow. "I can promise you, it wasn't that exciting."

"You underestimate yourself."

She called out to Martin and as he took photographs, she opened the bag and carefully spread the contents out on the bathroom counter. "The top few bills are hundreds, but after that, it's a few twenties and lots of ones. Looks good on the surface."

She pulled out a small black velvet bag and worked her finger into the drawstring. She removed a large gold coin. "What the hell?"

Bowman leaned closer. "It's not currency."

"No. Not currency." But the coin was perfectly formed. One side was smooth, and on the other was an embossed number six. "Six. Round Six?" She showed him the picture she'd just snapped of the notepad.

Martin glanced in his viewfinder. "I need another memory card. Don't touch anything."

"May I?" Bowman said, reaching for her phone.

She handed it to him.

"I'm texting it to my IT guy."

"Sure."

He typed a few quick numbers and as the image whooshed away, he handed her the phone back. "You were round five. The first games were in New Orleans and the sixth and seventh games were here."

Four previous victims. Her. Vicky. And possibly Cassie. "Do you think he only kills after winning a poker game?"

"I don't know. A man like him gets a taste for killing. He could very well have other scenarios that give him permission to kill."

There were so many runaways. Dozens could go missing and no one might notice. She dug into the dazed memories surrounding her missing days, searching for references to the number five. But she couldn't remember anything.

"Maybe forensics can pull a print."

"If they do, it will likely be Lewis's."

Bowman scanned the perfectly scrubbed bathroom and looked at the room again. "My guess is you'll only find traces of Lewis in the room. Lewis might not have been careful, but whoever is sponsoring this game covers his tracks."

Sharp returned, whistling when he saw the spread of cash. "Where would you hold a game like that?"

"Somewhere nice," Riley said, almost to herself. "A big private home. Jo-Jo said Vicky was going somewhere twenty or so miles west."

"We've plenty of houses like that in western Virginia," Sharp said. His cell buzzed again and a glance at the display had him rolling his eyes. "I can't complete a thought without getting interrupted."

When he was gone, Bowman spoke in a low voice. "The Shark's here because of you and Shield."

"Why Shield?"

"In New Orleans he sent Shield pictures of you and the girls he killed. You are the prize. Shield is the challenger."

"Is this all because he lost a damn hand of cards?"

"He loves a challenge and winning. Control is clearly a number-one priority for him. He lost you once, so now he's going for you again, and he wants to make sure Shield knows it."

"Damn."

"This time, he's also playing against Shield's brain and mine. It's beyond card games now."

"In New Orleans, did the forensic evidence suggest multiple killers?"

"We found the same DNA on each victim, which suggests one man did all the killing," Bowman said.

"So why does he want to share now? Why have Lewis kill Vicky?" Riley asked.

"I don't know."

"The Shark covers his tracks so damn well. I'm beginning to think there're no trails to this psychopath."

"There is one trail. You."

CHAPTER SEVENTEEN

Tuesday, September 20, 8:00 a.m.

Riley had been back in uniform and in the patrol vehicle with Cooper for less than an hour when the call came that Lewis's rental car had been found. Dispatch radioed in the report from a man who had spotted it parked at a country church at the western edge of the county.

Riley drove to the site and found the church at the intersection of two secondary roads. The abandoned church was a small building, painted with a graying white and sporting a tilting spire on a patchy roof. Several of the windows were broken and patched with plastic and duct tape. The grass around the building and a half-dozen worn headstones in a small graveyard had been recently cut. Time had long since passed this place by.

Out of the car, she hooked Cooper's line, donned gloves, and unfastened the strap holding her gun in its holster. She approached the car, a black Lexus covered in mud and peppered with bullet holes. The tires had been sliced and the windows smashed.

She allowed Cooper to sniff around the scene. Leaning in, she peered through one of the broken windows and spotted the keys in the ignition. The car matched the description of Lewis's rental car.

"Shame to waste such a good car," she said.

Blood splattered on the windshield and soaked the driver's seat. On the floor there were a half-dozen diet soda cans and an empty box of no-sleep pills. She popped the trunk release. Moving slowly to the back, she watched Cooper as he sniffed. The trunk was empty.

The door to the church opened, Cooper tensed, and she turned to see an old man shuffling toward her. She recognized him. He was Russell Hudson, the man who had found Vicky's body.

"About time the cops came out," he said.

"Mr. Hudson, you called this in?"

Hudson moved to within feet of her, making no effort to hide his curiosity as his gaze scanned her body. "Yeah. I called it. You ever find out who killed that girl? I still haven't been able to get on that field and cut the grass. The music festival promoter is calling me daily, asking about the case."

"We're working on it."

"Working on it doesn't get you off my land or get my work done. The promoter is talking about suing me for breach of contract."

Riley didn't rise to his anger. "Mr. Hudson, this car matches the description of her killer's car. It's an odd coincidence that you made the call both times."

Hudson's assessing gaze catalogued her from head to toe before he shook his head. "You think it's fun for me to take time out of my day to deal with this kind of thing?"

"An odd coincidence."

"All I know is that it's one more problem for me to handle."

"When did you first see the car?" Riley asked.

"This morning. Came by the church to check on a few things."

"The church has been closed for years."

"We get homeless people and the occasional teenager setting up shop inside. I chase 'em off."

"You see anyone when you arrived?"

"Nope. Just the car."

"And the car looked like this?"

"You mean, shot to hell? Yeah. Like that. Whoever got ahold of it had their fun and dumped it on me to clean up."

"You live in the area, right?" she asked.

"Up the road a few miles."

"And you didn't see anything out of the ordinary?"

"Nope, didn't see anyone. And I'm around a lot. I know my land."

Either this man knew more than he was saying or someone was baiting her, dropping clues like bread crumbs to lure her toward something. "Judging by the holes in the side of the car, multiple shots were fired. Did you hear any gunfire?"

"Nope. Didn't hear a sound. I reckon they shot it up and then parked it here." He shrugged thin shoulders, and she noticed the deep veins in his hands and the sallow complexion of his skin. "What did you say your name was?"

"Trooper Riley Tatum."

"Riley Tatum." He said her name as if testing. A lot of the old guys didn't see her as a cop or take her all that seriously. "Pleasure to meet you again."

"Yes, sir. How can I reach you if I have more questions?"

"I have a phone but no answering machine right now. Tired of the phone calls from the press and anyone else who has a gripe with me."

"No way to leave a message?"

"If I'm there, I'm there. If I'm gone, try again."

"Do me a favor and stay right here." She called dispatch and requested a second car.

"I've things to do."

"Yes, sir. Please stay where you are." Within three minutes a sheriff's deputy patrol car pulled onto the scene. She spoke to the deputy and explained the situation.

"My dog and I are going to walk the area and see if we pick up a scent." With the deputy and Hudson standing by, they moved around the car, Cooper dropping his nose to the ground and sniffing. The dog pulled Riley along the edges of the parking lot and then toward the woods. They were fifteen feet into the brush when she heard the rustle of branches. Cooper tensed and raised his head. "What is it, Cooper?"

The dog sniffed the air. She listened, her hand slowly sliding to the grip of her weapon. She spotted a mound of leaves, and as she moved closer, she saw the pale fingers jutting out from the pile. Carefully, she knelt and brushed away the thin layer of leaves. Lying beneath was Cassie's pale body.

***

Bowman pushed through the doors of the tech department and strode toward the large corner office of Garrett Andrews. In his late thirties, Andrews had been a Special Forces operative with Delta serving fifteen years on active duty before an IED exploded under his Humvee. The blast killed three of the four men in his unit. Garrett sustained burns over his back, and the doctors dug shrapnel and bone fragments from his body that left much of his arms and legs scarred. When he awoke in the hospital three days later, Shield, who'd only known him by reputation, was at his bedside. He offered Andrews a job at Shield Security. Andrews showed up eight weeks later and began helping with tech support.

"Find anything on the video?" Bowman asked.

Andrews sat at a desk that faced away from the window and toward a bank of ten computer screens. He didn't bother glancing up from them as a vague look of annoyance crossed his sharp features. "You gave the video to me yesterday."

"That's twenty-four hours ago. With your talents, that should be plenty for you." Andrews had triple majored in college, balancing an engineering degree with ones in mathematics and philosophy. He'd always amazed his roommates with his ability to recall every detail he read the first time through. His idea of studying for tests was skimming the textbook and getting to bed early.

Andrews grunted and reached under a pile of papers for the DVD. He pushed it into a computer and the image of Riley appeared on the screen.

Bowman squared his shoulders, sliding his hand into his pocket. Fingertips brushed the knife he always carried. He studied Riley's narrow face, more disturbed than he should be by an image taken over a dozen years ago.

"You said she's a cop now?" Andrews asked.

"That's right. Eight years."

Andrews sat back in his chair, folding scarred arms over his chest. "I haven't pinned the exact location. The painting on the wall does look like a Matisse, though I seriously doubt it is real."

"I know next to nothing about art, but I know that name. How do you know it's fake?"

"If it were real, it would be one of his lesser-known works, and even then it would be worth millions. Not likely to be hanging on a wall."

"Based on what Shield's informant told him, the Shark is wealthy."

"The furnishings in this room appear to be top grade." Andrews tapped a few keys on his computer, responding to a message that had nothing to do with their conversation. "I've isolated sounds in your tape. There's Mozart playing in the background and what sounds like someone clicking their fingers."

"Clicking their fingers?"

Andrews raised his hand and snapped. "Like that. A nervous habit, perhaps. Shadows on the walls suggest there are at least two other people in the room." Andrews advanced the video and they both heard gruff words spoken. The voice was male.

"He's hard to understand," Bowman said.

"There are two distinct voices. They don't sound young but aren't old. The one with the deeper voice is telling Riley she's lucky. He doesn't sound happy."

"Given the batting average for this guy, that's an understatement," Bowman said. "What about accents?"

"Neither had distinct speech patterns." Andrews held one side of a headset to his ear. "The men are talking about the winning player choosing if she lives or dies. The decision is made that Riley will live."

"Why let her live?"

"Riley was heavily drugged. In fact, judging by her pale skin and the way her eyes were turned back in her head, I wonder if they almost overdosed her. She wouldn't have remembered anything."

Bowman stopped the recording and studied her. "I see a faint bruise on her cheek. Knowing her, she resisted at some point."

"Maybe. I see no other major physical issues. That doesn't mean there weren't any."

Tension gripped in his gut. "Right."

Andrews sat back, pulled off his glasses, and rubbed his eyes. "So this prick left the DVD at her house?"

Bowman swallowed his anger, knowing he'd channel it when the time came. "He did."

"You say that like it really pisses you off."

"It does."

"We've not worked a case before, but word is you have ice water in your veins."

"Emotions don't get in the way of the work, but I care about all my cases."

Chuckling, Andrews replaced his glasses and grinned. "You didn't take your eyes off the screen when the camera was on her. When I talked about them hurting her, you clenched your fingers into a fist like you wanted to punch someone. Dude, that ice water is thawing. You've a thing for Tatum, don't you?"

Bowman ran his hand through his hair. "I don't know."

"I'll take that as a yes."

CHAPTER EIGHTEEN

Tuesday, September 20, 6:00 p.m.

Riley watched as Sharp knelt by Cassie's body, taking in the details now burned in her mind. The girl had been strangled, like Vicky, with a thin cord. Her nails and toenails were manicured, and her hair fashioned in soft curls that still hung around her face in a grotesquely odd way. Cassie wore the yellow dress, though it gapped around her waist and breasts.

Sharp approached Riley. "Tell me again how you found her?"

"Cooper and I responded to a call. When we found Kevin Lewis's car covered in bullet holes and blood, I decided to do a sweep of the area with Cooper and we found her."

"Where's Cooper?"

"In the SUV hanging out."

"Two bodies within a week, Riley. What the hell gives?"

"Bowman thinks it's the Shark."

"Yeah, I understand that. Is this all because of you?"

She tightened her jaw, wishing she didn't have to speak the words. "Yeah, I think so."

"You still have no memories of the time you were taken?"

"Only very vague ones. Smell of cigars. Sound of poker chips. Nothing concrete. If I had anything solid, I would have brought it to you."

Sharp muttered a curse. "The forensic guys didn't find anything on the cards you gave me."

"There was also a video delivered to me. It was shot during those missing days. I gave it to Bowman to analyze."

"Shit."

"He said his people have state-of-the-art equipment that can analyze it faster than anything we have."

A dark SUV arrived on the scene; she recognized it as Bowman's. Oddly, she felt tremendous relief. Bowman strode toward them, his long legs eating up the distance. Deep lines were etched around his mouth and eyes as if the frown had always been there. His gaze swept over Riley. "I received your text."

"Cooper and I found the missing girl."

He looked over at the car. "Who called in the car's location?"

"Russell Hudson."

"The man who found Vicky?" Bowman asked.

"Yes."

"Where's he now?"

"Sitting in the deputy's car," Sharp said. "And he is annoyed."

"Can I talk to him?" Bowman's tone made the question sound more like an order.

Sharp heard it, frowned. "Sure. But I want to be present."

"I want in as well," Riley said.

"No," Sharp said. "You stay clear of this for now."

"I might hear something you don't."

"No, stay away. I'll fill you in on anything that needs to be discussed. For now, I want you to clock out. Go home. I'll call you later. And, Bowman, I want to know more about the video Riley gave you."

"Understood," Bowman said. His stern expression told her she'd have no help from him. It wasn't her nature to cave, but if staying clear helped catch a killer, she'd give in for now.

She left, moving to her SUV with long deliberate strides. And when she slid behind the wheel, she couldn't help but fight overwhelming anger. As she watched Bowman and Sharp walk to the deputy's car, she smacked her fist against the steering wheel. "Damn it."

***

With Sharp beside him, Bowman approached the car. Before he reached the vehicle, he saw the anger etched in Hudson's face. Hudson was tugging at a loose thread on his pant leg as he tapped his foot. Bowman rapped on the door. The old man looked up, cursed, and got out of the car.

"Who are you?" Hudson demanded.

Sharp introduced Bowman and himself. "We'd like to ask you a few questions."

"Jesus, I'm tired of questions. I want you off my land, and I want to get my field prepped so I don't get sued by the festival. Shit, I knew I shouldn't have taken that deal. Too good to be true."

"What was too good?" Bowman asked.

"The music festival. But he offered so much money."

"Who offered the money?" Bowman asked.

"The music promoter. Cain Duncan."

The name didn't mean anything to Bowman, but he would put Andrews on it. "Why were you out here this morning?"

"I came out to check on the church and saw this car shot up to hell. I called the cops."

"And Trooper Tatum responded," Sharp said.

"Yeah, fancy that," Hudson said.

"Did you see anyone out here when you arrived?" Bowman asked.

"No. I didn't see nothing." He kicked the dirt and spat. "Someone's jerking my chain and I don't like it."

"What can you tell me about Duncan?" Bowman asked.

"He contacted me about six months ago. Said he wanted to hold an outdoor concert and said my land was the perfect location because it was close to the interstate and there were enough fields for parking."

"Have you met him?" Bowman asked.

"Talked to his assistant on the phone, but I haven't met him in person. He was on the television the other day getting interviewed. Press is all hyped about the bands he's got signed. I heard the motels in the area are all sold out and the restaurants are getting ready for more customers. Gonna be good for the area."

"I'd like to see the contract," Bowman said. He reached for his cell phone.

"Sure."

"Thanks for your time." He texted Andrews and asked him to pull up what he could on Cain Duncan.

"Even if Duncan isn't involved, just news of a concert brings in all kinds," Sharp said. "A magnet for runaways and anyone looking to make a fast buck."

"The perfect hunting ground for a guy like the Shark."

***

Riley parked in front of Duke's brick two-story colonial located at the end of a quiet residential street. The house had been picked by Maria, and had never seemed to be a match for Duke with his tattooed body and long hair. A rebel in suburbia, she used to say to him.

She knocked on the screened door, and when Duke poked his head out of the kitchen, he waved her inside.

"Hey, kid," he said.

The inside of the house was all Maria as well. Comfortable cushioned chairs, pillows on a plump couch, and soft pastels on the walls. The only hints of Duke were in a back room he called his cave. That's where he kept his extra-large television, worn recliner, and computer.

Duke was clearing the dinner dishes from the table, stacking them on his arm like a practiced waiter. The moment actually felt normal.

"Where's Jo-Jo?" Riley asked.

"The kid is upstairs now. She couldn't eat much of her meal, but she tried."

"That's saying a lot after what she endured."

"I think she's got your strength. And if she does, she'll find a way clear of the streets."

So many kids didn't make it or were so damaged by their experience that they spent the rest of their lives struggling. "I'm betting she's a fighter."

He carried the plates to the kitchen counter and scraped off the leftovers into the garbage disposal. "My money's on her."

"Have you told her that?"

"I did. I also told her there were times when I thought I'd end up in the void. I was so far gone in the gambling days that an hour couldn't pass without me thinking about the next turn of the cards. And then Maria held me with her big doe eyes and my life turned on a dime."

"You can be that person for Jo-Jo. That anchor. That rock. You did it for me."

A smile tweaked the edge of his lips. "You did me proud."

Emotion clogged her throat and for a moment she couldn't speak.

As he turned from the sink, wiping his hands with a towel, his gaze locked on her. "What gives?"

"That kid, Cassie. The one I was looking for. Cooper and I found her dead near the old church on Route 602."

"Damn."

Uncharacteristic tears glistened in her eyes. "I saw the kid a few days ago." She pinched her fingers to her eyes. "Duke, I think whoever killed Vicky and Cassie is sending me some kind of message."

A frown deepened the lines in his face. "Who would do that to you?"

"This is going to sound crazy, but it goes back to New Orleans."

"New Orleans?"

"You know what my life was like there."

"Sure, you told me."

"Something happened."

"What?"

The words caught in her throat. "I don't remember. But somehow I got away. I thought it was all behind me, but now I don't think it is." She glanced toward the stairs, thinking about the battered kid on the second floor.

"So you are starting to remember?"

"Bits and pieces."

He laid his hand on her shoulder. "It breaks my heart to remember you when you first stumbled off that bus."

Before she could respond, the house phone rang.

Swearing, Duke tossed the dish towel over his shoulder and answered it. "Duke Spence."

Instantly his expression darkened.

"Jo-Jo?" he asked meeting Riley's gaze. He motioned her forward and tipped the receiver so she could hear the caller's voice. "Who's asking for her?"

"A friend."

She recognized the voice instantly. She mouthed the name *Jax* to Duke.

He gripped the phone tighter. "Jax, what rock did you crawl out from?"

"You think you are smart, don't you, old man?"

"Smarter than your sorry ass."

"Tell Jo-Jo that her old friend's returning her call, and he hasn't forgotten her."

"You're returning her call."

Jax laughed. "That's right, she called me. She loves me and she misses me."

Duke mouthed an oath as he glanced toward the stairs. Then, in a lower voice so that Jo-Jo couldn't hear him, he said, "You're a piece of shit. And any piece of shit that comes near my house gets shot, no questions asked."

"Woo-hoo! You scare me, old man."

Riley had only seen Duke get mad once or twice in the last twelve years, but when he lost his temper, he transformed, and she saw hints of the man he'd been when he was gambling.

Jax laughed and hung up the phone, leaving Duke with the next move.

"I can't believe she called him. She asked for the phone to call her friend Sandy."

Riley muttered a curse. "Because at one time Jax was nice to her. He's the devil she knows. Give her time."

"If that bastard comes near my house, I'll put him down in the front yard. Jo-Jo might have pulled off the dumb-ass move of the century, but I'm gonna keep her safe until she gets a little smarter."

"That's what you did for me," Riley said. "Remember when my stepfather found me here? He offered to put me through college if I'd come home." She could still picture William walking up to Duke's restaurant as she'd been standing at the hostess desk rolling napkins around forks, spoons, and knives. "And I was scared enough at that point to go." Terror and then relief clashed in a confused explosion.

"Jo-Jo might recover enough that she won't want Jax's help, but I'll make damn sure she stays safe while she's under my protection."

***

When Riley's front doorbell rang at nine, she reached for her gun. She rose from the sofa. After leaving Duke's, she'd taken Cooper for a run in the neighborhood, showered, and changed into a pair of old cotton shorts and a T-shirt. "Who is it?"

"It's Bowman."

"Speak of the devil," she muttered. She put the gun back in the side-table drawer by the couch and unlocked the door. He stood on her porch, wearing the suit pants he'd had on earlier. He'd taken off the jacket, rolled up the sleeves, and loosened the tie.

"Come on in," she said. As he entered, she said, "Did you find out anything?"

"No smoking gun. Lots of forensic data collected."

She ran her hand over the tense muscles on the back of her neck. "This is insane. It makes no sense."

"No."

"Can I offer you a drink?"

"No. I came by to check on you."

"There was a card on the door from the security company. They will arrive first thing in the morning to install a system."

"They shifted around a lot of clients to work you into their schedule."

"Ah, the power of Shield."

A faint smile tipped the edge of his lips. "It's effective."

"You look beat."

"Nothing out of the ordinary."

She remembered the first time they'd stood alone. She'd gone to his room near Quantico. Since the first day of her training, she was drawn to him. He kept to himself. Seemed to put more distance between the two of them than he did with any of the other recruits. She was convinced the feeling was mutual.

When he opened the door of that room in Quantico, she smiled, and before she lost her nerve, she closed the distance between them with a kiss. He stood stiff, not kissing her back.

She moistened her lips. "Did I overshoot the runway?" she asked.

"Timing's not good."

"You have someone else?"

A muscle in his jaw tightened. "No."

"Good." Before her nerve abandoned her, she kissed him a second time. He didn't hesitate and wrapped his arms around her, pulling her into the room.

They'd spent the night making love, and she'd never felt so close to a man. And in the morning, he had ended it all.

Now they stood alone again. And despite his rejection five years ago, she still wanted to kiss him. She'd made mistakes in her life, but she always made a point to learn from them. Bowman was a mistake she would not repeat.

"Thanks for stopping by," she said. "I have an early call."

He hesitated as if he had more to say, but finally said, "Right. I'll keep you posted."

"Thank you." When she closed the door behind him, she realized her legs were trembling.

CHAPTER NINETEEN

Wednesday, September 21, 6:00 a.m.

Riley drove straight to the coffee shop, hurried inside, and ordered Martin's favorite blend. When she pulled into the station before the morning shift, her hope was to catch him before the day got rolling to see what he'd pulled from the clothes of Gilbert, Lewis, and now, Cassie.

She found Martin shrugging off his coat. He glanced up at her with a halfhearted glare.

She grinned. "I brought coffee."

"Double venti?" He eyed her, testing.

"With a shot of vanilla."

Martin's frown softened. "I assume this isn't out of the goodness of your heart."

"The Gilbert case. The Lewis case. Wondered if the lab had any matches."

Martin sighed. "Pulled hair samples from Gilbert's body and sent it off for testing. We're cross-checking DNAs, but you know how that goes. State lab is backed up. Also found similar carpet fibers on both bodies. Suggests they were killed in the same place."

"I don't suppose those fibers came with an address attached."

"Sadly, no." He sipped his coffee. "Lewis's rental car tire tracks match those found near Vicky Gilbert's body."

"Not a surprise."

"The car also had a significant dent on the driver's front fender. Bits of concrete and wilted flowers wedged in the damage. Looks like he clipped something."

"What, like a planter?"

"Maybe? That's Sharp's job to figure out."

"Right." Martin's comment was a reminder to her she was due to start her patrol soon.

Martin sipped his coffee, savoring the flavor. "I was also able to scrape skin from under Cassie's fingernails. She scratched the hell out of someone. There's DNA, but testing and matching will take time. I also pulled fibers from her clothes. Basically, I've a lot of forensic data, but until I have something to match it against, it's not going to be much help."

Impatience nipped at Riley. She had a scattering of puzzle pieces but had no larger picture that would help her connect them. In time the lab would give them more answers, but she couldn't shake the feeling that this killer would be long gone before any lab results came back.

"Thanks, Martin. You'll keep me posted?"

"Always."

As she pushed through the doors, Sharp rounded the corner. He shook his head. "I'm not surprised to find you here."

"Just dropping off coffee for Martin."

He frowned. "I will call you if I have news. I want this guy just as much as you do."

"I know."

"Riley, let me worry about this. You need your head in the game when you are on patrol. You're out there alone on the road, and I don't want you getting shot because you were distracted."

"I'll be fine."

"Be careful."

**

Traffic on the interstate was moderate, and Riley spent most of the day cruising a sixty-mile stretch. Traffic stops, an assist with interstate construction, disabled vehicles—it was all routine. She took a break in the late afternoon for lunch at a truck stop restaurant where she knew many of the girls like Vicky and Cassie worked. If anyone asked, she was just getting a bite to eat.

After taking Cooper for a walk, she entered the restaurant and ordered a burger and fries. There weren't many girls or much traffic around the place, but experience had taught her that could change quickly. A group of truckers arrived and suddenly the girls showed.

She leaned against her vehicle and unwrapped the burger. She had taken a couple of bites when her cell dinged with a text message. It was from Hanna. All was well. Good. At least one thing in her life was right now. She texted her back, reminding her to be careful. A grimacing emoji shot back.

Smiling, she bit into a fry. As she reached for a second one, a red Cadillac parked near the side of the restaurant. Sandy got out of the passenger side and Tony out of the driver's. Sandy glanced in her direction but turned and hurried around the side of the building where several big rigs were parked.

Tony pulled off dark sunglasses and walked toward her, his gait slow and steady. She wrapped up her burger, set it aside, and met him several feet from the car, knowing Cooper would bark if he got too close.

"Tony," Riley said, her hand shifting closer to her gun. "Sorry to hear about Cassie."

"I liked Cassie," he said. "I had plans for her."

She assumed his plans included working the girl until she was so used up no one wanted her. "What do you think happened to her?"

"If I knew, I might go looking for whoever hurt her myself." His gaze roamed over her. "Two dead girls who look like you. Someone with money has a type he likes to hurt. I'm wondering how much a man could get if you were up for sale."

Tension knotted her spine. Sharp's words of warning replayed. "You aren't making some kind of threat, are you, Tony?"

He grinned broadly, holding up his hands. "Don't be looking at me like you want to shoot me. I ain't a threat."

"Then why make the comment."

"More of a friendly warning."

She stood her ground. Cooper started to bark. He was search and rescue but very protective of her. "I'm not a kid like the other two. I know how to fight."

Tony tossed a tense glance at the barking dog. "Oh, I bet you are tough. But you be on the lookout, Lady Cop. Hate to see you get snatched. I like you."

She stood with her back to the car until he disappeared into the diner, and then she slid behind the wheel, locking the door.

As she pulled away, her cell rang. "Trooper Tatum."

"Trooper, this is Sheriff Fletcher up in the western part of the county."

"Yes, sir. What can I do for you?"

"Hoping you and your dog might head out this way. We have a man who is threatening to kill himself. He called 9-1-1 and said he's headed up into the mountains and is gonna shoot himself. He called local media, and they had him on the phone for a half hour talking to a reporter. But he hung up minutes ago."

"Did he say why he's upset?"

"Talking a lot about a debt he owes. He says he can't get out from under it. Says dying is the only way to get clear."

She checked her watch and calculated how long it would take her to drive the thirty miles west. "I need to clear it with the boss."

"Already done that."

"Text me your location. It should take me a half hour to reach you."

"Will do, ma'am."

As she pulled out of the lot and headed west, her phone rang a second time and she half expected it to be Fletcher telling her that the man had been found. She glanced at the number. Bowman.

She tucked the cell under her ear. "You must have radar."

"I do." Classic Bowman. "What's up?" His words were razor sharp.

"A man threatening to kill himself in the park and the sheriff can't find him. Cooper and I are headed west now. This guy has already called the media, so it's going to be a circus."

"Where?"

She relayed the location of the heavily wooded state park. "Cooper and I know it well."

"That's a big park."

"Command center has been set up at the south entrance."

"Who's going in with you?"

"There'll be a few deputies, but it'll be up to Cooper and me to pick up the trail."

"I hope the boys can keep up with you this time." Bowman had outpaced her on the trail and barely broken a sweat when he helped take down Carter.

"That's not my concern now."

"Be careful."

"Always."

She ended the call, pushed her foot on the accelerator, and flipped on her lights. She wove in and out of traffic until she pulled off the interstate onto the narrowing road and reached the south entrance of the park. She paused at the ranger's station and got directions to the search team. A half mile into the park she found a half-dozen cars parked with lights flashing.

She grabbed her backpack from the trunk that she always kept stocked with water, first aid supplies, power bars, rope, and anything else she might need for a long trip into the woods. Hope for a quick outcome but plan for the long haul.

Off to the left stood Potter next to his news van. At Potter's signal, the cameraman raised his camera and began shooting her. Both moved toward her, but two deputies stepped in their path.

She hooked the tracking line onto Cooper's collar. "Time to go to work, boy."

He barked, tail wagging. He loved the search, which was a great game to him.

With a slight tug he jumped down, sniffing the ground and wagging his tail. They strode toward a tall man dressed in a brown uniform. His trooper hat covered gray hair and a face tanned and lined by years in the sun.

"Sheriff Fletcher."

He towered over her, taking a long assessing look at her and clearly wondering if someone had made a mistake when they'd recommended her. "Trooper Tatum? You're the one who found Jax Carter?"

"Yes, sir." Despite so many search-and-rescue successes, her tall, thin frame always surprised those who had not met her in person.

"I've heard good things about you, ma'am. Hope you're as good as they say. But I must say, you don't quite look the part. It's rough country."

"I'm familiar with the area. Cooper and I trained in these woods. What do you have?"

"All I know is I got a man named Lenny who says he's betting he will kill himself before anyone can find him."

"Did Lenny say why he wants to die? Does he have a wife, family I can talk to?"

"All he said was that he was out of options. Said his wife and kids live out of state and can't do anything for him."

"Did you talk to him directly?"

"No, I did not, but I listened to the 9-1-1 recording and the conversation he had with Mr. Potter."

"He called Mr. Potter?" Riley asked.

"Yes, he did."

"And you're sure this is legit?"

"We won't know until we get into the woods."

Of course, they could not ignore the 911 call or Potter, who might have information that would help her.

"Can I talk to Potter?" she asked.

"Sure."

As Fletcher waved Potter past the deputies, she noticed the smirk he was trying to hide. He had to love this, especially after being stopped by the deputies when Riley arrived.

"Trooper Tatum," he said. "How can I help you?"

"I hear this man named Lenny called you. He said he was going to kill himself."

Potter's eyes danced with excitement. "Named this park and its waterfalls as his destination."

"Why did he call you?"

"Saw me on the news covering Jax Carter's arrest. Said my name was the first that came to mind."

"He tell you anything else that can help me?"

"I told you all I know."

"Okay. Thanks."

He held up his cell phone. "Care to make a statement before the search?"

"No, sir."

"Are you really going to go in after him?"

"That's my job."

Fletcher guided her away from the reporter and handed her a bag containing a shirt. "We found this in his car."

"Which is his car?"

"The blue Lexus parked right by the entrance."

"Do we have any idea what Lenny looks like?"

"The car is a rental and we're contacting the leasing agent for a photo ID they should have with the paperwork. I can text it to you."

"Right."

She knelt and held the bag with the shirt to Cooper's nose. He sniffed and snorted several times. "Lenny said he was going to shoot himself. Do you know what kind of weapon he's carrying?"

"No." Fletcher rubbed the back of his neck. "I don't like this any better than you. Sketchy on more levels than I can count."

Another news van arrived. "Who's coming into the woods with me?"

"We've got three deputies ready to go."

She met the sheriff's gaze. "What's your radio frequency so I can tap into your team?"

He rattled off the number and watched as she dialed in the setting.

She tested the radio several times before she hooked it to her vest. The deputies looked like they could each bench-press three hundred pounds, but she questioned their cardio strength. "I'm going to be moving quickly. Can your men keep up?"

"They're tough."

But could they keep up? As she faced the woods, a large SUV pulled up behind her car. She didn't bother a glance back as she hefted her pack onto her back and moved toward the woods.

"Trooper Tatum." The clear, deep voice was getting to be too familiar.

She turned to see Clay Bowman moving toward her. He wore dark BDUs, boots, and a lightweight long-sleeve shirt. "Bowman, what're you doing here?"

"I'm here to assist." Not a request, but an order.

"And you are?" Fletcher asked.

"Clay Bowman. Shield Security."

"And former HRT," Riley added. "He trains people like me."

Fletcher looked apprehensive. "But he's now a civilian."

"I'll sign any waiver you need me to sign," Bowman said. "But I am going in those woods."

Riley met Fletcher's gaze, now full of challenge. "He'll be an asset. We've worked together before."

Potter shouted, "Hey, I got our guy on the phone again!"

Fletcher swore under his breath and moved toward the reporter. "Can I talk to him?"

Potter nodded. "Lenny, will you talk to Sheriff Fletcher?" The reporter listened and nodded. "He said I can put him on speakerphone so everyone can hear."

"Go ahead," Fletcher said. When Potter held up the phone, Fletcher added, "Lenny, we've got a team here to help you."

"I don't want your help," Lenny said.

"You must want our help," Fletcher said. "Otherwise, you wouldn't have called us and the news station."

"I wanted him to know I was going through with it. He needs to see I kept my word."

"Who are you talking about?" Fletcher asked.

"It doesn't matter," Lenny said. His voice sounded calm, resolute. "Mr. Potter, make sure everyone knows I'm here and ready to die." The line went dead.

Bowman checked his watch. "He's controlling the situation, and I don't like it. It could be an ambush." He leaned in closer to Riley, his voice low enough so only she could hear. "How easy would it be for you to be lulled into a search like this and then vanish? Maybe Lenny is bait for you to overextend yourself and make a mistake."

She recalled Tony's comment just hours ago. Still, she held on to what she wanted to believe. "That's a little far-fetched. You're overthinking this."

"I'm paid to overthink. And it's what I do best." He moved to the trunk of his car and pulled out a pack, which he swung onto his back with practiced ease. "Ready?"

"Just try and keep up with me."

He grinned. "I'll do my best."

Riley and Cooper took point. Bowman's steady footsteps fell in step behind her, and the deputies kept up with her fast pace. Soon, though, the deputies' breathing became labored and she realized she'd burn them and smoke herself and the dog. That wouldn't do anyone any good.

Drawing in a deep breath, she adjusted her gait, and soon her heart rate and breathing slowed to a normal, steady pace. Bowman also shortened his stride, but she sensed he could have kept the faster pace much longer.

Riley turned to Bowman. "How many of these searches have you done?"

"Heard about the three fugitives who set off those bombs last year?"

"The ones that made it to the North Carolina Appalachian Mountains?"

"Those would be the ones. They were mine."

That arrest had captured national media attention. All the tracking experts who'd been interviewed about the search had only praise for the HRT team. And at the time, she'd been impressed by the team leader's skills.

Both paused to scan and listen, studying the sounds and sights of the woods. In the distance a creek flowed by. "Lenny mentioned the waterfalls in the northwest corner of the park."

"Roger."

They kept moving forward along the narrow path. The brush grew thicker and thicker.

"A lot of work for a man who wants to take his life," Bowman said.

"I don't pretend to understand his motives."

They broke through the thicket and into a small clearing at the foot of the waterfall. Cooper sniffed, his tail alert, his gaze sharp.

The primary path to the falls cut right, but Cooper pulled left toward a smaller footpath. She followed, not questioning the dog's nose.

"What's up that way?" Bowman asked.

"Another path to the falls."

The deputies cleared the woods and paused in the clearing.

"Take the path to the right," she said. "We're taking the left. One of us should make contact with him in the next ten minutes if he really is at the falls."

The deputies nodded and pushed onward.

She took out her water bottle and drank enough to match her perspiration rate given the heat and humidity. She gave Cooper a small amount of water while Bowman drank his own. When they were all hydrated, they left the clearing for the woods.

As the heat of the day rose, neither spoke. When they reached the base of the falls, the sun had climbed into a bright-blue sky.

Bowman looked up the steep slope leading to the top. "We shouldn't need climbing equipment to get up there."

"Agreed." She wrestled off her backpack and pulled off her sweater top, revealing a tank top that clung to her sweat-soaked body. Jamming the sweater in the top of her pack, she hefted the pack onto her shoulders, ready for the final push.

Bowman stood by watching for anything out of the ordinary. When Riley started moving again, he strode up the side of the mountain, taking point, his powerful legs making easy work of the terrain that grew steeper and steeper. She and Cooper held their own and kept pace, but her efforts weren't as smooth as his. She lost her footing once and slid a few feet. He paused, glanced back at her, but said nothing. When she regained her footing, he kept moving up. Higher and higher.

"Look," he said.

He pointed to a strip of red fabric dangling from a branch. "Seems like he wants us to find him. Take a break. You'll need fresh legs."

"Agreed." She sat on a rock and wiped the sweat from her eyes. "Why would a guy come all the way up here to kill himself? It makes no sense."

"No, it does not."

She rubbed the back of her neck with her hand. "People do all kinds of crazy stunts when they're stressed or under the influence. And some just don't want to go quietly but want to make their last act a show."

"Maybe."

"No theories on this guy?"

"I deal in fact, not theory. But I do know for certain that you will come out of these woods alive and well."

He had her back on the mission. Of that, she had no doubt. However, that confidence didn't extend to their personal lives. "I saw Tony today. He's the pimp that ran Cassie."

Bowman frowned. "Where?"

"Truck stop. My regular beat. He's also looking for the person who killed Cassie."

"So he wasn't the one that sold her that last time?"

"Apparently not. As tempted as I was to offer Jax and Darla up to Tony, I didn't want to out Sandy, who is still with him. He's the kind of guy that would make her pay for talking to a cop."

"What did Tony have to say?"

"Said there seems to be a high demand for women who look like Vicky and Cassie."

"And you."

"He said I should be careful."

Bowman reached for a branch and snapped it in his fingers. "He's right."

"I need to flush this Shark guy out. He needs to be caught."

Bowman looked up the last twenty feet of steep climbing. "I'm retaining point position."

"Cooper can take point."

"Not now."

The last ten feet were nearly hand over hand, and when he reached the top, he extended his hand down toward her. She readily accepted it, appreciating his strength when he pulled her to the top. Cooper climbed easily beside her.

They moved toward the falls where the river raced past, swollen by recent high rains. A cloudless, clear-blue sky touched the mountains. The view was stunning. "Lenny!" she shouted.

Her voice echoed, traveled, and bounced. Neither one of them moved or spoke as they listened. Water crashed and splashed. But no sign of the man.

"I'm Trooper Riley Tatum with Virginia State Police. I'm here to help you!"

Again Riley and Bowman stood in silence waiting for an answer. Wind rustled through the trees. Nothing moved.

She stared at the pool of water below, searching for signs of his body. Hell, if he'd fallen in the water, the current could have pinned him to the bottom of the deep basin. Where the hell was he?

Seconds later a gunshot rang out. She and Bowman both dropped into a crouch and reached for their weapons. "It came from the woods to the east," Riley said.

Bowman moved toward the gunshot while she and Cooper followed. The woods grew less and less dense, then opened into a small clearing. Leaning against a rock was a tall man with dark hair. He wore a suit, dress shirt, and shoes. His arms lay limp by his side. Clutched in his right hand was a revolver. There was a single gunshot wound in his head.

Bowman crept up to the man, his gun drawn. He pressed two fingertips to the man's neck. "He's dead."

"Why the hell would he come all the way up here? Look at his clothes and shoes. And those buffed nails. This is the last place a guy like this would come."

"There's a note in his front breast pocket."

"Let me get it." She handed him Cooper's tracking line while pulling latex gloves from her side pocket and tugging them on. Using her fingertips, she pulled out the white folded paper. A playing card flittered out to the ground.

For a moment, she didn't breathe as she stared at it. Carefully, she picked it up and turned it over.

It was the queen of hearts, and written on it were scrawled words that read, *I win. You lose.*

Bowman muttered an oath. Hand on his Beretta M9, he searched the woods around them. "That's the Shark's brand of cards."

"And he's talking directly to me."

Wind whispered through the trees. "We're chasing a killer who likes to play games."

Fear tightened her gut. "He wins. I lose."

"After we get off the mountain, I want you to go directly to Shield Security."

"Why?"

"For once, don't question. Do."

CHAPTER TWENTY

Wednesday, September 21, 6:00 p.m.

After they came out of the woods, Bowman followed her home. While she changed, he searched her house and around it, confirming no one had left a package or broken in. After she walked Cooper, they each got back in their SUVs and she followed him to the Shield Security offices.

Bowman stopped at the security entrance, showed his ID, and spoke to the guard. When Riley approached, the guard waved her through.

She drove up the winding road bracketed by thick trees, passing tall light posts outfitted with cameras. Probably infrared coupled with motion detection. State-of-the-art equipment. No other buildings lined the road, and she'd heard that Shield had purchased a couple of hundred acres. Not a cheap or easy purchase this close to Quantico and the DC area.

At the end of the road, a five-story building stretched along the landscape like a long, sleek animal. The front of the dark building was covered in smoked glass.

She parked and grabbed Cooper's long leash. Clay scanned her carefully, pausing on her freshly scrubbed face and the waves of brown hair draping her shoulders. His expression was neutral and impossible to read, but if she were standing in his shoes, she'd be making associations with the dead girl.

"I called ahead. They are waiting for you upstairs."

"Who's waiting?"

"The IT guy."

"Is this about the video?"

"You'll see."

As they made their way up the elevator and along the carpeted hallway, she was again made aware of his height. Most men his size had a tendency to lumber, but not him. He moved with an easy grace more like a wide receiver than a linebacker.

He held open a tinted-glass door for her as she entered. The computer room, as he called it, looked like something out of a science fiction movie. The state patrol had good equipment, but Shield must have an unlimited budget. Joshua Shield was clearly in this business to win first, profit second.

Shield moved toward her. He wore a light-blue shirt, red tie, and charcoal-gray suit pants. No jacket, which was likely his idea of casual.

"Trooper Tatum," he said, extending his hand. "Good to see you again."

She accepted it, noting restraint in his firm grip. "Mr. Shield. Pleasure to see you." He didn't hide his scrutiny as he studied her with a precision that logged every detail of her face. She found the cool calculation terrifying. "I understand you have some details about the video."

Instead of answering, he sidestepped by saying, "Would you like anything to eat or drink?"

Riley wasn't here to eat. "No, thank you. If you don't mind, the video."

He studied her an extra beat. "Thank you for sharing it. That took courage."

"If not for Vicky Gilbert, I wouldn't have. Not the kind of digital footage I want any of my colleagues in the police department to see."

"Strictly confidential," he said.

Shield led them into another room with a bank of computers and large screens spanning the walls. At the center sat a large man. His hands were as large as Bowman's, but they moved with a fast-paced dexterity as if he'd been on a keyboard since before he could walk.

Bowman laid his hand on the man's shoulder, and he turned to study Riley with the same cold efficiency as Shield.

"This is Garrett Andrews," Bowman said. "He is . . . what's your title, Garrett?"

"I'm the tech guy," he said, rising to extend his hand. Another firm handshake and eyes that missed very little.

She noted the scars on his hands but kept her eye contact. "I understand you learned something new."

"I did. My findings may upset you."

Good cops could put distance between themselves and death, tragedy, or whatever it was that stood in the way of them doing their job. Later, when they were alone, the fear, guilt, suppressed shame, or revulsion bubbled up. Most cops figured out how to deal with it. Some talked to a buddy. Others drank. Riley simply ran until her body was drenched in sweat and endorphins. Only then would the demons be temporarily calmed. "This tape isn't personal. It's evidence."

"Good." He turned back to his keyboard and typed. The video popped up on multiple screens. Riley kept her gaze steady, aware that Bowman was watching her reaction. She would not give him or anyone the satisfaction of seeing her squirm.

Andrews enlarged the image. "I've been over this tape several more times since I last spoke to Bowman. Basically, I have since been able to isolate several images in the video that confirmed that this was indeed shot in New Orleans. Note the mirror on the right. There's a faint reflection. Enlarge that and I find the outline of a building that matches a profile of a building in the French Quarter."

She leaned in, amazed at the sharp detail of the image. She had missed the reflection altogether during all her viewings. "So what's this building?"

"I obtained real estate records from the city planning office from twelve years ago. After a search, I found the building in the mirror and the one across from it—your hotel. I'm certain you were held in the Duval Hotel on the top floor."

Bowman met her gaze. "I called a contact in New Orleans. He checked out the property."

It didn't sit well that he was investigating without her input. Her back teeth clenched. "You hadn't mentioned that."

If he picked up on her annoyance, he didn't care. "I can't afford to have the Shark's people spot you near the hotel."

It took effort for her to back away from the anger and focus on the facts. Finally, she asked, "What did you find out about the hotel?"

"It has been owned by a shell corporation for the last eighteen years. Its penthouse is rented out on a monthly basis to high-level executives. We're now peeling through the layers of detail."

"Who was renting it during the time the video was made?"

"Records were lost," Andrews said. "Hurricane Katrina caused a massive power surge and fried the hotel's data banks."

"Damn," she said.

"The loss is unfortunate," Andrews said.

The lead had gone cold, which left only her. "I'm still the center of this storm."

Bowman nodded. "You are."

Impatience disturbed her. "Then do me a favor: keep me in the loop."

Silent, Bowman studied her.

"I don't want to be the last to know whatever you all discover." She didn't try to summon a smile. "I'm coming to this openhanded, which isn't easy for me. You investigate a scene, I'd like to know before a site visit, not after."

"If it makes sense logistically, I will. In this case, it did not."

"This cannot be a one-way street when it comes to information."

A muscle ticked in Bowman's jaw, but he nodded. "Understood."

"What else did you find out about the video?" she asked.

Andrews cleared his throat. "I believe three other people are in the room."

"How can you tell?" she asked.

"There's the man who takes your face in his hands, another with a cord in his hands, and the third is holding the camera. You can tell by the image that it's not stationary, but moving."

Riley was silent. How many people had witnessed her degradation firsthand?

Andrews pointed to the screen. "The man who takes your face in his hands is wearing a ring."

"I noticed that," she said. "It has a V shape."

"It's custom. I've not been able to trace it to any family, school, or society. Judging by the veins and skin, he was in his early fifties when this was shot."

"So we're looking for a man in his midsixties?"

"If he's still a player in the game," Andrews said.

"What do you know about the man holding the cord?"

"He's younger. Maybe early forties, and his body language suggests he's not enjoying this. His hands have a slight tremble and he flexes his fingers, in relief I think, when the old man turns and leaves."

"Even if other players were present, there'd be no incentive to speak to the police because they're accessories to murder," Shield said. "And there were four gamblers found dead in Vegas about eleven years ago.

No one ever connected their deaths to the girls, but now I'm not so sure."

"Is New Orleans the only place these men played before now?" Riley asked.

"We don't know," Bowman said. "They chose girls who fall off the radar easily. The mistake they made in New Orleans was killing four girls within a couple of weeks. Over the top, even for that city."

Riley swallowed. "And no one else survived?"

"None we've been able to track," Bowman said.

The weight of the young girls' murders settled squarely on her shoulders. "Why all the games? Why not just kill me?"

"According to my informant, this guy likes games," Shield said. "He bores easily, like a cat toying with a mouse. He lost you twelve years ago, and now he's determined to enjoy the kill this time."

"An ambitious man who wants to dethrone this card player might make a run at taking you," Bowman said. "Think about the woods today."

"Until he's caught," Shield said, "we need to keep you under surveillance."

She clung to calm composure. "I can't stop living my life. If this guy wants me, there's going to be no stopping him."

"I'd like to use an embedded microchip," Andrews said. "If you're taken, we'll be able to find you and the Shark."

She would have laughed if he didn't look so serious. "You're kidding."

Andrews didn't blink. "No."

"What kind of chip?"

"It's the size of a rice kernel. I'll insert it under your skin. It's not painful and can be removed after the case is closed."

She rubbed her arm. "Where under my skin?"

Andrews nodded. "On the inside of your upper arm. No one will see it."

She didn't like the idea of being tracked. But to wish and hope wouldn't get her anywhere. She needed to be smart. "When can you do it?"

"Now."

"Do it."

Bowman stood silent, watching as Andrews rose. "Follow me."

She and Cooper trailed behind him with Bowman and Shield on their heels. They moved into a sterile room where a large chair with an armrest sat beside a small table that was covered with a surgical drape. They'd been ready for her. Expected her to say yes.

"Am I that predictable?" she asked no one in particular.

"Bets were split whether you'd say yes or no," Shield said.

"Should I ask where you put your money, Bowman?"

"I bet on you," he said.

Had he really or was he now simply saying what would smooth the waters? "I'm always a safe bet."

She sat in the chair and raised her arm, revealing the long bruising scrape from the trek up the mountain today. Cooper settled beside her, and for his sake, she kept cool.

Bowman frowned. "That happened today?"

"I've done worse while training."

"You didn't say a word." The words sounded rough, as if he'd ground them between his teeth before he spat them out.

His irritation rankled her. "Complaining doesn't help, and Cooper notices when I'm upset."

Bowman didn't respond, but he wasn't happy.

Andrews donned latex gloves and approached her with a syringe. She hated needles, so she looked down at Cooper. Didn't make sense why they made her so jumpy or woozy, but they did. Realizing Bowman's gaze was locked on her, she sat a little straighter and stilled her arm, balling her fingers into a fist. She'd be damned if she'd go all light now.

Andrews rubbed her skin with an alcohol pad. "This next pad is going to numb the skin so that I can make the injection."

The cool, gentle swipe of the pad did not calm her nerves. "Okay."

"It's Novocain and will numb the site," Andrews said.

She held her gaze on Cooper. "Okay."

"Just a little prick," Andrews said. "And then you will feel a little pressure when I insert the microchip."

She drew in a breath, doing her best to look calm. "And when this is all over, you can get that thing out, right?" she asked.

"Yes, it's a simple procedure."

A minute later he said, "You're all set."

"That's it?"

"You're good to go."

"So do I need to avoid any microwaves or garage door openers?" Riley asked.

Andrews came close to smiling. "No."

Bowman and Shield stared at her, their expressions serious, with no hint of humor. She'd have called them on their stiffness if she weren't so twisted in knots. "Great. Then I'm good to go."

"Sit here for another few minutes," Andrews said. "I just want to make sure you don't have a reaction."

"A reaction? What does that mean?"

He pulled off his latex gloves. "It's different with everyone."

"Toss me a couple of examples, Mr. Andrews."

"Itching. Hives. Bleeding."

"Lovely." She rolled down her sleeve. "How long do I have to sit here?"

"Fifteen minutes. I'll get you some water to drink."

"Thanks."

When Andrews left, Shield said, "We're going to find the Shark."

"That's what I keep telling myself."

Shield left her alone with Bowman. He leaned against a table and folded his arms in front of his chest. "You have no color in your face."

"Get a probe stuck in your arm and see how you look."

"Until ten minutes ago you had a nice tan."

"It'll be back." She gingerly touched her arm. "So, who's going to be tracking my signal?"

"From this location, it'll be Andrews. Remotely, it'll be me," Bowman said.

She frowned, not liking the idea that they would know her every move.

As if reading her thoughts, Bowman said, "Look, Shield found you. And someone else found you and put that DVD on your porch."

And Hanna had picked up the package. Inadvertently, this killer had touched her life, and that bothered Riley more than her own safety. "Point taken. Who were the other girls killed in New Orleans? Do you have the profiles I requested?"

"I do."

"I want to see them." Andrews returned to the room, handing her water.

Bowman didn't speak for a moment, then nodded. "Okay. Come into my office."

She and Cooper followed him to a large carpeted office. Boxes filled with books, diplomas, and pictures lined the walls.

"You're not quick to settle in, are you?"

He sat behind his computer and tapped a couple of buttons. "I'll get to it."

As Cooper lay on the floor by the desk, she moved around to the credenza. She picked up the picture featuring a younger version of Bowman and a woman who looked up at him with adoring eyes. "Your wife?"

He glanced back, studying her holding the image of what must have been the key picture marking his past. "Yes."

"She's pretty. I'm sorry for your loss."

Deflecting the comment, he opened a file. "Is Hanna still in Georgia?"

"Yes, she is."

"Good. Better she's out of town."

"Agreed. I don't want this guy anywhere near her. She's seen enough to last a lifetime."

"She seems like a good kid."

"She is. And she's a hell of a sprinter and swimmer. No one gets past her."

"You said she wants to go to college."

"She's smart. Real smart, and it would be a waste for her not to get the opportunity. She's supposed to be working on her essays while she's traveling."

"She's lucky to have you."

"It's mutual." Riley didn't realize how much she had isolated herself until Hanna had come into her life. Suddenly, evenings weren't spent alone reading or working out but helping with math homework, driving Hanna to swim practice, or teaching her how to drive. The idea that anything bad could happen to the kid knotted her insides.

Bowman opened the file that featured the images of four girls he'd come across while doing his own research. "What kind of fantasy is this guy working out?" He clicked a button and a printer began to spit out copies. "Maybe you'll see something we all missed."

"I'm not sure what, but I'll look them over." Riley glanced at the time. "I need to get on the road. It's a solid forty-five minutes of driving. And I've an early shift tomorrow."

"Shield has suites in the building if you're too tired to drive. I've stayed here on a few late nights."

"I'll be fine. Rather sleep in my own bed." She glanced around, looking for Andrews. "Can you check with your buddy and see if he can cut me loose?"

A dozen rebuttals were written in the deep lines etched around the edges of his mouth and eyes. He collected the finished copies and handed them to her. "Sure."

Pushing away from the table, he walked around the corner to visit with Andrews. Riley rolled her head from side to side, turning her attention back to Vicky Gilbert's case as she leafed through the dossiers of the girls. If there wasn't a lead soon, the case would lose momentum.

Bowman returned seconds later with Andrews. The latter studied her closely as if searching for signs of trouble. Both men possessed an intensity, but when Andrews looked at her, she didn't feel as on edge as she did when Bowman was close.

"You feel okay?" Andrews asked.

"I'm fine. I need to get going."

"I've texted you my cell number," Andrews said. "If you have trouble with the injection site, call me. Don't go to your doctor."

She fished her phone from her back pocket and glanced at the screen. "You texted my cell? I assume Bowman gave the number to you."

"I suppose that was one other way of getting it," Andrews said.

"I'll walk you out," Bowman said.

"Sure."

With Cooper following, they moved out of Bowman's office to the elevators. He pressed the "Down" button and, when the doors opened, slid his hand over the door opening as she entered. The holding of the doors was something new for her. Made her feel oddly awkward.

In the elevator, his height and broad shoulders shrunk Riley's personal space to a bare minimum. And he knew it.

Bowman walked her out the front door and across the parking lot, which glistened from a recent rain. At her SUV he stood back, his hands in his pockets. "Let me know what you think of those files."

"I will." She opened the back door and Cooper jumped inside. "Unless I spot something, it's a matter of waiting for the Shark to make his next move. Either way, it won't be long."

"Agreed."

"This guy isn't going to quit, is he?" she said.

"Shield doesn't think it's over, and neither do I."

Absently, she rubbed the bandage on her arm. He was right, of course. She wasn't thinking like a cop but like a victim, and that wasn't smart. "I honestly don't get what the big deal is about me."

"Obsession isn't an easy thing to explain. But he's obsessed with you."

"Shield seems as driven."

"The longer you chase, the harder it is to give up. He wants this guy and won't stop until he's caught."

"Only this guy?"

"If it makes you feel better, he has a hit list of cases he plans to reopen."

"I just happen to be first on the list." She heard the fear edging the words.

His tone softened. "You're not in this by yourself anymore, Riley. You have me."

Alone in the parking lot, it was tempting to hand over the whole mess to Bowman. To lean in . . . But no. At this moment, she didn't feel strong or brave. She was exhausted and craving the normal life she'd worked hard to build. But she would not lean on anyone. That would be a slippery slope that would lead to dependence. She'd sworn when she'd stumbled off that bus and into Duke's care that she'd never be at anyone's mercy again.

Instead of reaching out to Bowman, she swallowed the tension rising up in her throat. "Thanks."

"Drive safe."

"Right."

As she drove off, she glanced in her rearview mirror and saw him standing there, staring at her until she vanished around the corner.

***

Bowman walked into Shield's office. The older man stood at his window, watching Riley drive away. He picked up his whiskey, took a sip, and grimaced as if it tasted bitter.

"I can see why the Shark is interested in her," Shield said.

Bowman's hands flexed. "We're using her."

"We are also saving her."

"We damn well better."

"You are taken with the woman. I don't blame you. She's remarkable."

Bowman shifted his stance, shaking change in his pocket. Self-recriminations rattled in his mind. He'd tried for a second chance the other night and she'd turned him away. Just because he wanted another chance with her didn't mean he deserved it. "She's tough but she also gets invested in those street kids. They're her Achilles' heel. Look how she tore after Jax Carter after he beat that girl. It wouldn't take much to lure her into a trap."

"Sounds like you want to be the one watching after her."

"Yes."

"Then go to her."

"We're on a case." He thought about the picture of Karen back in his office. Choosing Riley meant really leaving Karen behind.

"For a long time you thought your life ended when you buried your wife. The first time Riley crossed your path, I'm assuming there was a strong attraction as there is now. Then you were too raw with grief to take a second chance. Now, the single excuse standing between you and her is you."

Bowman stared into the darkness a long moment. "The Shark wants closure on his unfinished business."

"So for Riley's sake, let's end this."

***

Riley pushed through the front door of her house, immediately struck by the stillness inside. She'd become so used to having Hanna there that not having her around made the house feel off. Locking the door behind her, she unhooked Cooper's leash and tossed the file Bowman had given her on the small kitchen table. The dog padded into the kitchen, drank water, and walked straight into his crate. He laid his head down and closed his eyes.

By all rights, Riley should have been exhausted, but her mind buzzed. Rubbing her hand over the bandage on her arm, she set up her coffeemaker and turned it to "Brew." As it hissed and gurgled, she moved to the file and opened it, cringing when she saw the first image of a young girl murdered over a dozen years ago. She'd found very little information on the Internet when she'd searched before, but because the victims had been minors, their names had not been published. This file contained details the media had never known.

The first victim's name had been Angie Butler, and she was only seventeen when police found her body in an alley in the French Quarter. Like Vicky, she'd been strangled and playing cards had been shoved in her pocket. The next girl was Nadine West, age seventeen. Same MO. The third girl, Verity Coggan, had been sixteen. The last girl, Lana Smith, days short of eighteen. All had been found over a two-week stretch, and then no more bodies.

Riley arranged the pictures in a row. All the young girls had dark hair and brown eyes. All runaways. All like her.

"Damn." She turned to the coffeemaker and poured a fresh cup. Sipping, she moved back to the table and sat. Angie. Nadine. Verity.

Lana. Her gaze swept all four faces again, but this time it doubled back to Angie's. A distant sense of familiarity vibrated in her.

She sipped coffee and studied the girls' profiles.

What had been happening twelve years ago in her life? Her mother had been dying, and there were around-the-clock nurses taking care of her. So many people in and out of the house. William had been stressed and agitated more than usual, and he'd been gone a lot. Judging by the thick scent of cigar smoke and bourbon that clung to him and the clink of poker chips in his pants pocket, she knew he'd been gambling. There'd been trouble with the cops, but he'd downplayed it and she'd been too upset to care.

And he was close now and he knew where she lived.

She stared at the first victim's crime scene photo. Angie. She wore a dark T-shirt that set off vivid green eyes. What was it about this girl?

She snapped a picture of the victim's picture and texted it to Bowman with the message, There's something about this girl that bothers me. But I don't know what.

***

Cigarette dangling from his mouth, Jax rubbed his hands over his bare arms, staring up into the moonlight. Behind him, the door to the motor home closed, so he turned a fraction to see Darla walking toward him. A big part of him cringed as he thought about her chewing on his ear again. The bitch never knew when to shut up.

"We need to leave," she said. "We been waiting for over an hour and he ain't shown."

"He'll be here. He said he would be."

"He *said*. He *said*. Maybe he's a liar. Maybe he don't give two shits about us and he's leaving us hanging in the wind because he gets a kick out of it."

"Stop talking," he said as he pulled on the cigarette.

"Time to leave and find us a couple more girls. We can go to a new state and set up shop. It won't take me long to find them." She rubbed the back of her neck, arching her breasts toward him as if she wanted him to notice.

He noticed. But right now doing Darla was the last thing he wanted to do. He was as tired of those breasts as he was of her nagging.

Best to settle up, get his money, and make a new life.

She smoothed her fingers over his back and across his shoulders. "You're tense, baby."

He dropped the cigarette in the dirt and ground it out with his boot before he pried her hands off him and stepped out of reach. "Not now."

"Why not?" she asked, a pout in her tone. "You used to like what I did to you."

"Not now." His leg throbbed and he thought about that bitch Jo-Jo hiding out at Duke's. He'd go there and kill her if he thought he could get close enough to do the job. But the old man was tough as gristle, and he'd heard stories about Duke's younger days. When Duke wasn't gambling or drinking hard, he was breaking heads for the casinos. He didn't doubt for one second that Duke would shoot him dead without batting an eye.

"We can call Duke's again." She chuckled and it struck him that her laugh sounded more like a chicken's cackle. "Rattle his cage."

"No."

When she tried to touch him again, he moved out of reach. "Don't you go turning your back on me. I been with you through it all," she said.

Headlights loomed out on the road and he straightened. "That's him."

"Who?"

"Do me a favor and keep your mouth shut."

"Don't you tell me to shut up."

Rage roiled, and on reflex, he whipped his hand around and struck her squarely across the face so hard that she fell to the ground. She raised a trembling hand to her bloodied lip, staring up at him as if he'd lost his mind. He'd told her to be quiet. But she never listened.

Gravel crunched under tire wheels, and he turned away from her as if she were trash. Jax hiked up his pants and smiled as the car came to a stop. When the driver got out, he puffed his chest. "So what do you want? Coming to give me back what's mine?"

"Here to give you what you deserve."

CHAPTER TWENTY-ONE

Thursday, September 22, 6:30 a.m.

When Riley arrived at Duke's house, she was tired. She'd only logged a couple of hours' sleep last night. She found Duke sitting on the front porch, talking into his cell phone, his expression dark and his words muffled but tense. When she closed her SUV door, he straightened, grinned, and ended the call.

"You're looking a little rough," he said, standing as he tucked his phone in his pocket.

"Didn't get much sleep last night. And I could say the same for you."

"I got enough." He gave her an affectionate jostle to her shoulder. "So, what can I do for you?"

"How's Jo-Jo doing?"

"Moving slow but getting around. She's eating and her right eye isn't as swollen. But it still hurts for her to walk. Busted ribs."

"Any more problems with Jax?"

"Naw. I haven't heard a word from him."

"You should be on guard. That creep is out there stalking and waiting for his first chance to grab his meal ticket."

"I told Maria to keep Jo-Jo in the house." He nodded back behind him. "They're both up if you want to visit."

"Yeah. I'd like to touch base."

"Head on inside. I've another call to make. Supplier busting my balls on a delivery."

"Thanks."

He studied her closer. "You doing all right?"

"Nothing a little time won't fix."

"Get some rest."

"I'll do my best."

He grinned. "Liar."

She moved through the house that had always felt like home. Her blood pressure still dropped when she was here.

In the bright kitchen, Jo-Jo slowly stirred cereal in a bowl. Maria greeted Riley with a wide, welcoming grin and a hug.

"Where's Cooper?" Maria asked.

"In the SUV. I don't have long."

"Look who's in the kitchen. Jo-Jo made the big trip down the stairs this morning."

Riley sat down across from the runaway. "That's not a happy smile."

Jo-Jo looked up. "I don't like cereal."

"Really, cereal makes that kind of frown?"

"Easier to worry about this goop than my life."

The girl was dressed in well-worn but clean jeans and a T-shirt that Maria must have given her. In regular, age-appropriate clothes she looked like a normal fifteen-year-old.

"The way I look at it, your life took a major upswing. Like the universe reached out, grabbed you by the collar, and pulled you out of the abyss."

Jo-Jo cocked her head, her street smarts kicking into gear. "What're you doing here?"

"Thought I'd come by and see how you're feeling."

"I'll live."

"You're tough."

Jo-Jo lifted her chin. "Jax used to say he liked my toughness."

"Jax said nice things to you because he was manipulating you. He believes you're his property."

Fresh tears glistened in the girl's eyes. "Nobody ever said they loved me before Jax."

"And I bet he and Darla knew that. He's evil but also smart."

"He said some nice things to me and gave me presents. I felt special."

Maria set a cup of coffee in front of Riley, who smiled her thanks before reaching for the sugar and creamer.

"I know Duke and Maria have said nice things, too," Riley said.

Jo-Jo shrugged. "They have to. They're some kind of social workers."

"They don't have to do anything. They say what they mean. They don't lie. Neither do I."

"What's that mean?"

"Honey, Jax doesn't love you. Love doesn't hurt. A man who loves a woman does not beat her or pimp her out to other men. Jax says *love* because he knows you need to hear it, but he doesn't love you or any of the other girls, including Darla."

Jo-Jo's jaw clenched, but tears welled in her eyes. "That's not true."

Breaking the hooks Jax had sunk into this kid would take time. Riley would likely have to say this hundreds of times before it penetrated the girl's damaged self-image: "Real men don't bruise the women they love."

With trembling fingers the girl wiped away a tear. "Why are you really here?"

"I want you to understand that you have an opportunity to leave the streets. You can be someone different."

Jo-Jo glanced at her shorn fingernails and curled them into a fist. "It's not such a bad life."

"It's hell. But you've been trapped in it for so long you don't know the difference." Riley glanced at her watch. She needed to report in before patrol and knew one conversation with this kid would not cut it. "This place offers safety and a warm bed. You can give yourself a chance to sleep and heal. Maybe grab a couple of good meals. Then in a few days if you still think you want to find Jax, there won't be anything I can do to save you."

"I don't need saving. I can take care of myself."

"That's what I said when I landed on this doorstep."

"You stayed at Duke's?" Jo-Jo's expression conveyed disbelief.

"I did. I was a couple of years older than you are now. If I hadn't landed at Duke's then, it would have been just a matter of time before someone like Jax found me."

Doubt darkened Jo-Jo's eyes. "I can't picture that."

"Maria, is this true?" Riley asked.

Maria had been wiping the same spot on the counter for at least a minute. "Riley was in a bad place. Duke and I found her at the bus station. She was messed up. Could barely stand."

Riley could preach a sermon on what she knew about the streets and how they would chew up a girl like Jo-Jo. But she held back. The kid needed food and rest, not a lecture. "Give it a day or two. You've nothing to lose."

Jo-Jo ladled cereal with her spoon. "You're not going to change my mind about Jax."

"Maybe," Maria said.

Jo-Jo ate, wincing as her sore jaw chewed. She glanced around the modest kitchen as if she were afraid to allow herself to like it. "What if someone comes by here to get me?"

"Call me," Riley said.

The girl stared at her. "I bet you can kick some ass."

"I can."

She studied the scrapes on Riley's knuckles still healing from yesterday's search in the woods. "Jax must have been surprised as hell when he saw you on that mountain."

"He was. But if you want to hear the story, it'll have to be after my shift tonight. I need to roll."

A sigh leaked from Jo-Jo's clenched teeth. "Fine."

"Fine what? Does that mean you'll be here this evening?"

"Maybe."

Not a ringing endorsement, but Riley would take it. The girl's coloring was a bit better, and she'd had a chance to shower and wash her hair. Her road back to life was slow and frustrating. One step at a time.

"Can you walk?" Riley asked.

"Yeah."

"Good. Walk me to my car."

Jo-Jo followed Riley out to the gravel driveway where her SUV was parked. Duke was nowhere in sight. "Why is the car running?"

"My dog, Cooper, is inside."

Jo-Jo peered in the window. "He's not so scary looking."

"He's one of the best tracking dogs in Virginia. He helped me find Jax."

Maria stood at the front door. She didn't say anything but just watched, her expression worried.

Jo-Jo glanced back at Maria. "She always looks upset."

"She's worried about you."

"She doesn't know me."

"Better than you think. She's also looked at me that way more than a few times. If you haven't guessed, I can be hardheaded."

That coaxed the faintest smile. "No shit?"

"I'll be back this evening."

Jo-Jo shrugged her shoulders, but Riley knew the girl was simply afraid to hope. "Whatever."

Riley slid on her sunglasses and slid behind the wheel. She watched as Jo-Jo turned and slowly walked back toward the house. Her gait was uneven as she guarded her right side. Riley had cracked her ribs on a climb once, and they hurt like hell. Impossible to sleep and blinding pain if you sneezed. Tightening her fist, she imagined the judge sentencing Jax to dozens of years behind bars. But unless Jo-Jo was willing to press charges, he'd likely skate by with a year at the most.

***

Later that morning, when Riley was on I-95, her phone rang. It was Sharp.

"Credit card receipts show that Lenny left his home in Las Vegas five days ago and checked into a hotel about twenty miles from here. Rented the car you found at the park and bought one meal in a local restaurant. Other than that, he wasn't on anyone's radar."

"What about phone records?" she asked.

"Called his bookie in Vegas several times and a few other numbers that turned out to be burners," Sharp said.

"Have you considered asking Shield to run a search on the guy? His people might know a better way to trace them. They want to catch this guy."

"And we don't? Believe me, I want to bury him."

"I hear ya. Keep me posted?"

"You do the same."

"Will do."

When she pulled into her driveway that evening and got out with Cooper, she'd ended a long shift topped off by another visit to see Jo-Jo. She spotted a dark SUV parked in front of her house. Bowman stepped out of the vehicle in no hurry.

She almost asked how he knew she would be here, then remembered the chip in her arm. Terrific. "To what do I owe the pleasure?"

"Been thinking about the text you sent me last night."

"Walk with me. Cooper needs to stretch his legs."

"Sure."

Down the street, she turned onto a small path that cut through the woods behind her house. "Checking in?"

"Afraid so."

She laughed but heard the nervous buzz behind it. It was nice to have someone checking in on her, even if the arrangement was temporary.

"Sharp said the man who shot himself was Lenny Vincent. He's from Vegas and a gambler," said Riley.

"I know. I talked to Sharp an hour ago."

"Why would he kill himself like that? The forensic team hasn't finished its analysis yet, but there were hair fibers found in his car that appear to be from Cassie. The theory is that he killed her."

"I don't know. Andrews began reviewing his records this afternoon. He was in deep financial trouble, and he has a wife and two kids. I wish I knew the Shark's end game."

"How could Vincent know I would be the one to track him in the woods?" Riley asked.

"My guess was that it was a calculated risk."

The Shark's web never seemed to end. "I started reading the files you gave me, and I'll finish them this evening."

"Do you ever rest or drop your guard?"

"Rest?" Riley asked. "Now and then. Dropping the guard? Almost never."

They walked in silence for several minutes, and when they got close to the woods, she let Cooper off his leash so he could run.

"Would you like coffee?" Riley asked.

"That would be great."

When the dog returned, they moved inside and she unholstered her gun, placing it in a closet lockbox, then unstrapped her belt and hung it on a peg.

As they passed into the kitchen, she flipped on the lights. The kitchen table was scattered with the files she'd been reading last night.

As he leaned against the doorjamb, arms crossed, watching her, she set a coffeepot to brew. "Did you have any trouble on the road today?"

"Nothing out of the ordinary."

"Good."

She pulled the file of the first victim again and reread it. "Angie was seventeen years old, and she had been on her own since age fifteen. She worked in some of the casinos backstage as a grip for their stage shows, likely with a fake ID," Riley said.

"If she worked in the casinos, it makes sense she'd have caught the Shark's attention."

She tapped her finger on the papers. "That's not what bothered me. It was the fact that she worked with the stage crew."

"Why would that bother you?"

"Remember the T-shirt she was wearing? It's for a band called BANG."

His eyes narrowed a fraction. "Andrews researched the band. They were handled by Byline Entertainment," Bowman said. "He said they broke up five years ago."

"Byline," she said. "That's the company leasing Hudson's field."

"Really?"

"Yeah. Could it be that simple?"

He stepped closer and glanced down at the picture of the first victim. "Shield had an informant while he was working the cases in New Orleans. She was a casino dealer and a part-time singer. She was the one who first told Shield about the Shark and his possible connection to the dead girls. She was strangled to death shortly after she talked to Shield."

"This guy has eyes and ears everywhere."

Bowman pulled his phone from his pocket and dialed a number. "Andrews, this is Bowman. Check on a company called Byline Entertainment and cross-check their concert schedules with local murders that match the Shark's MO. Great. Thanks." He ended the call, carefully tucking his phone back into his pocket.

Riley moved to the cabinets and removed two mugs. She could feel his gaze on her, and simply the idea of him looking at her made her heart beat faster.

"He's not going to touch you," Bowman said. There was such confidence in his voice.

She faced him. "You sound sure of yourself. He's eluded you and Shield for twelve years. Why would now be any different?"

"He's moving very quickly. He's killed two girls, Lewis, and I'd bet my life he is behind Lenny's suicide. When a killer accelerates like this, the tendency is to get sloppy. I will catch him."

She poured two cups of coffee and pulled a carton of half-and-half from the refrigerator. "Duke says I can make coffee taste like ice cream."

"Black is fine."

"Have you eaten? I've a frozen pizza. You're always feeding me. Least I can do is toss a pizza in the oven for you."

He stood close, his energy radiating with such power her skin tingled. "Thanks. But I already ate."

"Probably best for us both. Hanna loves my frozen pizzas—but her standards aren't super high." She handed him his coffee and filled Cooper's water and food bowls. As the dog crunched on his dinner, she faced Bowman.

He stood at the kitchen threshold, leaning against the doorjamb with a casualness that belied the intensity of his gaze. "You said Hanna is at a triathlon meet?"

"Yeah. She's on a local team. The coach is great. She's taken the kids to some high-level meets."

"What's Hanna's best event?"

"Swimming. Considering she only learned how to swim three years ago, she's amazing."

"Is she getting any kind of scholarship money?"

"That's the hope."

A half smile tugged his lips. "Have her look at Virginia Military Institute."

"Your school, right?" When he nodded, she shook her head. "Wouldn't work. She hates authority more than I do."

"Where'd you go to college?"

"I did community college nights and weekends, worked it around a handful of jobs, and then commuted to George Mason in Fairfax for the final two years. After that I went to the academy."

She sipped her coffee. "So, how long were you married?"

He met her gaze as if she'd touched a nerve.

"You fiddle with your ring finger as if you expect there to be a ring."

He looked at his hand, shaking his head. "Karen and I were married for seven years. She died of pancreatic cancer five years ago. About six months before you and I met at Quantico."

They'd been together at Quantico, but they'd never really had a conversation about anything other than work, and when alone, they got naked so fast words only got in the way. "I'm sorry," she said.

He raised his coffee to his lips. "So am I."

She quickly chased away an awkward silence, saying, "You were one of the best instructors at Quantico and you do a good job of keeping up with me."

"Is that a compliment?"

"It is."

Riley braced her hands behind her on the counter. Less than six feet separated them, but there was a pull. She wanted to touch him. Kiss him. Last time she'd gotten in too deep with him. This time could be different. This time she could enjoy him and find a way to walk back to her life with her heart intact. She was older. Wiser.

She moved to a chair and sat, taking time to unlace her boots. "You finally get those boxes unpacked in your office?"

"Not yet."

She pulled off the first boot and went to work on the second. "You haven't committed to the job yet, have you?"

He shook his head. "No, I'm in it for the long haul, but it'll take some time getting used to not living like a nomad."

She bet the corner office had a paycheck to match. "It looks like a sweet gig."

"It'll be different. I'm looking forward to settling down."

She yanked off the second boot. "You'll adapt. I have faith."

"Thanks."

Hesitating a breath, she rose and met his gaze. He was watching her and she knew he wanted her. And God, but she wanted him.

Damn. Shoving aside doubts, she crossed to him but stopped inches short. He stared at her but made no move to touch her. She slid her palm up his chest and around his neck. His hands rose to her arms as she pulled his face toward hers. She was tall, but reaching his lips meant rising on tiptoe. Her lips touched his first, and she allowed herself a light kiss, half hoping that touching him, tasting him, wouldn't be as good as she remembered. She drew back, gently biting her bottom lip.

"You taste nice," he said.

She moistened her lips. "You, too."

He stared with an intensity that excited and unsettled her.

She lowered from her toes to flat feet and moistened her lips again. "So, did I just really embarrass myself?"

His fingers tightened gently on her arms as if he feared she'd back away. "No."

She searched his face. "I promised myself I wouldn't kiss you. I swore. And now here I stand. I've tossed my cards on the table and you're simply staring."

He tugged her toward him until her breasts skimmed his shirt. Carefully, he pulled her hair free and watched it fall around her shoulders. "I like seeing it loose."

"If you say *soft* or *vulnerable*, I'll punch you."

He smiled. "*Sexy.* Does that adjective work?"

The deep, smooth timbre of his voice made her hot. "I go out of my way not to be sexy."

He shook his head. "You haven't done such a good job, as far as I'm concerned."

He leaned in, traced her lips with his thumb, and kissed her, gently at first. But the touch set her body on fire. It had been so long since she'd really wanted a man that the sensation was a little unsettling. She kissed him back, not caring about anything but touching him.

He wrapped his arms around her waist and pulled her to him, pressing her against his erection. "I've wanted to do this since that first day I saw you in the woods," he said. "God, you were fierce."

"I was covered in dirt, scratches, and sweat."

"I was hot for you as you climbed up that mountain after Carter. Amazing."

She laughed, feeling playful. "Then it's been a while for you, Mr. Bowman. That wasn't one of my prettiest moments."

"You're confident. And that's sexy as hell."

She leaned into his chest and kissed him on the lips. He threaded fingers through her hair. She moved her hand along his flat belly to his erection.

He groaned, and his hand tightened around the strands of her silky hair.

Her hand slid down the front of his pants, savoring the feel of his erection. When he muttered an oath, she pressed harder.

He clutched her hand. "Where's the bedroom?"

She pulled him down the hallway and closed the door behind them. He pinned her against the door, caressing her breasts as he kissed her.

Breathless, he pulled her toward the bed as he sat on the edge. She straddled him. He sucked in a breath, his hands on her hips. Fire blazed inside her.

She slid her fingers up his chest and around his neck. "If you've wanted me all this time, you've certainly done a good job of hiding it."

"Good to know." He kissed her again, this time more deeply, moving his tongue into her mouth and exploring. Her mind swirled, brushing aside any thoughts or worries that lingered from the day. It was just him. The two of them.

He stroked her breasts, teasing her nipple under the soft cotton fabric until it hardened. She moaned, dizzy with desire.

As she reached for his belt buckle, he touched her face, allowing his calloused thumb to trace her jawline and then her lips. She unfastened his belt, but before she could free him, he leaned into her, pulled her under him, and kissed her as he pushed her against the bed. As rumpled sheets and blankets pressed into her back, she was vaguely aware that she'd not made her bed today and nearly laughed at the absurdity of the thought; she was thinking about an unmade bed when she was ready to give her body to a man who had proved before he could leave her when the sun rose. She should have been leery of lowering her guard again, but she wasn't.

He reached for the end of her shirt and tugged it over her head. He traced the flat midline of her belly, an intense expression on his face, as he reached for the hook between her breasts and unfastened her bra. He pushed the bra aside and held her breasts.

"Beautiful," he murmured. He leaned down and kissed her, and she savored his touch as he teased the tips of her nipples until they were hard.

When he drew back and reached for the buttons on his shirt, she was breathless. As he unfastened the shirt, she undid the button of her waistband and wriggled out of her pants. She settled on the bed, watching him as he shrugged off his shirt and pants. His body was lean, corded muscle and just looking at him made her hot.

When he lay on top of her and kissed her again, his erection pulsed against her. She dragged her fingertips hungrily along his six-pack, arching her breasts and belly against him. Just as it had five years ago, being with him like this simply felt right.

His hand cupped her breast, teasing the nipple into a hard peak before he pulled his fingertips over her flat belly. It was as if he remembered what excited her. When those fingers dipped lower and began to circle in a maddening, exhilarating pace, she hissed in a breath, knowing she'd not last long at this pace. She shifted, spreading her legs.

Neither spoke as he positioned himself and pressed the tip of his erection against her moist center. When she spread farther for him, he met her gaze and pushed inside her. She drew in a breath as her body expanded, and for a moment, neither moved. Slowly, he began to slide in and out of her, testing and teasing her. She traced her hands down his sides and grabbed his hips, goading him to move faster.

Bracing his hands on either side of her head, he looked down and watched as he moved in and out of her. The raw desire on his face left her breathless.

"So sexy," he whispered. "I've imagined this moment dozens of times over the years."

In the darkest parts of the night, when she felt most alone, she'd also dreamed of him.

He moved faster. Sweat glistened between her breasts and on his back. The desire in her built, heating with each thrust, and when his fingertips touched her pulsing sex, she all but exploded under his touch.

A moan escaped her lips and her fingers dug into his back. "Oh God."

"Not yet," he whispered.

His fingers slowed for a moment and when she whimpered in protest, a devilish glint sparked in his eyes. She'd prided herself on absolute control, and now she had none.

He rose and kissed her taut nipple, gently capturing it between his teeth. He licked, suckled, taking his time as if he savored every taste.

When she thought she'd go mad, he began to move faster. Coherent thought vanished in a whirlpool of sensation that pulled her deeper and deeper until it overwhelmed her. Her body exploded with a riot of sensations. Bowman pushed faster and faster until he released.

He collapsed against her, his heart beating hard against her chest. He nestled his face in the crook of her neck, and for a moment neither moved as they struggled to catch their breath. Only as her heart slowed did her mind clear.

He gently rolled off her, closing his eyes for a moment, but already her mind buzzed and she wouldn't allow herself to nestle close to him. Sex was one level of intimacy but cuddling more so. A gentle breeze blew over her naked skin as she searched around for her T-shirt.

He traced those fingers over her spine, and this time the touch surprised her. "You're running away," he said.

"Not running. I don't want to crowd you."

He grabbed her hand, halting her slide off the bed. A gentle tug and she faced him. He'd tucked his other hand behind his head, staring at her with an unvarnished curiosity that made her want her T-shirt all the more. "You aren't crowding me."

The time for her coyness had passed. "Look, I know the last time we hooked up, it meant more to me than it did to you. I get that. I'm trying not to make the same mistake twice."

"It was a tough time for me. You were a perfect light in the darkness, but I wasn't ready to feel good or be happy. I woke up that morning and for the first time didn't think about Karen, and I felt guilty as hell."

She braced for another rejection. "It's okay."

"I'm not that guy anymore."

She shook her head. "I'm not the same gal. My life has more complications than it did before."

"Hanna's a good kid."

"She is and she's also a teenager with abandonment issues. It's not always easy. We're a package. Like Cooper and I are a package on the job."

He traced her jawline with his thumb.

"I understand."

A muscle tensed in his jaw as he stared at her. Without a word, he tipped his head forward and kissed her. Against her lips, he whispered, "You're better than I remember. And a few hours isn't going to cut it for me."

His hand came up and stroked her breast and she leaned into the touch, every nerve in her body firing again.

"I love your hair," he said as he raised a lock of it to his nose. "It still smells like roses."

When he entered her the second time, her breath caught in her throat and she had to fight not to rush to orgasm. It had been too long since she'd been touched like this.

He rose, staring at her with an intensity that stole her breath. He moved faster and faster while the heat built inside her so quickly she couldn't stop it. Within seconds her body tensed and she climaxed, the sensations rolling over her like crashing waves.

"Riley," he said.

He kissed her as he thrust deeper inside her, and within seconds, climaxed even harder than the first time. Finally, he rolled on his back and stared up at the ceiling. Despite what they shared, she couldn't read his expression. She'd promised herself this would be casual. She would not get invested. But she'd dealt with enough liars to know she was lying to herself.

Her phone rang, and as she sat up to get it, he grabbed a handful of her hair and playfully tugged.

"I need to check. Hanna is traveling."

He released her, relaxing back against the pillow. This was a man who understood duty.

She found her pants on the floor and unclipped her cell phone from the waistband.

"Tatum, this is Sharp. I thought you might like to know we have two more bodies."

Her thoughts went to Sandy, to Jo-Jo, and other girls she'd spoken to over the last few days. "Who?"

"Not over the phone. You have to see this. I'll text you the address."

"Okay, I'll be right there." She hung up, holding the phone close to her chest before she squared her shoulders.

Bowman traced his hand over her back. "What?"

"They found two bodies. Sharp won't say who."

"I'll go with you."

"Thanks. Second set of eyes might pick up something."

She quickly dressed in jeans, a T-shirt, and ankle boots before going to get Cooper. "Work time, Cooper."

No matter what time of day it was or how little sleep they'd both had, Cooper was always ready to work. After Riley texted the address to Bowman's phone, she pulled on her belt and holstered her gun. She ran fingers through her hair and made a ponytail.

At the front door, Bowman grabbed her arm and tugged her close, kissing her on the lips.

She smiled, and without a word, they each got into their vehicles. Twenty minutes later they arrived at the rural scene.

Several marked local and state cars were at the scene, as was the news van with Eddie Potter. The man must live on the police scanner.

Potter spotted her and started to move toward her. She heard Bowman get out of his SUV and slam the door closed, but she didn't dare look back. The last thing she needed was Potter suspecting a connection between her and Bowman.

She moved toward the reporter, her hand outstretched. "Mr. Potter, you keep long hours."

"I couldn't pass this up. Can you tell me anything about the victim?"

"I just arrived. I suggest you talk to Agent Sharp."

The reporter's face soured. "Tried that. Would rather not get my head bitten off again."

She forced down a smile. "Well, if you'll excuse me, I do need to check in."

"You'll double back and talk to me?"

"Can't make any promises."

Bowman had moved across the field toward the yellow crime scene tape and caught Sharp's attention. As she moved toward them, she heard Sharp's deep voice. "We don't know much at this point. I checked local property records on the way out here. No connection to the victims."

"Who are they?" Riley asked.

"Jax Carter and Darla Johnson," Sharp replied.

"What!" Riley didn't hide her surprise.

"Go look for yourself."

Sharp handed them latex gloves, which they each donned before ducking under the tape. Riley walked up to Martin as he snapped pictures. "Mind if Mr. Bowman has a look? He's worked his share of homicides."

"Sure. I don't mind."

Bowman followed Riley into the crime scene. They stared at thick ropes tossed over a beam and wrapped around the man's and woman's necks. The two dangled, their heads slumped forward, mouths agape, and the settling blood darkening their limp fingers. "Have you checked their pockets yet?" Riley asked.

"Not yet," Martin said. "I'm still photographing the scene."

"Mind if I check?" Bowman asked.

Martin stood back. "Let Agent Sharp do it, and I'll photograph him."

Sharp stepped forward and reached into Carter's back jeans pocket. He found a wallet stuffed full of money. "Not a robbery." He dropped the wallet into a plastic evidence bag and checked the other back pocket. Sharp pulled out a playing card. It was a joker.

"Another card?" Martin asked.

Sharp held up the card and studied the morbid smile of the joker in the center. The very ordinary card wasn't like the ones found on the dead girls. "I suppose this is some kind of message."

"They both were bit players in all this," Bowman said. "And whatever they did, the Shark didn't like it."

***

The Shark stared at the videotape of the girl sitting in the chair. Drugged and nearly unconscious, she possessed the physical beauty he always craved. Long dark hair. A slim face. Tapered hands. Like Angie. All were angels damaged and ruined by the streets, all of whom he set free from this world's pain and suffering.

Angie had been dead for twelve years, but he still couldn't forget her. He'd thought killing her would cleanse her from his senses, but she had burrowed deep under his skin and pierced his soul. Even now, she invaded his dreams, laughing at him, calling him common. *"You're pathetic,"* she said.

Killing her was never the plan. He'd wanted her to love him and to understand the depth of his feelings. But instead of acceptance, she'd laughed and turned away from him. *She'd shown him her back.* Disrespected him—something she'd never have done if not for the streets.

On that long-ago night, he'd snapped, grabbed her, and spun her around. Still, his frustration had amused her. She'd pouted as if looking at a small harmless child. He never remembered wrapping his hands around her neck. He was so lost in his own grief, he didn't hear her choke and gasp as he squeezed until the smile vanished and panic bloomed in her gaze. Her fingers, long and delicate, rose to his, trying to pry them free as pain distorted her features.

Her killing should have satisfied him. But even after all these years, he still heard her laughter. He still saw her in his dreams, mocking him.

The girl on the tape was not Angie. She was Riley. But she was so very similar to Angie that they could have been sisters. He traced the computer screen with his index finger; the sight of her could make him weep. She didn't look damaged, but he knew the streets had ruined her as they had destroyed Angie.

"I've won," the other player said.

Twelve years hadn't dulled the sting of disbelief. For the first time, he'd lost.

"Pay your debt," the winner said. *"Give me my money and the girl."*

Watching the recording, the Shark reached for a glass of bourbon and drank it in one gulp, wincing as the liquid burned his throat. She had been so drugged, she barely noticed his touch.

Refilling the glass, he raised it to his lips and stared at Riley's image, picturing the cord wrapping around her neck. He imagined her rapid pulse beating against the cord. The need to kill her—to kill Angie again—burning so strong.

Shoving aside the countless regrets he still attached to the day he lost Riley, he curled his fingers into fists, remembering what the video recording *didn't* capture.

"You aren't doing her any favors," the Shark said. *"She's been on the streets. She's damaged. She'll never be right."*

"That's my problem. Not yours."

"You're making a mistake. Kill her."

"Not today."

"Why the hell not?"

"Conscience? Hedging my bets. Who knows?"

The Shark cursed. *"Take your money. Take the girl. And be grateful Lady Luck favored you today."*

Now twelve years later, he wanted a rematch. He was all in.

***

Riley stayed at the crime scene for hours. She hoped that there'd be some bit of evidence that would tell her anything about this killer who had landed in her backyard and was circling around her like a stalking panther.

It was after eight when she walked through the back door of her house after disarming the newly installed alarm. Standing in the utility room, she didn't turn on the light as she stripped off her clothes, shoved them in a garbage bag, and tossed them outside. They smelled of death, and she did not want the stench coming into her house.

She locked the door behind her, checking it twice, and moved to the shower. Andrews had told her to keep the bandage dry for a couple of days, so she wrapped plastic wrap around her arm and turned on the water. When it was hot, she stepped under the spray, washing off the scent of the crime scene.

She dried off her hair and body and slipped into an oversized shirt before she unwrapped the plastic from her arm. She inspected the small insertion site, and the gravity of the Shark's reach struck home.

Threading her fingers through her wet hair, she moved into the kitchen and pulled out yesterday's leftover chili from Duke's. She popped it in the microwave and hit two minutes. Her doorbell rang and, without a thought, she reached for her gun. She moved to the side of the door. "Yes?"

"It's Duke."

She opened the door. "What brings you here?"

"I came to check on you."

"Alive and well. Come on inside." He moved into the house. She glanced around, seeing Hanna's extra junk shoved in a corner and her own coat draped over a chair by a stack of magazines and papers. She didn't care that Duke was seeing the mess but remembered Bowman had seen the chaos that came with a teenager in her home. She'd scared him off once before, and if she didn't now with her more complicated life, she'd be shocked. "I was heating up some chili. Can I offer you some?"

He slid his hand into his pocket. "Naw, had my fill of it today. I heard about Jax and Darla."

"Isn't that something? Guy tangles with the devil and gets nabbed."

A frown deepened the lines in his forehead. "What does that mean?"

She smoothed her hand over her head, knowing anything she said to Duke wouldn't be leaked. "Without going into a lot of detail, the man that Bowman is chasing might have killed them."

"The man who killed Vicky? I thought he was dead."

"There's another man who's setting up these poker games. The stake in the game is a girl with a very specific look."

"Shit."

"You used to gamble a lot. Did you hear of games like that?"

"Life-or-death games. Sure, I heard rumors. But I always figured it was a lot of hype."

"Yeah. I don't understand it myself. But if Jax and his girlfriend knew anything, they took it to their graves."

"Can't say I'm sorry they're dead. Scum. I told Jo-Jo. She didn't say much, but I know she'll sleep better tonight knowing they're no longer a threat."

"How's she doing?"

"It's going to be a long haul. And girls like her sometimes never completely leave the street behind. They're scared. At least she has a decent chance now."

"That's all anyone can ask."

He snapped his fingers, as if remembering the reason for the visit. "Maria wants you and Hanna to stay with us until this is over."

"Thanks, but I'm not leaving my home. But I will take you up on the offer to keep Hanna."

He allowed his gaze to roam the house, settling on the windows and the back French doors that opened to a small backyard. "Riley, we don't like the idea of you being here alone. It scares the hell out of us."

"I'll manage. I even have a fancy new security system courtesy of Shield."

He shook his head. "I can tell by the tone of your voice that your mind is made up."

"It is."

"When is Hanna due back?"

"Tomorrow."

He took a step forward and wrapped his arms around her. She relaxed into the embrace, thinking this is what it must feel like to have a father that loved her. "You're going to be okay, kid."

"Right."

He kissed her on top of her head and stepped back. "I know you've had a long day, so I'll go. Lock the doors after I'm gone. Call if you need anything."

Unshed tears tightened her throat. "Will do."

When she locked the door behind him, she leaned against it.

CHAPTER TWENTY-TWO

Friday, September 23, 6:03 a.m.

Riley's ringing phone woke her up minutes after six, and she realized she'd overslept. She pushed up and grabbed it, glancing at the number. She didn't recognize it. Groaned. Then remembering Hanna was traveling, she shoved the phone against her ear and said, "Tatum."

"Riley, this is Hanna."

She sat up, glancing at the red digital numbers glowing from the nightstand. The girl sounded agitated—no, terrified, just as she had when she'd first found her. "Honey, what's wrong? Where are you?"

"I'm at this house." She pulled in a breath as if trying to stem the tide of tears. "And I don't know how I got here."

Riley swung her legs over the side of the bed, her heart kicking into high gear. Her thoughts jumped to the Shark. "Are you sure you're not in the hotel room?"

"No. I remember the hotel room. We woke up early to get on the road. An hour ago, we were at a gas station. I went to the counter to get a drink. I drank about half, but it tasted funny, so I threw it out. I said I was going to be sick, and some man helped me out to the alley to throw up. I passed out. And now I'm here."

"Where is here?" Standing, Riley frantically searched for her clothes. Fear circled around her.

Hanna began to cry. "Riley, I'm scared."

She glanced toward the other side of her bed, noting only the faint impression of Bowman's head still etched in the pillow. She struggled to keep her voice calm. "I need you to take a deep breath. Stay focused, Hanna."

"I'm trying."

"You're doing just fine." She hurried to her dresser drawer, where with trembling hands, she yanked out jeans and a clean shirt. "Do you know where the house is? Do you remember any part of the ride?"

"I don't remember anything."

"What about sounds. Did you hear anything?"

"No." She drew in a ragged breath. "You're supposed to come. He said there will be a car outside for you."

Panic rose. She'd thought Hanna would be safe out of town, but now she could see that was foolish. The Shark had found her. She struggled to keep her voice calm. "Who is he?"

"I don't know. I do know the car will be there in three minutes." She started to weep. "Riley, I'm scared."

Her heart hammered as her mind raced to the next step. "It's okay, Hanna. I'll be there. I'm coming for you."

Silence filled the line.

"Hanna!" When the girl didn't answer, Riley shouted her name again. God, this was her kid, and it was her fault that Hanna was now in danger.

"He said to leave your phone and gun," Hanna finally said.

"Okay, honey. I'll do whatever it takes. Tell him, I will do what he says."

"He's watching." Hanna's voice cracked with fear. "Riley, hurry."

"Okay." The line went dead, leaving Riley to stare at her cell. As a cop she'd been trained to act in times of stress and to not panic. But all the scenarios she'd ever run had never involved her own child.

She set the cell on the rumpled sheets of her bed and tugged on her jeans and a black long-sleeved shirt that covered her bandage. "Bowman, if I ever needed you, it's now."

She shoved her feet into ankle boots, grabbed her phone and a hair tie, and fastened her long hair into a bun. She smoothed damp palms over her jeans and opened the gun box that contained her service weapon. She shoved her weapon in an ankle holster and strapped it under her pant leg. She also grabbed a pocketknife, which she slid in her boot. She dialed Bowman.

"Riley," he answered.

Bowman's deep voice was tense, cutting, and she nearly broke at the sound of it. God, she needed him now. But instead of giving in to the tears, she dug deep and fell back on her police training. "The Shark has Hanna. He's sending a car for me in three minutes and I have to go."

"Riley, don't get in that car."

"I don't have a choice. Let's hope Mr. Andrews knows his stuff." She didn't dare say *tracker*, as her cell phone was likely compromised.

"Don't go." His voice was diamond hard.

She rushed to the window and saw the black sedan pulling up in front of her house. It was the car she'd seen when she'd been running days ago. Getting into the car was akin to signing her death warrant. The Shark had come back to kill her. But she wasn't ready to die and there had to be some way to save Hanna and herself. "I have to go. He'll kill Hanna if I don't. Don't call the cops."

"Riley, do not get in that car. Wait for me. I can be there in twenty minutes."

"I don't have twenty minutes. I don't have one minute. I have to go now."

"Damn it, Riley! Do not go!"

The anger and frustration in his voice nearly broke her heart. She didn't want to do it this way. She didn't. But there was no other play right now.

She hung up the phone, tossed it aside, and squaring her shoulders, walked out the front door, pulling it closed behind her. The windows were tinted and the passenger-side rear door popped open just a crack. She opened it, sat down on the rich leather seats, and stared at the dark partition dividing her from the front seat.

"Where's Hanna?" she shouted.

"Close the door." The calm voice came over the speakers.

"I'm not doing anything until you tell me who's got my kid and where she is!" The more time she could delay, the more time Bowman had to find her.

"Shut the door or get out now. You've got ten seconds and then Hanna dies."

Her options gone, she shut the door. "Where is she?"

"You'll see her soon." The car began to drive.

***

Bowman swung his legs over the side of his bed and clicked on a light. The echo of Riley's voice, filled with fear and pain, ricocheted in his head. The sense of helplessness he'd felt when his wife was sick crept from the darkness as he reached for his jeans and a T-shirt and crossed the room to his computer. He wasn't fighting a faceless disease this time but a psychopath whom he would find and destroy. And Riley was not a vulnerable runaway anymore. She was a smart woman and one of the best police officers he'd ever met. He was banking on the fact that she'd find a way to buy time.

He hit the "Return" button to bring up the screen and opened the tracking program. Riley was on the move and headed west fast.

He dialed Andrews, who answered on the second ring. "Check your monitor."

"I'm looking at it now. Did Riley say where she was going?" Andrews asked.

"No. She called me and said the Shark has Hanna. She is now in a car sent by the Shark."

"Have you called the cops?"

"I have a good idea what he'll do if the cops roll up."

"Do you need my help? I can be ready in five."

Bowman rose and moved to the corner of his bedroom where he kept his gear. "Notify Shield and then suit up and follow the signal. I'm leaving now."

"Consider it done."

***

Though the windows in the car were tinted and Riley couldn't see where they were driving, she'd been on the move thirty minutes, and judging by the feel of rolling land around them, she knew they'd headed west. At one point they'd slowed to cross what felt like train tracks.

She didn't know her specific location but knew this area of the state was home to some rich horse farms. The car slowed and turned to the right, moving unhurriedly down what sounded like a gravel drive. When the car stopped she tensed, fingers curled into fists. Her door unlocked.

The driver said, "Ms. Tatum, he is waiting for you."

"Who is he?"

"You need to exit the vehicle."

Riley got out of the car and stared at the driver's-side tinted window, which did not open. She knocked on the door and shouted, "Where are we?"

The window opened, but the stone-faced man did not look at her. "He is waiting for you. Go inside." He gestured toward the house.

Riley stood at the top of a circular drive that curved in front of a three-story brick house complete with a porch that wrapped around the front. Twin large planters filled with bright-yellow flowers and trailing ivy stood on either side of the wide front door.

Wind whispered through the trees. Fine gravel crunched under her feet as she crossed to the front door. She was all alone. Exposed.

She climbed the steps and stopped at the door. As she raised her hand to lift a brass lion-head knocker, footsteps echoed on the other side. The door snapped open.

Standing before her was a smartly dressed older man with sharp green eyes and pale skin. Leaning on a cane, he was thin in a brittle kind of way but possessed a dynamic energy that made it impossible to ignore him. His suit was cut from a charcoal-gray cloth—handmade, judging by the quality—and his shirt was sewn from fine linen. The tie was Hermès.

"Welcome, Riley. I've been waiting for you."

The sharp angles of the man's face struck a familiar chord in her memory. "Mr. Duncan. I saw you on the news talking about your music festival."

He smiled. "I wasn't sure if you'd caught the interview. We met formally that one time years ago. I know you don't remember me, but I've been tracking your career for years."

"Why are you doing this?"

He held out his hand, indicating she should enter. "This isn't a conversation to be had on the front porch. You're my guest, and I'd like to offer you a drink."

"I don't need a drink. In fact the last time I had one of your drinks, I didn't wake up for seven days. Where's Hanna?"

"She's fine. Safely tucked away upstairs. But if you want to know more, you'll have to come inside."

Tension tightened Riley's chest. She always identified her exits no matter where she was, but this house was so large she had no way of knowing how to escape. She stepped inside, and he slowly closed the door behind her with a click that echoed off a two-story-high foyer crowned with a massive crystal chandelier. A large staircase carpeted in red wound to a second-floor hallway that vanished somewhere in the mansion.

The foyer was carpeted with a handmade Indian rug and furnished with a round mahogany table, which displayed a crystal vase filled with red roses that perfumed the space with a soft scent.

She thought about the tracker in her arm and knew Bowman was paying attention. "No one notices street girls vanishing from multiple cities. And concerts draw girls, don't they?"

"They do. And moving around has been helpful. As much as I would like to have stayed in New Orleans, I was a little too greedy twelve years ago and it almost ruined me."

"I remember the concerts that summer. There must have been a half dozen."

"It was a good gig. Kept me in town six weeks. But handling all those venues is stressful and I found I couldn't resist setting up games."

"How many games have you set up over the years?"

"I've lost count."

"And none of the other players turned on you."

"A man like me develops a knack for spotting people who enjoy killing. In all the years, I've had two issues, if that's what you want to call them. The first was losing you and the second was Kevin. I thought I had the guy figured out, but it turns out he had no stomach or spine for mercy killing. He became too much of a liability."

"Did he kill Vicky or did you?" She knew the answer but needed to keep him talking to give Bowman time. She needed any time she could squeeze from this madman.

"He killed her." Duncan flexed his fingers and stared at them as if they'd betrayed him. "I wanted to kill her. I really did. My hands used to be so strong, and I could steal life with the twist of a cord. But my hands don't work like they used to. See, I'm sick. I have heart disease. The simplest movements exhaust me. It won't be long before I won't have the breath to talk."

His death wouldn't be painful enough as far as she was concerned. And as much as she wanted to take joy in his suffering, her goal now was to get Hanna and survive.

"You've won so much in your life," she said. "Money, prestige, and I don't know how many poker games. And now you're losing to your own body."

"Not having control is frustrating." He smiled. "As you must know by now, I'm not a good loser. When I fell sick, it became a bit of an obsession."

"Who did you lose to?" She wanted to know the name of the bastard who had risked her life on the turn of cards. "That's bothered me most since all this began."

"Someone you know."

She'd crossed paths with so many over the years. "Who?"

Instead of answering, the Shark deflected. "Did you know the man who beat me won half a million dollars and you were allowed to go free? I was blown away. I'd never lost before."

"It must have been a frustrating blow."

"You can't imagine." He smiled as if he were talking to a kindred spirit. "I lost track of you right after the game, but never him. I followed his exploits over the last dozen years and was amused by his efforts to appear legitimate."

"Appear?"

"He is an addict like me, and no matter how much he swears he's gone legit, I know he hasn't. I've heard about some of his private games.

He's always been one of the best, being most careful not to lose too much when the cards turn on him."

"Are you talking about my stepfather, William Charles?"

His eyes sparked with amusement. "Good guess, but wrong."

Her temper burned in her gut, but she refused to give it free rein. This bullshit guessing game would keep him talking.

"I even thought it might be Shield," she said.

He chuckled. "He's a true gambler at heart. The way he rolled the dice and left the FBI to start that company. And he was in New Orleans during the killings, wasn't he?"

She'd thought her guess had been too wild to consider. "Is it Shield?"

"No."

The only other gambler she knew in her life was Duke. But he didn't even play lotto scratch cards. He even frowned on the coin game heads or tails.

The Shark tugged at his shirt cuff, adjusting the square gold cuff link. "When I became sick, I searched him out. He didn't see me, but I saw him. And who should I see talking to him? You. I almost wept. It was as if it were all meant to be."

Who had he seen her talking to? Dread surrounded her, teasing her and prodding her to surrender to her inevitable loss. "Who is it?"

He shook his head. "Not yet. Ask me who killed Cassie."

She checked her frustration and fear. Keep playing his game. Buy time. "Who?"

"Lenny Vincent, a Vegas gambler. Lenny was willing to make one final bet for me so that I'd leave his family alone. I thought he did well for a man who had never been in the woods before."

"When I saw the playing card, I knew it was you."

"You're the final round. I want to end the games as a winner."

"You're talking about betting my life—a stake you don't own, but stole."

He laughed. "Those kind of details bore me."

"What if I choose not to play?"

"You have a choice now, Riley. You can participate in the game as you did twelve years ago, or I can play the game with Hanna as the stake. Not my first choice, but there must be a stake in the last game."

"Aren't you worried that I'm wearing a wire?" she said.

"There are so many signal jammers within a two-mile radius of this house that no signal will travel beyond these walls."

Whatever hope she had for Bowman's help was dashed. She was truly alone. "And you'll kill Hanna if the player loses."

"That's the risk. Her champion, if you want to call him that, beat me twelve years ago. Maybe he'll get lucky again. Maybe not. Either way, there must be a stake in the game. You or Hanna. Choose."

She stared at him, angry and frustrated, knowing she had no real choice. "What if my champion loses? What about Hanna?"

"After the game, I'll take her back to your house. She'll live."

"How can I trust you?"

He cocked his head. "I never break my word, Riley. You're living proof of it. I'm disappointed you even need to ask."

"And if my champion wins? We both walk free?"

"Absolutely."

She smoothed her hands over her jeans, not having the faintest clue how she was going to save Hanna and maybe herself. To buy time and ensure Hanna's survival, Riley knew she had to play. "All right. I'll play."

A smile curved the edges of his lips. "I'm glad. You don't know how much this all means to me." He held out a hand, indicating she should move toward a set of pocket doors. "The game is waiting. Are you sure I can't get you a drink? I promise it won't put you to sleep this time because I want you awake for the final round."

"Pass."

The doors opened to a lush sitting room. The furnishings were a mix of modern and old, eclectic, but very expensive. A man she assumed had been her driver stood in the corner.

"I want to see Hanna," she said.

"That wasn't part of the deal," the Shark said. "And I gave you my word she is fine."

"You don't rank very trustworthy in my book." She shook her head as she reached for her ankle holster and drew her gun. She pointed it at him. "So consider this a renegotiation. I'm not playing if I don't see her."

The Shark studied her with a mixture of annoyance and respect. "I bet myself you wouldn't come here defenseless. You are too smart for that. And I know you can shoot me. But remember if you do, Hanna is dead before you clear this room."

"Where is she?"

"She's fine. And I'll really enjoy winning this game." He looked at the driver. "If Riley hands you her gun, then you can bring Hanna here."

Riley's grip on the weapon tightened. This was her only defense. But she'd seen the bodies of the girls he'd killed. He wouldn't hesitate to kill her child. Going against all her training and instinct, she handed it over.

The Shark seemed even more pleased by her distress. He nodded and the driver vanished behind a door.

"Who is the man who bet me in the game?"

"You'll see him in a moment."

The door opened and Hanna stumbled into the room. She was drugged, but she was functioning enough to walk. Her vacant gaze rose to Riley and she started to cry, moving toward her in fast but awkward steps. "Riley."

Riley wrapped her arms around her, holding her close. The girl trembled in her arms. "It's okay, baby. No matter what, you're going to be fine."

Hanna's tears dripped onto Riley's shoulder. "Riley, I'm scared."

"I know." It took all her strength to cling to her composure and sound calm. "But you'll be fine."

Hanna buried her face in Riley's shoulder. "What about you?"

Riley pulled Hanna back so that she could see her eyes. "Don't worry about me. I'll be okay."

"But he's got us both here."

She brushed a stray strand of hair from the girl's eyes. "Put your money on me, because I plan on winning."

The Shark checked his watch and snapped his fingers. "Take Hanna away."

Riley nearly broke as the girl clung to her and begged to stay. "Where are you taking her?"

"There's a nice soft bed for her to lie upon while we play the game."

Hanna gripped Riley's shirt. "I don't want to go."

"It'll be fine." The lie barely stumbled off her tongue; it sickened her to say it. But until she figured out who all the players were in this game, she had no choice. "I'll come find you soon."

"I don't want to go."

"You have to," she whispered into the girl's ear. "You have to. I promise to come for you."

"You swear?" she gasped.

"Yes," she said with a conviction that surprised her.

"Lock her in her room and then stand guard outside the house."

The driver nodded and took Hanna by the arm, pulling her toward the door. The girl cried louder while Riley's stomach knotted.

When it was the two of them, she faced the Shark. "Who's the other player?"

He smiled. "You are about to find out."

***

Bowman drove the backcountry roads in his black SUV at speeds bumping eighty miles an hour as he monitored Riley's signal on his phone. The signal was growing stronger, so he knew he was getting closer. She was less than three miles from him. Just a little more time . . .

And then in a blink the beep went dead.

"Shit." He tapped the console on the dash. He grabbed his cell and dialed Andrews. On the first ring he heard, "Andrews."

"I lost the signal," Bowman said.

"I see you on my map. When did you lose the signal?"

"Moments ago."

"How far ahead of you do you estimate she is?"

"I don't know. Fifteen minutes. Twenty. The scanner says she's about three miles from me."

"Give me a second to check the area homes."

Bowman eased off on the gas pedal, knowing he should stop and wait for Andrews, but too worried to sit still. "Hurry up."

"I'm calculating."

"Need it yesterday."

Silence followed and then Andrews said, "There's a large estate twenty clicks due west on Route 602. It's called the Sheffield Estate. It was built five years ago by . . . shit. It was built by Byline Entertainment."

Bowman cursed. "Vicky's body was found in the field rented by Byline for the concert. The Shark is a brazen bastard."

"What do you need?" Andrews asked.

"Feed directions into my GPS. And tell Shield. I want all the troops in on this op."

"Consider it done. Bowman, I've been watching Riley's video over and over trying to dig every detail out of it. I've isolated a sound. I think I know who's playing for Riley's life."

***

Riley sat in a large red straight-backed chair with thick walnut armrests. Like everything in the house, it was the finest of its kind. The Shark felt as if he deserved the best.

He sat at the table and carefully arranged the chips, clearly excited about the game.

She couldn't resist goading him. "What does your opponent get if he wins?"

"He won't win."

"But what if he does?" she challenged. "Does he get another half-million dollars this time?"

"This time he does get a sizable amount of money, but more important, he gets his freedom and my promise that I'll never bother him again."

"He doesn't want to be here."

The Shark shrugged. "I actually think he does. Made me twist his arm, but I saw the change in his eyes when he accepted the challenge."

"Why him?"

"How can it be a rematch unless we have all the players from the first game?"

"You sent Lenny into the woods. You bet I'd be the one to find him."

He smiled. "Betting is a hard habit to break."

The Shark seemed to know all the angles of his opponent before the games began. "Why my type? What's the deal with dark-headed runaways?"

"You are searching for motivation. That's your cop mind working. Very good."

She knew enough about interrogation to know that he'd talk more if she sounded as if she empathized. "I would wager some woman must have hurt you very badly."

"I never thought I had a type or could really care about anyone until Angie."

Angie had been the seventeen-year-old runaway. "How did you meet her?"

"She was following one of the bands. Young, wise beyond her years, but ultimately a lost soul."

"And you wanted to help her." She nearly choked on the words.

His smile faltered. "I loved her. I tried to save her from the streets until I realized she was too damaged to save."

"How was she damaged?"

"She couldn't control herself. I promised her the world and realized she was seeing other men." For a moment his face took on a faraway expression. "She looked so much like you."

"What happened? Why did you kill her?"

"I was gambling large to impress her. I took risks I'd never taken before. When the last card turned and I realized I'd won, it was thrilling. I went to her immediately and told her what I'd won for her. But the moment I took her in my arms, I knew she'd cheated on me."

"How could you tell?"

"I could smell another man on her. When I called her a whore, she just laughed. It was her taunts that sent me into a rage. She was an ungrateful bitch."

"Maybe she hadn't cheated on you."

"She had. I know it. I know women cheat, and yet I believed she was different. If I hadn't loved her so much, I wouldn't have killed her. My emotions ran so deep."

"And after she was dead?"

"I missed her almost immediately. I wanted to forgive her, but she was gone. And then I started to see her face in some of the faces of the young runaways that summer. The urge to gamble returned. And so did the urge to kill."

Riley wanted to keep him talking. She was stealing time on the slim hope Bowman would find Hanna and her. "What was it about the girls that reminded you of Angie?"

"The ones I liked the best were smart and real survivors. They were strong. Scrappers like Angie. They weren't afraid of me. I wanted to see the fight in their eyes when I strangled them. Angie fought me to the end."

He raised his focus, allowing it to trail over her face and hair. "I prefer it when your hair isn't tied in a knot."

Panic tugged at her composure, but she shoved it aside, refusing to show him any fear. She took her hair tie out, tipped her head downward slightly, and ran her fingers through her hair. "How much do I remind you of Angie?"

"More than any of the others." His voice deepened.

She curled a strand of hair around her finger. "When this is over, the first thing I'm going to do is cut my hair."

He laughed. "Angie would have said something like that."

"You also killed the singer," she pressed. "Shield's informant."

His expression sharpened. "That pretty girl asked one too many questions."

"I'm not Angie. Unlike her, I'm getting out of this alive."

Smiling, he shook his head. "You're avoiding the real question. Don't you want to know who was willing to risk your life for a card game?"

Yeah. That was at the top of her list. But right now she needed more time. "I'm more interested in you. Think all this rage means you have mommy issues?"

He laughed. "No. I loved my mother very much. And if you think talking will delay the game, you're wrong."

"I'm thinking your mother didn't love you at all."

The savage smile vanished.

Ah, she had hit a nerve. "Did Angie remind you of Mommy? Is that why you could never really trust her?"

Despite his age he moved quickly, raising his hand up like a cat and striking her across the face. The unexpected impact sent her head flying back as pain rocked her skull and shot through her jaw. She tasted blood.

He flexed his fingers as his breathing quickened. She was hurting, but he was also struggling.

Carefully, she touched her bruised lip. "You hit like a girl." If she provoked his temper, his judgment in the poker game might slip. Battered and bruised was a small price to pay if the other player won and she and Hanna got out of this alive.

Seething, he raised his hand to strike again but stopped. "It's time to play."

"Hard to believe someone like me could scare the hell out of you."

He leaned close so that his face was only inches from hers. "You do not scare me."

"Liar."

The old man shook his head. "You are trying to provoke me."

"Just calling it like I see it."

He smiled. "I think your strength is your best quality." With the buzz of a bell, the man who had vanished returned. "Bring in the other player."

"Yes, sir," the man said.

She wasn't expecting to recognize the player, but when she turned and saw the familiar face, she felt as if she'd been punched hard in the gut. She blinked, shaking her head as she tried to will the sight of him away.

"Duke?" she whispered, her voice tight with fear and anguish. "This can't be true. You haven't gambled for twenty years."

He looked at her bruised face. A sense of resignation deepened the lines around his eyes and mouth.

She sat there stunned as the pain of betrayal cut into her. Duke. How could it be Duke? This had to be a mistake. He'd said once she was like a daughter to him, like family. Tears tightened her throat. "Duke, you met me at the bus in Virginia. You took care of me. You protected me."

He sat at the table, staring at the sealed deck of cards. "Riley, I put you on that bus in New Orleans."

"I don't understand."

He shoved out a sigh. "Gambling gets in your blood. You think you can control it, but it's always there, lurking. I was in New Orleans and the fever to gamble hit me hard. I heard the Shark was in town and I wanted to test him. When I found out what the stake was, I went looking and I found you on the streets. I was so sure I'd win. I didn't think anyone would get hurt. And they didn't."

"And if the cards hadn't gone your way, would you have killed me?" Duke didn't answer.

"The Shark had already killed four girls in New Orleans," she said.

Duke shook his head. "I had nothing to do with those games."

"You had to have known about the girls."

"There was nothing I could do for them. And I was so sure I could save you when I won." He stared at her. "You were in a bad place in New Orleans. I saw how afraid and hungry you were. It was a matter of time before the streets ate you alive."

"You *knew* this killer was out here."

An angry frown deepened the lines on his face. "And he knew where I lived and where you were. He knows about Maria. If I'd spoken up, we'd all have been killed. I had no way out."

"So you let him go free?"

"Shit, Riley." Pain mingled with anger. "Don't you get it? Not a day goes by that I don't regret this."

"Why can't I remember you and the game?"

"The drugs I gave you wiped out your memory," the Shark said. "It was designed to make you forget several days before the game so if he did win, I could set you free without worries."

She couldn't look away from Duke. "And you won? What happened? Why didn't you dump me back on the streets where you found me?"

"I couldn't. You could barely walk, and it would've been like throwing you to the wolves. So I put you on a bus and made sure I met the bus. I brought you here. I saved your life."

"But you're risking it again now."

"He's going to kill Maria if I don't play."

"We've talked enough. Time to play," the Shark said.

Both men sat at the table. The dealer, while both men watched, broke the seal. The cards were elaborate, like the ones in her pocket and Vicky's backpack and Cassie's pocket.

"Who put the cards in my pocket?" Riley asked.

"I did," Duke said. "It was one of the Shark's stipulations. Win or lose, he wanted to leave his mark."

"I trusted you," she said.

Duke dropped his gaze to the cards, his eyes sharpening. She'd seen that look when he'd been talking to Jax on the phone. This was a man she didn't recognize, because now she was getting a glimpse into his darker days as a younger man. The gambler. The man who'd lived for over two decades on the turn of a card.

Her mouth still throbbing, she sat, knowing she could berate Duke, but right now she needed his focus on the game. Her life and Hanna's depended on him winning.

"We'll play one hand," the Shark said. "One hand decides it all."

Duke nodded.

The Shark looked at his dealer. "Would you get Riley some ice for that cut on her lip?" the Shark said. "I think it's swelling."

"Yes, sir."

When the dealer approached her with a white linen cloth filled with ice, she accepted it. *Play nice, Riley. Your shot will come.*

"We're playing five-card stud, Riley," the Shark said. "You know how the game is played, don't you?"

"I do." She gripped the cloth, wondering if she could wrap it around the Shark's neck and kill him. She looked to the closed doorway and windows. On the slim chance she could fight her way out of here, she'd never get to Hanna in time. She might as well have been handcuffed to the Shark.

***

Bowman cut the lights to his SUV when the GPS told him his last turn would be around the next bend. He slowed and pulled to the side of the road. Grabbing his gear, he unholstered his weapon and screwed a suppressor on the end. He hurried along the edge of the road, knowing that going directly up the driveway was too risky. The Shark must have surveillance posted around the property. He reached for his radio. "Andrews."

"Here."

"Anything on satellite? What do you see?"

"The house is lit up. I see three vehicles. Looks like there are two men standing guard."

"Two?" Bowman asked.

"Is that a concern?" Andrews asked.

"No. I'll contact you when it's over. Where's the cavalry?"

"Ten minutes out."

"Everyone comes in quiet. No sirens."

"Understood."

"Out." He clipped the radio to his belt and, gun in hand, moved through the woods toward the house. The early-morning sun allowed him to navigate at top speed. "Just buy me ten more minutes, Riley. Just ten more minutes."

***

"Did you bring the money?" the Shark asked.

Duke set a worn backpack on the table. "Two hundred grand. It's what I have left from our last game."

"Two hundred grand?" Riley shook her head, fearful if she said more, she'd lose her temper.

Duke unzipped the backpack. "For every dollar I put in, the Shark staked one hundred. I had only five grand in New Orleans."

"And my life to risk," she said.

Slowly, Duke unpacked the money and set it on the table in neat stacks. "The plan was to turn it into half a million and save you. And I did it, Riley."

The Shark snapped his fingers. "I've got twenty million to cover that bet."

Duke carefully removed his watch and set it precisely beside him. Riley wondered if the act were a ritual from his gambling days.

The dealer gave the Shark and Duke twenty poker chips, each representing $1 million. Each player was then dealt one card that remained facedown. Neither player would discover the card's value until the last moment of the game. The second card was dealt faceup.

Duke's second card was a queen of hearts; the Shark's was a nine of hearts. The Shark had the lowest-ranking card, so the rules required he bet first. He pushed in five chips. With no expression on his face, Duke matched the Shark's bet.

Riley shifted in her seat, doing her best to focus on the fact that Duke was off to a good start.

Duke's third card was an ace of clubs; the Shark's was a seven of hearts. Because Duke had the two best cards, it was his turn to bet. He wagered four chips. The Shark matched him and raised him another four chips. Duke accepted the challenge, and now both players had staked $13 million.

Riley could barely breathe. Duke was pulling better cards, but that could all change.

Duke's fourth card was a queen of diamonds. The Shark received a ten of hearts. Still holding the better hand, Duke bet three more chips. The Shark matched him. The pot was $16 million.

Riley studied Duke's calm face. He appeared to be in total control, as if he expected to win. A part of her dared to hope the game would go in their favor.

The fifth and final cards were dealt. Duke got the queen of clubs, the Shark the eight of hearts. Duke pushed his remaining four chips into the pot. The Shark matched the bet. Both were all in at their limit.

All that remained was to turn over the first card. Odds were overwhelmingly in Duke's favor. The Shark would have to produce a six or jack of hearts to win.

Duke turned over his card. Queen of spades. He had four of a kind.

Riley held her breath.

The Shark tapped his finger twice on his card and paused for a long moment. He smiled at Riley before turning it over. Jack of hearts.

"A straight flush," the Shark said. "I win. Riley dies."

The blood drained from Duke's face.

She gripped the towel, which she twisted around the ice until it was a hard ball. Her mind still could not fully process this. Yes, Duke had bet her life twelve years ago, but he didn't know her then. Surely, now after all this time, he would find a way to save her. He had to be pretending, playing along with all this until he found a way to save them.

Duke did not rise from his seat. He sat frozen, his fingers clenched.

"Time to pay up," the Shark said.

Duke curled his fingers. "I can't do it. I can't."

"If you don't, I'll have a few of my associates visit your house and they'll skin your wife alive while you watch."

When Duke looked up, tears glistened in hard eyes. "Riley and Hanna have nothing to do with this."

The Shark rose and circled around Duke. "We played. Lady Luck chose me. Now you have to pay your debt."

Duke looked in Riley's direction but didn't make eye contact. "I'm sorry."

She faced the Shark. "Hanna can walk away from this unharmed?"

He nodded. "I am a man of my word."

Her grip tightened on the towel. A strike to Duke's temple would hurt like hell and might buy her some time, but then what? There were three candelabra on the sideboard. Get to those and she had a weapon. "You're not going to kill me. My God, Duke, you've been like a father to me."

The Shark said nothing as he reached for his phone. "Maria will die so slowly."

Duke stood but didn't move forward.

The Shark dialed. "I'm calling my man stationed outside your house."

Duke's jaw tensed as his eyes sharpened with a desperate panic.

The Shark spoke clearly and slowly. "Are you outside of Duke's house? Good. Instead of starting with Maria, start with Jo-Jo, that girl from the streets. I want Maria and Duke to hear her screams first."

"Stop!" Duke pushed away from the table, his hands clenched as he moved toward Riley.

Riley stood up. "Duke, you will be no better than him if you do this."

"I can't worry about that." As Duke reached for her, she swung the ice cloth and caught him on the jaw. He stumbled back, holding his hand to his stubbly chin. She pulled the ice pack back and twirled the towel, ready to strike again.

The pain energized Duke, heating the fire in his eyes. He rubbed his chin, and cursing, he lunged forward with more speed than she anticipated. She readied to swing when the Shark came up behind her and hit the side of her knee hard with his cane. Her knee buckled as pain shot up her leg. Her leg crumpled, and she hit the ground hard.

She blinked, trying to fill her lungs with air and clear her head. She managed to roll onto her side and push herself halfway up before Duke shoved her in the chest and slammed her flat against the carpeted floor. Her heart raced as she fought pain. She would not die this way.

Duke straddled her, sitting hard on her midsection and knocking the wind from her. She tried to gasp in air and reach her boot, but he pinned her arms with his knees. She managed a feeble punch to his side, but he didn't seem to notice. He quickly pulled a long cord from his pocket and wrapped it around her neck.

"Please don't fight," he said.

She spat in his face.

"You thought Duke was so noble," the Shark said. "Who do you think killed Jax and Darla?"

Riley searched Duke's gaze, expecting some kind of denial. But she saw none. "Duke?" she rasped.

Duke tightened the rope. "Yeah, I killed them both. They didn't deserve to suck up any more oxygen on this planet."

"Think about it, Riley," the Shark said. "Why did he really help you?"

She looked into Duke's eyes, unable to pull in a breath to speak.

"Shut up, old man," Duke said.

The Shark towered over her. "You deserve to know why he really put you on that bus. He gambled that I'd want a rematch. He gambled that I'd come looking for you and he'd get another chance to win big again. You were nothing more than a walking poker chip."

Tears welled in her eyes as she tried to wedge her fingers under the rope. But her movements were slowing. Her vision was graying.

For the second time in her life, she teetered close to the abyss. With her last breath, she screamed.

***

Bowman moved as quiet as a cat through the dark, and when he saw the two guards, he assessed the order in which he would take them out. The one on the right was taller, thicker, and had the look of a linebacker. Not quick, but likely threw a hard punch. The one on the left was muscled but with a leaner frame. Bowman guessed he was the faster of the two, so he would be the first to go.

He raised the gun and fired. The larger of the two guards fell. The second guard barely had time to react before Bowman fired again. The man dropped to the ground.

Bowman approached both cautiously, and confirming they weren't a threat, he searched the pockets of the leaner man. Nothing. He shifted his focus to the other man's pockets, where he found several keys in his jacket.

He grabbed the keys and rushed to the front door. Methodically he began trying each in the lock. The first didn't work. Neither did the second. Inside the house, he heard Riley scream. *Hang on, Riley.* Cursing, he shoved the next key in the lock. It released the tumblers. Gripping his gun, he opened the front door and then the double mahogany doors of a parlor. He surveyed the scene and in a split second identified the threats. An unknown male. An old man who must have been the Shark. And Duke on top of a still Riley.

Bowman fired twice, hitting the first man center of mass in the chest and killing him. The Shark looked up at him, his dark eyes narrowing with hatred, as he raised the phone. Knowing the man's capacity for violence, Bowman didn't question that the phone call meant death for someone. Lives were nothing to this killer. Only winning mattered.

Bowman fired the kill shot, striking the Shark in the chest. For a moment, the old man gripped the phone to his ear, trying to suck in a breath so he could speak. But as blood blossomed through his gray jacket, he couldn't articulate any words. He staggered a step and dropped the phone.

Realizing the old man was neutralized, Bowman ran toward Duke. Propelled by rage, he grabbed Duke's head and twisted until his neck popped and his body went still. Duke's fingers went slack and his body, limp. Bowman shoved him aside and unwrapped the cord from Riley's neck. He sat her up. "Come on, baby, breathe."

For a moment she was still. Then Riley gasped in air, raising her hands to her marked neck.

"It's okay," he said. "It's over."

"Hanna! Here somewhere. Please find her."

Bowman hauled Riley up and sat her in a chair. He handed her his backup gun. "I'll find her. Shoot anything that doesn't look right."

"With pleasure."

***

Riley's head spun and her vision was blurry as she looked at the bodies that lay around her. The old man lay on his back, his dark eyes staring sightless at the ceiling, his fingers inches from his cell. In the corner, the dealer. And Duke.

As she looked at Duke, hints of pity mingled with overwhelming hatred and anger. He'd been her savior. Her mentor. And he'd been lying to her for years. Tears welled in her eyes; she wiped them away with the back of her hand.

"Riley?" Hanna's broken voice cut across the gaming room, elbowing out all other thoughts.

Riley rose and set the gun on the poker table. More tears welled and spilled down her cheeks as she hurried to Hanna. Her knee pounded with pain, her jaw hurt, and her throat ached. But she didn't care. Hanna was alive.

"Honey, are you all right?" She hugged Hanna, checking her for any signs of injury. "Did they hurt you at all? God, I am so sorry."

The girl began to cry and collapsed against Riley, clinging to her. "I was so scared. When I woke up, there were two men in the room."

Riley cupped Hanna's face in her hands. "Did they hurt you?"

"No. They didn't."

Riley kissed her on the cheek, smoothing her hands over the girl's head, needing a moment to control her own emotions. She'd come close to losing everything that mattered.

She looked up and saw Bowman. He checked the men in the room to make sure none were alive or capable of threat. When he confirmed the room was secure, he went to her.

He touched her bruised cheek. "Are you okay?"

"I'm fine." She smiled at Hanna. "We're fine."

"Thank God."

She reached out and touched his face. "Thank you."

He leaned into the touch and laid his hand over hers. "I thought I lost you."

She shook her head. "I'm not going anywhere."

"Good," he said.

EPILOGUE

Eight Weeks Later

Sweat dripped into Riley's eyes as she, Hanna, and Cooper finished up their run through the park. It had taken a couple of weeks for her bruises to heal, but she was physically her old self again. As they rounded the corner of their street, she noticed a black SUV parked in front of her house. Bowman stood by the car, dark glasses covering his eyes, his arms folded.

She'd not seen him in nearly two weeks and had begun to think the baggage of a teenage kid had scared him off. As always, he was impossible to read. Despite all the unknowns dancing between them, her heart beat a little faster as she stopped in front of him.

"Hey, Clay," Hanna said. "How's it going?"

He tugged off his glasses and tossed a warm smile at the girl. "It's good. How are the applications?"

She groaned for effect, but it wasn't a tortured kind of sound, more like a normal teenager reaction. "You sound like Riley."

"She's a smart lady. Best to listen to her." He reached in his coat pocket and pulled out a white envelope. "This is for you."

"What is it?" Hanna asked.

"Read it."

She glanced at Riley, who shrugged. She had no idea what it contained. Hanna tore open the envelope. Her mouth dropped open as she read and then looked at Bowman, tears glistening in her eyes. "Is this for real?"

"You still have to get into college and keep your grades up senior year. So it's not a freebie by any stretch."

"What is it?" Riley asked.

Hanna handed her the paper. "Shield Security has a scholarship fund. If I get into college, they'll pay my way."

Riley's breath stilled as she read and reread the words. She was shocked, pleased, and taken aback. "This is very generous."

"I looked up her grades," Bowman said. "She's doing a hell of a job. College is the right path for her."

Nothing he could have done would have touched Riley's heart more. "Thank you."

As she stared at him, she knew, as she'd known for weeks, that she loved him. No one had ever made her feel so complete and whole as Clay Bowman.

Hanna took the letter back from Riley. "Can I accept this?"

The pure excitement in the girl's face made it impossible for her to say no. "Yes."

Hanna squealed. "I need to call Julia."

"Can you take Cooper?" Riley asked.

"Sure." She took his leash and ran with him into the house.

Riley watched the girl bound into the house full of all the joy and happiness a girl her age should feel. She looked up at Bowman and found him staring at her. Her heartbeat skipped. "That's pretty amazing."

He carefully folded his sunglasses and tucked them in his pocket. He moved to within inches of her. Energy snapped between them. "You're amazing."

After Bowman had killed Duke and the Shark, the cops had been called and Agent Sharp and his team arrived at the scene. There'd been lots of questions not only from state police but the FBI. In the end, Riley's past was laid bare. And she discovered being open about her own life had been very freeing and had helped Hanna, who was more at peace with her own past.

Bowman had been by her side in the first weeks, but she'd not seen him in the past ten days. They'd spoken on the phone a couple of times, but their conversations had had more to do about the case than it did them.

She wanted him to pull her into his arms. "I figured we scared you off."

"You had your hands full with the FBI and the Shark case, and after I gave my statements, Shield sent me to Texas to look into another set of cases that might have been related to the Shark. We think we can now link Duncan to over two dozen killings in twenty different cities."

"Two dozen." The number was staggering when she tried to picture all those young girls.

"How's Maria doing?"

"Duke's funeral was hard. There must have been a hundred people there. He touched so many lives." It would be a long time before the pain of Duke's betrayal eased. "I guess you heard the forensic data linked him to Jax's and Darla's deaths."

"I did hear that."

"All these years I saw him as some kind of savior. And he really was. He was good to me. He did help so many kids off the street. I believe there was goodness in him. It scares me that there was also so much darkness." How had she not been able to see it?

"Jo-Jo still with Maria?" he asked.

He'd not been around, but he was keeping tabs. "Jo-Jo and Maria seem to be good for each other. Hanna and I were over there last night. Maria's still crying a lot, and Jo-Jo is actually stepping up and taking care of her. Maria had no idea about the Shark or how Duke really found me. Maria wants to keep the restaurant and the shelter open. In her good moments, she's refusing to let Duke shatter what they built. In her bad moments, well, I hope I can be there for her."

He ran his hand up her arm, sending a shiver through her body. "How're you? How is your department handling this?"

"Paid administrative leave, but I'll be back on the job in a couple of weeks. Gave me time to spend with Hanna, and I finalized the adoption."

"Hanna must be pleased."

"She is." She smiled. "She's been practicing signing her name as Hanna Tatum now."

"Good for her." His hand wrapped around hers. "And Sharp?"

"Agent Sharp is the man of the hour. He's being hailed for leading the investigation that caught a wanted serial killer. He wants to give credit to Shield, but he refuses."

"That's the way we like it. No media. No press."

"You should take the credit."

"Credit has never mattered to me." Bowman traced his thumb over her palm. "I've missed you."

A sigh shuddered through her, testing her promise to be cool about this. "I've missed you."

"I don't want this to be over for us." He clasped both his hands around hers. "And part of my being away for the last two weeks was about saying good-bye to my own past. I wanted to make sure my head was on straight this time. I never want to hurt you again like I did five years ago."

"And you can let it all go?"

"Never forgotten, but it's behind me."

She closed her eyes, cherishing the words before she forced herself to look at him. "Are you sure?"

There was no hesitation in his expression. "I wasn't ready for you the first time we met. You were everything I wanted, but I needed more time."

"You were in a bad place."

"Not anymore."

"I'm not in the same place either. I'm not free to pick up and go like I could then. My life is more complicated."

"Hanna's not a complication. And I like knowing where you are." He rubbed the healing scar on her arm. Andrews had removed the chip the day after the Shark was killed. Bowman tugged her closer.

As her breasts touched his chest, her senses jumped as if jolted by electricity. She glanced at the damp tank top that clung to her skin. "I'm covered in sweat."

He smiled, tracing the outline of her collarbone with his finger. "I like your body when it's glistening with sweat. Especially when it's naked."

She leaned in and kissed him on the lips. "I have a fondness for your naked body as well."

When her breasts brushed his chest, he grinned. "What do you say I treat Hanna and her friend Julia to pizza and a movie?"

She steadied, needing to make sure he understood that having Hanna in her life was a nonnegotiable fact. "She's in my life for good, you know. She'll be around a lot. We're a package deal."

He kissed her again, this time allowing the full force of his passion. "That's fine with me. What about sending them out for pizza?"

She gripped his shirt in her hands, savoring the feel of his chest beneath her palms. Already, she was imagining them alone, naked and in her bed. "That sounds even better."

THE FORGOTTEN FILES BOOK 2

THE DOLLMAKER

by Mary Burton

Monday, October 4, 3:00 p.m.

The Dollmaker touched his newest creation's face gently, knowing it was still tender. The redness and swelling had faded, and the skin had shed the damaged cells leaving whole, healthy skin in its place. Still, her face would be sensitive to touch and he didn't want to hurt her.

Her skin warmed his fingertips as he traced the outline of her thin dark eyebrow, then slowly along high cheekbones dotted with freckles, and finally over bright-red heart-shaped lips.

She was perfect.

A living doll.

Four weeks ago when he'd first taken her, the woman's face had been lovely in an ordinary sort of way. She was in her late twenties with long limbs, a trim waist, and small round breasts. But she'd reached her full potential, which sadly was destined to fade with time. So he'd intervened, snatched her from her predictable life, renamed her Destiny, and enhanced her beauty by painstakingly tattooing her face.

Experience taught him that the best tattoo art began with detailed prep work. And knowing Destiny deserved the best, he took his time, first cutting off her brown hair, then shaving her head and eyebrows until the skin was as smooth as glass. Next he applied alcohol to clean the skin so there'd be no risk of infection.

Only when the canvas was ready did he reach for the first tattoo gun loaded with the finest of needles. It took a full day of meticulous work to cover the key portions with the base coat of white ink. And though there were times when his hands ached and his back stiffened, he refused to rush. Finally, when all the pale color had been applied and the blood wiped clean, he tattooed gracefully arching eyebrows. Next came the rosy blush of color on the cheeks. Stippled freckles. Heart-shaped lips. He saved the eyes for last, permanently lining the upper and lower lids with a steady hand.

Toward the end of the transformation, she began to wake, so he set up a fresh IV bag of propofol so she drifted off to sleep again.

After the job was complete, he wrapped her head and face, knowing that the healing process was critical to the best tattoo work. Infection and neglect ruined tattoos. He changed her bandages twice daily, knowing his work at this stage was akin to an open wound.

For her safety, he kept her drugged and hydrated with the IV bag that hung over a special reclining chair. And as she slept, he spent hours embellishing and ironing the clothes that would match her flawless features.

Once, he had allowed his doll to partially wake so she could see how beautiful she was becoming. She had roused from her deep slumber and immediately tried to sit up.

Her long delicate fingers tried to rise to her bandaged face. "What's wrong with me?" she said, her lips still swollen.

Gently he laid his hand over hers. "Shh. You're safe," he soothed. "You're fine. Your body just needs time to heal."

"My face." She tried to raise her hands but discovered straps bound them to the chair. "What's going on?"

"No touching yet," he said.

She stared at him through a haze of drugged confusion. "My face hurts."

He reached for a bowl of oatmeal and ladled a small amount on a spoon. "I know. It's healing. Soon you will be just fine. But you need to eat now. You won't heal properly if you don't eat."

Panic brightened the color of her eyes. "What happened? Was it an accident?"

He teased her mouth open with the spoon and she opened, like an obedient child. "I'm making you perfect. Don't worry. I am taking great care of you. When you wake up again, it will be over."

She ate a few bites before she shook her head. "I can't eat any more."

The Dollmaker looked in the bowl and saw that she'd almost eaten half. Not as much as he hoped, but sufficient. "Enough for today." Setting the bowl aside, he reached for the nearly empty IV bag and replaced it with his last bag of propofol. Soon she was in a deep sleep.

As the tension relaxed from her face, he couldn't help but be pleased. The extra sprinkle of freckles across the bridge of her nose was exactly the right amount, and he was glad now he'd not added more.

Ten days had passed since he'd first done the work, and he now stood back and studied her. All the hours of labor and the extra days of healing had been worth it. The colors were vibrant and vivid, the lines clear and sharp.

He'd dressed her in a plaid skirt and a white top that was formfitting but not overly tight in a vulgar sort of way. He turned toward the collection of wigs and vacillated between blond and auburn. Finally, he chose the blond wig with long locks that curled gently at the ends. All the wigs were natural, the best on the market. He'd even taken extra care to trim the bangs on this particular model so that delicate wisps of hair brushed the tops of her painted brows.

The Dollmaker carefully settled the wig on her head, centered it, and braided it into two thick strands. He slowly rolled on knee socks, savoring the silky smoothness of her calf, then folded the white cotton neatly at the top. He slid on patent-leather shoes and fastened the buckles so that they were snug but not too tight.

The finishing touches included a small bracelet with a heart charm on her left wrist, and on her right hand, a delicate ring on her pinky finger. He painted her fingernails a pale pink, fastened on delicate earrings, and dabbed hints of perfume behind her ear and on her wrist.

He stepped back, pleased. She was his living doll. A perfect mate.

He lifted her listless body and placed her on a red couch in front of a photographer's screen. He angled her face to the side and propped it up with a silk pillow. He arranged her curls around her shoulders and fluffed her skirt. Reaching for his camera, he snapped a couple of pictures. Glancing in the viewfinder, he frowned, not liking what he saw. Her eyes were closed. And to have the right effect, they needed to be open.

Time to wake up.

"Destiny," he whispered close to her ear. "Time to rise and shine."

When she didn't stir, he pulled an ammonia caplet from his pocket. But before he snapped it, he stopped to admire her again. He ran his hand over her cheek, along the smocked edge of her blouse, and over the swell of her round breast. Drawn by her seductive lure, he squeezed her nipple. His body hardened, and unable to chase away temptation, he slid his hand under the skirt and touched her between her legs.

She wasn't ready for him yet. But she soon would be. He needed to wait.

Drawing his hand back, he snapped the caplet, and held it close to her nose. She inhaled sharply as the acrid smell chased away the haze.

His doll glimpsed her creator with a lovely face of bewilderment. Yes, her open eyes completed the look.

He snapped his fingers. "Time to wake up."

She stirred and her eyes fluttered, but the sedatives still lingered. She was confused as she stared up at him. "Where am I?" she asked. "Am I getting better?"

"You're perfect."

She blinked, focused, and looked down at her hands, now tattooed white like her face. She tried to rub off the ink, and when it didn't smudge, confusion turned to worry. She pushed off the couch, but her legs wobbled as her head no doubt spun.

"Not too fast, Destiny. It will take time for the drugs to clear."

She staggered a step, crumpled to one knee. "What's happening? What have you done to me?"

"I've made you perfect."

She looked at her delicately painted fingernails, and as her gaze rose she caught her reflection in a large mirror he kept in his studio. She froze, shocked. Tears mingled with disbelief. "What have you done!?"

He didn't like the judgment in her voice. A perfect doll didn't judge. It didn't get angry. A perfect doll was still.

"Shh," he said. He put his camera aside and reached for a drink cup with a straw. "It's okay. You're fine."

With a trembling hand, she touched the wig and then her bow lips. "I look like a freak!"

Worry crowded out his happiness. "Don't say that. I've made you perfect."

"I'm a monster!" Her hands began to tremble. Red-rimmed eyes spilled more tears.

He hated to see a woman cry. "Don't be ungrateful."

Shaking her head, she raised her hand to her head and the wig "My hair?"

When she tried to tug the wig free, he brushed her hand away. "Don't do that," he said, trying to remain calm. "It took me a lot of time to get it just right."

"It's not my hair. Not my skin." She forced herself to stagger toward the mirror. Her face inches from her reflection, she gawked.

"You must be pleased with the work. You're one of my best creations."

She rubbed the round blush on her checks and the dots of freckles. Worry ignited in her eyes. "What have you done to me?"

"I've made you beautiful." He snapped more pictures, enthralled by this instant of discovery. She might be shocked now, but she would be beholden to him when she realized the beauty of his work.

Her fingers curled into fists. "You have ruined me."

"I've made you a living doll."

With a yank she pulled the wig off and smoothed her hand over her bald head. She screamed. The shrill sound cut through his head, shattering his calm.

With growing horror she glanced wildly around the room at the large four-poster bed, the rocking chair, and the small table with tea set. When she saw the door, she stumbled toward it. Her knees wobbled as her skirt skimmed the top of her shins.

She yanked on the knob, and realizing it was locked, she screamed. "Let me go!"

"No one can hear you."

She pounded her fist on the hard wood, crying for help and mercy. "You've ruined me."

"You need to calm down. It'll be all right. I have taken such good care of you."

Her eyes blazed hate and disgust. "You have ruined me, you fucking freak!"

Her harsh words belied the angelic features. "That's not necessary."

"Like hell it's not! Let me out of here! Let me go!"

As her raw words mingled with more weeping, he knew he had to silence her. Dolls were not supposed to speak, and Destiny was not supposed to cry.

He moved to his worktable and hurriedly dumped a powder into a glass. As she shrieked louder and pounded on the door, he added fruit-flavored water because he knew she'd like the taste.

Mixing the drink with a straw, he stood beside her. "Here, drink," he said, raising the straw to her lips.

She slapped at his hand. Red drink sloshed on her white skin. "Get away from me. I'm not drinking anything else."

"You have to drink," he coaxed. "It will help you, and when you wake up, you will be just like you were."

"How can I be who I was? This shit is all over me." Her hands clutched into fists, she slowly slid down the wall to the floor, her legs crumpling under her like a real doll.

"I promise. Drink this and you will be fine. You'll see." He pressed the tip of the straw to her lips that now always smiled. "Drink."

"I don't want to drink." She tried to stand but couldn't rise. "I want to go home."

"And I want you to go home."

The Dollmaker wiped the tear from her cheek with his fingertip, pleased that her face remained unspoiled. No smudged mascara. No faded blush or lipstick. "It's okay."

She stared up at him, eyes large with fear and hope. Finally, she sipped, her throat and mouth clearly parched.

When she finished, he pulled the straw away and dabbed the corners of her mouth. "You like the taste of cherry, don't you?"

She nodded.

"That's a good girl."

As she stared up at him, her breathing hitched as she tried to suck in air. She drew a stuttering breath. "What's wrong?"

"It's okay. This is what's supposed to happen." The Dollmaker smoothed his hand over her bald head, already eager to put the wig back on her. "Soon your lungs won't work at all and you will stop breathing forever."

"What?" she gasped.

"Don't worry. I'll be right here with you. I would never leave you alone at a time like this."

"You're killing me?" Her voice was now a hoarse whisper.

"No. I'm finishing the job."

The doll tried to speak, to scream, but her lungs were paralyzed. She was afraid, but her fear would soon fade. Gently, he tilted her back so that he could peer into her eyes and watch as the life drained from her body.

Her hand rose to his arm in one final attempt to cling to life. Her grip was surprisingly strong for someone who teetered so close to death.

He let her hold on to him, smiling and touching her cheek gently. "Shh. Just let go."

Her fingers twitched and slackened a fraction. No more tears pooled or ran down her painted cheeks. Death pulled.

The Dollmaker leaned forward and kissed those still-warm lips. Slowly her fingers slackened and her hand fell away, and all the remaining energy faded from her body.

When her eyes closed, he removed a clean tissue from his pocket and wiped her face, savoring the peaceful stillness that settled over her.

God, she was a perfect creation. In all his years of practice, he'd never made anything so beautiful.

"Death has made you my permanent little Destiny doll."

He kissed her lips again, savoring the sweet tranquility. "I wish I could keep you forever, but we only have a few hours. But, don't worry, I'll be as careful as always. You'll see how much I love you."

ABOUT THE AUTHOR

Photo © 2015 Studio FBJ

New York Times and *USA Today* bestselling novelist Mary Burton is the highly praised author of twenty-six romance and suspense novels and five novellas. She lives in Virginia with her husband and three miniature dachshunds.